THE BURNING SHADOW

ALSO BY JENNIFER L. ARMENTROUT

The Darkest Star

THE BURNING SHADOW

Jennifer L. Armentrout

A TOM DOHERTY ASSOCIATES BOOK

New York

This is a work of fiction. All of the characters, organizations, and events portrayed in this novel are either products of the author's imagination or are used fictitiously.

THE BURNING SHADOW

A Tor Teen Book
Published by Tom Doherty Associates
120 Broadway
New York, NY 10271

www.tor-forge.com

The Library of Congress Cataloging-in-Publication Data is available upon request.

ISBN 978-1-250-17574-8 (hardcover)
ISBN 978-1-250-25806-9 (international, sold outside the U.S., subject to rights availability)
ISBN 978-1-250-17575-5 (ebook)

Our books may be purchased in bulk for promotional, educational, or business use. Please contact your local bookseller or the Macmillan Corporate and Premium Sales Department at 1-800-221-7945, extension 5442, or by email at MacmillanSpecialMarkets@macmillan.com.

First Edition: October 2019

Printed in the United States of America

0 9 8 7 6 5 4 3 2 1

For you, the reader

ACKNOWLEDGMENTS

Thank you to my stellar agent of awesome, Kevan Lyon, and my extraordinary editor, Melissa Frain, for believing that Luc needed his own story. Thank you Taryn, for helping to spread the Luc love all around the globe, and a huge thanks to the amazing team at Tor—Saraciea, Elizabeth, Anthony, Eileen, Lucille, Kathleen, Isa, and Renata, and the rest of the excellent team. Thank you Kristin, for stepping in when needed and for helping get the word about my books and me out there into the world. I'd lose what's left of my mind if it wasn't for Stephanie Brown, but don't tell her that; I need to keep her on her toes. Writing is such a solitary experience, so the following friends and people I love have helped in so many different ways—Andrea Joan (except when you incessantly text me about your Prometheus theory); Jen Fisher (especially when you bring me cupcakes); Jay Crownover and Cora Carmack (you're basically the same person now); Andrew Leighty (when you text about the weird Snaps you receive); Sarah J. Maas (except when I read your books and feel like a loser); my husband (when you're not interrupting me); Hannah McBride (when you're not texting me for the ApollyCon budget); Kathleen Tucker (side-eye for days); Valerie, Stacey Morgan, Tijan, Jessica, Krista, Sophie, Gena, Kresley, Brigid, Jen Frederick, and so many, many more.

To my JLAnders, you guys rock my socks. Thank you, for supporting my rock and me, and entertaining me with all your posts.

And finally, none of this would've been possible without you, the reader. Thank you for allowing me to continue pursuing my dreams.

THE BURNING SHADOW

I

"Just put it in your mouth already."

Blinking rapidly, I lifted my gaze from the steaming bowl of tomato soup to where my mom stood.

That was a string of words I sort of never wanted to hear come out of her mouth ever again.

Her blond hair was smoothed back into a short, neat ponytail, and her white blouse was impressively wrinkle-free. She wasn't so much staring as she was glaring from where she stood on the other side of the island.

"Well," came the deep voice from beside me. "Now I feel super uncomfortable."

The woman I'd believed to be my birth mother up until a few days ago appeared remarkably calm despite the fact that the dining room was still in shambles from the epic death match that had taken place less than twenty-four hours ago. This woman did not tolerate disorganization of any kind. However, the taut corners of her lips told me she was seconds from becoming *Colonel* Sylvia Dasher, and it had nothing to do with the broken dining room table or the shattered window upstairs.

"You wanted grilled cheese and tomato soup," she said, punctuating each food item as if it were a newly discovered disease. "I made them for you, and all you've done is sit and stare at them."

That was true.

"I was thinking." He gave an elaborate pause. "That getting you to make me grilled cheese and tomato soup was too easy."

She smiled tightly, but it didn't reach her eyes. Eyes that were brown only because she wore specially designed contacts that blocked the Retinal Alien Check—RAC—drones. Her real eyes were a vibrant blue. I'd only seen them once. "Are you worried that the soup is poisoned?"

My eyes widened as I lowered the perfectly toasted buttered bread and melted cheesy goodness to my plate.

"Now that you mention it, I'm worried there's arsenic or maybe some random leftover Daedalus serum in it. I mean, I feel like you can never be too sure."

Slowly, I looked at the boy sitting next to me on a stool. *Boy* wasn't exactly the right word to use to describe him. Neither was *human.* He was an Origin, something *other* than Luxen and human.

Luc.

Three letters, no last name, and pronounced like *Luke,* he was an utter enigma to me, and he was . . . well, he was special and he knew it.

"Your food is not poisoned," I told him, inhaling deeply as I tried to interject some common sense into this rapidly deteriorating conversation. The nearby candle, one that reminded me of pumpkin spice, almost overwhelmed his unique, outdoorsy scent that reminded me of pine needles and fresh air.

"I don't know about that, Peaches." Luc's full lips curved into a half smile. These were lips that I had recently become well familiar with. Lips that were as completely distracting as the rest of him. "I think Sylvia would love nothing more than to get rid of me."

"Is it that obvious?" she replied, her thin, fake smile narrowing even further. "I always thought I had a rather good poker face."

"I doubt you could ever successfully hide your rampant dislike of me." Luc leaned back, crossing his arms over his broad chest. "I mean, the first time I came here, all those years ago, you pointed a pistol at me, and the last time I came here, you threatened me with a shotgun. So, I think you've made it pretty clear."

"We could always go for a third time," she snapped, her fingers splaying across the cool granite. "Third time's a charm, right?"

Luc's chin dipped and those thick lashes lowered, shielding astonishingly jewel-tone eyes. Amethyst. The color wasn't the only thing that gave away the fact that he was rocking more than *Homo sapiens* DNA. The fuzzy black line surrounding his irises was also a good indication that there was only a little bit of human in him. "There won't be a third time, *Sylvia.*"

Oh dear.

Things were . . . well, awkward between her and Luc.

They had a messy history that had everything to do with who I *used* to be, but I'd thought the whole grilled-cheese-and-tomato-soup thing was her waving a white flag—a weird offering of a truce, but an offering nonetheless. Obviously, I'd been wrong. From the moment Luc and I had walked into the kitchen, things had gone downhill fast between the two of them.

"I wouldn't be too sure of that," she remarked, picking up a dishcloth. "You know what they say about the arrogant man."

"No, I don't." Luc dropped his elbow to the island and propped his chin onto his fist. "But please enlighten me."

"An arrogant man will still feel immortal." She lifted her gaze, meeting his. "Even on his deathbed."

"Okay," I jumped in when I saw Luc's head tilt to the side. "Can you two stop trying to out-snark each other so we can eat our sandwiches and soup like normal human beings? That would be great."

"But we're not normal human beings." Luc sent me a long side look. "And I cannot be out-snarked, Peaches."

I rolled my eyes. "You know what I mean."

"He's right, though." She scrubbed at a spot on the island only she could see. "None of this is normal. It's not going to be."

Frowning at her, I had to admit she had a point. Nothing had been the same from the moment Luc entered—actually, *reentered*—my life. Everything had changed. My entire world had imploded the moment I realized just about everything about me was a total lie. "But I need normal right now. Like, really badly need normal right now."

Luc's jaw clamped shut as he returned to staring at his sandwich, his shoulders unnaturally tense.

"There's only one way you're going to get normal back in your life, honey," she said, and I flinched at the endearment.

It was something she always called me. Honey. But now, knowing she'd only been in my life these last four years made the simple, sweet word seem wrong. Unreal, even.

"You want normal? Cut this one out of your life."

I dropped my sandwich, shocked that she would say that—not just in front of Luc but that she would say it in general.

Luc's head shot up. "You already took her from me once. That's not going to happen again."

"I didn't take her from you," she fired back. "I saved her."

"And for what, *Colonel* Dasher?" Luc's smile was razor sharp. "To give yourself the daughter you lost? To have something you knew you could hold over my head?"

My heart squeezed painfully in my chest. "Luc—"

The dishcloth wrinkled under Mom's fingers as her hand balled into a fist. "You think you know everything—"

"I know enough." His voice was too soft, too even. "And it's best you don't forget that."

A muscle thrummed along her temple, and I briefly wondered if Luxen could have strokes. "You don't know her. You knew Nadia. This is Evie."

The gulp of air I inhaled got stuck in my throat. She was right and she was wrong. I wasn't Nadia. I also wasn't Evie. I had no idea who I really was.

"They are not the same," she continued. "And if you really do care for her—for Evie—you'd walk out of her life and let her go."

I jolted. "That's not—"

"You think you know her better than I do?" Luc's laugh could've frozen the Alaskan wildlands. "If you think she's your dead daughter, then you're living in a fantasy world. And if you think that me walking out of here is what's best, then you don't know shit."

My gaze darted between them. "Just FYI, I'm sitting right here. Totally present for this argument that is about me."

Both ignored me.

"And just to be really, painfully clear," Luc went on, "if you think I'd walk away again, then you've obviously forgotten who I am."

Was the dishcloth starting to smoke? "I haven't forgotten what you are."

"And that is?" Luc challenged.

"Nothing more than a killer."

Holy crap.

Luc smirked. "Then you and I should get along famously."

Oh my God!

"It's best that you remember you're only a part of her life now because I'm allowing it," she retorted.

Luc kept his arms crossed. "I would sincerely love to see you try to keep me away from her now."

"Don't push me, Luc."

"In case you haven't noticed, I've *been* pushing."

Bluish-white energy flickered over Mom's knuckles, and I just lost it. All the violent, raw emotions swirled inside me like a cyclone, lashing through every part of my being. This was too much—just too much.

"Stop it! Both of you!" I shot to my feet, and the barstool toppled over, cracking off the floor and startling both her and Luc. "Do you guys really think any of this is helping right now? At all?"

Luc whipped around on the stool, his odd eyes slightly wide while Mom stepped back from the island, dropping the dish towel.

"Have you guys forgotten that I almost died last night because a psychotic and slightly suicidal Origin had a *T. rex*–sized bone to pick with *you*?" I pointed at Luc, and his jaw hardened in response. "And have *you* forgotten that you've spent the last four years pretending to be my mom? Which is scientifically impossible because you're a Luxen, something else you've lied about?"

Mom's face paled. "I'm still your mother—"

"You convinced me that I was some dead girl!" I shouted, throwing my hands up. "You didn't even adopt me. How is that even legal?"

"That's a really damn good question." Luc smirked.

"Shut up!" I swung on him, my heart racing and my temples beginning to throb. "You've also done nothing but lie to me. You even made my best friend become friends with me!"

"Well, I didn't exactly make her become your best friend," he replied, slowly unfolding his arms. "That happened organically, I'd like to think."

"Don't bring logic into this," I snapped, my hands tightening into fists when the lines of his mouth softened. "You two are driving me out of my mind, and I barely have any of it left. Do I need to remind you of what happened in the last freaking forty-eight hours? I learned that everything I knew about myself was a lie and that I was pumped full of alien DNA courtesy of a serum I can barely pronounce, let alone spell. And if that's not messed up enough, I found a classmate super-duper dead. Andy's eyes were legit burned out of his face, and then I was literally just dragged through the woods and had to listen to the bizarre ranting of an Origin who had hard-core abandonment issues!"

Both stared at me.

I stepped back, breathing heavily. "All I wanted to do is eat a damn grilled cheese sandwich, eat some freaking soup, and be normal for five seconds, but both of you ruined it and—" Without warning, a wave of dizziness swept over me, making my chest suddenly feel hollow. "Whoa."

Mom's face blurred as my knees went weak. "Evie—"

Luc moved so fast I couldn't have tracked him even if I were not weirdly seeing double at the moment. Within what felt like half a second, he had a strong, steady arm around my waist. "Evie," he said, cupping my cheek and lifting my head. I hadn't even realized it had lowered. "Are you okay?"

My heart was pounding too fast, and my head felt like it was weighed down with cotton. Pressure settled on my chest as my legs trembled. I was alive and standing, so that meant I was okay. I had to be. I just couldn't get the words out at the moment.

"What's wrong?" Worry threaded every syllable of Mom's voice as she drew closer.

"Dizzy," I gasped, squeezing my eyes shut. I hadn't eaten anything since sometime the day before, and I'd only managed to get one bite of food in before they had started to argue, so being dizzy wasn't all that surprising. Plus, the last week . . . or month had been a bit *much*.

"Just breathe." Luc's thumb dragged over my jawline, making long, soothing strokes. "Take a few moments and just breathe." There was a pause. "She's okay. It's just that she was . . . she was hurt pretty badly last night. It's going to take a bit for her to be 100 percent."

I thought that was weird, because this morning I'd felt like I could've run a marathon, and I didn't normally feel like running unless a horde of zombies was chasing me.

But slowly, the weight lifted from my head and chest, and the dizziness faded. I opened my eyes, and the next breath I took got stuck in my throat. I didn't realize he was so close, that he was hunched over so we were eye level, his face only inches from mine.

A thoroughly perplexing mix of emotions woke deep inside me, fighting to get to the surface—to get me to pay attention to them, to make sense of them.

His bright gaze met mine as a lock of wavy bronze hair toppled forward, shielding one of those stunning, abnormal purple eyes. I took in the features that were pieced together in an inhumanly perfect way we mere mortals truly couldn't accomplish without a skilled surgical hand.

Luc was beautiful in a way that a panther in the wild was, and that was what he often reminded me of. A sleek, captivating predator that distracted with its beauty or lured its prey in with it.

There was a daring twist to the corners of his full lips, tilting them up. Early October sunlight streamed in through the kitchen window, glancing off sharp cheekbones, highlighting them and creating alluring shadows under them.

I was staring at his lips again.

When I looked at him, I wanted to touch him, and as I stared at him wanting that, that teasing grin of his kicked up a notch.

My eyes narrowed.

Only a few Origins could read thoughts as easily as it was for me to read a book. Luc was, of course, one of them. He'd promised to stay out of my head, and I think he did most of the time, but he always seemed to be peeping when I was thinking the absolute most embarrassing thing possible.

Like right now.

His grin became a smile, and a flutter picked up in my chest. That smile of his was as dangerous as the Source. "I think she's feeling better."

I jerked away from him, breaking the embrace as warmth crept into my cheeks. I couldn't look at her. Sylvia. Mom. Whatever. I didn't want to look at him, either. "I'm okay."

"I think you should eat something," she said. "I can warm up the soup—"

"I don't really want to eat anything," I interrupted, my appetite nonexistent at this point. "I just don't want you two to fight."

Mom looked away, her small chin jutting out as she folded her arms over her chest.

"I don't want that, either," Luc said, his voice so quiet I wasn't sure Mom heard him.

My chest squeezed as I met his gaze. "Really? Seemed like you were more than willing to fight."

"You're right," he said, surprising me. "I was being antagonistic. I shouldn't have been."

For a moment, all I could do was stare at him, and then I nodded. "There's something I need to say, and both of you need to hear it." My hands curled into loose fists. "She can't keep me away from you."

His eyes deepened to a violet hue, and when he spoke, his voice was rougher. "Good to hear."

"Only because I can't be kept or forced to do anything I don't want to do," I added. "That goes for you, too."

"Never would imagine it didn't." He was closer, moving toward me as silently as a ghost.

Drawing in a shallow breath, I faced Mom. Her face was pale, but beyond that, I couldn't read anything in her expression. "And I know you don't want to try to force Luc and me apart, not now and not after everything. You were mad. You guys have a messy history. I get that, and I know you two may never like each other, but I really need you guys to pretend that you do. Just a little."

"I'm sorry," Mom said, clearing her throat. "He might've been willing to argue with me, but this was on me. I invited him for lunch, and then I was unnecessarily rude. He obviously has reasons to not trust me or accept any of my actions in good faith. If it were the other way around, I would feel the same as he does." She drew in a deep breath. "I'm sorry, Luc."

Shock splashed through me as my eyes widened, and I wasn't the only one staring at her like I didn't understand the words coming out of her mouth.

"I know you and I are never going to like each other," Mom continued. "But we need to try to get along. For Evie."

Luc was as still as a statue in one of the few museums that had survived the alien invasion. Then he nodded. "For her."

In my bedroom later that evening, I found myself sitting on the edge of the bed, staring at the corkboard tacked full of pictures of my friends and me. I didn't even know when I started looking at them, but I couldn't take my eyes off them.

Luc had left shortly after #grilledcheesegate, which was for the best. Even if they sort of smoothed things over, it was best if they got some space between them. Probably a whole zip code worth of space. I wanted to be hopeful that they could get along, but I also knew that may be expecting too much from both of them.

I sighed, my gaze crawling over the photos. Some of them were photos of us just chilling or goofing off. Others showed us in Halloween costumes or dressed up in fancy dresses, hair and makeup on point. Me. Heidi. James. Zoe.

Zoe.

She'd been the first friend I'd made at Centennial High four years ago. We'd hit it off immediately, both of us having suffered—or at least thinking we had—unimaginable loss after the invasion. Our little party of two quickly expanded to include Heidi and then, eventually, James. The four of us had been thick as thieves, but Zoe had been lying, too. Just like Luc. Just like Mom. Zoe had been ordered to be my friend, to watch over me because Luc couldn't, and maybe Luc had been right earlier. Maybe she was made to become my friend, but we'd become best friends all on our own. Who knew? I didn't. And we'd never know.

My stomach grumbled once more, and I knew it was time to go downstairs, because my stomach felt like it wanted to eat itself. Part of me hoped Mom had holed herself up in her bedroom. I felt terrible for thinking that, but things were always super-uncomfortable after a fight, and I didn't have the brain space to deal with it. The moment I hit the foyer and heard the TV on, I knew I wasn't that lucky.

Taking a deep breath, I squared my shoulders and entered the living room. An episode of *Hoarders* was playing on the TV, and I shook my head as I continued into the living room.

She was at the island, a bottle of mustard, loaf of bread, and a packet of deli meat spread out before her. There was even a bag of sour cream and cheddar chips, my favorite. Roast beef. She was making roast beef sandwiches, and it was apparent, based on the fact there was only mustard on the bread, that she'd just started.

Mom looked up as she picked up the packet of meat. “Hoping you’re hungry.”

My steps slowed. “How did you know I was coming down? Were you listening for sounds of life outside my bedroom door?”

“Maybe.” A sheepish look crossed her face. “I was planning to coax you out with this if you didn’t.”

I stopped to stand behind the barstool that I’d knocked over earlier. “I am hungry.”

“Perfect.” She motioned at the barstool. “It’ll be ready in a few moments.”

“Thanks.” I sat down, letting my hands fall to my lap as I watched her drape a slice of roast beef over the bread and then another. I had no idea what to say as the silence stretched out between us. Luckily or unluckily, she knew exactly what to say.

“If you’re still upset with me, I completely understand,” she said, cutting right to the point in typical Colonel Dasher fashion. Another slice of roast beef went onto the sandwich. “I apologized, but I know I said things today to Luc that I shouldn’t have, and you were right. After everything, you didn’t need that today.”

I loosely folded my arms in my lap as I looked around the kitchen. “Luc . . . He did sort of start it. I mean, he didn’t need to bring up the whole pulling-a-gun-on-him thing, and I know you two are probably never going to get along, but—”

“You need him,” she answered for me, placing the bread on the meat.

Warmth hit my cheeks. “Well, I wouldn’t say that.”

A faint smile tugged at her lips as she looked up at me. “You are as much a part of him as he is a part of you.” Her smile faded as she shook her head. “Luc thinks he knows everything. He doesn’t.”

Thank God Luc wasn’t here to hear her say that.

“And he especially thinks he knows why I did what I did when I decided to . . . help you become Evie, but he doesn’t. He’s not in my head,” she said, and I wondered if she realized that Luc could read thoughts. She had to. “And I know he doesn’t trust me. I can’t blame him for that.”

“But you stopped my fath— You stopped Jason from trying to shoot him,” I pointed out. “And you weren’t the only one keeping secrets. So was he. It's not like you've given him any other reason to not trust you. The same goes for him."

She nodded as she reached for the bag of chips. "You're right. Maybe we'll try it again, and next time, we'll have better results."

"Maybe," I murmured.

"You don't sound too certain."

"I'm not," I admitted with a laugh.

A wry grin appeared as she dumped some chips onto the paper plate, next to the sandwich. "But something you can be certain of is that I am your mother. I may not be her by blood or by certificate, and I may have only been in your life for these last four years, but you are my daughter and I love you. I would do anything to make sure you're safe and happy, just like any mother out there would."

My lower lip trembled as my chest and throat burned. *Daughter. Mother.* Simple words. Powerful ones. Words I wanted to own.

"I know you're mad about how I kept everything from you, and I understand that. I suspect it will take a long time for you to get over that. I don't blame you. I wish I had been more up front with you about him and who you were. The first time he showed up here, I should've told you the truth."

"Yeah, you should have, but you didn't. We can't change any of that, right? It is what it is."

Mom looked away then, smoothing her hand over the front of her shirt. She'd changed out of the blouse and into a pale blue cotton shirt. "I just wish I'd made different choices so that you could have made different ones."

I lifted my gaze and looked at her—really saw her. Something about her seemed off. Mom looked at least a decade or so younger than her age, but she seemed paler than normal. Her features were drawn, and there were faint lines around the corners of her eyes and deeper grooves in her forehead that I'd sworn hadn't been there two weeks before.

Despite all the lies and all the million things I still didn't understand, concern blossomed. "Are you okay? You look tired."

"I *am* a little tired." She reached up, lightly touching her shoulder. "It's been a while since I tapped into the Source."

A tremor coursed through my entire body. She'd used the Source when fighting Micah. "Is that normal?"

"It can be when you haven't used the Source in a while, but I'll be fine." She smiled then, a faint but real one. "Eat up."

Feeling a little bit better about everything and almost normal, I scarfed down the sandwich and chips so fast it was amazing I didn't choke. Once I was done, I was still hungry. Dumping my paper plate in the garbage, I went to the fridge and stared inside, debating if I wanted to go to the trouble of cutting up the strawberries I spotted and smothering them in sugar or if I wanted something easier.

"When you're done cooling yourself off standing in front of the fridge, there's something I want to show you," Mom announced.

I snorted as I grabbed a packet of string cheese. Walking over to the trash can, I pulled off the wrapper and tossed it into the trash. "What?"

"Follow me." She turned, and I followed her to the front of the house, to the French doors that led to her office. She opened the doors, and my steps slowed.

A tiny part of me didn't want to go into the office.

I'd found pictures of her in there, the real Evie, hidden away in a photo album. I'd always been told that we didn't have any old photo albums. That Mom hadn't had the chance to grab any of them during the invasion. I'd blindly believed in that, but now I knew the truth, and I knew why there could be no photo albums.

I wouldn't have been in them. The real Evie would've been.

"You remember the night you called me while I was at work because you thought someone was in the house?" she asked.

The question caught me off guard. She was talking about the night I'd been here alone and had heard someone downstairs. "Yeah, I'm probably not going to forget that until I'm eighty. You thought I imagined it."

"You didn't." She turned to her desk. "Someone was in here, and they did take something."

I opened my mouth, but I couldn't get any of the words out. That was probably a good thing, because most of the words building on my tongue were curses. Finally, I found my voice. "You said nothing was taken."

"I was wrong. I wasn't hiding anything from you. I just didn't realize until this afternoon. I was organizing my office when I discovered it," she said.

I had no idea how she could organize her office any more than she normally had. For Pete's sake, her office was already more organized than a monthly planner.

Unease surfaced as I stared at her. "What was taken?"

She reached into the desk drawer and pulled out that damn photo album, placing it down on the desk. She opened it to the blank pages. "When I was in here straightening up, I happened to open up the album. I hadn't looked through it in a while, but I noticed it then. There were pictures of Jason's daughter here. Other birthday pictures and a few candid ones." Her fingers lingered on the blank pages. "Those were taken."

Confused, I lifted my gaze to hers as my thoughts whirled. "It had to be Micah. He'd been . . ."

"He'd been what?"

He'd been in this house before, while I'd been sleeping. He'd scratched me—*choked me.* I'd thought it had been a nightmare until he'd admitted to me what he'd done. A shudder rolled through me. Mom didn't know about that. Crossing my arms, I stared down at my bare feet. The purple nail polish had begun to chip on my big toe.

Micah hadn't admitted to taking the photos, and he also claimed that he hadn't killed Andy, one of my classmates, or that poor family in the city. He'd owned up to Colleen's and Amanda's deaths, and Luc and I had just assumed he'd been lying.

What if he wasn't?

And why would he take pictures of the real Evie? He knew who I was from the beginning. He didn't need picture proof. Knots twisted up my stomach as I lifted my gaze to hers. "What if it wasn't Micah? Why would someone take them?"

The line of her mouth thinned until the upper lip was nearly gone. "I don't know."

2

We will not be silenced! We will not live in fear!" April Collins's voice carried from the front of the school Monday morning, the sound like rusted nails on my nerve endings. "No more Luxen! No more fear!"

My steps slowed as I squinted against the glare of the sun. April was lifting a bright pink poster, shaking it as the small group of classmates behind her continued to chant, "No more Luxen! No more fear!"

A teacher was trying to usher April and the others in through the front door, but the young woman wasn't having much luck. She looked like she needed about two more large cups of coffee to deal with this.

It was way too early for this nonsense.

I should've stayed home like Mom had wanted, just to avoid seeing April riling up the students. Then again, I would've been bored out of my mind, and Mom would've stayed home. If I wanted to see my friends and if I wanted to see Luc, like I planned to later, that meant I had to go to school.

And apparently deal with April.

Good news was I hadn't had any more dizzy spells even though I hadn't gotten a whole lot of sleep the night before. First, I couldn't stop thinking about the missing pictures even though it had to have been Micah who had taken them, and when I did finally fall asleep, a nightmare had woken me hours later.

I'd been back in the woods with Micah and Luc . . . he had been hurt badly and—

Cutting those thoughts off as a chill swept down my spine, I powered forward. April had taken to protesting outside, at the front entrance in the mornings and the parking lot after school let out, both places where she was bound to be seen by the registered Luxen who attended our school.

Looking around, I didn't see Connor or any of the other Luxen, and I hoped that meant they'd made it into the school before April started. Most people were ignoring them. Only a few others stood around, watching. A girl I didn't recognize, possibly a freshman or sophomore, was yelling back at them, but whatever she was saying was drowned out by April and her group's chants.

My fists tightened as I picked up my pace, hurrying down the steps that led into the front of Centennial High. As I neared the group, April spun toward me, her long, blond hair reminding me of a tail as it whipped along with her. She lowered her stupid poster that literally had NO LUXEN written in large block letters with an actual glitter pen.

Shaking my head, I focused on the RAC drone hovering by the doors, scanning the eyes of the students to ensure that no unregistered Luxen were present. What the creators of the drone didn't realize was that Luxen and Origins had figured out a way around them with the contacts they wore. Sometimes I wondered how long it would last, the safety the contacts afforded. The government would have to figure it out eventually, but then again, look at how long most of the Luxen had been here without a lot of the branches of the government or the general populace knowing they were here. Decades and decades, if not longer.

"Hey, Evie!" April called out. "Want to join us?"

Without even looking at her, I extended my right hand and my middle finger as I kept walking toward the glass doors.

"That's not nice." April fell into step beside me. "You shouldn't treat friends like that, but I'll forgive you. Because I'm nice like that."

I stopped, facing her. Things were tense between us. April and I had never been all that close, but she was someone I'd once considered a friend even though she'd always been abrasive. "We're not friends, April. Not anymore."

Her brows lifted. "How are we not friends?"

"Are you serious right now?" I demanded.

The poster tapped off her thigh. "Do I look like I'm joking?"

"You look like a bigot who's pulled her hair back a little too tightly," I snapped, and her cheeks flushed pink. Maybe it was the almost dying thing this weekend, but I had absolutely no filter. "I've tried talking to you about the horrible stuff you're saying and doing, but that was like talking to a brick wall. I don't know what's happened to you, April, who didn't hug you enough as a child, but whatever it is, it's no excuse for this crap."

Her eyes narrowed. "And I don't know how you can stand there and defend Luxen—"

"We've already had this conversation." I cut her off before she could bring up my supposed father. "I'm not having it again, April."

She gave a small shake of her head and then inhaled deeply through her nose. Determination pinched her features. "They can kill us, Evie. With a snap of their fingers, you and I both could be dead before we took our next breath. They're dangerous."

"They're wearing Disablers," I told her even though I knew that only registered Luxen wore them. "And while you're right, they can be dangerous and they could kill us, so could any person around us. We're just as dangerous, and yet you don't see anyone out here protesting us."

"Not the same thing," she argued. "This is our planet—"

"Oh, come on, we don't own this planet, April. It's a freaking planet, with more than enough room for all the aliens in the world. The Luxen here have done nothing to you—"

"How do you know that? You don't know what has or hasn't been done to me," she fired back, and my brows lifted. I doubted she'd been dragged through the woods recently. "Look, I get we have different opinions, but you don't have to be rude to me just because we don't agree on this. You just need to respect how I feel."

"Respect how you feel?" I laughed dryly.

"Yeah, that's what I said. Don't know what's so funny about that."

"What's so funny is that you're wrong, April. This isn't just about having different opinions and respecting that. I don't like pizza. You think pizza is great. We can agree to disagree, but this is about right and wrong, and what you're doing is wrong." I took a step back from her, having no idea how she couldn't understand what I was saying. April had always been difficult to deal with and often had opinions that made me want to throat punch her, but this? "I hope you see that someday."

April's chest rose with a deep breath. "You think I'm going to be on the wrong side of history, don't you? That's where *you're* wrong, Evie."

"Is it true?" Zoe demanded the moment she appeared by my locker, her tight, honey-colored curls pulled back in an impeccably neat bun I could never master.

Opening the door, I looked over at her. I had no idea what she was talking about. "Is what true?"

"What?" She stared at me. Cocking her arm back, she punched me on the arm. "Are you serious?"

"Ouch." I rubbed at the spot. That wasn't a light punch, but I was grateful for it, because things had been a little weird between Zoe and me this morning. Not bad or anything like that, but just like we both were walking on eggshells around each other. Not exactly a huge surprise there. I was still processing the fact that we hadn't organically become friends or that not only was Zoe an Origin—like Luc—but that she had also known me when I'd been Nadia.

Zoe was obviously worried that I was holding things against her, but I really wasn't. Things were weird, but she was still my friend—one of my best friends, and I wasn't going to let how our friendship started destroy what we made of it.

Plus, almost dying made me realize how pointless grudges were while driving home the whole you-never-know-if-you'll-have-a-tomorrow kind of thing. Unless holding a grudge involved April. With her, I was going to cuddle and feed and water that grudge.

Zoe cocked her head. "You got into it with April this morning?"

"Oh. Yeah. That." Shaking out my arm, I pulled my English textbook out and shoved it onto the shelf.

Zoe looked like she was going to hit me again, so I leaned away. "You had all morning to mention you got into it with April. I just heard some girl I'm not even convinced goes to school here talking about it while I was in the bathroom."

I grinned. "It wasn't a big deal. She tried to talk to me, and I wasn't having it."

Zoe caught my locker door as it started to close on its own. The orange and tan bangles around her slim wrist clattered softly. "Not a big deal? I need to know exactly what you said to her that apparently caused her to throw her poster at Brandon."

My brows shot up. "She did that?"

She nodded. "Yep."

An evil little giggle rose in the back of my throat. I told her what I'd said to April as I grabbed my history textbook and shut the door. "I guess I got under her skin."

"Sounds like it. God, she's the worst."

I nodded as we edged around a slow-moving younger student. "So, what did you do yesterday?"

"Nothing much. Just watched this really sad documentary about coma patients."

Zoe watched the weirdest things.

"What about you?" she asked.

"Luc came over," I said in a low voice. "Mom made him grilled cheese and tomato soup."

"Wow." She nudged my side. "That's awesome."

"Well . . ."

"It wasn't?"

"At first it was. He and I sort of hung out for a while first and talked." I could feel my stupid cheeks warming. "But things went south between them pretty fast. They argued and it got ugly. Both ended up apologizing."

"Even Luc?" She sounded surprised.

"Yep. I guess things are okay now, but they're never going to be fans of each other."

"Really can't blame them," Zoe said. "They have a . . ."

"Messed-up history? Yeah." We entered the cafeteria. It smelled like burned pizza. "But I think it's big that they both apologized. I think they're going to try the best they can."

"I would've loved to have been a fly on the wall when you yelled at both of them," Zoe said as we went through the line. "You're scary when you get mad."

I laughed at that, because when I got mad, all I could do was yell. If Zoe or Luc got mad, they could burn down entire houses with a flick of their wrists. The idea of Zoe thinking I was scary was laughable.

After I loaded my plate up with what I thought might be roast beef but sort of looked like stew, Zoe grabbed a pizza, and I tried not to puke over her poor life choice.

James was already at the table, munching from a bag of chips. His size was super-intimidating to most, but he was a big cuddly teddy bear who hated confrontation . . . and Foretoken. Couldn't quite blame him considering the one and only time he'd been there, he'd met the meanest Luxen ever.

Grayson.

Ugh.

The Luxen had basically told James he'd reminded him of one of the victims in the old movie *Hostel,* and how creepy was that?

As soon as we sat down, James demanded, "So, what is the best *Taken* movie? One. Two. Or three?"

I stared at him.

"There are three of them?" Zoe asked.

His mouth gaped, and a chip fell out, causing me to giggle. "How do you not know there are three of them?"

"I haven't seen any of them," I admitted.

He blinked at me. "If I were wearing pearls, I'd be clutching them right now."

Heidi dropped into the seat next to James, her crimson-colored waves brushing against cheeks that were way paler than normal. Immediately, my stomach twisted as instinct blared a warning.

Zoe must've picked up on it. "What's wrong?"

"Do you guys know Ryan Hoar?" she asked, and my stomach sank. The last couple of weeks, when someone asked that, good news did not follow.

Chip halfway to his mouth, James looked over at Heidi. "Yeah, he's in my art class. Why?"

"I don't know who that is," Zoe said.

"He's kind of tall and skinny. Usually changes his hair color a lot. I think the last time I saw it, it was green," Heidi explained, and that sounded vaguely familiar.

"Actually, it was blue on Friday," James corrected. "I haven't seen him yet. Art is my last class."

"You're not going to see him," Heidi said, placing her hands on the table. "I just heard from his cousin that he died over the weekend."

"What?" James dropped the bag of chips. "He was at Coop's party Friday night."

Immediately, I thought of Micah. It couldn't be, could it? Micah was dead, but that didn't mean he hadn't done it before Luc ended it. "Was he . . . killed?"

"No." Heidi shook her head. "He caught the flu or something and died from that."

"The flu?" James repeated as if he couldn't quite believe what he'd heard. "Like the sneezing and coughing flu?"

Heidi nodded. "Yeah."

"Wow," I murmured, unable to think of anyone I knew that had actually died from the flu.

Zoe stared down at her plate. "That's sad."

"Yeah," Heidi agreed.

James said nothing as he sat back, hands falling to his lap. A hush fell over us, and just like that, I learned . . . or I remembered that a natural death, an unexpected one, was just as heavy as an unnatural one.

And death was a constant companion, with or without dangerous aliens.

3

Touch it."

"Nope," I said, focusing on the open textbook as I lay curled on my side. I'd been at Luc's apartment for about an hour, and I needed to study because I had a feeling I was going to have a quiz in history, but within that hour's time, I'd probably managed to read about one paragraph.

If that.

Not only was Luc incredibly distracting, I kept thinking about Ryan. I didn't know him at all, but he still lingered in my thoughts. To die from the flu at such a young age? That was scary—scary and sad, and I could almost hear my mom's voice in the back of my head, lecturing about the importance of flu shots.

The school had already suffered too many losses.

"Come on, Evie, touch it," Luc cajoled, and I fought the way my lips twitched in response to his deep voice as I traced idle circles along the soft blanket.

"No, thank you."

"I'm far more interesting than whatever you're reading."

That statement was annoyingly true. Reading about the Gettysburg Address, something I was confident was covered every single year in school, wasn't exactly edge-of-your-seat reading.

"Touch it," he persisted. "Just a little. You know you want to, Peaches."

I lost the battle to ignore him and my gaze flicked from the textbook to the long, lean body stretched out beside me. He smiled, and a flutter picked up in my chest. That smile of his was as dangerous as the Source.

"Touch it." Luc let his head fall to the side.

I shouldn't be touching any part of Luc, because things with him had a tendency to spin spectacularly out of control in the best and worst possible way.

"Peaches," he murmured.

"What do you . . . ?" I trailed off as I saw what he wanted me to touch.

The tip of one finger glowed bright white like a mini lightbulb. I sucked in a shallow breath, torn between wanting to pull away and inch closer. "Are you ET?"

Luc chuckled. "I'm way hotter than ET."

"That's not saying much, you realize that, right? ET is like this lumpy thing made of Play-Doh," I said, staring at his finger. What I saw was no light. It was the Source, a power not from this Earth but brought here by the aliens. Only the Luxen, hybrids, and Origins could harness the energy to varying degrees. Some could heal with it. Some could move objects. All could kill with it.

And Luc was adeptly skilled at all uses of the Source.

"Why do you want me to touch it?" I asked.

"It's a surprise, Peaches," he said. "Because I know you missed me while you were at school."

"I didn't miss you while I was at school."

"You shouldn't tell lies, Peaches."

I shot him a look, but the truth was, he did randomly pop up in my thoughts throughout the day, and it was always followed by a dipping motion in my stomach. I had no idea what that meant, if it was something good or bad, but it *was* weird. I'd spent a decent amount of time with him, so how could I miss him already? I used to go entire weekends without seeing my ex, Brandon, and not really miss him. Actually, if I was being honest, I hadn't missed him at all.

"Okay," I said after a moment. "I did miss you."

"A lot."

"A little," I corrected, fighting a grin as I stared at the white glow in his finger and then lifted my gaze to those stunning eyes. "Why do you want me to touch it?"

He was quiet for a moment, and the teasing eased from his features. "Because this is something you *used* to love doing."

My heart lodged itself in my throat. He meant it was something Nadia loved to do.

When I first learned of who I was, hearing that name—*Nadia*—made me sick to my stomach, but now I was thirsty for the knowledge, to know what she liked and disliked, what her dreams were, what she had wanted to be when she got older. If she was like me, scared of nearly everything, or if she was brave.

I wanted to know what it was about her that had captured the heart of someone like Luc.

Drawing in a short breath, I lifted my hand, trusting that Luc wouldn't let the Source harm me. The warm glow was pleasant, like basking in the sun, and it sent a trill of electricity dancing up my arm. The moment I pressed my finger against his, the room exploded with light. I gasped, starting to jerk back.

"Look," he urged softly. "Look around us."

Eyes wide, I tugged my gaze from where our fingers had disappeared under the glow, and when I saw his room, I couldn't believe what I was seeing.

Luc's apartment was one large, open space with the exception of a bathroom and closet. From where we were on the bed, I could see straight into the living room and the kitchen that appeared rarely used.

But every square inch—the large sectional couch and television, the end tables, and even the guitar displayed by the floor-to-ceiling windows—looked like it was covered with twinkling, floating, warm white Christmas lights.

"What is this?" I watched as one of the dazzling lights drifted past my face. It was so tiny, the size of a needle point.

"It's the molecules in the air lit up." His breath coasted over my cheek. "The Source can bond and interact with those molecules and the atoms that create the molecules. Normally you wouldn't be able to see them since they're too small, but the source magnifies them, and when you see one, you're actually seeing thousands of them."

Everywhere I looked, I saw the dancing little balls of light. "Is that how you can use the Source to move things?"

"Yes."

"It's beautiful." Awed, I took in the stunning sight before me. I wanted to reach out and touch one of the dazzling lights, but I didn't want to disturb them. "I think it's the most beautiful thing I've ever seen."

"It's not the most beautiful thing I've seen." His voice was different now, deeper and thicker. As if I had no control over myself, I turned my head toward him.

Luc's gaze snagged mine, and a shivery feeling spread over my skin. Every inch of my body became aware of his.

My heart sped up. "I used to do this with you?"

He didn't nod or move, but somehow, he seemed closer. I inhaled the unique pine-and-spice scent of him. "You used to make me do this at least once every day."

"Once every day? That seems excessive."

"It was in the beginning," he admitted, and there was no mistaking the fondness that had crept into his tone. "When you were really small—really young, I'd get annoyed because you'd followed me around for hours until I made the fireflies come."

"Fireflies?"

"Yeah." Thick lashes lowered, shielding his eyes. "That's what you called the lights. Fireflies."

"They do kind of look like fireflies in a jar." With those intense eyes not focused on mine, it was easier to concentrate on what he was sharing with me. "Did you get mad at me when I'd ask you to do this?"

"I was always annoyed with you when we were younger." He chuckled as he pressed the palm of his hand flat against mine. The contact sent another ripple of electricity through me, causing the tips of my fingers to tingle and the dancing lights around us to pulse. "When I wouldn't do this for you, you'd go to Paris, and then he'd guilt me into doing it even though he could've done the same thing."

"I wish I remembered Paris." Especially since Luc spoke of him as if he were like an older brother or father to him and to me.

"I can help you remember." His thumb slid along the side of my hand. "Because a lot of my memories were yours."

You were all my good memories.

Pressure clamped down on my chest, threatening to seal off my throat with emotion. That's what Luc had said to me when I asked if

I'd been a part of his rare good memories, and I believed him. I just couldn't find those memories.

Sometimes I couldn't reconcile the two very different worlds—different lives. The Nadia that Luc claimed was bold and brave, kind and strong. The Evie that thought of Sylvia as her mother and had no idea what she was doing half the time. The monster known as Jason Dasher and the hero celebrated all around the States who had never been my father. I had memories of the man, mourned his death, and I actually never met him.

How messed up was that?

Worse yet, sometimes I didn't even feel *real.*

Like, did I really love taking photographs, or was that just because it was something Nadia liked? And if that were the case, did it matter because, at the end of the day, I *was* Nadia? Did I not know what I wanted to do with my life because I had no idea who I really was, my likes or dislikes? Could I trust anything I wanted when I didn't know if they were my desires, or the real Evie's, or Nadia's?

Did Luc call Nadia *Peaches,* too?

"Come back to me," Luc whispered against my cheek, and I sucked in a sharp breath.

Blinking, I focused on features that were both painfully familiar and heartbreakingly not. "I'm here."

"You went someplace else." Lifting his other hand, he caught a loose strand of my pale hair and tucked it back behind my ear. His hand lingered, slipping to the nape of my neck. "Do you see these lights?"

My brow furrowed in confusion. "Yes."

"Do you feel my hand against yours?"

"I do."

"And do you feel this?" He slid his hand around the side of my neck, gently pressing his thumb to where my pulse started to pound as his eyes searched mine.

"I feel that." I'd have to be dead to not feel that.

"You're real, Evie. It doesn't matter who you used to be or who you thought you were. You are real, and I see you."

Air caught in my throat, and my lungs felt like they might burst.

"And I never once called Nadia *Peaches.*"

He'd been reading my thoughts. "Luc—"

"I couldn't help it. You were broadcasting your thoughts loudly." His thumb moved, smoothing over the skin just below my ear.

It would be wise to pull away and put some distance between us, but I didn't move. I couldn't. A thrill lit up my veins, and a ridiculous amount of warmth poured into my chest. "So, it's . . . it's all mine, then?"

The question might've sounded ridiculous to anyone else, but I thought Luc understood. "Yeah." His voice was rough as he drew his hand up, dragging his thumb under my jaw. "It's all *you*."

A heavy exhalation left me. I couldn't describe how it felt. It was just a nickname based on the lotion I loved to wear, but still, it wasn't something that belonged to the Evie before me or to Nadia. It was me, right here and right now, and I latched on to that desperately.

Luc's hand tilted my chin to the side. Heat climbed down my throat, flushing my skin. Luc had lips that were as soft as satin and hard as steel. I had no idea how one thing could be both, but his lips were, and I knew this, because I'd touched them, tasted them. Those lips were so close to mine—the closest they had been since we'd last kissed, and that seemed like an eternity ago even though it had only been a few days.

I'd been his first kiss—well, Nadia had been his first kiss—and I was confident that I had been his last.

"Evie." Luc said my name as if it were a prayer and a curse.

I took a breath, but it went nowhere. His forehead touched mine, and I swore my heart stopped right then and there. Low in my stomach, muscles clenched once more.

Luc was so close that I felt his lips curve into a smile near my mouth, and if I turned my head just the scantest inch, our lips would touch.

Would he want that?

Would I want that?

I wasn't sure. The night we'd kissed, we'd done more. We'd been chest to chest, our bodies tangled and moving together, but Luc had stopped before it had gone that far, and we weren't boyfriend and girlfriend. There'd been no labels, no definitions to speak of. Not that we needed to be together to *be* together. There was just this expectation that there could be more, there could be *everything* if I'd just reach out and take it.

I wanted to reach, but I . . .

I was *afraid.*

Afraid of Luc realizing what I feared I already knew. That he was in love with a girl who no longer existed, and ultimately, wouldn't he be disappointed? I was terrified of letting myself feel those kinds of emotions that could lead to a broken heart. Scared that I would always be second best, or worse yet, a cheap imitation of the real thing.

Did Luc even see me when he stared into my eyes, or did he see the ghost of Nadia and didn't realize it yet? I wasn't sure if he even knew what he wanted, if he really wanted this with me, whoever I was.

"I always want that," he whispered against my lips.

Startled, I jerked back and broke contact. The lit atoms flickered and then fizzled out in a series of crackles. My gaze swung to Luc's face.

One side of his mouth kicked up as his gaze collided with mine. "All you have to do is ask, Peaches. All you have to do is tell me what you want, and it's yours."

I opened my mouth as my cheeks warmed. At a loss, I reached for the soda on the nightstand, taking a huge gulp. A slight tremble rattled the can as I placed it back on the nightstand that was bare except for a silver lamp.

"So . . ." I cleared my throat, searching for something to say. "How did you meet Paris?"

"It's kind of a funny story," he replied after a moment. "He tried to kill me."

"What?" My head whipped toward him. I had not been expecting that. "How is that funny?"

He grinned. "It was shortly after I'd escaped the Daedalus. I was around five, I think?"

I stared at him. "He tried to kill you when you were five?"

"Well, me at five was like a normal human at sixteen for all intents and purposes, but yeah, he'd been blackmailed into hunting me down with this other group of Luxen. They were supposed to capture and bring me back. That's not how it went down, though."

I had a feeling I could guess what happened.

"They, of course, weren't as prepared as they should've been when they found me. All of them except Paris had no issue with what was being done. I could tell." He tapped his finger to the side of his head. "So, I saved Paris."

In other words, he'd killed the rest of them . . . at five years old. I blinked slowly. "How were they blackmailing him?"

"They had his siblings," he answered. "A brother and a sister."

Oh God. "What happened to them?"

Luc looked away then. "We tried to find and free them, but they were killed once the Daedalus figured out Paris had teamed up with me instead of killing me."

"God," I whispered, thinking there were a lot of moments like this for him. People trying to kill him or control him, experiment on him and use him. "Are you sure you had good memories?"

"Many."

I wasn't so sure about that, and I was thinking that maybe it was a little bit of a blessing that I couldn't remember my childhood. And I wished I could . . . change that for him.

I looked away from him, my gaze landing on where my camera sat on my backpack. I'd brought it with me, planning to finally go through the pictures, but it sat untouched.

There was something I wanted to do, but it was kind of weird. Like, super-weird.

"Nothing is weird to me."

I sighed. "You're in my head again."

"Guilty as charged." When I looked at him, he arched a brow, utterly unrepentant. "What is it that you want to do, Peaches?"

"I want to take your picture." My face felt as if it were on fire. "And I know that sounds creepy—"

Interest filled his expression. "That sounds hot."

"Not that kind of picture!" Now my entire body was burning. "I just . . . you have such interesting lines. Your face, I mean. I want to capture them on film." I rose, wiping my suddenly damp palms as I turned away from him. "God, saying that out loud does sound creepy as hell. Just forget—"

"You can take as many pictures as you want."

"Really?" I faced him, clasping my hands together. Excitement thrummed to life. "You don't think it's weird?"

Luc shook his head, sending messy waves tumbling in every direction.

I glanced at my camera and then back at Luc. The question came out before I could stop myself. "You said Nadia—you said I was always interested in taking pictures?"

He nodded this time. "You liked to take a lot of the outdoors. Fall was your favorite. Then winter, but only when it had snowed. Otherwise, you didn't like taking those pictures, because—"

"Everything looks dead in the middle of the winter," I whispered, and when he nodded again, I felt a little dizzy. "It's weird. You know? That there are pieces of Nadia in me. I guess they've always been there." I walked to my bag and picked up the camera, wrapping the strap around my arm. "Do you think there's any of Evie in me?"

Luc was quiet for a moment. "I don't know. I didn't know her."

I fiddled with the buttons on the camera. "I was thinking last night that it seemed wrong to replace her, you know? Like it's an insult to her memory. It makes me feel gross."

"It wasn't of your choosing, though. You didn't wake up one day and decide to take over her life. Sylvia—" He cut himself off when I looked over at him. His shoulders were tense, the line of his jaw harsh, turning the beauty of all those lines more brutal than warm.

I lifted the camera then, snapping a picture before I lost my nerve. He didn't seem to mind.

"Don't put that kind of guilt on yourself," he said. "You didn't make that choice."

I knew what he was saying. Mom had made that choice, to replace the real Evie with me. She hadn't needed to do that. A part of me thought it wasn't wise to talk about Mom with him, especially after what happened the day before, but the words, the truth of it all, bubbled up. "She could've given me any other identity."

"Yeah, she could've." Luc held still as I slowly approached him. "Kind of makes you wonder why she did that."

My fingers halted several inches from his face. "It does." I drew in a shallow breath and then touched his chin. His entire body gave the slightest jerk, and I pulled my hand back. "Sorry. I was just going to—"

"No, it's okay." His eyes were a brighter shade of violet as he caught my hand and brought my fingers back to his chin.

Throat inexplicably dry, I tilted his head back and to the left so the sunlight caught the side of his face again. "I think she did it because she missed the real Evie."

"People do the strangest things for love."

Carefully, I brushed a thick lock of hair back from his face. His eyes closed as the tips of my fingers grazed his forehead. Warmth crept into my cheeks as I stepped back. "Don't move."

"Your wish is my command."

My lips twitched as I lifted my camera, adjusting the focus until I snapped a picture of him. I took several as I moved toward the foot of the bed, attempting to capture all the striking angles while feeling incredibly self-conscious.

Lowering the camera, I walked back to him, turning his chin so he was looking straight at me. I wanted to ask him to smile, but I was too embarrassed to do so.

"Are you going to look at the ones you just took?" he asked.

I shook my head. "Not until I'm done."

"That's different."

My gaze lifted to his, and I saw that he was smiling. Not a big one. That kind was rare for Luc, but this was a lopsided grin, and when those strands of hair flopped back onto his forehead, there was this adorable rakish look to him.

I snapped a pic.

"From before, I mean," he clarified. "You'd look at every picture after you took it. But you never took portraits. Do you take a lot of them now?"

"Not a lot, but I've taken photos of Zoe and Heidi, even James. But more candid shots, you know? Like when they're not paying attention to me." I switched the mode to black-and-white. "I guess that's something that is all me."

"It is."

Smiling, I lifted the camera and took another shot of him in black-and-white, and then I went over to him to readjust his angle.

Luc caught my fingers as he snagged my gaze, and my entire body locked up. He dragged them over the line of his jaw, to his parted lips. His warm breath danced over the tips of my fingers. He pressed a kiss to one finger. A tight, hot shiver curled low.

"I like this," he said, kissing my next finger.

"Like what?" Did I sound as breathless as I felt?

"You taking pictures." Another kiss on another finger. "I like that you're involving me in something you like to do."

An incredible whooshing sensation swept through my chest, more than a flutter, like an impossibly sweet swelling. "I like . . ."

He stared up at me through thick lashes, his mouth centimeters from my last finger. "What?"

I felt warm and dizzy as he held my gaze. "I like you . . . being involved."

One side of his mouth kicked up. "I know," he said, and then before I could respond, he nipped at my pinkie, a quick bite that sent a bolt of awareness through me.

My stomach hollowed as I sucked in air that seemed to do nothing to alleviate the sudden, intense throbbing.

Luc's smile turned downright wicked as he lowered my hand. His gaze flicked over my shoulder. "We'll have to take more later."

I opened my mouth, but a knock at the door silenced me. I stared at him dumbly as he rose, still holding on to my hand. "How do you do that? Know when someone is about to knock?"

"I'm that special." Luc led me down the step and into his living room. "Like a snowflake, unique and pure."

I snickered as he let go of my hand and went to the door. From where I stood, I saw Kent's blue mohawk when Luc opened the door.

"What's up?" Luc asked, dragging a hand through his hair.

"We got a problem."

4

Unease churned in my stomach as I sat on the edge of the couch. A problem could be anything from someone stubbing their toe to a raid on the club. Anything was possible here.

"Sorry to bother you guys." Kent cocked his head to the side, and I had no idea how the weight of his mohawk didn't topple him over. He waved at me. "Hi, honeybuns. Glad to see that you're okay. You dying would've sucked."

I waved back up at him. I hadn't seen Kent since before Micah's attack. He hadn't been a part of the cleanup.

He refocused on Luc. "It's Officer Bromberg. Again. This time, he's refusing to leave until he speaks to you."

"Officer?" My heart plummeted. "Is something going on?"

"Nothing to worry about, Peaches." Luc pivoted, heading into the kitchen. "Bromberg is with ART, and he likes to come in here and throw his weight around, because he knows we have unregistered Luxen here." Luc grinned at me as he pulled out a contact case. "He just can't prove it."

ART? That meant there was an Alien Response Task Force officer down there, and I had no idea why that wasn't something to worry about.

"Which is why I'm lingering up here," came a deep, familiar voice from the doorway. A tall, dark-haired Luxen stood in the doorway beside Kent. Daemon Black. "I'm too lazy to put the contacts in."

"Or too afraid," Luc quipped as he popped the lenses in, changing the color of his eyes from a vibrant purple to a dark brown. "You should've seen him the first time he did it. I thought he was going to vomit."

Daemon shot him a look.

"I can't stand the idea of contacts, either. The whole sticking my finger in my eye—no, thank you," I chimed in, and one side of Daemon's mouth quirked up.

"That's because you're not supposed to stick your finger in your eye, Peaches," Luc replied.

I ignored that comment. "Are you sure we shouldn't be concerned with this officer being here?"

"It's fine." He swaggered over to the door. "Thought you were leaving?" he said to Daemon, and as they both stood there, eye to eye, I wondered if Daemon would think it was creepy if I took their picture.

Probably.

So, I resisted.

"I am in a bit." He strolled into Luc's apartment as if it were his own. "I'll keep Evie company while you're occupied, though."

Luc's eyes narrowed, and I'd swear Daemon's grin kicked up a notch as he dropped onto the couch beside me, throwing his arm along the back of it.

"I'll be back shortly," Luc said, sending one last, long look before hooking a finger along the back of Kent's collar, spinning him around.

Kent waved goodbye, and then the door was swinging shut behind them, and I was sitting side by side with Daemon Black. With his black wavy hair and chiseled features, he was just as stunning to look at as his emerald-green eyes were.

Alien DNA did a body good.

Fiddling with the strap of my camera, I stared at the television, unsure of what to say. The TV was turned on to one of the news channels, but the volume was so low that I couldn't hear what they were saying. There was a breaking news banner along the bottom, something about a quarantine situation in Boulder, Colorado.

"You don't have to worry about the officer," Daemon said, looking over at me. Those emerald-green eyes were so bright, it was slightly unnerving. "Luc has it handled. This is just another normal Monday for him."

"I don't think it's normal to have ART officers show up like that." I lowered my camera to my lap. "I mean, what if he were to find proof of any number of unregistered Luxen here?"

"Then Luc will take care of it."

"Take care of it? As in 'take care of' the officer?"

"You probably aren't ready for that answer."

I opened my mouth but promptly snapped it shut. I wasn't stupid. Didn't take a genius to figure out what Daemon meant, but suspecting that Luc would silence the officer in the forever-and-ever kind of way was not the same thing as hearing Daemon confirm it.

So, I changed the subject.

"You haven't gone home yet?" I asked.

Daemon shook his head. "I'll be leaving tonight, once it's dark. I would hang around to make sure everything is cool here after that shit with Micah, but I need to get home. My girl is about to have our first baby, and I need to be there with her."

"Baby? Congrats!" I immediately pictured Daemon snuggling an infant, and my ovaries might have exploded a little. "Being away has to be really hard right now."

"It is. Coming here and getting the packages is something I need to do, but I'm not missing another second of Kat's pregnancy," he said. *Package* was the code word for unregistered Luxen. Daemon and others were moving them from their temporary hideout here at the club to someplace safe, where they could live without fear and without being forced to wear a Disabler. Where they were moving those Luxen to, I had no idea. No one had filled me in on that part yet. "This is the last trip I'll make for a while, so you'll probably be meeting my brother soon."

"Cool," I murmured, thinking about how dangerous it was, what they did, and the risks they were taking. "Have I met your—"

"Wife. Her name is Kat, and you two have met a couple of times." Daemon's gaze flickered away. "Luc will probably be pissed at me for telling you this, but the first time Kat and I saw you, you were dancing."

My heart stuttered. Daemon had seen me dancing? I couldn't believe it. I loved dancing, but I only did it in the privacy of my bedroom, where I could flail around like a cracked-out Muppet baby and no one could judge me. But Nadia danced in front of people—people like Daemon?

"I was?" I asked, throat parched.

He nodded.

I guessed Nadia—the old, unfamiliar me—had larger lady balls than I did.

Go figure.

What little I did know of Nadia's life told me she was a braver, stronger, and all-around more badass version of me.

He nodded. "It was at Harbinger, another club Luc owned. It's no more now, destroyed after the invasion, but we saw you there. You were a couple of years younger than Luc, and you were up on a stage just dancing away. You were really good. That was before . . ."

I nodded slowly, processing this little tidbit of information. I knew what *before* meant. Before the other Luxen, the ones who hadn't been living here for decades unknown among the human populace, had invaded. Before millions of people and Luxen were killed in an all-out war. Before, when I was known as Nadia Holliday, and before I became so sick that I had been dying of a blood cancer that no Luxen or Origin could heal.

I hadn't known there had been another club, and based on the timeline that I knew, I quickly did the math. My eyes widened as I shook my head. "Luc owned a club at thirteen or fourteen?"

A wry grin appeared. "Yeah, that was about my reaction when I first learned who Luc was. But that was before I even knew Origins existed. Anyway, later that night, while Kat and I were talking with Luc, you popped your head into the room. The way he reacted to us seeing you, to us learning you existed, I knew right then and there, Luc and I had something in common."

My brows pinched. "What? Mind-numbing good looks?"

Daemon's response was a slow curl of the lips that hinted at deep dimples.

Wait. I said that out loud?

I sort of wanted to smack myself. Hard.

"Well, we do have that in common, but that's not what I was thinking," he replied smoothly. His grin faded. "Can I give you some unasked-for advice?"

"Sure," I said, curious. Probably had to do with my driving since I almost ran him over once before. Totally not my fault, though. He *had* appeared directly in front of my car without warning.

Daemon was quiet for a long moment. "Luc and I would do anything to protect the people we love."

I stilled, unable to take more than a shallow breath as I stared at the male Luxen. I didn't know how to respond to that.

"I would beg, plead, barter, and kill to protect Kat," he continued, voice low, but every word struck me like thunder. "Nothing in this world would stop me, and there's nothing that I wouldn't do—and it's the same for Luc when it comes to you."

The next breath I took got caught in my throat as a brightness whirled through my veins. An undefinable amount of joy became a balloon in the center of my sternum, filling me up. I felt like I could float right up to the ceiling. To be loved like that? I'd seen that kind of all-consuming powerful love whenever Emery looked at my friend Heidi, so I knew that was real, and to know that Luc felt—

Luc felt that way about Nadia, though.

The reminder popped that whole balloon and sent me whizzing back to reality.

Things between Luc and me were complicated, and it had nothing to do with the fact that I was a human and he was an Origin, and everything to do with *who* I used to be.

A girl Luc had loved and lost—a girl he *still* loved.

A girl who used to be me.

A girl I couldn't remember no matter how hard I tried.

"Luc loves Nadia, and I'm not her," I said, sliding my suddenly damp hands over my jeans. "I may have been her once upon a time and I might look like her, but we're not the same person."

Daemon fell quiet as he studied me. "You might not have those memories, but that doesn't mean you're not her and that Luc doesn't feel the same about you as he did when he knew you as Nadia. And he was a kid then, Evie, and he already was willing to sacrifice everyone around him to save you."

Something about that tugged at the fringes of my memories. There was a flash of familiarity, but it was gone before I could grasp it. "What do you mean?"

"Do you really want to know?"

I wasn't so sure, but I nodded. "Yes."

He sat back, looking toward the television as he rested his ankle on his knee. "Do you know that Kat was captured by the Daedalus?" The Daedalus had been a secret division of the Department of Defense that had been responsible for assimilating Luxen into the human populace long before they'd invaded, and then for an atrocious series of horrific experiments with both Luxen and humans. "How it all went down?"

I shook my head.

"We were trying to free my brother's girlfriend, and we did so going off information Luc provided us even though he knew one of us would get caught and that the other would do anything to free them. The whole time, he was planning for it. He needed one of us on the inside, one of us who'd be exposed to all the different serums, especially the new ones that were developing. In a way, he set us up."

I thought I knew where this was heading, and I also thought I might be sick.

"Luc sent us in there to get the last serum that he knew the Daedalus had created, in an attempt to heal you. It was called the Prometheus serum," Daemon went on. "That serum was for you. Kat and I could've died. We didn't, but people did die, Evie, and I'm telling you right now, he'd do it all again knowing how it ends."

"Who died?" I whispered, chilled to the bone.

"A lot of people. A lot of good people died in the process of it all."

A name came to mind. "Paris?"

"He was one of them."

I opened my mouth, but I didn't know what to say. I couldn't believe it. Paris had died because of Luc.

Because of me.

As much as Luc talked about Paris, he never mentioned this. Not once.

"If Luc was the mastermind behind you all getting captured by the Daedalus and for people dying, then how are you friends with him?" I asked.

"Friends with Luc?" Daemon chuckled, and it was admittedly a nice sound even though I wasn't sure what was so funny. "I think you mean, how can I look past the fact that he almost got Kat and me killed? Easy. Because I would do the same thing if those shoes were on my feet."

"Really?" I gaped at him.

"Damn straight. If it were Kat who was dying and there were a chance I could save her, I'd throw everyone in this building under the bus, including you." He lifted a shoulder as I blinked at him. "Luc and I have an understanding."

"That's an . . . interesting understanding." Pushing a strand of hair out of my face, I glanced at the television as I chose my next words. "He did those things for Nadia, because he loved her—I think he's still *in* love with Nadia, and she's basically dead, Daemon. She and I couldn't be any more different."

He leaned toward me, bright green eyes meeting mine. "If Kat lost all her memories tomorrow and she didn't know who she was or who I was, it wouldn't change a damn thing about how I feel for her. I would still love her just as much as I did the day before."

I swallowed hard. "That's not really the same thing. You two have been together. It's not like she disappeared for years and then resurfaced with no recollection of her life before."

His eyes flashed with something dark. "Kat has disappeared on me before. Nothing like what happened to you and Luc, but time apart doesn't make that kind of love lessen. Just makes you more protective of it and makes you willing to do things others won't to make sure nothing like that ever happens again."

Tearing my gaze from his, I stared down at my checkered socks with little white ghosts all over them. I didn't doubt for one second that what he was saying about his feelings for Kat was 100 percent true, but things *were* different between Luc and me.

"And here's where my unsolicited advice comes into play. Whether you believe Luc is still in love with who you used to be or who you are now, it doesn't matter. He will do anything to make sure you're healthy and whole, and that means you need to be careful."

It took me a hot second to formulate a response to that. "Why would I need to be careful?"

"People like Luc and me? We aren't the bad guys, Evie, but we aren't the good guys, either. Do you understand what I'm saying?"

"Not really."

Daemon's gaze slid back to mine. "You have power over him and his actions, and because you don't even realize it, that makes him very dangerous."

I cast a skeptical look at him. "I don't see how I have any power over him, how that would make him dangerous, or how what he does or doesn't do is my responsibility."

"I'm not saying it's your responsibility. It's not. What Luc does is all on him. What I'm saying is you need to be aware of what he's capable of."

"I'm aware. I've seen it firsthand."

"You've seen a little of what he's capable of. So have I, and I like to think I'm a badass. My legion of fans would agree." A quick smile appeared, flashing deep dimples. "But he could take this whole block down with a snap of his fingers."

My eyes widened as my stomach dropped. I'd seen Luc uproot trees as tall as skyscrapers, but take down a whole block? "You're being a little overdramatic, right?"

Shaking his head, he turned to the television. "My sister."

I frowned. "What?"

"My sister is on TV."

The volume turned up without anyone touching it, and I figured that was courtesy of Daemon and his nifty alien talents. I twisted toward the TV.

I recognized the man. Senator Freeman appeared on half of the screen along with the skyline of New York City. He was the senator of one of the midwestern states. Oklahoma? Missouri? I didn't know, but the man was extremely anti-Luxen and in favor of tightening the ARP—Alien Registration Program—policies that President McHugh was trying to get passed through Congress, along with repealing the Twenty-Eighth Amendment, which afforded Luxen the same basic rights as humans.

He wasn't alone on the screen. There was a girl, a stunningly beautiful young woman who was the feminine mirror image of Daemon.

"Dee?" I said, pulling the name out of the recesses of my memory.

"Yeah, that's Dee."

"What's she doing on TV?" I was assuming that she was like her brother, unregistered.

"Doing God's work," he said, and then smirked.

The female Luxen was absolutely poised, her midnight hair pulled back from her face and her emerald-green eyes shockingly bright. I couldn't tell where she was. The background was just a plain white wall.

Senator Freeman was worked up over something, his cheeks ruddy and lips thin. "You keep saying that your kind aren't dangerous, that you can be trusted, yet there has been a steady increase of Luxen-on-human violence."

"There is no evidence that the unfortunate acts of violence against humans have been at the hands of the Luxen, only speculation—"

"An entire family in Charleston were found just this morning, burned from the inside out," Senator Freeman viciously interrupted, his tan cheeks deepening in color. "Are you saying that one of your people didn't do that?"

There wasn't so much as a flicker of response on Dee's face as she calmly stated, "There are many things that could explain their deaths other than an altercation with a Luxen—"

"Like being struck by lightning?" He scoffed.

Dee ignored the comment. "None of these senseless deaths have been officially linked to any Luxen, but there is staggering evidence of violence *against* Luxen—"

"Oh really?"

She nodded. "Videos of beatings loaded onto the internet—"

"Videos of United States citizens defending themselves."

"God, will he let her get one full sentence out?" I muttered. "How can anyone have a conversation with this dude?"

"He interrupts because he doesn't want to hear what she's saying," Daemon said, one hand tapping off his bent knee. "He doesn't want anyone else to hear it, either."

"I don't know how she doesn't lose her mind and flip a table."

"You've met me, right? She's had twenty-two years of practice dealing with someone who continuously interrupts her."

I grinned. "You must've prepared her well."

"Looks like it."

Dee wasn't flustered in the least as the senator slipped into another tirade about how Luxen were committing wholesale genocide against humans, which was an exaggeration even if a Luxen or a group of them *had* been responsible for the recent murders—even the recent murders Micah had been responsible for. He claimed he had nothing to do with them, but we knew better.

"She's so young." I brushed my hair out of my face. "I'm surprised that she's the one doing these interviews." Her youth was another thing I could tell irritated the senator, simply based on the way he spoke down to her. He was the definition of condescending and patronizing, and I had a feeling he probably spoke to *all* women like that.

"There are not many older Luxen left," Daemon said. "Most were killed during the invasion and the fallout afterward. Dee's kind of become our unofficial spokesperson."

"That's brave of her."

"It is. Most unregistered Luxen want to lie low, not wanting people to know their face. She's well protected, but most importantly, she's fearless."

"Archer?" I asked. "You?"

"All of us." His gaze flicked to me. "An entire community protects her."

"There's nothing to fear from a Luxen," Dee was saying for what had to be the millionth time. "We are no more dangerous than humans—no more evil or innocent. We are not monolithic, Senator Freeman, just like the human race isn't. If we were to judge the entire human race based on the rather extraordinary number of serial killers, mass murderers, rapists, racists, and so forth, how would that make you feel?"

"Oh, good question." I glanced back at Daemon. His head was tipped back, exposing his neck. "Bet he totally ignores that."

"I would not be willing to take that bet."

"If there's nothing to fear from a Luxen, then why aren't we having this conversation face-to-face?" Senator Freeman asked with a well-practiced smirk, ignoring Dee's point like I knew he would. "Instead, you're squirreled away in some undisclosed location."

Dee's steely green gaze fixed on the camera. "Because no one needs to be afraid of us, but we can't say the same thing about you. About *humans*."

5

I have a surprise for you.

Staring at the text message Luc sent while I was in history class, I volleyed back and forth between excitement and trepidation.

He had a surprise?

I glanced up at Mr. Barker. He stood in front of the chalkboard, green smoothie in one hand like always, a piece of chalk in the other. Whatever he drank every day was something that would never, ever get close to my mouth. I liked meat and carbs and sugar, and that stuff looked like a garden threw up in his cup.

The screen on my phone flashed again from where it was hidden under my desk, signaling another text.

Meet me at your car.

The corners of my lips turned down as I quickly typed back *now* with about five dozen question marks, along with 🤔.

A second later, I got a response. *ASAP. The surprise is in a box. And it could suffocate.*

I nearly knocked my phone out of my lap as I quickly typed *WHAT?* Then I followed it up with a reminder that I was in the middle of the class.

Come out as soon as you can, then.

As soon as I could? Like I could just come and go from school as I pleased? This was a problem when you were friends with someone who obviously had no structured education and followed absolutely no rules.

It had been two days since Officer Bromberg had shown up at Foretoken, demanding to see Luc. I had no idea what the officer had really wanted. When Luc returned and after Daemon left, Luc had brushed off my questions, claiming that the officer's visits were rather routine. I wasn't sure if I believed him or not. Part of me suspected he wasn't telling me the whole truth because he didn't want me to worry.

Which was annoying.

Straightening in my seat, I glanced over my shoulder at Zoe. She was staring at Mr. Barker, a dreamy smile plastered across her deep brown cheeks while she tugged one tight honey-colored curl straight and then let it bounce back.

Zoe had a bit of a crush on Mr. Barker. So did half the school. Mainly because he did have an amazing smile.

My gaze traveled over the class. Most of my classmates looked half-awake, including Coop, who kept blinking to keep his eyes open. His blond head rested on a fist while the other hand hung limply off the desk. Considering how much the guy liked to party, it wasn't entirely surprising to see him like that. I didn't know Coop well, but I wondered how he was doing after Andy's body was found outside his parents' home, where he'd been hosting the party. Did Coop also know Ryan?

News of Ryan's untimely death had been all that anyone was talking about this morning, but by the time lunch rolled around, it was like everyone had accepted it.

Until someone sneezed.

And then there were looks of fear, as if every sneeze was spraying a flu virus that had possibly killed a teenage boy. When I'd talked to Mom about it, she'd told me that the flu could kill, especially if someone had underlying health conditions, and that sadly most people didn't even realize they did until they got sick.

The phone vibrated against my thigh again, and I looked down.

I'm vaguely afraid of pandas, just so you know.

Pandas? What in the world? I grinned. The bubble appeared, showing that another text was coming. Mr. Barker was droning on about conquistadors or something, and I got another text.

Pandas are like one of the most misleading creatures in the entire animal kingdom. They're fluffy and cute, so you think they want to hug you, but in reality, they'll rip you limb from limb.

I had no idea how to respond to that.

Wait. I think that's koala bears. Those things are evil bastards.

And I had no idea how to respond to that, either, so I texted back *I'll be out in twenty minutes.*

That's a long time.
What will I do for twenty minutes?
Someone might try to take me.
I am that needed.
And wanted.
It's hard being me.
So
Hard

Oh my God, Luc was a mess.

Shaking my head, I dropped my phone into the front pocket of my bag and tried to focus on the rest of the class, but there was a strange flutter in my stomach and an even stronger one in my chest. Like I was buzzing. I'd never felt that way with my ex, Brandon, or any random dude I'd harbored a crush on. I didn't know what to make of the feeling, but it felt like a first of something major.

The next twenty minutes were the longest minutes of my seventeen years of life. When the bell rang, I popped out of my seat like I had springs attached to my feet.

"You're in a hurry," Zoe pointed out as she shoved her history textbook into her bag.

"Yeah, Luc's been texting me." I kept my voice down. "He said he had a surprise for me in a box, and he's worried it's going to suffocate or something."

"Oh God." Her eyes widened. "That literally could be anything he has in that box. Seriously, Evie. Anything."

"I know. That's why I need to hurry." I slung my book bag over my shoulder.

"You need to text me later and tell me what he has," she ordered.

"Will do." I waved goodbye to her and James, who, with his red-rimmed eyes and dazed stare, looked like he'd just woken up.

James wiggled his fingers at me, yawning.

Out in the hall, I hurried through the throng of students, making my way to the back entrance. It was way too easy to leave. All I had to do was open the doors and then walk out into the early October sun.

I cut through the manicured lawn and then up the steep hill, heart thumping heavily. I really had no idea what Luc could have in a box. If it was some kind of pet, Mom would flip.

She didn't do animal hair of any kind, and I wasn't sure how I felt about scales or furless pets in general.

I trekked across the asphalt of the parking lot, the flutter intensifying in my chest as I spotted my car and the guy lounging against it.

Luc stood with his long legs crossed at the ankles, leaning against the driver's door. He was wearing that gray, slouchy knit beanie that I had a thing for and his reflective silver aviators. My steps slowed as my heart sped up.

Today he wore a shirt that, ironically, featured a spaceship beaming someone up, and it said in bold, white letters, GET IN, LOSER.

He was holding a box. A small white one wrapped in red ribbon. There was definitely not a kitten or a puppy in the box. It was only big enough that maybe a very large tarantula or a lizard would fit.

I would straight-up knee him in the man parts if he had a damn furry spider in that box.

He looked up as I approached, those full lips tilting in a small smile. "There you are. I was starting to worry that maybe I was going to have to come in there, raise some holy hell, and get you."

I eyed the box. "You do realize that I have at least two more classes?"

"I do." He pushed off the car and leaned in, his warm breath dancing over my ear as he said, "But what I have planned for you is much more fun."

The skipping motion danced through my insides. "Does it have to do with whatever is in the box?"

"What's in the box is just the beginning."

I stared at the box in his hand. There were no holes to let any amount of air into it. "Is it a panda?"

"Don't think a panda would fit in this."

"A koala bear, then?"

"Dear God no. We'd all die if that were the case."

The corners of my lips curved up. "I don't think koala bears are that aggressive."

"Yes, they are, Peaches. They're demons disguised as fur balls. Ask an Australian."

"I don't know any Australians."

"I do." He shifted the box under his arm. "Let me see your car keys."

I narrowed my eyes. "Why do you need my keys, and what's in the box? I thought you were worried about it suffocating."

"I need your keys because I'm taking you somewhere, and you'll get the box once we're in the car."

Perhaps I should turn right around and head back into school. That would be the smart thing. I shouldn't be skipping, especially with Luc. But the curiosity got the best of me, as did something far stronger—something that felt *familiar.*

"Okay," I said, reaching into the pocket of my bag. I pulled out my keys, unlocked the car, and then handed them over to Luc. "If I get in trouble, I'm totally blaming you."

"It'll be worth it." He grinned as he slipped past me, opening the car door without even reaching for it.

Lazy.

Tossing my bag in the back seat, I hurried around the rear of the car and climbed into the passenger seat. The box was now in Luc's lap, and it wasn't moving around like there was anything in it.

Anything alive, that is.

Turning on the car, he looked over at me as he dragged his lower lip between his teeth. "You ready for your surprise?"

I nodded.

Luc handed the box over. "Be careful with it."

The box wasn't light, but it wasn't all that heavy, and as I placed it in my lap, nothing inside moved. I glanced over at Luc. "What's in this box?"

"It'll ruin the surprise if I tell you." He eased the car out of the parking space. "Open it."

Wary, I slipped my fingers under the red, satiny ribbon, sliding it off. Drawing a deep breath, I lifted the lid, prepared for something to spring out and sting me in the face.

Then I saw what was in the box.

I opened my mouth.

I closed my mouth.

And then a loud laugh burst out from me as I stared into it, not really believing what I was seeing.

"His name is Diesel," Luc explained as he pulled out of the parking lot, turning right. "He likes to be cuddled and held."

"Luc, it's a . . ." Another laugh escaped me as I shook my head. I couldn't believe what I was even staring at.

It was a *rock*.

A hand-size, oval-shaped rock nestled in cotton balls. And it wasn't just a normal rock. It had a face—a face drawn by a black marker. Two round eyes that had purple eyeballs. Eyebrows. An angle-shaped nose. A wide smile. There was also a lightning bolt drawn above the right eyebrow.

"It's a rock, Luc." I looked over at him.

"His name is Diesel. Don't judge him for the shape and form that he comes in."

I stared at him, mouth hanging open. "Was he attacked by Voldemort?"

"Maybe." That half grin appeared. "He's lived a very interesting life."

Slowly shaking my head, it took me a couple of moments to even formulate a coherent response. "You made me leave school early because you had a rock for me?"

"Now, Peaches, he's a pet rock, and I didn't make you do anything."

I gaped at him. I couldn't even remember the last time I'd heard the words *pet* and *rock* used in the same sentence.

"And where was I supposed to keep him while I waited for you to get out of class?" he asked. "The trip to school already scared him since I was moving so fast."

"I don't even know what to say right now," I murmured. Diesel the pet rock smiled back up at me. "Thanks?"

"You're so very welcome."

I blinked as I stared down at the rock, fighting a silly grin, because this whole thing was just so stupid and silly that it was actually sort of amazing.

"So, learn anything interesting in class today?" he asked, and when I looked up, I realized we were on Interstate 70, heading west.

"Not really." I held on to the box. "April was protesting again. We kind of got into it."

"What happened?"

"Nothing much." I stared out the window. Shopping centers gave way to tall elms and oaks, their leaves a stunning array of golds and reds. "She's . . . I don't know. Sometimes I don't even understand how Zoe could've been friends with her."

"Zoe has amazing restraint."

"If you spent any time with April, you'd understand how amazing that restraint really is," I said, looking over at him.

It struck me then how much my life had changed in a matter of weeks. A little over a month ago, I couldn't even fathom being in my car right now, going Lord knows where, with someone like Luc, while I was supposed to be sitting in class, stressing over what the hell I was going to do when I graduated. Every single aspect of my life, from the minor to the extreme, had changed. Some were in major ways, and others, like right now, were small and barely noticeable, but crept up on me.

Evie from two months ago wouldn't dare to do something like this. I didn't skip school. Hell, I'd been almost too afraid to go into Foretoken the first night with Heidi.

But now?

This was an adventure. This was fun despite all the insane things that had happened and were sure to come. I needed this.

I looked down at Diesel and smiled against the sudden burn in the back of my throat. I hadn't realized until this very moment that I needed this—the goofy-as-hell pet rock and this trip to wherever.

Glancing over at Luc, I wanted to hug him. Maybe do more. Like kiss him. Except that might cause him to wreck, and I liked my car.

"Peaches?" Luc was waiting.

Flushing, I was grateful that for once he didn't appear to be peeping on my thoughts. "I just want to kick April in the face. That's all I have to say."

He chuckled. "Please try to refrain from doing that, or at least make sure I'm there first to witness it."

Laughing, I let my head fall back against the seat. I saw a sign for US-340 West and, underneath it, the words *Harpers Ferry.* I repeated them absently. There was something familiar about it. I knew it was a town in West Virginia, but there was something more about it. Had I been here before or heard of the town? "Are we going there? Harpers Ferry?"

"Yeah. We're about thirty or so minutes out from there now. It's a small, old town. Famous for John Brown, an abolitionist. When he raided the federal armory in town with the intention of arming the slaves, it basically led to the Civil War a year later."

All of that sounded familiar. The Civil War was covered extensively in class last year, but I couldn't shake the odd tingling sensation at the nape of my neck.

"It's also kind of known for the fact that it sits right at the juncture of the Potomac and Shenandoah Rivers," he was saying. "Beautiful town, luckily virtually unscathed from the invasion."

I nodded, hearing what he was saying, but at the same time, consumed by the sense of being here before. But I knew I hadn't. At least not that I remembered, so unless—

Holy crap.

Was I remembering coming here as Nadia? Or was it just common knowledge picked up in school buried in my subconscious?

The tingling sensation increased throughout the remaining drive. The scenery was beautiful, especially when we crossed the bridge and I was able to see the town, off in the distance, situated on the face of the mountain that was a stunning kaleidoscope of yellows and burgundies. My fingers itched to grab my camera from the back seat, but I was frozen, soaking in the white-tipped waves of the river under the bridge and the view of a distant church.

A nervousness lit up my veins. Stomach twisting in raw knots, I fell silent as Luc turned right at a small hotel and I got my first close look at the town as it dipped and rose, houses scattered over hills and valleys. He'd taken another right, and as we crested the next hill, the homes and businesses tightly stacked together struck a chord in me.

Lower Town.

I blinked, my fingers gripping the box in my lap. We were driving into what was called the lower town, a street packed with quaint restaurants and locally owned shops. How did I know that? Was that covered in class? Or . . .

Reaching a stop sign, Luc waited until a group of people wearing sun visors and carrying cameras crossed. Tourists. He then turned left onto cobblestones and into the parking lot for what appeared to be a train station.

"You okay over there?" Luc asked as he turned off the car.

I nodded. "Yeah. It's just . . . I don't know. This place seems familiar, and I don't know if it's from school or if . . ."

"Ask me, Evie."

I swallowed and slowly looked over at him. Luc had removed his sunglasses, tucking them into the visor. "Did we come here before?"

Violet eyes met mine. "Yes."

I sucked in a short breath. "I feel like I know this place, but I don't know if it's because of school or something else."

Luc was quiet for a moment. "We came here a lot. Actually, it was one of your favorite places. There's an old cemetery you liked to take pictures of."

A strangled-sounding laugh escaped me. "That's dark."

His grin was quick. "The cemetery wasn't what you loved the most."

"What was?"

Looking away, he opened the driver's door. "You'll see."

For a good minute, I sat there, trying to decide if I was ready to do this. This was the first time I was truly going somewhere I used to frequent as Nadia, a place that meant something. What if I went wherever Luc was taking me and I didn't feel anything? Just nothing?

What if I felt something?

The possibilities were equally terrifying, and while there was a tiny part of me that wanted to stay in the car with my pet rock, I wasn't that Evie anymore.

I couldn't be that Evie anymore.

With a shallow breath that did nothing to ease the pressure clamping down on my chest, I opened the door and climbed out, carefully placing the box on the seat.

The window was cracked, but I left it like that. Luc was staring at me, and I grinned. "Letting air in, you know, so Diesel doesn't get too hot."

A wide, beautiful smile traveled across his features, momentarily stunning me. It was a rare smile. A real one that reached his eyes, warming them.

"Look at you, already thinking of Diesel."

Laughing, I closed the door and joined him. "So, where are we going?"

"You'll see." He started walking, and I knew he was slowing down his pace so I didn't have to speed walk to keep up with him.

We crossed over to the sidewalk, passing several places that were grilling or baking something that smelled amazing. Luc maneuvered us so that he was on the left, closest to the street, a weird move I didn't fully understand. As we walked down the sidewalk, our progress hindered by the people taking pictures and their sweet old time, my left hand brushed his right, sending a jolt of awareness through me.

Was he going to take my hand? And hold it?

My heart gave a silly little skip at the thought.

We hadn't held hands before, at least not that I remembered.

Then up ahead, to the right, I saw the Gothic-style church I'd spied from the bridge. As we grew closer, I could see how ancient it was, built out of reddish-tan stone, with white trim outlining the steeple.

"That's beautiful." I could feel my eyes widening. "God, it has to be old."

"It's St. Peter's Church."

We stopped to cross the street, and I felt one of his fingers brush over the top of my hand. Heart thumping heavily, I turned my hand palm up, extending a finger along his. Luc didn't hesitate. His fingers immediately closed around mine, his grip warm and strong. It was such a simple gesture, but it was huge to me.

"I think it was built in the early 1800s," he said, voice rougher than normal. "It's also haunted."

My head snapped toward him. "What?"

Luc was grinning as he led me across the street to the wide set of steep steps that led up to the church. "Yeah, supposedly by a priest or a nun . . . or a chupacabra."

"Chupacabra?" I laughed.

"I think it was a priest or reverend. A man of the clergy." He guided me to the stone courtyard of the church, past the crowds taking pictures. We were getting looks—well, he was. Not because of his eyes. Because of that face and his height. "We did a ghost tour down here once with Paris."

My smile faded at the mention of the deceased Luxen's name.

"You got so scared, you started crying." Luc was looking ahead. "You made us leave halfway through the tour and take you home."

"You're lying."

"Never." He slid me a sidelong glance, eyes twinkling with mischief.

We went past the church, onto another narrower trail that consisted of earthen-stone steps leading up a rather steep hill surrounded by trees. To the right, there were stone ruins behind the trees, remnants of a brutal past. My calves were burning by the time we reached the halfway point, proof I needed to, like, walk more. Luc's hand remained around mine, all the way to a collection of smooth boulders that a few people stood on.

Immediately, I turned to our left and that tingling feeling from earlier resurfaced, but this time, it was all over my body, like I'd walked into a cobweb.

"This is Jefferson Rock." Luc nodded at the shale rocks that appeared precariously piled on top of one another, perched on the edge of the cliff. Four stone pillars held the top rock up.

Luc was explaining why it was called Jefferson Rock, something to do with Thomas Jefferson, but there was a buzzing in my ears. A small child raced past us, toward the stone steps we'd just climbed, followed by a ragged-looking father.

I was drawn to the rocks. Slipping my hand free from Luc's, I walked over, legs jerky, and I stopped, placing a hand on the boulder as I stared out over the Shenandoah.

I could never catch him.

The words came out of nowhere, raising the tiny hairs all over my body. Dizziness swept over me, sudden and acute. Air seized in my lungs. I didn't know if it was because of the height or—

"Careful," Luc murmured, suddenly beside me, a hand on my lower back. "Really don't want to go diving after you."

I drew in a breath to speak, but nothing came out. White flashed behind my eyes, and suddenly, I didn't see the roaring river down below or the blue, cloudless sky.

I saw a boy running past the church and up those old, ancient steps. He was laughing, and the sun turned his hair bronze. He was running too fast, and I couldn't catch up to him.

I could never catch him.

I tried—I always tried.

And he let me catch him by the rock, when our clothing was

covered with dust and sweat dotted our skin, and I'd kissed him. I'd stretched up on the tips of my red-and-white sneakers, looped scrawny arms around his neck, and I'd kissed him.

The memory fragmented as quickly as it had formed, disappearing like raindrops in the sun.

"Evie?" Concern filled his tone.

"I . . ." I couldn't catch my breath as I stared into his eyes—the eyes of the boy I kissed right here, years ago. "I *remember.*"

6

Luc had taken my hand again, leading me away from the people crowding Jefferson Rock, farther up the trail and to the grassy knoll that bordered the cemetery.

Nothing about the irregular rows of white and gray tombstones was familiar to me. Some of them were decayed with age, others glossy and new, but the sensation of invisible fingers along the back of my neck continued.

Luc sat, tugging me down with him in the plush grass. From where we were, we overlooked the river cutting through the valley. The hand he held trembled in his tight grasp. "You remember?" he asked, his voice rough as if his throat were thick.

I rubbed my palm over my leg, nodding as I swallowed hard. "I remember you running up the steps, and it was like we'd done that so many times before and I could never catch you, but then I did. You . . ." I squeezed my eyes tight and then reopened them. "You let me catch you, and I kissed you. I stretched up, threw my arms around you, and kissed you. Is it real? The memory?"

His striking features were pale as his hand spasmed around mine. "It's real."

The next breath I took got stuck as I curled my fingers around his. I closed my eyes again, seeing him as a boy—his features the same but softer and younger, his body familiar but thinner. I inhaled sharply as a cool breeze lifted my hair, tossing it over my face.

"It was right after the invasion and things had begun to calm down. We came back to see if anything here had been impacted, and it was like the only place for miles around that had been untouched."

"That's strange."

"It was, but the day we came here . . . it was a good day. You were feeling good." He let go of my hand, and when I opened my eyes, he was tugging the beanie off his head. "It was after you were given the—"

"Prometheus serum?" I said, and those wide, questioning eyes shot to mine. "Daemon told me about it."

Luc stared at me for a long moment. Tension crept around his mouth, and then he exhaled heavily. "The Prometheus serum seemed to work for a few days. You had more energy. You weren't nauseous at all. You could eat. And all those *goddamn* bruises that covered you had started to fade. I was still cautious. Didn't want you out running around, but you wanted to come up here, and who was I to deny you?"

Luc stared out over the valley. "Sometimes I wonder if you knew the serum hadn't worked beyond giving you a respite from the disease. Looking back, I think you did." Lifting his hands, he scrunched his fingers through his hair. "Anyway, that was the day you kissed me, and damn, it takes a lot to catch me off guard, but you'd managed to do just that. I had . . . these feelings for you. I didn't like them at first. I didn't even understand them." His fingers curled around the short strands of hair. "And I'd always thought you saw me as a brother. That's all I could let myself think. I was young. You were even younger."

I didn't know how anyone could look at Luc as only a brother other than someone who was legit his sibling, but I kept that to myself.

"But you kissed me and . . ." He dropped his hands as he tilted his face to the sun, eyes closed. "It broke me in a way I didn't even know you could be broken."

"That doesn't sound good." I felt like I needed to apologize.

"It was . . ." He lifted his hands, shaking his head. "It wasn't bad, Evie. Not at all." A quick smile appeared and then disappeared. "Do you remember what you said to me afterward, while I was staring at you like an idiot?"

I shook my head. "No, I don't."

"Do you remember anything else?"

"No. Just that, but as soon as I saw the sign for the town, I felt weird. I told you that." I threaded my fingers through the grass. "Is that why you brought me here? To see if I'd remember anything?"

"Yes? No? I don't know. Mainly, I brought you here because it was someplace I knew you used to love. I've been wondering if you'd still feel the same."

Taking in the ancient trees and the valleys and rivers below, I could see why I'd loved this place. There was a calming effect to it, being close to civilization and yet somehow surrounded by nature and rich history. "I think I could grow to love it again."

He was silent and then asked, "Do you want to stay or leave?"

I knew if I said I wanted to leave, he would be standing faster than I could finish the sentence, but I didn't want to leave. "Not yet."

"Okay." His throat worked on a swallow.

Companionable silence fell between us as I watched the limbs move in the wind, shaking loose dying leaves and sending them fluttering to the ground. The scent of river and soil surrounded us, and if it hadn't been for the million steps we climbed to get here, I would've raced back to my car for my camera.

"What did I say to you?" I asked, remembering what he'd said. "After I kissed you?"

Luc was quiet for a long moment. "You said, 'Don't forget this.'"

I stilled. God. Maybe I had known that the serum hadn't worked, because that was a hell of a thing to say.

"How ironic is that?" He chuckled, but it was without any lightness. "Like I would ever be able to forget what it felt like for your lips to touch mine. Like I could ever forget you."

"It was me who forgot." Tears pricked my eyes as I pulled my knees to my chest and wrapped my arms around my legs. He couldn't forget me, and I'd forgotten him. "I'm sorry."

His gaze shot to mine. "For what?"

"I don't know." I lifted a shoulder and rested my cheek on my knees. "For all of this? Because it seems easier to not have these memories."

"No. Not at all." Luc leaned over, bringing his face close to mine. "I cherish every single memory I have of us. Even the sad ones. I wouldn't trade a second of them for anything, because I had my memories and you had a second chance. You lived."

More tears clogged my throat, and I closed my eyes. "And you lost me," I whispered. "I lost you."

"Did we lose each other?" he asked, and then I felt his fingers on my cheeks, chasing a tear that had sneaked free. "You and I are here right now, aren't we? Somehow, you found me, and I'm not someone who believes in happenstance. I don't think it was a fluke that you walked into Foretoken with Heidi. I think it was something that was bound to happen and I . . ."

I opened my eyes, finding his. "What?"

"I was just waiting."

"It really is a pet rock." Heidi was staring at Diesel, who now rested in a nice little bed of cotton and rolled socks on top of my nightstand. "Holy crap."

It was after school the following day, and it had been a while since the three of us just hung out. Zoe was in the computer chair I never used, toeing herself around my bedroom, and Heidi and I sprawled along my bed.

"I don't know if that's the strangest thing I've seen in a while or the most amazing thing." Heidi's chin was propped up on her fist, and her crimson-colored hair was pulled up in a high, messy topknot. "I think pet rocks stopped being a thing before we were born, but I think it's the most amazing thing."

"It is." I smiled into my comforter. "I can't remember the last time I laughed so loud."

Zoe shook her head as she toed herself closer. "Part of me was hoping it was, like, a snake or something."

My eyes widened. "I do not do scales of any sort."

"I know. Then I could've had it." She grinned at me. "By the way, did you get your Halloween costume?" she asked Heidi.

She nodded. "Sure did."

"What are you dressing up as?" I asked.

"Rainbow Brite," she answered, and I laughed. "Didn't see that coming, did you?"

"Actually, I kind of already think of you as Rainbow Brite, so . . ." I looked over at Zoe. "What about you?"

"I think I'm going as Wonder Woman." Her arms flopped over the sides of the chair. "Or maybe Daenerys? Not sure. You?"

"I have no idea."

Heidi's brows knitted. "You're coming to Foretoken with us, right? I figured your anti-Foretoken oath has officially been broken."

"Yeah, it has, and I'm going, but I haven't really thought about it. I'll figure something out. I have time." Sitting up, I glanced at the television and saw the breaking news banner along the bottom of the screen. "Something is going on."

Heidi followed my gaze as I leaned over her, but the remote was still too far away. "What's going on in Kansas City?"

Zoe lifted her hand, and the remote flew from the edge of the bed to her hand. I shot her a jealous glare as she turned the volume up.

A male reporter was on the screen, his brown hair cropped close to his skull. I vaguely recognized him. "We've just received a statement from officials concerning the alarming activity at the apartment complex in Kansas City. Jill, can you update us?"

A dual screen appeared, revealing a dark-skinned woman in a pale pink turtleneck. She was standing across the street from a several-story, gray brick building that was cordoned off by yellow tape and partially blocked by ambulances and fire trucks. "Yes, Allan, we've just received word from Sergeant Kavinsky that this apartment complex on Broadway is under a complete quarantine at this time. There's been no official statement, but we do know that the situation began last night when a coworker of one of the tenants came to the building to check on an employee of"—she glanced down at something she held in her hand, off-screen—"a local advertising and marketing firm who had missed work both Thursday and Friday and had no contact with the employers. It was this coworker who discovered several severely ill individuals inside the complex—all of whom, we are told, are now deceased."

"Yikes," I whispered as Heidi sat up and leaned into me.

"We have also been told that the coworker has been quarantined, as there are fears of exposure to whatever has sickened and perhaps killed the tenants of this building," Jill continued. "This apartment complex has fifteen units, and from what we have been able to gather, all tenants in the complex are accounted for inside." She turned her body, angling slightly toward the building. "We have also exclusively learned that one of the deceased tenants of this building, a Lesa Rodrigues, worked at a Luxen outreach facility in Kansas City. Now, we contacted this group and are currently waiting for a response, but this situation appears to be very reminiscent of the event in late September at a home outside of Boulder, Colorado, where a family of five were found dead, their bodies showing signs of a massive, destructive infection of some sort. The father of that family, a Mr. Jerome Dickinson, was a property manager at a Luxen subdivision."

The camera zoomed out, capturing the activity on the sidewalk below the apartment. There were several people in white biohazard suits disappearing behind one of the fire trucks as the reporter continued to speak.

"Sergeant Kavinsky has said that they do not believe that there is any threat to the community at this time; however, they are asking that people try to stay away from the apartment complex and the Luxen outreach facility on Armour Street. We have received word that the facility is also currently being quarantined as a preventive measure until they can determine if there is any risk to the public. The nearby buildings here, which house many businesses, will also be closed until further notice." She faced the camera once more. "Now, a source close to this investigation who has seen the bodies of the deceased is saying that the condition of the remains are nearly identical to those in Colorado, leading this person to believe that the individuals in this complex, like the family in Boulder, have died of some sort of virus or infection. This source is saying that even though authorities are not publicly stating this yet, it is believed that the infection occurred after close contact with a Luxen."

Oh no.

Heidi stiffened against me, and my stomach sank all the way to the floor. A massive, destructive infection like . . . like possibly a flu? Like the kind of flu that killed Ryan?

"That's bullshit," Zoe spat.

"If you remember, the cause of death for the family in Boulder is believed to be partially from a hemorrhagic-type fever and a cytokine storm—the body's overwhelming reaction to an infection. Sometimes you will see that in severe flu cases or with other viruses, but officials investigating the Boulder family have stated that while they believe that was an isolated case, whatever had sickened and killed the family has not been seen before."

The male reporter suddenly returned to the side of the screen, replacing the image of the apartment building. “And now we have an entire building quarantined with possibly the same sickness, hundreds of miles away.”

Jill nodded. “It hasn’t been confirmed, but our sources suspect that it is the same illness that struck down the family in Boulder.”

The male journalist’s gaze turned somber. “With the increasing acts of violence and terror in cities all across the nation, this surely will help President McHugh’s push to repeal the Twenty-eighth Amendment and increases the likelihood of legislation such as the Luxen Act and reinstatement of the Patriot Act, which is legislation backed by President McHugh, being passed.”

Jill agreed while I stared at the screen.

Beside me, Heidi swallowed thickly. “Do you think it’s possible that whatever Ryan had is what these people died of?”

“I don’t know,” I murmured. “They said that whatever these people had wasn’t a threat to the community, and we’re like a thousand miles from there, but . . .”

“But you guys heard what I heard, right?” Zoe asked, turning to us. “Sounds like they’re gearing up to blame the Luxen for whatever made these people sick.”

“Mom!” I yelled the moment I heard her come home that night, close to midnight, my feet thumping off the steps as I headed downstairs and into the foyer. There was one person I knew who was well familiar with viruses and biological gross stuff that could be passed from one person to the next. Mom. She was a fountain of knowledge since she worked at the United States Army Medical Research and Material Compound at Fort Detrick in Frederick.

I didn’t know how she could still work for a government that had operated and sanctioned the actions of the Daedalus, but then again, there were many in the government who were fighting for the Luxen, and I figured it was safe to assume that there were also many like Mom, Luxen who were hidden in plain sight. And after everything I’d experienced and seen, I knew you couldn’t make any changes if you weren’t in the thick of it. Sitting by the sidelines or hiding only aided the opposition.

“In the kitchen,” came the response.

A candle was burning somewhere, filling the open space with the scent of pumpkin and caramel. I hurried through the living room, where everything was neat and had a place, past the dining room table that had to be replaced after the showdown with Micah, and found her standing at the kitchen island, placing her briefcase and purse on it.

Her hair was smoothed back into a ponytail, and there wasn't a single strand out of place. I didn't need a mirror to know that mine was gnarled and resembled a bale of hay at the moment. There was always this inherent grace and elegance about Mom and the way she moved, and I just sounded like a herd of horses clopping down the steps.

She lowered her keys. "Should I be worried that you just ran down the stairs at breakneck speed?"

"Not exactly." I hopped onto the stool. "I have a question for you."

"I might have an answer." Mom walked to the fridge and grabbed a bottle of water, sitting it on a gold-colored coaster. It was new. She had a habit of collecting coasters like some people collected expensive purses or shoes.

"Can humans get sick from a Luxen? Catch something like a cold or a flu?"

Mom stared at me for a moment. "You've seen the news."

"Yes." I tipped toward her, resting my feet on the lower bar of the stool. "A whole apartment building in Kansas City has been quarantined, and it seems like everyone is sick or dead inside. The reporters are talking like it's some kind of infection passed from Luxen to humans, but—"

"Luxen cannot make humans sick, Evie." Reaching up, she placed two fingers to her temples as if she had a sudden headache. "There is no known cross-species disease. Luxen—we—don't even get sick, not like humans." She briefly closed her eyes. "If those poor people are sick from some kind of virus or infection, it is not from Luxen. If anyone is saying that, it's an unsubstantiated opinion not remotely based in the science or any of the extensive research that has been done."

That's what the girls and I thought. "Then why would they put that out there like that? You know how people believe whatever they hear or see. They read a stupid post on Facebook about killer spiders hiding under toilet seats, and even though that makes no sense, they believe it and share it five million times. People are going to believe this."

Mom shook her head as she lowered her hand to the gray granite island top. "The idea of Luxen carrying some kind of unknown virus that can infect humans is far more salacious than carbon monoxide poisoning or a virus like influenza, which is probably the actual source of these illnesses. After all, it is flu season."

"They're saying that Ryan—that boy I told you about—died of the flu. I know you said that the flu can kill, but is it really that deadly? And could it be the same virus that killed the people in Kansas City and Boulder?"

"I think it's unlikely that it's the same strain, but every year, there are cases of H1N1 and other strains that are quite deadly. Plus, like I told you before, it can be extremely dangerous for those with compromised immune systems. People just don't report on that kind of stuff, because it's not going to get the ratings they want."

"What those reporters were saying is so incredibly dangerous," I murmured, turning my gaze to the small window above the sink. "People already . . ."

"People already fear us," she finished for me, her voice so quiet, I had to look at her. "People are already going to assume and think the worst of us, and that is why I must be careful. That is why Luc must be careful. " A chill skated over my skin as my eyes met the exact same shade as mine. Her contacts were a warm brown. "And that's why you must be careful."

7

It was my brother's fault," Emery said, running a hand over her head, catching the shoulder-length, raven-black strands in her fingers. Her hair was buzzed close to the skull on one side, and I was *this* close to totally copying her hairstyle. "I love Shia and miss him every day, but it was his fault."

It had been two weeks since the trip to Harpers Ferry and the quarantine situation in Kansas City, and luckily, there hadn't been any more situations like that.

Cooler and more logical heads were prevailing. So far. Many human doctors and scientists were on TV nightly, as was Daemon's sister, Dee, attempting to dispel the rumors that there was some kind of virus being passed from Luxen to humans. They were making headway, thankfully, because there'd been no more cases of the mysterious virus.

Somehow, the three of us had gotten on the topic of what happened to Emery's family during and after the invasion, while we were in Emery's apartment above Foretoken. Before I'd learned that Emery was a Luxen, I'd been told that her family had died, but I never knew how.

"There were a lot of Luxen here who weren't happy with having to live like humans. They thought that they should be in control," Emery explained as she sat back. "That we were the higher lifeforms, so why were we living in the shadow of humans? My mom was still alive then, and so was my other brother, Tobias. They were like me, having no problem living like humans. I mean, it would've been great to have things out in the open. Pretending to be human isn't easy."

"Because of having to force yourself to slow down and move like a human?" I asked, vaguely remembering Zoe explaining why she always came in dead last in gym class.

Emery nodded as she glanced at Heidi. "It takes more energy for us to slow down. Not to mention, it's exhausting always being aware of how fast we're moving and how we're behaving, so it would be nice to live out in the open, but not in the way they wanted. To Shia and others like him, it was never about equal rights. It was about dominating humans and proving we were stronger, smarter, and better in every aspect. They helped the invading Luxen."

I drew in a short breath as I sank into the thick cushions.

"Shia helped them, and when the war began, he was on the other side." She bit down on her lip, looking at the menu from a bakery down the street that offered all variations of cupcakes humanly possible. "We tried to get him out. You know, to get him to see that what they wanted to do wasn't right. Wasn't any better than what the humans are trying to do now. He wouldn't listen, and it happened right after the war—during the first wave of raids, where they were just rounding up Luxen and . . ."

And killing them.

My memories of the time after the invasion weren't real . . . or at least, they weren't *my* memories. Or maybe the memory of the fear and confusion had been mine and that trauma had broken through the fever, forever implanted. Either way, it had been a scary time for humans and Luxen alike.

"He'd been spotted before, during the war, and they couldn't tell Shia and Tobias apart. Not that it mattered then. They both were killed, and my mother tried to intervene. She was slaughtered right along with them. It happened so quickly. They were alive one moment and dead the next." Her lower lip trembled as she gave a short shake of her head. "I don't even know how I escaped. It's a blur to me now, but I got out of there."

"You don't have to talk about this," I told her, my heart squeezing as Heidi rested her cheek on Emery's shoulder. "I mean, I don't want you to feel like you do."

"No. It's okay." Emery's smile was brief. "It's good to talk about these kinds of things sometimes. You know?"

I nodded. "What did you do afterward?"

"Moved from city to city, trying to keep a low profile. I met some other Luxen along the way, others like me who were unregistered and just wanted to live. I ended up in Maryland after hearing about this place where unregistered Luxen could be safe."

"Foretoken?"

Emery nodded. "Didn't believe it, even after I first met Luc. Couldn't figure out how he, at the time being like fifteen or sixteen, could remotely guarantee anyone's safety, but he took me in and got me straight."

"Got you straight?"

Heidi glanced at Emery before speaking. "Let's just say Emery was on a very understandable, destructive path."

"I wasn't taking care of myself. Not eating right and . . . there are drugs out there that have the same kind of effects on us as they do on you," she said, and *that* I hadn't known. "Ketamine. Some narcotics." She rubbed her hands together. "Heroin. It takes twice the dose—sometimes more than what a human can withstand—for it to have the same effects, but I fell down that rabbit hole."

Oh God, I didn't know what to say. *I'm sorry* didn't feel like it would cover it. All I could do was offer her no judgment, and that's what I did. Luxen or human, not everyone who went down that path did so because they woke up one day and decided to trash their life. Some ended up there because of human doctors overprescribing pain medications. Others, like Emery, were trying to escape trauma, and I could understand that.

Empathy was power.

"When I met Luc, I had no idea he was an Origin. I had no idea they even existed. I couldn't figure out how he spent ten minutes with me and seemed to know my deepest secrets."

"He was reading your thoughts?" I guessed.

A quick smile appeared. "Yeah, and he knew right off the bat that I had a problem, and me getting clean was his only condition of helping me. And he did, he and Grayson and Kent. It wasn't easy. Hell, there are still days . . ."

"Never again." Heidi cupped Emery's cheek, guiding the Luxen's gaze to hers. "Right?"

"Right," Emery whispered.

Feeling I was creeping on an intimate moment, a vulnerable one, I lowered my gaze to the menu. I saw the glorious lists of cupcakes, but I wasn't processing the words.

I was thinking about what Emery had just shared.

Not only had Luc provided someplace safe for Emery, as he had for countless others, he'd also gotten her clean. God. That was no small feat for humans.

Luc was no miracle worker, but he was . . . well, he was just Luc.

"Okay, now I really need some cupcakes." Emery's laugh was shaky. "What do you want, Evie?"

"Um." I glanced back at the menu. "Can I have all of them?"

Before the girls could respond, there was a knock on the door, and Emery called out, "Come in."

I twisted around, and my heart gave a little jump when I saw it was Luc. I hadn't seen him earlier, but I figured he was around somewhere. At once, I noticed his shirt. It was gray with a picture of a panda in the middle. It read WARNING. PANDAS ARE BEARS. And then underneath, in smaller print, was STILL NOT AS BAD AS KOALA BEARS.

Immediately recalling his text rant, I grinned.

Luc's gaze immediately zeroed in on me. He didn't need to look around; it was like he knew exactly where I was sitting from the moment he opened the door.

"I'm coming to crash the girls' party." He walked up to where I sat. "Because I know you guys missed me."

"We were just sitting here, talking about how much we missed you, and we were wondering what you were up to," Emery responded, grinning.

"Actually, we were almost in tears over the fact you hadn't blessed us with your presence yet," Heidi chimed in. "Right, Evie?"

"Right," I replied dryly.

"You guys warm my soul." Luc tugged gently on a strand of my hair, and I looked up at him. "I have a surprise for you."

I immediately became very, very wary.

Heidi, on the other hand, clapped excitedly, vaguely reminding me of a seal. "I'm so excited to see what this is."

"Same," Emery echoed as she kicked a long leg onto the coffee table.

Admittedly, I was, too, because I really had no idea what Luc had for me today. Diesel the pet rock wasn't his last gift. There hadn't been any more trips to Harpers Ferry or anywhere, but there'd been a lot of surprises.

A lot of weird ones.

"It's a private one." Luc's grin was downright wicked.

My eyes widened.

"That makes it all the more interesting," Heidi said.

"That it does, but . . ." He tapped the bridge of my nose, and I swatted at his hand. "Can I steal you away?"

I glanced over at them, and after a moment, I nodded. "Can you guys get me one of the Butterfinger cupcakes?"

"You mean, like, three of them?" Heidi corrected me.

I laughed as I rose, dropping the menu on the coffee table. "Yes. Text me when they're here."

"Will do." Emery handed the menu to Heidi.

As I stepped around the couch, Luc pushed off the back of it and took my hand. Warmth exploded across my cheeks, because I knew damn well both Heidi and Emery were watching, and I'd never hear the end of it.

But I didn't pull my hand free. I let him lead me out of Emery's apartment and down the hall. "Where are you taking me?"

"It's a surprise, Peaches."

"I'm not sure I like your surprises."

"You don't," he replied. "Because you *love* my surprises."

I arched an eyebrow. "Yeah, I don't know if we're in agreement. I loved Harpers Ferry, but the rest of them? Not so sure about that."

"Now what makes you say that?" The door to the stairwell opened before we reached it.

"Diesel," I reminded him.

"What about my handsome boy?"

We climbed the stairs. "He's fine."

"I know he is, because he's sitting right on your nightstand."

The stupid rock *was* sitting there. It was the last thing I'd seen when I'd fallen asleep the night before and the first thing I saw upon waking.

I glanced over at him, finding him grinning at me. "Okay, what about last Sunday? You asked me to come over because you had a surprise, and the surprise was a marathon of all the James Bond movies."

"James Bond is amazing."

"I hate those movies," I pointed out as we reached his floor.

Luc bent his head toward mine, coming just short of his lips brushing my cheek as we stopped in front of his door. "I know."

When he spoke, I felt his breath, and a tight, hot shiver curled its way down my spine.

"And I still like you even though James Bond is a classic and you have no taste," he added, opening his door with a wave of his hand.

"How was that a surprise?"

"You didn't know it would happen, now did you? Pretty sure that's the definition of a surprise." He pulled me into his dimly lit apartment. The blinds were drawn, blocking out most of the afternoon sun.

"Pretty sure that surprises should be something the person receiving the surprise is interested in." The door swung shut behind us.

"Don't think that's what it means." Luc tugged me forward, and I went, stopping directly in front of him.

I had to tilt my head way back to meet his shadowy gaze. "How about the day before that? You said you had a surprise when I came over and you handed me cheese and bread."

"The surprise was that you were going to make me a grilled cheese sandwich," he explained.

I looked at him blandly. "What about the Chia Pet?"

Luc chuckled, and it was a nice sound, dancing off my skin. "I still can't believe you managed to kill a Chia Pet in a week."

"It was defective," I muttered. "And it was a Mr. T Chia Pet! Like, how did you even find one of those?"

"I have Chia Pet connections."

I stared at him. "That's . . . special. Look, I'm just trying to point out you have a history of surprises that I either don't like or have no idea the purpose behind."

"All my surprises have purposes. You shall see." Still holding my hand, he led me onto the raised platform of his bedroom. It was much darker in this part of the room; I could only make out the shape of his bed. "This is a special surprise that involves no cheese, bread, or James Bond."

"Or Chia Pets?"

Another chuckle sent my stomach tumbling in the most pleasant way. "I don't hate Chia Pets enough to bestow another one on you."

I frowned.

"I hope you like this one." His hands went to my shoulders, and in the darkness, he turned me around. His hands stayed there, the weight oddly comforting. "Ready?"

"Yeah?" I strained to see into the darkness.

A moment later, the ceiling lamp flicked on, momentarily stunning me. It took a second for my eyes to focus as I scanned the room.

Then I saw it.

It was lying on the bed, a framed photograph that was roughly sixteen by twenty. The moment I saw it, I knew what it was.

A photograph taken from the cemetery in Harpers Ferry, overlooking the lush green valleys and the greenish-blue rocky river of the Shenandoah. And I knew in my bones and in every cell of my being that I had taken that picture. I didn't remember snapping it, but my fingers twitched nonetheless.

My lips parted as I shook my head, and a part of me thought that if Luc hadn't had his hands on my shoulders, I might sink right through the floor.

"I . . . I took that."

"You did." His voice was by my ear, quiet.

"I don't remember taking it, but I know I took that," I said. "How does that make sense?"

"I wish I could answer that."

The next breath I took got stuck as I leaned into him, letting the back of my head rest against his chest. "Did you have it all this time?"

Luc's hands slid off my shoulders and down my arms, stopping just above my elbows. "You took it one of the last times we went there, and you loved the picture so much, you talked about getting it printed out and framed, but . . ."

I closed my eyes and swallowed hard. "Ran out of time?"

"Yeah," came his gruff reply. "We ran out of time."

"But here it is."

Luc was quiet for a long moment. "After I got set up here, I started going through some of the stuff I'd brought with me. I found your old camera; I still have that, if you want to see it. Anyway, I started looking at the pictures and saw this one. I printed it out and got it framed about three years ago."

He'd had this for three years? My eyes opened, and my lashes felt damp.

"I didn't hang it up. I don't know why. I kept it in one of the extra rooms here." He lifted a shoulder. "I thought you should have it, since it's yours. You can keep it here or you can take it home—"

Spinning around, I didn't stop to think about what I was doing. I just did it. Probably much like I'd done that day by Jefferson Rock, when I'd been a different girl and he'd been the same boy.

I threw my arms around his neck and stretched up onto the tips of my toes. His hands moved to my hips, steadying me as I brought my lips to his.

And I kissed him.

It wasn't much of a kiss. A quick peck on his lips that still somehow short-circuited my entire system. It was like touching a flame, and when I pulled away and stepped back, my hands trembling as they slid down his chest and then off him, I was surprised that my lips weren't burned—though they did tingle.

Luc stared down at me, his lips parted and the centers of his cheeks slightly flushed. He looked like a feather could knock him over.

"Thank you," I said, taking another step back as I clasped my hands together. "I love this surprise."

For a moment, there was no reaction from him. His features and body were as impassive as a statue, and then a wide, beautiful smile broke out across his face. Being on the receiving end of it, I felt like I needed to sit down and take a moment to soak it in.

"Anytime, Peaches," he murmured. "Anytime."

Walking to history class Friday afternoon with Zoe, I smothered a yawn. A nightmare had wakened me shortly after falling asleep, and then Luc had called, and I ended up staying awake for several hours, watching a funny web series on my laptop while Luc did the same from his apartment. I fell asleep with Luc's laughter in my ear, and that was as nice—no, as wonderful—as the picture he'd given me.

I'd taken it home with me and had hung it above my bed, and I thought—or hoped—it was level.

"Do you think we have a quiz today? I feel like we're long overdue for one."

"God, I hope not, because I don't even know how to spell my name right now," she said.

I laughed. "It's three words."

"Look," she said. "Don't underestimate my inability to spell right now."

"I'll try not—" My right shoulder jerked forward as someone bumped into me. Turning, my mouth dropped open. "Whoa, Coop. Good afternoon to you."

The tall, blond boy lurched past us, shuffling through the classroom. He didn't apologize, didn't even seem to notice that he'd nearly knocked me over. I straightened the strap on my bag, eyeing him. He looked a mess—a hot mess. His striped navy-and-gold shirt was so wrinkled it looked like he'd pulled it on at the last minute, and his usually styled hair was sticking up in every direction.

I glanced over at Zoe. "What in the world?"

She shook her head. "He looks hungover."

"As if you'd know what that looks like."

"Oh, I will never forget over the summer when you decided to taste each bottle in your mom's liquor cabinet," she replied. "That is not something I'll ever forget, thank you very much."

Cringing, I could almost taste the liquor. It was like gasoline going down and bad life choices coming back up. "God, don't remind me."

"Hey, at least we can forget about it while checking out Mr. Barker."

"You are so hot for that teacher," I told her.

"Ain't no shame in my game," she said as we walked past the podium.

Coop took his seat in the middle, looking as pasty as a powdered doughnut. A sheen of fine sweat dotted his forehead. Did he have a fever? Thinking of Ryan and the families in Kansas City, I resisted the urge to cover my entire face with my shirt. I doubted this virus, if it was a flu, was still lingering around.

"Hey, Coop?"

He lifted his head, and his cloudy gaze met mine. "Hey."

I let my bag slip off my arm. "Dude, you look like crap. Are you okay?"

"I feel like crap." He ran his hand over his cheek.

"You probably should've stayed home." I slid into my seat and starting digging around in my bag.

"Yeah," he muttered. "Got an exam next period. Probably hit the nurse's office after that."

Zoe dropped into the chair behind me. "You do not look like you're going to make it until next period."

"Thanks for the vote of confidence." Coop cradled his head in his arms. Within a couple of seconds, he looked like he was out. I dropped my bag on the floor as Mr. Barker walked into class, and like every day, he had that gross-looking smoothie in his hand.

I started nibbling on my pen as something as wonderful as the photo Luc gave me and falling asleep to his laughter occurred to me.

Things felt . . . well, they felt normal.

I was still somewhat hungry, even after lunch. Zoe and I were no longer walking on eggshells with each other, and she was currently eyeballing the teacher like she was starving, and all of that was a normal Friday. It had been a normal week, actually.

Muscles I didn't even realize were tense relaxed. I needed this—the normalcy—because that was how I would deal with everything that happened. And I was dealing. Totally. Because the only other option was to curl up in a corner somewhere and rock back and forth, and while I had no idea who I really was, I knew that wasn't me.

Realizing that Mr. Barker had started to lecture, I scribbled down as much as I could of what he was talking about, ignoring Zoe as she repeated nearly everything Barker said under her breath . . . with a really bad English accent.

I had my cheek smashed against my fist and my pen hovering over the paper when the door opened. A low-level hum entered the room. Mr. Barker didn't stop talking as I peeked up and spotted the RAC drone enter the class.

Drones.

Ugh.

The thing hovered about five feet off the floor, its black spindles whirling as it moved down the first aisle, stopping at each person to scan their retinas.

No matter how many times I saw them at the mall or in class, they freaked me the hell out. Like, what if it got hacked and started poking people in the eyes with one of its spindle things at the bottom?

Never once had I seen it poke someone's eye out, but that didn't mean it wasn't a reasonable fear.

Even though I knew Zoe had her contacts in and it never hit on her before, my palms still felt sweaty as I thought about how every day at school she sat through this. Hidden just by a pair of contacts. And the others—the Luxen who couldn't hide what they were? My stomach soured. Some thought the RAC drones were necessary. Part of me could even understand why they'd feel that way, but it was still an atrocious abuse of privacy. Even worse was that there was a percentage of the population who didn't even consider that, since they didn't think Luxen deserved the same basic rights.

The drone beeped, a sound I honestly didn't think I'd ever heard it make. The little drone was on the third aisle, waiting beside Coop's seat. His chin was dipped, and sweat had dampened the hair at the nape of his neck. He wasn't looking up like he was supposed to.

"Coop," Mr. Barker called out, a frown pulling at his mouth.

Coop didn't respond.

The center of the drone spun, and it beeped again.

Mr. Barker frowned as he rested his textbook on the podium and stepped in front of it. "Coop." He spoke louder, harder. "You'd better not be asleep."

Coop wasn't asleep. His knuckles were bleached white from how tightly he was gripping the edge of his desk. His large frame trembled.

I laid my pen down and shifted uneasily in my seat. Concern filled me. I didn't know Coop all that well, but I didn't want to see him get in trouble.

"I think he's sick," a girl named Kristen said. She was sitting next to Coop but was leaning away from him. "He really doesn't look good at all. Does he have that flu that killed Ryan?"

Murmurs of worry rose throughout the class as Mr. Barker strode down the aisle. "Coop, what's going on?"

Coop slowly lifted his head. I could only see his profile, and he was paler than he'd been when he'd entered the class. The drone locked into place, lining up with his eyes. The white light pulsed once and then twice.

The light flipped red.

A screech emanated from the drone, a low siren that increased until it sounded as if a police car were roaring through the classroom, and it was all that any of us could hear. I froze in my seat, eyes wide.

What was happening?

A tiny voice in the back of my head told me I knew what was going on even though I'd never seen it happen.

"Hell," I heard Zoe say under her breath.

A great sense of foreboding took hold, sending an icy shiver spiraling down my spine.

The RAC drone had hit on Coop, picking up alien DNA.

8

Face pale and drawn, Mr. Barker started backing up as chairs screeched across the floor. "Everyone stay calm," he said, not sounding very calm at all. "I need everyone to keep calm and stay in their seats."

Zoe was already standing, but I was a statue in my chair, my heart pounding like a drum.

This was impossible.

The drone's siren wailed as someone shouted over the noise, "Something's wrong with it! Coop is a human!"

More shouts of protest joined the first, but the drone kept screeching. Did it make mistakes? I had no idea. I'd never heard of that happening, but it had to be, because Coop was human. He wasn't a Luxen, a hybrid, or an Origin.

Unless he was like Zoe, hiding what he was?

But why wouldn't Zoe have said anything if that was the case?

The drone inched back as Coop lumbered to his feet. He swayed as he let his head fall back. Sweat poured off his face, traveling down his neck in beads. A rosy flush mottled his once pale cheeks.

Coop opened his eyes, and the air punched out of my lungs as someone screamed. Blood seeped from the corners of Coop's eyes, coursing down his cheeks and into the corners of his open mouth. His chest was heaving as if he couldn't breathe.

Oh no.

No. No. No.

Mr. Barker stopped backing up, and his lips moved wordlessly. Or maybe he was saying the same thing I was, but the drone was drowning out the sound.

Coop doubled over, retching and gagging. Liquid the color of blood and black tar spewed from him, splattering off the floor and the legs of chairs.

Gasping in air, I pushed out of my seat and took a step back, bumping into Zoe. Her cool hand gripped my upper arm.

"Coop," I whispered, heart pounding. "Oh my God, Coop—" I started toward him without thinking.

Zoe's fingers dug into my arm. "Don't. Something is so not right here."

That was the understatement of the year.

Just then, Mr. Barker rushed toward Coop, concern replacing the confusion. He reached Coop, gripping the boy's arm. "What's wrong, Coop? Tell me what's—"

Everything happened fast.

Coop swung his arm out, catching the drone with his forearm. The drone flew across the room, smacking into the side of another student's head. The wailing of the siren stopped. Someone screamed as the boy went right down, out before he even landed, his face making a sickening cracking sound as he hit the floor. Blood pooled around him.

Suddenly, Mr. Barker was *flying* across the room. I jumped back as our teacher slammed into the window and then went *through* it. Shards of glass flew like missiles, cutting through clothing and skin.

Coop had thrown him.

That wasn't normal.

Holy crap, none of this was normal.

Shouts and shrill screams pierced the air, and Coop just raged out, picking up chairs and tables and throwing them. They broke apart against the chalkboard. Those close to the door bolted, but Zoe and I and everyone else near the broken windows were trapped.

"We've got to get out of here," Zoe said, her gaze darting around the room. Coop was tearing the classroom apart.

"Really?" I breathed, yelping as a chair winged over our heads. "You think?"

"You got any ideas? Because—"

Coop ripped the leg of a chair off, just tore it right apart, breaking wood and metal. His strength was inhuman. He whirled and pitched it. The leg flew toward us—toward Zoe.

I didn't think.

Spinning around, I pushed Zoe hard. She toppled sideways, and I followed. What felt like a piece of ice hit my left cheek a second before the chair leg crashed through the window directly where Zoe had been standing. That was how it felt at first, like an icicle was dragged across my cheek, and then it burned as glass rained down on us, catching in our hair.

"Evie!" Zoe's eyes went wide. "Your face."

Crouching next to her, I touched my face with a shaky hand and winced. "I'm . . . I'm fine."

"You know you didn't need to do that," she whispered through clenched teeth as she grabbed my wrist, pulling my hand away. Blood tinged the tips of my fingers.

We both jumped when something shattered near us again.

"I have to do something." Zoe still held on to my hand. "He's going to hurt more people. I have to—"

"No." I pulled on her arm, my wide gaze swinging toward her. "You can't. If you do . . ." I didn't need to finish the sentence. If Zoe intervened, it would expose her to every single person in the class; the world didn't know about Origins or hybrids. They'd think she was an unregistered Luxen, and unregistered Luxen . . .

They *disappeared*.

Zoe squeezed her eyes shut as she sucked in a ragged breath. Something else crashed above us, and she opened her eyes. "Evie, I have—"

"Everyone down," a male voice boomed. "Everyone down on the floor now, palms flat against the floor."

Officers dressed like SWAT members filed into the room, wearing all black and helmets that shielded their faces. They carried rifles, the long and scary kind. They didn't look like the Alien Response Task Force. Not at all.

Zoe pulled me down to my knees. Within seconds, our bellies were on the floor, our heads down. Coop turned to them, still on his feet.

"This will be our last warning," came the voice again. "Stop or we will stop you."

No. No. No. They couldn't shoot Coop. He was sick. They couldn't—

It sounded like a zapping noise, a succession of rapid electricity firing. Coop jerked as the hooks dug deep into his shoulder. I expected him to go down. A Taser was no joke.

But he didn't.

Coop took a step forward, toward the men.

Another Taser fired. The hooks snagged him in the belly, and he kept going. He didn't slow, knocking a chair aside even as a third Taser hit him in the leg. He was *still* standing, *still* charging toward them.

How was that possible? Tasers and stun guns even affected Luxen.

Classmates were prone on the floor, their faces pale, some bloodied, and all of them had their eyes squeezed tightly shut. I saw the boots of the officers at the doorway to the class. I saw Coop.

Three Taser shots and he was *still* standing.

"One more step and we will put you down!" one of the officers shouted. "Come on, bro. Don't make us do this. Stop!"

"Please," I said under my breath, my fingers squeezing Zoe's until I could feel the bones in her hand. "Come on, Coop, please just stop."

Coop didn't.

Blood was leaking from his nose and eyes now. And that blood didn't look right. There was a bluish-black tint to it, and it *shimmered.*

Oh my God . . .

He threw his head back and roared. The sound caused me to jolt and Zoe to curse. Coop screamed so loudly and deeply, like he was being torn apart from the inside. There was a cracking sound—a sound of bones snapping.

One of the officers with the long rifles stepped to the head of the pack. It sounded like a firework. A quick pop. Then a dime-size hole appeared in the center of Coop's right thigh. His leg gave out, and he stumbled. Two of the officers launched over the overturned tables, tackling Coop. He fought them, throwing one of them off and breaking free. It took four officers to bring him down—four officers, three hits of a Taser, and a bullet to the leg.

And he was still screaming, and all the while, I heard his bones breaking.

We were kept on the floor, on our bellies with our hands palms down until after Coop was removed from the classroom. It felt like an eternity stretched out—even though it had only been minutes—until an unfamiliar voice ordered us to stand and to leave the room in an orderly fashion.

Escorted out of school, we weren't allowed to go to our lockers or to stop. I stayed close to Zoe, and I didn't remember the walk to my car or how I ended up in the passenger seat with Zoe driving, since she had her own car, but there we were. Without asking, I knew Zoe was driving to Foretoken.

That made sense, because after what we'd just seen, Luc had to be told about it. Maybe he could even shed some light on it, because I had no idea what had happened to Coop. All I knew was that whatever happened to him sure as hell was not some flu.

I held my book bag close to my chest and stared straight ahead like a little robot. After what had happened, the buildings reaching into the sky, the manicured lawns in front of the homes, and the cars filling the roads felt a little fake.

Did the woman in the van at the stoplight beside us have any idea that Coop threw a teacher through a window? And then seriously injured another student? Did the driver of the city bus flying through the intersection know that Coop had vomited blood and the good Lord knows what else before freaking the hell out?

Was Mr. Barker going to be okay? Or the guy that had smacked his head on the floor? I didn't know.

Since I'd figured this was going to hit the news soon, I'd texted my mom and let her know that I was okay. I hadn't heard back from her, but that wasn't uncommon. She was probably squirreled away in a lab somewhere.

The normalcy of today had been all too brief.

Squeezing my bag as if it were a giant stress ball, I exhaled long and hard. God, they'd shot him with a Taser. Shot him multiple times and with a real live bullet, and he still didn't go down.

"You okay?" Zoe asked as we pulled onto the street toward Foretoken.

I nodded. "You?"

"No. Not really."

"Me neither," I admitted. "I can't believe that happened."

Zoe didn't respond, and neither of us spoke as she parked and we crossed the busy street. Clyde met us at the front entrance, ushering us in with a grunt of acknowledgment. A Mr. Potato Head on the front of his shirt peeked out from behind a pair of blue-jean overalls.

He caught my arm, his grasp surprisingly gentle for such a large hand. I looked up at him, and he nodded at me. "Face."

I didn't know what he was referencing.

The piercings in his eyebrows and cheeks glimmered in the bright ceiling lights as he jerked his chin at my face again and let go of my arm. "Got blood on your face, girl."

"Oh." I reached for my cheek. There was a dull sting there that I'd forgotten about. "It's just a scratch."

"Luc'll see it and react like it's a gunshot wound," he grumbled, and Zoe snorted her agreement. Clyde reached into his back pocket and pulled out a red-and-white handkerchief. "It's clean."

I didn't get a chance to protest. Clyde was quick as he played nurse, carefully wiping away the trace of blood.

"Thank you," I said when he was done.

He grumbled something again. "Luc'll probably still see it."

I really hoped not.

Clyde walked away then, disappearing into the darker recesses of the main club floor. I turned, following Zoe toward the employee entrance. It was always strange to me to see the club like this, empty of people and chairs on tables.

We'd just reached Luc's floor when the door swung open, and there was Luc, dressed in jeans and a camouflage shirt that said YOU CAN'T SEE ME.

I squelched the laugh crawling up my throat, because in light of things, it seemed inappropriate.

"Emery just told me what happened. Heidi told her," he announced, his gaze flickering over Zoe to me. "Are you okay?"

"Yes." I let go of the railing as I glanced at Zoe. "What do you know?"

"That some kid flipped out in class and threw a teacher through a window?" He held the door open for us.

"Yeah, that's, like, one-tenth of the story." Zoe walked through. "Is Heidi on her way?"

"I guess so." Luc frowned as I slipped past him. I made it about a step, and then suddenly, he was in front of me.

I stumbled back. "God. I hate when you move like that."

"You're injured," he said, lifting his hand and placing his finger on my cheek. Only then did he look to where Zoe waited by his door. "What happened?"

Dammit, Clyde was right. "Injured? I'm not—"

"You have a cut." His jaw was hard as his chin dipped down. "How is that not being injured?"

"I'm totally fine."

A muscle flexed along his jaw.

"She pushed me out of the way of a chair leg that had been turned into a projectile," Zoe explained. "I already told her that wasn't necessary."

Pulling away from Luc, I spun toward Zoe. "How was that not necessary? You could've ended up with a chair leg in your head."

"I would've moved out of the way before that happened." She paused. "I'm fast like that."

"She wouldn't have gotten hurt." Luc tugged on the sleeve of my shirt, and I faced him. "And while it was rather admirable of you to look out for her and I'm sure Zoe appreciates it—"

"I do," Zoe chimed in.

"It wasn't necessary," Luc finished. "You know what she is."

"Just so everyone is on the same page, if anyone throws a chair leg at the head of someone I care about and I can intervene," I said, "I'm going to intervene. I'm not just going to stand there."

"Peaches—"

"Except for you," I told him. "I'm going to let it hit you in the head because you have a thick skull."

One side of his mouth curled up. "I'm okay with that."

I rolled my eyes. "Whatever."

Placing his hand on my lower back, he leaned down and whispered, "I'd take a thousand chair legs to the head if that meant you stayed out of harm's way."

I had no idea how to respond to that. Saying thanks seemed wrong. Thankfully, I didn't have to, because Zoe started telling Luc what had gone down, and we made our way into the room next to his, an open space with couches, giant beanbags, and a TV that was obscenely large. Kent joined us, Cokes in hand and his mohawk all perky and upright.

It occurred to me as Luc and I sat on the couch and Zoe and Kent occupied one of the beanbags that I had never seen any of them in Luc's room.

By the time Zoe finished with what happened, I'd drunk almost all my Coke and Kent was staring at her, slowly shaking his head. "That's impossible," he said. "RAC drones don't hit on humans."

"I know," she replied. "But that's what happened. And if he was wearing contacts and in hiding, I would've sensed it."

"It was like he had a fever or something. He said he was going to go home after he took an exam. He was talking, and then he just snapped and started throwing up that stuff." I rested my Coke on my knee as I looked over at Luc. "Is it possible that he might've known a Luxen and was healed by one? That he began to mutate?"

Kent shook his head. "Mutation doesn't look like that. Yeah, you get sick and all, but you don't rage out like that. Right, Luc?"

Luc, who'd been awfully quiet through the whole discussion, leaned forward and rested his hands on his knees. "When the Daedalus was trying to re-create mutation, they were developing serums that were administered to humans who'd been mutated. LH-11 was one of them, as was the Prometheus serum."

Muscles in my neck clenched. Those were the serums Luc had set Daemon and Kat up to retrieve for him—for me.

"The serums were designed to speed up the mutation and enhance it. They often didn't work, causing the subject to rapidly mutate and, in some cases, rage out," Luc explained. "So if he was given something like that, then it could explain the strength and the rage."

"But how would that be possible?" I asked. "The Daedalus is gone, so even if he was somehow healed by a Luxen on such a level that a mutation began, how would he have been given one of those serums?"

"We have some of them," he said, sitting back. "Just in case of emergencies."

I really didn't want to know what kind of emergency would warrant that. "But you're Luc, and this is Foretoken. I can see you guys getting your hands on these serums, but other Luxen?"

Luc looked over at me. "It's not impossible, but yes, it's unlikely. If that's what did it, then there's someone else out there who had ties to the Daedalus."

"How bad would that be if that's the case?" Kent asked, rocking forward into a sitting position.

"If it was some Luxen who saw the mutation start to take hold and gave the serum, then it really sucks for them," Luc explained.

"Wait. If he was healed, wouldn't he have a trace?" I looked over at Zoe. "Wouldn't you have seen it?"

"Traces can fade during mutation. Fever sort of burns them off," she explained. "But I didn't see a trace on him at all, and I think I would've seen one."

Luc's brows pinched. "Then I really don't know what could cause a spontaneous mutation with those kinds of results."

I stared at him, beyond unsettled that Luc didn't know, because Luc seemed to know everything.

"Then maybe we're looking at this wrong. If it wasn't a mutation, what could have caused it?" Zoe asked.

No one answered.

But I thought of the people in the apartment complex, sickened by some sort of virus that the reporters had tried to insinuate was something passed from Luxen to human. Mom had said that was impossible, but what if she were wrong? The people in Kansas City had gotten sick and died, just like Ryan had a few weeks ago. Granted, Ryan could've just had the flu, but what if there were something like the flu that humans were catching from the Luxen?

9

No one knew what happened to Coop in the days after he spewed brackish blood all over the class before being shot with three Tasers and a bullet, but local and national news had picked up the story and speculations were wild, ranging from the belief that he had caught this mysterious Luxen virus to the possibility that he was doing some drug called ET, which apparently involved shooting oneself up with alien blood. I was almost 100 percent positive that wasn't even a thing since neither I nor anyone I knew, including Luc, had ever heard of anyone doing that.

On the news every evening there were random, middle-aged people with some vague medical background talking about the risks of this new high sweeping the safe suburbs of America. They claimed Luxen blood, when mixed with opioids, became a powerful stimulant that could cause massive internal bleeding and death.

It all sounded like some kind of sensationalized fictional report, but people believed it.

We'd learned that Mr. Barker was going to be okay, as was the student who'd hit his head. Neither had returned by the following week, and it was doubtful Mr. Barker was ever going to come back, but they were okay.

Coop was probably not okay.

Out of all the media covering what happened at our school, out of the speculation and rumors, no one knew what was being done to Coop, and there were no answers. Not even when his parents appeared on television shortly after the incident, demanding to be allowed to see their son, and that wasn't just weird.

There was something very wrong with that.

"You should come," Zoe was saying to James as we walked up the hill to the parking lot after school, pulling me from my thoughts.

"Everyone will be dressed up. It's a Halloween party. Come on, it'll be fun, and we all need a little bit of fun right now."

"There is no way in hell I'm going to Foretoken," James responded. "We could be in the middle of an all-out zombie apocalypse, and that could be the only safe location in the entire world, and I still wouldn't go there."

I snorted as I pulled my camera out of my bag, having spied the gold and burgundy leaves shimmering in the afternoon sun.

"That seems a bit excessive, don't you think?" Zoe asked. "I mean, what if the cure were there?"

"Nope. I'd stick my arm out the window and get bitten by a zombie before I'd step foot—"

"No more Luxen! No more fear!"

Stopping, I jerked my head up and stared at the entrance to the parking lot.

"You have got to be kidding me," James muttered beside me as we got a good look at what was going down. "Do they ever get tired of this?"

"I think the answer is *no,*" I muttered. "And I'm really getting tired of hearing that chant. Like, *really* tired."

A group of students were sitting in the middle of the parking lot, blocking at least a couple dozen cars from leaving. The ring leader of the dumb sit-in stood in the middle, her thin body vibrating with hostility.

Ugh. April.

I hadn't talked to her since that morning in front of the school. Obviously, the conversation had gone nowhere. Worse yet, her protest group had doubled in size since everything had gone down with Coop.

She was holding a stupid hot-pink sign with an oval-shaped alien face slashed out as she shouted, "No more Luxen! No more fear!"

Her minions chanted with her, holding their own stupid signs. I recognized my ex among them, and that was, like, double embarrassment for me.

"We will not live in fear anymore!" April shouted, thrusting her idiot sign in the air above her. "We will not be murdered in our homes and at school! We will not be made sick. We will—"

"Shut up?" I shouted, earning a few chuckles from the peanut gallery behind us, but a lot more looks of scorn.

April spun toward us, and her bright red lips thinned. "We will not be silenced!"

I rolled my eyes. "I can't believe I was ever friends with her."

"You know, I've thought that a hundred times." James shifted his book bag up onto a broad shoulder. "I have no idea why you guys were friends with her. She was never nice."

"I'm not sure." I glanced over at Zoe, who was staring at the group with an impressively blank face. James didn't even know the half of it. I would never know how Zoe had managed to even talk to April all these years, being what she was. Wasn't like Zoe could draw attention to what she was, but in one of my many fantasies that involved slapping the blond ponytail off her head, all of them included the look on her face when April realized that one of her friends for years was part alien and she'd had no idea.

That would never happen, but still, picturing it brought a smile to my face.

"Thank God the three of us are always late and we're parked in the back." Zoe shoved her tight, caramel curls out of her face. "We can just ignore them."

"Yeah, but they're not as lucky." James jerked his chin in the direction of the small group standing to the right of April and her crew.

My shoulders tightened as I recognized Connor and the younger Luxen, Daniel. There were two others with them, and their cars were completely blocked by the circle.

"Crap. I didn't even see them there." Zoe crossed her arms over her lilac sweater as she looked over her shoulder. "Where are the teachers? They don't see any of this going on?"

Considering the huge audience the group was drawing, the teachers had to know something was happening out here.

Irritation snapped to life. I'd tried talking to April once about her anti-Luxen crap, but that had been as successful as talking to a brick wall. Worst part was that Connor and the other Luxen couldn't do anything. With the Disablers on their wrists, they were virtually human, but if they stood up for themselves, they would be labeled the aggressors, "proving" whatever crap April was shouting.

"Hey, April!" I lifted my camera and snapped a picture of her. "How about a picture to commemorate your bigotry?"

April dropped her pink sign. She stalked toward me, her pale blue eyes narrowed. "I swear to God, Evie, if you take a picture of me, I will break your stupid camera!" She grabbed for it, but I danced backward, keeping it out of her reach. "I'm being serious."

"So am I," I shot back, keeping a good grip on my camera. Probably a good time to mention the fact that I did take a picture. "What? Are you worried about having actual proof of how stupid you are?"

Zoe snorted. "I doubt she cares."

"No one asked you." April held up her hand, placing her palm inches in front of Zoe's face. Zoe's brows flew up, but April zeroed in on me. "You shouldn't take people's pictures without their permission."

"Are you for real right now?" I demanded. "You're blocking half the parking lot."

"So? That's our God-given right." Her head bobbed as she spoke. "Freedom of speech and all. We're protesting *them*." She jabbed a finger in Connor's direction. "They made Coop sick!"

"And Ryan!" some girl shouted from April's group. "They killed him."

"They didn't make anyone sick," Zoe snapped.

"You obviously don't know what you're talking about!" April volleyed back.

"Thought you needed a permit for this." James stepped in.

"It's the school parking lot," April shot back. "We don't need a permit and, again, it's our right."

"What about their rights?" I demanded.

"Their rights?" April smirked. "What rights? This isn't their planet."

"Their rights to come to school and be able to leave without having to deal with you all, and yeah, last time I checked, they did have rights."

She rolled her eyes. "They don't deserve them."

"Oh my God." Sickened and yet somehow not surprised that she would say something like that, I wanted to put as much distance between us as possible. "You're terrible, April. Just go protest someplace else where the rest of us decent human beings and Luxen don't have to see or hear you. Or better yet, stop being a horrible human being." I sidestepped her and nearly walked into Brandon.

"Evie." He stared down at me, his sign dangling from his fingertips. "Are you really okay with them being here?"

"She is." April crossed her arms. "She's a traitor to her species."

I rolled my eyes at her. "Yes, I'm totally okay with them being here, and you didn't have a problem with them before. What's changed?"

Brandon glanced over at the Luxen. The group of protestors were still in front of their cars. "I wised up, that's what changed." His blue eyes—eyes that I used to find so pretty—searched mine. "They killed your father—"

"Shut up," I snapped, shoving past him as April and Zoe started arguing with each other. "You have no idea what you're talking about. At all."

Brandon caught my arm, yanking me to a stop. "What do you mean I have no idea? Your father *died* fighting them. Of all people, you should be the last person supporting them."

"My *father* was a shit human being." My gaze dropped to where his fingers were digging into my arm—the same arm that Micah had broken in this very parking lot.

Confusion poured into his face. "What? Your father was a hero, Evie."

God, I wanted to vomit. He really had no idea. "Let go of me."

He frowned. "Why? So you can run over to them and make sure they're okay? Hold their hands? I heard about you escorting that little Luxen shit to class."

"Let go of me so I don't break my camera on your stupid face," I said, tugging on my arm. His grip tightened, and I winced as a burst of sharp pain flared up my arm. "I'll be really pissed if I break my camera, but if you don't let go, it'll be worth it."

"Really?" Brandon exclaimed. His eyes widened with shock, but he didn't let go. "You'd hurt me and not them?"

"I'd prefer to hurt no one, but if push comes to shove, I'd gladly hurt you over them." I glanced at the group of protestors. They were on their feet, looking at one another nervously. "Want to know why? You're the one grabbing me. Not them."

"Dude, let go." James was suddenly by my side, and even though he was a nonconfrontational teddy bear, he was bigger and broader than Brandon by far. James snatched my camera from my hands.

"I really don't want you breaking this over his face. You love your camera, Evie."

That was true.

Brandon's gaze darted to James, and then he dropped my aching arm. "I don't get you guys. They killed Colleen and Amanda. They killed Andy, and you guys act like it's not a big deal? What's wrong with you all?"

"No, they didn't, Brandon. They had nothing to do with their deaths."

"How do you know that?" he fired back.

I wished I could tell him exactly how I knew, but I couldn't. I'd known Brandon since I started going to this school, nearly four years. We hadn't dated that long, only like three months, but we'd been friends before and after. Brandon had seemed like a good guy—smart and kind—but he looked like a complete stranger to me now. "What happened to you? You were never like this."

"What happened to *me*?" he challenged. "I woke up, Evie. I saw what was really happening—what they're doing to us."

He was so asleep it wasn't even funny. "What do you think is happening?"

"They're taking our rights, Evie. They're taking our jobs and government assistance from us," he argued. "They're making people sick. They're killers."

They could be killers—I'd seen it with my own eyes—and while there was a part of me that was beginning to wonder if there was something to this whole Luxen virus thing, Brandon was so wrong. "So are humans," I told him. "We kill just as much as the Luxen do—more if you look at our history and look at all the diseases we pass to one another, mainly stupidity. They're not shooting up schools or theaters. They're not killing unarmed teens and hiding behind a badge. They're not gassing innocent people or blowing up buildings. They're not—"

"Human," he cut me off. "They're not human, Evie, and they are killing people—entire families. Watch the news."

Disgusted, I shook my head. "They're more human than you are right now."

"Oh my God!" April shrieked, spinning around. Out of the corner of my eye, I saw that the Luxen were in their cars, and since the protestors had started to scatter, they were able to get out of the parking lot. "Look! They're getting away. Dammit!"

Brandon whipped to the side, his cheeks flushing as the carful of Luxen left the parking lot. His head swung back at me, and I smiled brightly up at him.

"You guys can't even protest efficiently." Zoe flicked her fingers in April's face, causing the girl to flinch. "Kind of pathetic."

"Dammit," Brandon growled.

"Just so you know, I have lots of secondhand embarrassment right now," I told Brandon. "For you guys." I paused. "And for myself, because I actually dated you."

His face turned bright red. "You did more than just date me, you stupid—"

"Use nice words, Brandon." James smiled at the smaller guy. "Very nice words."

Brandon's jaw flexed as he snapped his mouth shut, glaring at me. "Whatever," he said.

I lifted my hand and extended my middle finger.

Turning away, he muttered something under his breath that sounded an awful lot like *Luxen lover,* the edges of his sign crinkling under his fingers.

"It's okay." April hurried to Brandon, looping her arm around his. "They're not going to be a problem much longer."

"Keep dreaming," Zoe called after them as they stalked off.

April's arm shot up. She flipped us off.

"Your nail polish is chipped!" Zoe added, grinning as her eyes flashed in my direction. "God, I want to hit her."

"You and me both." I started walking toward my car.

"If I agree, does that make me a bad person?" James asked.

"No," Zoe and I said at the same time.

Walking ahead, Zoe looked over her shoulder to where April and Brandon had disappeared. She shook her head. "I'm worried, though."

I stopped in front of my car as James handed my camera back to me. "About?"

Zoe exhaled heavily as her gaze flicked between James and me. "I'm worried they're eventually going to do something really stupid . . . and really dangerous."

IO

I woke up in a cold sweat, gasping for air as I scratched at my throat, searching for the fingers I could still feel digging into my skin.

Not real. Not real. Not real.

Drawing in deep, shuddering breaths, I forced my hands away from my neck. No one was here choking me. It was a nightmare. I knew this, but I still shoved the blanket down my legs and scrambled to my knees, heart thundering against my ribs as I scanned the bedroom.

Moonlight seeped under the curtains and traveled across the floor and along the foot of the bed. I scanned the familiar bookshelves and heaps of clothing. The TV placed on the dresser, left on but turned down low because I'd been having a hard time falling asleep without the light, flickered from one blood-splattered crime scene to the next.

Forensic Files.

I really needed to stop falling asleep with that playing, though I found the dude who narrated the show to have an oddly relaxing voice.

The door to my room was still closed, as was the bedroom window, both locked even though I knew there were a lot of creatures out there that locks couldn't keep out.

But it was just a nightmare.

I knew this, but I still flipped on the lamp that sat atop the nightstand. I saw Diesel the rock smiling at me.

Sliding off the bed, I darted into the bathroom, hitting the switch on the wall. Bright light poured into the narrow space as I lifted my shirt with trembling hands.

My stomach was bare of scratches or bruises, just like the rational, logical part of my brain said it would be. I was okay. I would be okay. Micah was dead, and I was—

I didn't know *who* I was.

Nausea twisted sharply in my stomach, bringing me to my knees with a harsh grunt. Grasping the cool, porcelain base of the toilet, I lost everything I'd eaten the night before. Tears sprang from the corners of my eyes as my throat and chest burned with the force of the tremors racking my body. The retching sickness came on fast and powerfully, ending in painful dry heaves until all the muscles went loose and my body gave out.

I found myself lying sideways on the cold tile of the bathroom floor, curled tightly, trembling as I squeezed my eyes shut. I pressed my lips together and counted each breath I inhaled through my nose. I had no idea how much time passed. Five minutes? Ten? Longer? Slowly, I unfurled my legs and shifted onto my back, opening my eyes to stare dully at the ceiling.

I'd heard his voice in the nightmare. Micah's. He'd been ranting about Luc and warning us that *everything* was already over, just like he'd done in the woods.

Neither Luc nor I had any idea of what he was talking about, but those words were like ghosts lingering in the recesses of my mind. Had he actually been trying to tell us something, or were they just the words of someone who wanted to cause as much pain and terror as possible before dying?

I wanted to hate Micah, and I did, but I also felt . . . God, I also felt pity for him, and I didn't like the stuffy, ugly feeling that pity left behind. It stained my skin like an oil slick. I hated him for that and for what he'd forced Luc to do—to kill him. I knew that haunted Luc, because he'd felt responsible for Micah, for all those Origins. I despised Micah for how he'd hurt and terrorized me.

Micah had been a murderer, but he had also been a victim. Created in a lab, he was bred from a Luxen and a hybrid to be the perfect human—the perfect soldier. Given God knows what kind of drugs, Micah might've looked to be my age, but he was only ten years old. He might've been extremely intelligent and extraordinarily manipulative, but he was also just a child who'd needed to feel *wanted* and had felt abandoned and betrayed by Luc.

I hated him, but I still pitied him. I felt bad for all those kids Luc had to . . . take care of because they had turned *bad*.

But Micah was definitely dead, and I was lying on the bathroom floor in the middle of the night.

Groaning, I sat up and slowly rose to my feet. Shuffling to the vanity, I turned the water on and then bent over, scooping the icy water and splashing it across my face. I sucked in a sharp gasp but did it again, letting it soak my skin and most of my hair. I reached for the mouthwash, swishing it around until the taste of the bile was gone. Then I lifted my eyes to the water-spotted mirror and gazed upon the girl who stared back at me.

I recognized the heart-shaped face and damp, blond hair sticking to cheeks that were flushed a faint pink. The large brown eyes were mine, as were the parted lips and slightly pointy chin that really didn't match the rest of my face.

That was me.

"My name is Evie." I cleared my throat as I placed my hands on the vanity, steadying myself. "My name is . . . Nadia Holliday?" I shook my head. "No. I'm not her. I'm Evie Dasher."

I wasn't her, either, now was I?

But I was Peaches . . .

I ran my hands down my face as I stepped back from the sink. And I had remembered something of Nadia. The kiss. Our first kiss. I may not have any other memories of my time as Nadia, but I knew in my bones that had been my first kiss, too.

A ding from my phone startled me. I turned from the mirror and flipped off the light, hurrying to my bed. I found the phone half buried under a pillow and picked it up, my stomach twisting and dipping when I saw Luc's name on the screen.

Can't sleep. You?

I sat down on the bed. A strange mix of fluttering anticipation and trepidation replaced the churning nausea, and I wasn't sure if that was better or worse.

Since the day in Harpers Ferry, things had shifted between us. What I was beginning to feel for him, or had *always* felt for him, was all over the place. How could I untangle those feelings from a past I couldn't remember and a present that left me entirely confused?

Can't sleep, either, I texted back.

A moment passed and then, *Let me in.*

Let me in? Crap! Shooting off the bed, I spun around and stared at my bedroom window. Was he—

There was a soft knock.

He was totally outside my window.

I hurried over before one of our neighbors just happened to notice him perched on my window like a hot pterodactyl.

"Evie?" came the muffled voice. "Is Diesel sleeping?"

A grin tugged at my lips. I probably shouldn't let him in, but I wanted a distraction after that nightmare.

That's what I told myself as I pushed the curtains aside and shoved the window up. That letting him in had nothing to do with that distraction being Luc. Cool night air rushed in. "My mom is home."

"I know." Moonlight sliced over his striking face.

"You shouldn't be here."

Luc grinned as he offered a can of soda to me. "I know."

"You just don't care?"

"About getting caught? Nope."

Shooting him a dark look, I snatched the can out of his hand and then stepped back. "If she catches you, it's really not going to win you any brownie points."

"She won't catch me."

Like a large cat, he came through the window and landed nimbly, quietly on his feet. He straightened to his full height. I wasn't exactly short, but Luc still towered over me. He turned, closing the window.

Soda can in hand, I desperately tried to ignore the fluttering deep in my chest as I checked the bedroom door, making sure it was locked. Then, drawing in a shallow breath, I faced him.

He was wearing a plain white T-shirt and a pair of gray-and-burgundy flannel bottoms. His hair was a mess, waves sticking up in every direction, and he looked utterly adorable, which was a word I never thought I'd use to describe Luc.

But there was something boyishly charming about him as he stood there, his eyes heavy with the cobwebs of sleep. In that moment, when he looked like he'd just shuffled out of bed, I could almost forget what he was.

"You came all the way here in your pajamas?" My gaze dipped. "And barefoot?"

"My feet didn't even touch the ground." He gave me a cheeky grin as his gaze drifted over me in a quick perusal. "I like the shirt."

Glancing down at myself, I frowned. The shirt I wore was at least three sizes too big. It was a shapeless tent, and as long as I didn't start to do jumping jacks, there was no way he could tell that I wasn't wearing a bra. A whole lot of leg was on display since the shirt only reached the middle of my thighs.

But Luc had seen a lot more than my legs.

"What do you like about it?" I asked.

One side of his mouth curled up. "There is an unmeasurable list of things I like about this shirt, but the QUEEN OF THE NAPS written across the front of it is in the top three."

"Oh." I looked down again. Yep. My shirt did say that. Apparently, I'd forgotten how to read. I wondered what the other two things were, but I didn't have the courage to ask.

His gaze flicked from me to the space above my bed. A slow smile appeared, and I knew he was staring at the framed photograph of the picture he'd given me. I'd decided to take it home that night, and after nailing several holes in the wall above my bed, I'd finally gotten it level.

At least, I thought I did.

"*Forensic Files,*" he said after a moment, tilting his head toward the television as I grabbed the hem of the shirt, tugging it as far it would go. "I think you're the only person who can fall asleep with that on."

While his back was to me, I all but darted toward the bed, still holding on to the hem of my shirt as I dived under the covers. "Probably why I have nightmares."

Luc turned to me, and even though I couldn't see his eyes, I could feel his gaze as I tugged the soft blanket to my waist. He took a step and then stopped. "That's not why you're having nightmares."

Letting go of the blanket, I looked up at him, my chest clenching. "Why would you say that?"

He picked up my laptop from where it rested and sat at the foot of the bed. "You've been through a lot of shit, Peaches. You've seen me kill Luxen, and you've stumbled across dead bodies. You were hurt by Micah and learned that your entire life was a lie. You're bound to have some nightmares."

"Do you?"

"Almost every night."

A different kind of pressure clamped down on my chest. "What kind of nightmares do you have?"

He was quiet for a long moment. "Things that have already come to pass," he said and then quickly moved on. "What woke you?"

"Micah," I said, telling the truth instead of lying or avoiding his question like I normally would.

"Micah's dead. You said that yourself." His head turned in my direction and in the shadows of the room our eyes met. "Which is probably why you're having nightmares."

"I know he's dead, it's just . . ."

"You've been through a lot," he repeated. "I wish Micah were alive so I could kill him all over again."

"Don't say that. I know you didn't want to kill him, and I know killing him bothers you."

Luc tilted his head to the side. "Why do you think that?"

"Because I remember what you told me about the other Origins, and I could tell that what you had to do is something that's stayed with you."

"It has, but Micah was different."

"How?"

"Because Micah did something that none of the others did." He rose with the laptop in hand and walked to the head of the bed. He sat beside me, on the other side—*his* side. Not that he had a side, but he sort of, kind of did. "He hurt you. I don't regret a thing I did to him."

I sucked in a shrill breath. "You don't mean that."

"I do. There's not an ounce of regret in me. He deserved it—deserved worse. He hurt you, Evie."

"He also killed other people, but—"

"I don't care about that."

My mouth dropped open as a lock of hair fell across my cheek.

"When he broke your arm, he was already in his coffin." He leaned against the headboard, stretching out his long legs. "Him attacking you again, hurting you like he did? I just put the final nails in."

My gaze lifted to his, and I drew in a shallow breath and spoke the truth. "I don't know what to say to that."

He stared at me a moment longer and then nodded. "You don't need to say anything."

I reached up to push my hair out of my face, unsure if I believed him or not.

Luc snapped toward me, his long, warm fingers circling my wrist. "What happened to your arm?"

The contact of his fingers sent a pleasant jolt up my arm. I followed his gaze as he lifted my arm, examining it. At first, I didn't know what he was talking about, but then I saw the blue smudges marring the inside of my forearm.

"These are fingerprints." His mouth pulled taut. "Who did this?"

I shook my head. "There were some idiots protesting Luxen at school today, and things got heated."

His head cocked to the side. "Who did this, Evie?"

My gaze snapped to his. Barely leashed violence churned in his eyes, matching his tone. There was no way I was going to tell him what happened, and I immediately started thinking about puppies with fluffy, wagging tails and kittens chasing balls.

Luc's eyes narrowed.

"It's nothing," I told him.

"Sure as hell doesn't look like nothing." He finally looked away as he lowered my arm to his thigh. "No one should be touching you in a way that leaves a bruise behind."

I had to agree with that last part.

"I'm sure the Luxen appreciate you standing up for them, but you need to be careful."

"I am."

He folded his hand over the bruises. "This tells me you're not careful enough." His palm began to warm. "There are people out there who are so controlled by their hate and their fear that they will not think twice before harming someone in the name of whatever they believe in. Even people you thought you knew."

The warmth rolled up my arm, washing over my elbow. "Are you healing me?" When he didn't say anything, my eyes widened. "Luc, you shouldn't do that. It's just a bruise." I kept my voice low as I tugged on my arm. "What if—?"

"Nothing is going to happen from a quick healing." His other hand had folded over mine, and his thumb slid back and forth along the center of my palm. "You're not going to mutate."

"How do you know?"

A lopsided grin appeared as his lashes lifted. "I know all, Peaches. Haven't you learned?"

"You're not omnipresent." A pleasant tingling swept over my skin.

He chuckled. "That's *omniscient,* Peaches."

"Whatever," I murmured, letting my head fall back against the headboard. We needed to talk more about Micah and how Luc really felt, but the tingling warmth was beyond distracting.

His fingers slid away from the bruised area, and I knew without looking that the bruises were gone, but his fingers kept searching, kept caressing. "You won't have the trace. The—"

"Andromeda serum," I finished for him. "I remember, but just because I don't have a trace, does that mean I can't be mutated?"

His hand smoothed over my upper arm, sending a tight shiver down my spine. My right leg curled. "Not through me healing you."

I turned my head to him. "Origins can't mutate humans?"

"Correct." His palm, calloused over, slid back down my arm. He kissed the center of my hand and then laid it back in my lap. "I remember you mentioning a couple of days ago that you like *BuzzFeed Unsolved*?"

"I did." Heidi had introduced me to *BuzzFeed Unsolved,* and Ryan and Shade were quickly becoming my favorite two humans—well, I *assumed* they were human and not Luxen. Nowadays, you really couldn't tell. Not when there were many Luxen out there, unregistered and using those contacts to hide their eyes from the RAC drones.

Human or Luxen, I could really go for Ryan's dramatic storytelling and Shade's hilarious wry wit.

"Want to watch a few episodes?" he asked, picking up my laptop.

"Yeah." I reached over, pressing my finger to the reader to unlock it.

I snuggled down as Luc searched for the episode that had something to do with the Mothman in West Virginia. I struggled to ignore how close we were, shoulder to shoulder, thigh to thigh. Somehow his legs were under the covers now, and the soft material of his pajama bottoms rasped against my bare legs, leaving me feeling like I needed to shove the blankets off by the time he got the video going.

I tried to pay attention, but within minutes, my thoughts took me back to one of the many things that had driven me to my knees in the bathroom. Had he done something like this with Nadia? Stayed up and watched videos because she—I—couldn't sleep?

I peeked over at him, hating and loving the tugging motion in my chest when I saw the faint grin on his face as he watched Ryan and Shane traipsing through a forest. Somehow he'd known I was awake, and while there was a part of me that did want to know how, I was also afraid to find out.

Because what if it were some kind of bond, some weird alien bond he'd forged with Nadia that had guided him to my room tonight, because of all the times he'd tried to heal me as Nadia? Maybe he wasn't able to mutate me, but could there have been some bond created?

How did Luc know I was having nightmares? Mom didn't even know I was spending many nights a week like this. I didn't want her to worry or feel guiltier than she already did.

And she already had enough to feel guilty about.

From what I gathered from Emery, repeated healings could link a human to a Luxen or an Origin on some kind of metaphysical level. I had no idea, but I really hoped Luc and I weren't connected like that, because it seemed super-weird and invasive.

"Hey," Luc said.

Pulling myself from my thoughts, I looked over at him. "Yeah?"

"Are you a magician?"

"What?" I laughed out loud as I glanced at the laptop screen. Shade was standing on the side of a dark road near Point Pleasant, West Virginia, making loud, weird animal sounds.

"Because whenever I look at you, everything else disappears."

"Oh my God," I said, rolling my eyes.

"Someone needs to call the cops."

I bit down on my lip.

"Because it's got to be illegal to look as hot as I do—wait. I meant *you*. Got to be illegal to look as beautiful as you do."

Laughing under my breath, I shifted onto my back. Luc had the worst pickup lines I'd ever heard in my entire life, and nothing distracted me more than his ridiculous one-liners. "You're a dork."

"Got an even better one." He scooted down so our heads were resting on pillows. "Was your father an alien?"

"I don't want to see where you're going with this."

"Because there's nothing like you on earth."

"Please stop."

"Never." There was a brief pause. "You must be a broom, because you've swept me off my feet."

"You're a cornball of epic cornball proportions."

He was closer, our mouths inches apart. "But you miss me when I'm not here."

Closing my eyes, I let out a little sigh. I did miss his stupid shirts that were always so random. I missed the way he could irritate me one second and make me burst into laughter the next. I missed the dumb, mysterious little half grin that seemed to always be on his face, like he was in on all the universe's secrets. I missed him randomly showing up at my bedroom window like a freak with a fresh, chilled can of Coke. I missed the way he sometimes seemed like he couldn't take his eyes off me. I missed the way he looked at me, because no one, especially not Brandon, looked at me like I was the only important person to him in the whole world. I missed—

"I miss *you* when you're not here, Peaches."

I even missed that idiotic nickname.

Taking a shallow breath, I opened my eyes and saw that his were closed, those thick lashes fanning his cheeks. "I miss you."

11

"God," Heidi groused Friday during lunch, drawing my gaze from my lunch tray. I thought it was Salisbury steak and gravy, but I wasn't entirely sure, because the slab of meat also vaguely resembled meat loaf and tasted like wet cardboard. "What have we done to deserve this?"

I looked up at the same time Zoe did, both of us scanning the packed, brightly lit cafeteria. We saw her at the same time. April. Heading straight for us, cutting between tables and people, her long ponytail snapping behind her. I had no idea why she was walking toward us. How could she not realize none of us wanted anything to do with her? We'd made that painfully clear.

Plopping my elbow on the table, I groaned. "Not today, Satan."

Zoe sighed, dropping her peanut butter sandwich onto her napkin. "I'm not in the mood for her."

"Who is ever in the mood for her?" Heidi pressed her cheek into her fist as I placed my plastic fork down, just in case I caved to the urge to turn it into a projectile.

April reached our table with unerring speed, her pale eyes flashing as her gaze zeroed in on me. "What did you do?"

"Me?" I looked around the table, confused. "I haven't done anything."

Squeezing in between Heidi and Zoe, she planted one French-manicured hand on the table and leaned forward, pointing the other directly in my face. "That's bullshit."

"I'm out." James stood, snatching a handful of chips off Zoe's plate before he spun, leaving us to deal with April.

Everything in me focused on the slim finger inches from my face. How easy would it be for me to reach out and snap it back? Too easy.

One side of my lip curled up as my skin prickled with the desire to hear the crack—

I caught myself lifting my hand. Shocked, I leaned away from her finger as my heart hammered against its cage. Was I going to break her finger? Not that anyone would blame me if I did it, but I wasn't a violent person.

At least I didn't think I was.

"I don't know what you think I did," I said after a moment. "But you really need to remove your finger from my face."

"And you need to remove your body from my presence," Zoe added, leaning as far as she could to her left.

"I'm not talking to you." April glanced down at Zoe, her lip curling. "Are you wearing overalls?"

Zoe's dark brows lifted, and then she looked over at me. "Remind me that she's not worth it."

"She's not." I met Zoe's stare and then looked up at April. "I honestly have no idea what you're talking about, and your finger is still in my face."

"You really don't know that some guy accosted Brandon outside of his house this morning?" April's finger was still in my face, getting closer.

"Accosted?" Heidi giggled. "Sorry. That just sounds funny."

"Someone jumped him? You can safely assume it wasn't me."

"No shit, but the guy jumped him because of you," April snapped back, and a sense of knowing invaded me. "Got him outside of his car and then proceeded to break every single bone in his hand."

My mouth dropped open, and I had a sudden, sinking suspicion that I knew who it was.

"And then told him if he ever looked at you or breathed in your general direction again, it would be the last thing he ever did." April was practically humming with rage as she hissed, "And the guy was a Luxen. He had those freaky eyes."

My jaw was officially on the table. Luc. It had to have been Luc, but I hadn't told him the night before. I had made sure not to even think Brandon's name.

Immediately, I thought about what Daemon had told me—had basically warned me.

"He's been at the hospital all morning, and he'll have to wear a cast for three weeks," April ranted, and there was a part of me that was surprised that was all Luc had done.

"Then maybe Brandon shouldn't grab people like he did yesterday." Zoe picked up her sandwich and took a huge bite. "Just saying."

Had Zoe told Luc?

"You tell your Luxen freak to stay away from Brandon—away from us—or he'll regret it."

I couldn't help it. A laugh burst out of me as I imagined telling Luc to stay away from them *or else*.

April's cheeks went a mottled red. "Do you think I'm funny?"

"Yes." I nodded.

"We'll see just how funny you think it is." Then she flicked the tip of my nose.

I jerked back out of surprise, and there was no stopping the red-hot burst of anger. I reacted without thinking. My fingers wrapped around hers before she even had a chance to pull her hand back.

Surprise widened her eyes, and then her glossy red lips curved into a smirk. "Do it. I dare you, Evie."

The bone was fragile. I knew that. Hell, I knew firsthand exactly how frail bones could be and how easily they could break. My skin heated as I inhaled through my nose, holding her stare. I could easily do it. I wanted to. Probably more than I wanted to do anything in my life.

And that was kind of messed up.

I didn't care, though.

"Evie." Zoe's soft voice snapped me out of it.

Blinking, I dropped April's hand as if her touch scalded me. Unnerved, I clamped my hands together in my lap.

April's smirk grew. "Didn't think so." Straightening, she twirled around, nearly smacking Heidi and April in their faces with her ponytail.

Heidi was staring at me. "I really thought you were going to do it. Honest to God, I thought, *Holy shit, she's going to break April's finger,* and I didn't know if I should stop you or applaud you."

I laughed, but it sounded as forced as it felt as I met Zoe's stare. "Did you tell Luc?"

"No. I didn't."

Then how did . . .

I twisted around, my gaze swinging exactly to where the Luxen usually sat. They were all there, all except one.

Connor.

Whipping around, I pulled my phone out of my backpack and fired off a quick text to Luc.

We need to talk.

It was a little before five when Luc texted back. He didn't question why I was texting him. His response was *Meet me at Walkers.*

Walkers was a burger joint not too far from my house, and it served amazing pan-fried hamburgers. Like, old-school, not even remotely healthy kind of hamburgers. I hadn't been there in ages, but I always gave them a look of longing every time I passed the usually packed parking lot.

As I grabbed my small purse off the front seat and climbed out of the old Lexus that had belonged to the man I'd thought had been my father, it felt like a nest of butterflies was fluttering around in my chest.

Why in the world was I so nervous?

I had no idea.

Okay. That was a lie.

I was nervous because I'd kissed him two days ago. It wasn't much of a kiss, but I'd done it. Even though I'd seen him since then, I was . . . I was crushing on Luc.

Despite the fact I was 100 percent confident he'd broken Brandon's hand. Not that Brandon hadn't deserved it, but Luc couldn't just run around breaking people's hands.

Closing the door, I hopped up on the sidewalk and made my way to the all-glass door. There were flyers plastered all along the front windows of the diner. Most looked like they'd been there a while and were offering things for sale or for free. Someone had a litter of adorable black-and-white kittens.

But one of the flyers stood out. Kind of hard not to notice it since it was right in the center of the door and used big, bold letters.

LUXEN NOT WELCOME HERE.

Underneath the words was the standard alien face, the oval-shaped head and big, black eyes. The circle-backslash symbol was over the top of it for, I guess, aliens who couldn't read?

That had to be new. The last time I was here, they weren't banning Luxen from eating their artery-clogging pieces of heaven.

Why would Luc pick a place that discriminated against Luxen?

Then again, I wasn't exactly surprised by that.

Opening the door, I was immediately surrounded by the drool-worthy scent of fried meat and onions, a combination that only worked in diners. Holding my purse, I scanned the round tables in the middle as I stepped forward. I didn't see him. What if he wasn't here yet? What if—

There.

I saw Luc.

The fact that all I needed to see was a little bit of his hair over the red vinyl booths and knew it was him made me want to throat punch myself. Ugh. Crushes were stupid.

I cut around a tableful of kids and started toward the back of the diner. To the right of where he sat, a TV was on, broadcasting some news station.

Luc didn't look up as I approached the table. He was focused on something on his phone. "Peaches," he said. "Even in this place full of grease, I can still smell peaches."

Brows knitting, I slid into the booth across from him, placing my bag beside me. "You do realize how weird that is, your fascination with peaches?"

"It's not my fascination with peaches. It's my fascination with *the* Peaches. You. Is that creepy?"

"Yes," I said, drawing the word out while this horrible part of me that existed deep, deep inside got kind of . . . giddy.

"I also don't care that it's weird. I'm living my best life over here." He finally looked up then, and I . . . God, my breath did this little catch thing. Those eyes. The violet color was startling, no matter how many times I saw them. He was—

"Extraordinarily handsome? So much so that you find yourself wondering how such a perfect specimen could be sitting in front of you?"

My jaw unhinged as heat infused my cheeks.

"So hot that you almost can't believe I'm real?" he continued. "I know. I have a hard time believing I'm real, too."

"That is not—"

He leaned in, resting his chin on his palm. A lock of wavy hair fell forward, brushing his brows. "That's not what you're thinking?"

I sucked in a shrill breath. I was not thinking that *exactly,* but yeah, some sort of variation. "Get out of my head, Luc."

He chuckled under his breath.

My eyes narrowed. "Do I need to remind you that you said you wouldn't read my thoughts? We've only had this conversation a million times."

"I said I would *mostly* not read your thoughts. And like I've said before, sometimes you're so loud there's no stopping it." He shrugged as his gaze flickered over my shoulder. "About time. I'm thirsty."

An older woman appeared, placing tall sodas in front of each of us, along with straws. "Two Cokes." She winked at Luc. "Your orders will be out shortly."

I waited until the waitress left and then leaned forward. "Aren't you worried about being here since they're anti-Luxen?" I asked. I couldn't tell an Origin apart from a Luxen, so I doubted the owners of Walkers could. And I doubted they'd see a difference between the two even if they knew. Luc wasn't wearing contacts. If a RAC drone roamed in here, the poo would hit the fan.

One side of his mouth kicked up. "Do I look worried?"

"No. You look pompous and arrogant."

The smirk spread into a grin. "I think those are two great looks on me."

"Pompous looks good on no one, dude," I replied dryly. "And just FYI, I wasn't thinking about you being hot."

That was, in fact, a total lie.

Luc grinned as he arched a brow.

Oh my God, he was doing it *again*. "Luc—"

"I ordered you a bacon cheeseburger, no tomato and no pickles," he interrupted, picking up one of the straws.

Completely thrown off guard, I started to ask how he knew I didn't like pickles or tomatoes on my burgers, but then it hit me. "I didn't like them then, either?"

His gaze flicked to mine and then away. "No. You liked to eat them separately. Garden tomatoes—"

"Cut up and with salt?" I whispered.

Those eyes met mine again. "Yes. Pickles were okay as long as—"

"They aren't on anything." Sitting back, I dropped my hands into my lap. "Wow."

A long moment passed. "So, you wanted to see me? I know you miss me even though it was just last night you were snuggled up against me."

"I was not snuggled against you." Was I? I honestly didn't recall. He'd been gone when I awoke this morning.

He shoved the straw into my drink. "You were wrapped around me like an octopus."

I glared at him.

"By the way, just going to remind you that you told me last night you missed me."

I had. "I must've been high."

"On my presence."

Snorting, I picked up the straw wrapper and started folding it into tiny squares. "I texted you because we need to talk about Brandon."

"Who is that?" He sat back.

I shot him a bland look. "You know exactly who he is. Especially since you broke his arm this morning."

"Oh, that guy." He watched me, focusing on my fingers. "I broke his hand, actually. Not his arm. What about him?"

My fingers stilled. "What about him? You broke his hand."

Luc nodded, sipping his drink. "That I did."

I stared at him for a moment. "That wasn't okay, Luc."

"It wasn't?"

The waitress appeared just then, placing two plates stacked with burgers and fries in front of us. "Anything else you two need?"

I shook my head, and Luc said, "Not at the moment, but thank you."

The older lady nodded and then pivoted around, hurrying off to another table.

Luc grabbed the ketchup bottle and then proceeded to drown his burger in it. "He shouldn't have grabbed you in the first place." He offered the bottle. "And he should definitely not have grabbed you hard enough to leave bruises."

I took the ketchup. "I agree, but that doesn't mean breaking his hand is okay. This is not an eye-for-an-eye society."

"You're right. It's a hand-for-a-bruise society." Luc bit down on his burger, and miraculously, none of the ketchup seeped out and hit his shirt. That alone had to be a result of alien superpowers. "We're going to have to agree to disagree."

I sighed. "Luc."

"Do you know that a lot of people pronounce my name like *Luck*?" he asked as I took a smaller bite.

Ketchup smacked off the table. I sighed again.

"No. I didn't know that. And don't try to change the subject."

Half his burger was already gone. "Did you know that sometimes, when you're asleep, you make little animal noises?"

Lowering my burger, I frowned. "What?"

His lips pursed as a thoughtful expression settled across his face. "Last night, when you fell asleep once Shane and Ryan got to the brewery, you were making these little cub-like noises."

My head slowly tilted to the side. "For real?"

"For reals."

Warmth crept into my face. "You're lying."

"I'd never do such a thing." His eyes gleamed. "By the way, I left around four, and I'd swear Sylvia had already left the house."

"She's been going into work early." Rolling my eyes, I took a bite of my hamburger. "And stop trying to change the subject, you freak. You cannot run around and break people's hands, Luc."

Finishing his burger, he moved on to his fries. "I can run around and do pretty much whatever I please."

"I am going to throw this hamburger in your face."

His lips twitched. "Please aim for my mouth."

"You're ridiculous."

"Among many other things." Picking up a fry, he pointed it at me. "Look, I know that my reaction to learning that a guy grabbed you hard enough to leave bruises may be seen as excessive, but if he touches you again, I'll do worse."

"Luc, seriously—"

"He hates Luxen, right? He thinks they don't deserve basic rights and there's nothing better than a dead Luxen?" He tipped forward, voice low. "They feel the same way about those who support the Luxen, interact with them, and protect them. He feels the same way about you, and he proved that when he grabbed you."

My stomach took a little tumble.

"So, he needed a really good warning to stay the hell away from you." Luc popped the fry in his mouth. "And if I hadn't done it, Connor would've, and since Connor is registered and tracked, that wouldn't have ended well for him."

"It might not end well for you. You may not be registered, but it's not like you're invisible." I reached for the napkin to wipe my fingers. "Hell, you're in here with no contacts, and I have no idea how no one realizes what you are."

"Because appearances can be deceiving, Peaches."

My eyes narrowed as I roughly cleaned my fingers. "How so?"

"Well, there may be an anti-Luxen sign on the front door of this fine, greasy establishment, but our waitress? One of the rare older Luxen. Unregistered and hidden in plain sight."

I stared at him.

"And that happy group of teens over there? Not a single one of them are human." When I started to look behind me, he stopped me. "Don't be obvious, Peaches. The owners?"

"Luxen?" I whispered.

"A Luxen female and her hybrid husband. The older couple that everyone thinks are the owners are actually decoys. They're just two humans that have known the real owners for over a decade."

Placing the napkin on the table, I picked up my Coke as I mulled this over. "They really are hidden in plain sight."

Luc smiled. "We're safe here."

My gaze connected with his, and a weird flutter started deep in my chest like there was a nest of hummingbirds attempting to buzz their way out. Which was so stupid, because he irked me just as much as I liked him.

Which was a lot.

Luc picked up a fry, popping it into his mouth. He didn't break eye contact. Not once.

Heat pricked at my skin as Luc's lips kicked up. A humming, burning connection flared to life. The buzzing in my chest spread to my stomach. More intense than before, and I knew that could only mean one thing.

Trouble.

Big trouble.

12

Growing up, I loved Halloween—Halloween and Christmas. Or at least I thought I did. Who knew if I really did since I had no real memories beyond the last four years, but every Halloween I could remember, I loved dressing up and watching scary movies while gorging on candy.

This year was different. Everything felt off, and it wasn't just because I was actually at a club instead of at Zoe's or Heidi's house, sitting next to Luc and staring at him like—

"You're staring at me."

Blinking, I jerked my gaze away from Luc. I had been staring at him. It was kind of hard not to when he was sitting there, his head tilted slightly to the side and a mysterious smile curling the corners of his lips.

"No, I'm not," I muttered.

"Uh-huh. Looked like you completely dazed out over there. What are you thinking about?" Luc asked.

That was a loaded question, because it felt like I was thinking about everything. Lifting a shoulder, I scanned the crowded dance floor of Foretoken as columns of vibrant purple light streamed from the ceilings, gliding over the churning bodies. I'd lost sight of Heidi and Zoe in the crush of angels and sexy cats, Black Panthers and vampires. What *wasn't* I thinking about?

My head was running a million miles a minute and not really conducive to being at a club. I felt like I was better suited for staring morosely out of a coffee shop window.

"Peaches . . ."

I looked over at Luc. He sat beside me, one arm thrown along the back of the couch. His other hand rested on his thigh, his long fingers tapping. He was the picture of lazy arrogance, but I knew he could spring into action at any moment. When I didn't answer, the hand behind me tugged on one of my pigtails.

I pulled my hair away from his fingers. "You're not just going to read my thoughts?"

"You don't like it when I do that."

"Has that stopped you before?" I squinted, thinking I'd caught a glimpse of Zoe's super-cute Wonder Woman costume, but it wasn't her. She'd disappeared with a college-age guy, and I had a feeling that tonight would end in shenanigans of the fun and naughty kind.

"More than you realize, Peaches."

I shot him a look, and he grinned at me. "I'm just thinking about . . . everything."

His head inclined. "That sounds like a lot."

"It is." And it really was.

He was quiet for a long moment. "A penny for your thoughts?"

I laughed, thinking I hadn't heard that saying in a while. Truth was, I wasn't quite sure I could make sense of the mess of thoughts or explain the weird restlessness invading every cell in my body.

I felt like I should be out there, dancing with my friends and having fun, instead of sitting here, too afraid, too in control, too *whatever* to just let go and be who I used to be.

And I didn't want to talk about any of this.

Twisting one of my pigtails into a rope, I looked over at him. Those eyes were shadowy in the dim light, but the heaviness of his gaze was still there, intense and consuming.

"Did we ever go trick-or-treating? You know, as kids?" I asked after a moment.

"That was random." He chuckled. "We did a couple of times."

"We did?" My gaze tracked its way to his.

He nodded. "I'd never gone before you. Never really had any interest in it."

My brows lifted. "How could you not want to dress up and go get candy?"

"I wasn't exactly a normal kid."

"You're not exactly a normal guy right now."

He laughed again, shoulders rising and falling, and I liked the sound a lot. Sometimes too much. "True."

Shifting toward him, I drew a leg up. “Tell me about it? Like, what did we dress up as, and did you have fun?”

“We had fun.” He dragged his teeth over his lower lip. “Paris would take us to the best subdivision, the ones where they handed out full-sized candy bars.”

“Nice.” I laughed, letting my hair go and then twisting it once more.

His lashes lowered. “He’d make us dump our bags at the end of the night and evenly count them out, but you always ended up with more.”

“Because you gave me the candy?”

“Hell no. I worked hard for that candy. Halfway through the night, you’d somehow trick me into carrying your bag. I had tiny arms back then. That crap was heavy, so I wasn’t giving away any of it.” He reached over, stilling my fingers around my hair. “You’d wait until I went to sleep and would sneak into my room and steal it.”

“No way!” I let him pull my hand from my hair.

“Hand to God, I’m telling you the truth, my sexy little Big Bird.”

“For the third time, I’m not dressed up as Big Bird!” I exclaimed, pointing at my yellow tights that I’d paired with a pair of jean overall shorts and a long-sleeve yellow shirt with my other hand. The yellow beanie and the pair of ski goggles I’d found at a thrift shop completed the costume. “I’m a minion.”

“You’re a sexy minion.”

“Whatever.” I grinned. His costume consisted of a black shirt that read in white lettering I DON’T NEED A COSTUME. PEOPLE WANT TO BE ME.

God, that was such a Luc shirt.

He was quiet for a moment, and the teasing eased from his tone as a distant look crept into his face. “The first Halloween, you dressed up as Princess Leia, and I went as Han Solo.”

I snorted. “For real?”

“Yep. Except you demanded to have a light saber.”

My gaze dropped to where he held my hand, his fingers threaded through mine. It seemed so effortless, the whole holding-of-hands thing, so why was I so hyperaware of it? I cleared my throat. “Leia should’ve been a trained Jedi. Fight me.”

“That’s not a fight I will win.” His thumb moved over my palm.

"The second year, you went as a princess, but somehow, you got your hands on a pair of nunchucks, and you became a ninja princess. I still have no idea where you found a pair of nunchucks."

I really wished I could remember how I'd gotten my hands on them, because that sounded really bizarre. "And you?"

"I went as a ghost. Sheet and all."

"Creative."

He snorted. "One year we went as outlaws. I was Jesse James, and you were Belle Star."

"Belle Star?"

"She was a famous outlaw believed to have hung out with Jesse James," he explained, and now that I knew we'd been dressed as outlaws, I thought that sounded adorable. "Neither of us really knew who they were. It was Clyde's idea. You . . . were sick one year and couldn't go." His voice grew quiet. "You'd been so excited to go. Halloween and Christmas were your favorite holidays, but you were just too sick." There was a pause. "That was before we knew what was wrong with you. Paris thought it was the flu."

I tensed as I watched him close his eyes. It hadn't been the flu.

"You cried and cried because he wouldn't let you go. It . . . got to me." He rubbed at the center of his chest with the heel of his hand. "Anyway, I went out for you, determined to bring back more candy than you'd ever seen."

My heart stuttered in my chest as I lifted my gaze to his. Immediately, the image formed of a little boy with messy bronze hair and mischievous purple eyes, going out to get Halloween candy like a soldier going through his drills. Was that another rare memory or just my imagination? I decided it didn't matter, because I liked the image enough to file it away.

"And did you?" I asked, thinking I already knew the answer.

His gaze met mine. "Of course I did. You had a thing for Mounds bars. I got you enough to last half a year."

"Really?" I smiled. "I love Mounds, and I know no one else who likes them. Zoe nearly vomits in her mouth when I eat them in front of her."

"Because they're disgusting?"

I rolled my eyes. "They're not disgusting. They're delicious heaven made of coconut and chocolate."

"Your taste in candy is about as bad as your taste in movies." He was close again, his mouth inches from mine.

My heart rate kicked up. "And what about before? Was I a fan of James Bond?"

"Yes and no. You thought James Bond should've been Janet Bond."

I laughed, but it quickly faded. "Sounds like Nadia was ahead of her time."

"*You* were ahead of your time," he corrected softly.

The next breath I took hitched in my throat, and I didn't know what to say. It was weird. I was like a volleyball, bouncing back and forth from accepting that I was Nadia, that she was me, and then feeling like she was a completely different person.

All I did know was that I didn't feel like *her* right now.

"Nice costume," Kent remarked as he dropped into one of the chairs next to the couch. He was definitely in costume, wearing striped black-and-white tights and some kind of ruffled shorts that were secured just above the knees with an elastic band. His white shirt had puffy sleeves and large buttons up the center. There were large teardrops painted under his eyes.

"She's Big Bird," Luc offered.

I was going to punch Luc. "I'm a *minion*."

"And you're adorable, honeybuns." Kent kicked his feet onto the small glass table.

"What are you dressed as?"

"You don't know?" He sent me a boyish grin that hinted at dimples. "I'll give you a hint."

"Okay."

Kent leaned over, his brown eyes wide. "*We all float down here.*"

"You're Pennywise!"

"Kind of." He rocked back, lowering his eyebrows as he pointed at the teardrops under his eyes. "I'm emo Pennywise."

"Emo Pennywise?" I laughed as I looked him over. "I see it now. I like it. Are you as psychotic as the normal Pennywise?"

"I like to think I'm the version of Pennywise who still eats children but then feels bad about it afterward. Not just because I imagine children would give you indigestion but because eating children would make me feel like a glutton and I have a gluten intolerance.

I feel like kids would be full of gluten," he explained while Luc blinked slowly. "And it would be tiresome, you know, having to lure kids into sewers to nom nom on them. I imagine when I wasn't eating children, I'd mope around, bemoaning how hard my life was and how everyone misunderstood me."

I stared at him. "You've put a lot of thought into this."

"I have."

"To a scary level, Kent."

That grin grew and dimples appeared. "I know."

"I knew there was a reason I liked you so much," Luc chimed in. "You're the perfect kind of weird."

"That I am." Kent smiled happily, which was a weird look with the tears and all. "Where's Grayson?"

"Probably out on the streets, stealing candy from kids," remarked Luc, and I snorted.

I could actually picture Grayson doing just that.

Pulling my legs up, I circled my arms around them as I watched the people dancing, and nervous, antsy energy built inside me. As I watched the bodies moving in tune to the music, the urge to get out there and move my body along with them crept over me. The restlessness from earlier returned with a vengeance. There was a desire to let the music seep into my skin and muscles, to throw my head back and let the rhythm guide the way my body moved. I'd had that desire before, and now I thought I knew why.

It was something I used to do as Nadia, so why couldn't I do it now?

"Oh, there he is," Kent murmured, and I looked up, following his gaze.

It was Grayson.

The tall, blond Luxen dropped into the chair opposite Kent as he pulled out a Blow Pop. He also wasn't dressed up. I doubted he'd ever celebrated Halloween. Probably hated Halloween and Christmas and Valentine's Day and every holiday there ever was. He paused, unwrapping his Blow Pop as he looked over at us. "What?"

"You're so pretty," Kent said with a grin.

Grayson arched an eyebrow at him. "Everyone looks like they're having an amazing time." His tone could've dried out the Everglades. "So glad I came down here."

"You didn't have to," Luc pointed out.

"And not bless you all with my presence?" Grayson smirked. "I would never be so selfish."

I rolled my eyes but kept my mouth shut. Grayson wasn't a fan of mine. I had no idea why. I'd never done anything to him. At first, I'd thought it was because I was human, but he had no problem with Kent.

My gaze drifted back to the dance floor, and once again, I could feel the tension tightening my muscles. I could do it. Go out there, find the girls, and dance. I could.

I didn't budge.

But Luc did.

Pulling his arm off the back of the couch, he rose, offering his hand. "Come on."

Dammit.

He'd read my thoughts.

I didn't move as I shot him a look. There was no way in this lifetime I was going to let him drag me out onto that dance floor.

Luc wiggled his fingers. "Trust me."

I froze.

Luc had never asked me to do that. Once I had asked if he expected me to trust him, and he'd responded that he'd never asked that of me.

And now he was?

That was kind of a big deal.

Truth was, I did trust Luc. Not when I first met him, but I knew now that he wasn't going to make me do something I didn't want to or wasn't ready for. Aware of Grayson and Kent watching, I unfurled my legs and placed my hand in his.

Luc tugged me off the couch. "You all know where to find me if you need me," he said as he led me around the glass table. "Just make sure it's important."

"In other words, someone had better be dying." Kent grinned, and I shook my head. "Got it, boss."

Luc didn't lead me to the dance floor, thank God. He guided me around the floor and back down the hall, toward the entrance marked EMPLOYEES. Most of the letters were scratched out, leaving only the word PLOY behind. We didn't speak as we went up to his apartment, not until we were inside, the door closed behind us. One of the lights near the couch flipped on, casting buttery yellow light.

"What are we doing?"

Luc walked around so that he stood in front of me. There was a secretive twist to his lips, one that caused a curl low in my stomach. Without saying a word, he carefully took off the beanie and ski goggles I wore, dropping them on the couch.

I lifted a brow. "Luc."

"You'll see." He pulled his phone out of his pocket, thumbing through something before sitting it on the arm of the couch.

Having no idea what he was up to, I let him take my hands in his. A moment later, a steady beat echoed from his phone, just the clap of drums, joined by the riffs of the guitar.

The tiny hairs all over my body rose as Luc pulled me toward him, placing my hands on his chest. The song. I remembered it had been playing the first time I'd walked into the club with Heidi.

Don't fret, precious, I'm here . . .

Step away from the window, go back to sleep . . .

There was something more about the song, though . . .

Luc's hands dropped to my hips, and I stopped thinking about the song. "Just close your eyes," he said, "and let go."

That was harder to do. I stared up at him with wide eyes. Dancing with him was no easier than dancing in the club with a bunch of people I didn't actually know . . . or like . . . or care about.

His grin kicked up a notch as he started to sway his body in tune to the beat of drums. His eyes closed, thick lashes sweeping down, and as his body moved fluidly mere inches from mine, my heart rate kicked up.

"Close your eyes," he repeated.

Heart thumping, I did as he said. I closed my eyes and focused on the feel of his heart thrumming under my palm. He was dancing, and I was just standing there. And I could dance. I knew I could, but I wasn't even trying.

I could at least *try*.

And I had a feeling that Nadia tried everything.

"You don't have to be like you were." His lips brushed my ear. "You just need to be *you*."

Drawing in a stuttered breath, I found the beat and started to move against him, and it felt like an eternity for me to lose the stiffness in my legs and my arms and to find the beat of the music, but I did.

And the music, the beat of the drum and the rhythm, unlocked something deep inside me—something that tasted like *freedom,* and that feeling resonated through me, my limbs and my body.

Luc didn't speak as I danced with him, and I didn't open my eyes. I didn't let myself think that I was in Luc's apartment, dancing with him in yellow tights and overalls. I didn't let myself think about the past—our past—or the future. There was nothing but the music and the beat of the drums, the beat of Luc's heart.

I let go.

Moving my shoulders and my hips, I slid my hands down Luc's flat stomach and then I lifted them above my head, because that's what I felt like doing. What I *wanted.* I spun around, and Luc's hand slid from my hip, across my lower stomach, sending waves of tight shivers throughout my entire body. I felt his chin graze my neck as the beat picked up.

I didn't know how much time passed, but the song became something else and the air around us became thicker. Sweat dotted my forehead, and when I reached up to free my hair from the pigtails, I didn't stop dancing.

Neither did Luc.

My back was pressed to his front, and as our bodies moved together, there was a different kind of heat invading me that had nothing to do with embarrassment or self-consciousness and everything to do with the feel of him, the unique scent of him. The heavy air shifted around us, and when Luc spun me back to him, I knew this was no longer about proving I could still dance.

That I was still *her,* because that was what this had been about.

Now it was about something more.

There was a power in this. A freedom I relished. I was on the tips of my sneakers as I slid my arms around his neck. His head lowered, forehead pressing against mine. A rush of power flowed through Luc, transferring to my skin as our bodies surged with the beat, fusing together in all the right, interesting places. It was like the night on his bed, when there'd been less clothing between us. Memories of that night danced in my head like half-naked Luc sugarplums.

Feeling dizzy and warm, I opened my eyes. Luc lifted his head, and there were pinpricks of white light in his pupils.

One large hand drifted up my side, following the dips and rises of my body all the way up, over my neck. His thumb stopped briefly on my pulse and then continued until his fingers splayed over my jaw, cradling my cheek.

My fingers curled around the short strands of hair at the nape of his neck.

"I think . . ." His thumb dragged along my bottom lip, causing me to suck in a short breath as he brought my chin down. Our gazes connected and held. "I think I'm getting a little distracted."

"By what?" I asked as I pressed into him—

The arm around my waist tightened as a low sound rumbled from him. "By *this*."

I froze, eyes widening as my cheeks flushed. Oh my, holy llama babies everywhere, I could feel just how distracted he was.

I didn't pull away from him. Instead, I got even closer, which didn't seem possible before but was. We were chest to chest, hip to hip. Heat seeped through my skin, turning my muscles to liquid. There was a rush of new and powerful sensations. I felt empty and aching and wanting.

Groaning, he dropped his forehead to mine once more, his hand sliding to my hip, guiding mine against his. A sharp burst of pleasure lit up my veins. Our mouths were so close, I could taste him on my tongue.

Kiss me.

I didn't speak those words. They never left my mouth as my hands opened and closed against the cotton of his shirt. His head tilted and his nose skated over my cheek and then to the other side of my jaw. His lips brushed the hollow just under the bone and then again above the place where my pulse beat wildly. I couldn't breathe. My eyes drifted shut. I wanted him to kiss me. I needed him to—

Luc shifted, and suddenly, we were moving. I was up and then I was down, and a stuttered heartbeat later, I was on the couch, lying on my back. Luc hovered over me, one hand planted in the cushion next to my head, the other gliding down my throat, his touch as light as wings, and his hand didn't stop there. It coasted down the center of my chest, the soft contact burning through the denim and the thin, loose shirt. He was barely touching me, but my back arched as I clamped my mouth shut, sealing off the sound and the words I knew were seconds from spilling from my lips.

I like you.

The music stopped as his gaze followed his hand, leaving a wake of throbbing heaviness that was full of promise.

I want you.

A tremble coursed through his arm as his fingers reached my navel and then slid along my side, to my hip. Slowly, he lifted those impossibly thick lashes, and the pupils of those extraordinary purple eyes were diamond white, intense and consuming. I became aware of my hands resting on his chest, his stomach, and as he leaned in, my blood thundered through me.

"You," he spoke. "It's only ever been you. Before. Now. Later. There's been no one else. There . . . just can't be."

My lips parted as his words sank through the haze. Wait. Did he mean what I thought he did?

A knock on the door jolted both of us. Disbelief thundered through me as Luc swore under his breath and his eyes drifted shut. His striking features were all hard lines and lush, parted lips.

The knock came again, and this time a voice followed. "I'm sorry. I know you're busy, but this can't wait."

His eyes opened, and those pupils were still a shining, bright white. He didn't look like he was going to move.

I wasn't sure I wanted him to.

"I'm sorry," he said, and in a blink of an eye, he was on his feet, pulling me upward into a sitting position.

"It's okay." Dazed, I shoved several strands of hair out of my face as Luc made his way to the door, opening it.

A tall form stood there, and I immediately recognized the black, wavy hair and stunning green eyes—eyes that widened as they caught sight of me sitting on the couch, most likely looking like a sweaty mess. He stared at me like he'd never seen me before, but that wasn't the case.

"Daemon?" I hadn't known he was back in the city, especially after he'd said he wasn't leaving his wife.

"No." He continued to stare at me, looking a little thunderstruck. "I'm Dawson."

Whoa.

Good thing I was sitting. It was Daemon and Dee's brother—the rare third Luxen sibling. Having now seen all three of them, two in person and one on TV, it was like spotting a unicorn.

I'd never seen a full set of Luxen triplets. Daemon, Dawson, and their sister were the first, and I knew they were a rarity since most were killed in the invasion and afterward.

I blinked several times, stunned that they were nearly identical like Luc had said. Good Lord, it was like seeing a mirror image of Daemon. I squinted as I studied him. Well, there were small differences. Dawson's hair was slightly longer and curlier, and his voice wasn't as deep as Daemon's.

But that was all.

Freaky. Cool. Also, again, sort of freaky.

"Have we . . . um . . . met before?" I asked, feeling awkward, but we could've been best friends forever when I was Nadia and I'd have no idea.

"Briefly," Luc answered as he shifted so that he was between Dawson and me, and I could no longer see the Luxen. Luc was just as tall and marginally broader. "This is *Evie,*" Luc said, stressing my name as I rose from the couch and stepped to the side so I could see Dawson.

Dawson nodded. "Nice to meet you, Evie."

"Same." I smiled at the Luxen that was somehow familiar and yet a stranger.

"Sorry to have bothered you two, but this can't wait. Something's happening with the girl," Dawson explained. "I think she's dying."

13

Girl?" My stomach dropped all the way to my toes. Immediately, I thought of my friends, but if it were one of them, wouldn't Dawson have said so? Plus, they were down below, having fun. They were fine. "What girl?"

Luc hesitated.

My gaze flicked from Dawson to him. "What's going on, Luc?"

"Her name is Sarah," Luc answered as he stepped out into the hallway. "And I thought she had the flu or something." He said the last part to Dawson.

I had no idea who Sarah was, but the flu? "Like the flu from Kansas City kind of flu?"

"I don't know, Peaches."

Following Luc out into the hall, I realized Dawson hadn't come here alone. Grayson was waiting.

"What is she doing out here?" he demanded.

My eyes narrowed, but then Luc looked over his shoulder at me as if just realizing I'd followed him out into the hall.

"Give me a moment," Luc said, and then he took my hand, taking me back into his apartment. The door mostly closed but didn't shut the whole way. "You should probably stay here, wait until I get back. This shouldn't take long."

I stared at him for a long moment, somewhat stuck between disbelief and irritation. "Just a few minutes ago, we were on that couch and your hands were on me—my hands were on you."

Luc's eyes slammed shut as he made a low growling sound. "Don't remind me. I'm trying everything not to think about it at the moment."

My cheeks flushed at the sound, sending shivers down my spine.

"The point is, we were just really, awfully close right then, and we've been closer—"

"Not helping," he all but moaned.

The tips of my ears burned. "And something is obviously going on and you want me to just sit here and wait for you to come back?"

His eyes opened, and the pupils were bright white again. "Pretty much."

"That's not how this works, Luc. I want to go with you."

"Not sure if that's wise, Peaches."

"Why?" I planted my hands on my hips.

"Because if there's even a small chance that girl does have some kind of weird virus, I don't want you to get exposed to it."

I didn't want to be exposed, either. "I didn't catch anything from Coop, and he sat right next to me."

"Maybe, but it's more than that. You were a part of this world before, but you're not anymore. What goes on here doesn't touch you. What I do doesn't touch you."

"But I am a part of this world. My mom is an unregistered Luxen. One of my best friends is an Origin, and the other is dating a Luxen. I've been shot up full of alien DNA and not in the fun way."

Luc opened his mouth as his brows lifted.

I didn't let him say anything. "And then there's you—there's you and me, and I'm trying to figure out what you and I mean. I can't do that if you push me out of this world—your world."

"Okay." Something akin to respect glimmered in his eyes as a slow smile tugged at his lips. "Then let's get you knee deep in this world."

The moment Luc and I stepped back out into the hallway and started toward the stairwell door, Grayson opened his mouth, and I knew he was about to say something ignorant. Luc silenced him before he could.

"She's here because she wanted to be." Luc's tone brook no room for argument, and I resisted the urge to stick my tongue out at Grayson. "What's her condition?"

Dawson was watching the three of us curiously as he easily kept up with Luc's long strides and they started down the steps. "She's awake, but, well, not quite sure that's a good thing."

"Can you walk any faster?" Grayson snapped from behind me. "You're about as slow as a three-legged turtle."

The corners of my lips pulled down. The way he said *you* was as if he were speaking of a mutant cockroach crawling along the floor. "You can always walk in front of me, you know."

"I don't trust you behind me."

I laughed. "What in the world am I going to do to you?"

"Anything is possible," he shot back.

"Gray?" Luc called out from several steps ahead.

"Yes?"

"Shut the hell up."

Grayson muttered a curse under his breath, and then he said, louder, "Look, I'm just not sure you want her to see this."

"See what?" I held on to the railing as I rounded a landing. Grayson was still behind me, and I was willing to bet he was engaged in a massive internal debate over whether or not to push me down the steps.

Dawson glanced at Luc before speaking, and I supposed whatever he saw in Luc's expression was interpreted as permission.

Everyone always looked to Luc first before doing anything.

Well, everyone except for me.

"I was moving a group yesterday, and there was a couple—a Luxen and a human girl—Sarah," Dawson said. "We ran into some problems and had to come back here."

Was it the relationship between this Luxen and human girl that caused a problem? Relationships between Luxen and humans were currently illegal. If the human was under eighteen, their guardians faced substantial fines, and if they were over eighteen, they could face prison time.

Heidi was taking a huge risk to be with Emery, but love was worth it. I truly believed that, so I was thrilled for Heidi. She had the kind of love for Emery that made a slicing motion in my chest that was both scary and hopeful, and it was obvious Emery felt the same way . . . but that didn't mean I didn't worry about them.

We reached the third floor, and my eyes tracked Luc down the wide hallway, my gaze lingering on the breadth of his shoulders.

Since the general public didn't even know Origins existed, they'd assume Luc was a Luxen if they saw his eyes or caught him using the Source. So, if we got together, it would be a risk, too.

Wait. Was I planning to get involved with Luc? Well, I'd just told him I was trying to figure out what we were, and that was the truth. Maybe I hadn't realized that until this very moment. Plus, a couple of minutes ago, I'd been willing to wrap myself around him like a horny octopus, so . . .

Luc slowly turned his head and looked over his shoulder at me, his eyebrows raised as he mouthed, *Horny octopus?*

Oh my God! My hands curled in fists, but before I could yell at him, Dawson was speaking again.

"We ran into trouble just outside of Virginia," Dawson was saying. "One of those damn recovery teams spotted us, and there was a fight. Two Luxen were killed, one of them being the human's boyfriend."

My heart clenched for the couple I didn't know as I looked at Luc again, surprised that he hadn't mentioned any of this since I showed up at Foretoken this evening. Dread formed like lead balls in my stomach. Did Luc go out on these missions? He hadn't mentioned it, but Luc never really said what he did with his time, and he sure as hell hadn't told me about any of this.

Instead, he took me into his apartment and danced with me.

"Was she hurt in the fight?" I asked, refocusing on the topic at hand.

Dawson shook his head, sending black waves in every direction. "Archer met us halfway and took the rest of the Luxen, but the girl . . ."

"What?" Confusion swirled.

"Without the Luxen to vouch for her, she wouldn't be welcome where they were going," Luc answered, slowing his steps so I was now beside him. "And like I said, she's sick."

Luc had said that.

The door suddenly opened at the end of the hall, and I saw Kent and his emo Pennywise face pop out. "I have never been happier to see you guys than I am right now. Even happier than if you'd brought me a bucket of Popeyes chicken," he said as Grayson snorted behind me. "There is some really weird shit going on in here, and I feel like

I need an adult, and I also wish Chas had never come down to get Grayson and me."

Chas? It took me a moment to place a face to the name. He was the Luxen that had been beaten so badly by Micah, I was still shocked that he was alive. I hadn't seen him in what felt like forever.

Kent stepped aside, opening the door wide so Luc could enter, and I could finally see into the room. A harsh gasp parted my lips the moment I saw this girl. She was in front of a narrow bed, stringy blond hair hanging around her sunken face in thin, limp clumps.

Sarah was standing, but like Dawson had said, I wasn't sure that was a good thing. She looked like death stood beside her. Coop hadn't looked like this, and I thought he'd appeared bad. This was far more severe.

When Luc spoke, his voice was quiet and soothing as if he were speaking to a cornered, sick animal. "Hey, what are you doing out of bed? Did you need something? We can get it for you so you can rest."

The girl staggered to the side, shoulders hunched forward as she lifted her head. Thick, black veins appeared under her skin.

"Good God," I whispered, taking a step back, but I bumped into Grayson as he came forward. He crowded me into the room. This was not the same as Coop. He did *not* have black veins.

A ragged, wet-sounding cough shook the girl's entire body. "I . . . I don't feel well."

"Understatement of the year," Kent murmured as Dawson edged around the wall.

Luc ignored him. "I know. That's why you should be back in bed, so you can get better."

I didn't think she was going to get better.

"Should I get her something?" I asked, wanting to help. "Maybe water?"

"Does she look like water will help her?" Grayson retorted, shooting me a look that showed just how dumb he thought I was. "I don't think a bucketload of penicillin will help her."

I hated to admit it, but Grayson sort of had a point. "You really didn't need to say that out loud."

"What?" he replied. "I'm just being honest."

"How about you try being tactful?"

Grayson opened his mouth, but Luc looked over his shoulder at him. The Luxen quieted. Finally. I focused on Luc. It was hard not to recognize the way he stood with his shoulders squared and his legs spread widely as if he were blocking Sarah from me, like he'd done with Dawson earlier.

Was he worried she was going to sneeze on me?

I peered around Luc.

The girl's thin arms were folded across her stomach. "Where is Richie?"

"You know he's not here anymore, but I'm here. So are Kent and Dawson. We're friends. Even Grayson. Remember?" Luc asked, and I guessed Richie must have been the poor girl's boyfriend. "I'm taking care of you, Sarah, and I think it's best if—"

Sarah doubled over and heaved violently. Bluish-black bile spewed, splattering the floor, and it looked like it almost . . . *shimmered*.

I clasped my hand over my mouth, because *that* did look familiar.

Grayson pulled a Blow Pop—Sour Apple—out of his pocket and slowly began to unwrap it. "That's disgusting."

Sarah vomited again, and the stuff that came out of her did not look normal. It was like she'd swallowed a gallon of oil and blue paint, and it was coming back up.

Braver than I ever would be when someone was throwing up something that looked like that, Luc started toward her, but halted when Sarah threw her head back. Whatever substance was coming out of her trailed down her chin and covered the front of her wrinkled shirt.

"They . . . did *sssomething* to me," the girl gasped, heaving. "They did *sssomething* to me—"

Her back bowed at a deep, unnatural angle. Something cracked, reminding me of a dry twig being snapped. I gasped as Sarah fell forward, dropping onto her knees and palms. Her arms popped from their sockets. Her hips spread. More oily, thick liquid hit the floor.

Her bones kept snapping, just like Coop's had.

Dawson had stopped moving. "What the hell is—?"

Sarah's head wrenched back as her mouth stretched into a silent scream that seemed like it would tear her cheeks apart. Those inky veins rose from her skin—from her face, throat, and arms.

Luc was suddenly in front of me as he threw out his arm,

thrusting me back. Horror swamped me as her body contorted in a series of snaps that reminded me of milk being added to Rice Krispies.

I would never eat cereal again.

Sarah collapsed, sank into herself, her upper body meeting her bent legs. She didn't move. Didn't seem like she even breathed. The veins retracted, disappearing under the skin.

Sarah's shoulders lifted as she dragged in a deep breath and then kept lifting with several more breaths. She was alive. How was she alive?

"I think she might be a zombie," Kent whispered. "Get ready. Head shot, guys. Head. Shot."

Luc's exhale was audible. "Seriously?"

Kent nodded. "I've seen this in movies. I'm telling you, if she gets up after that, this is some kind of zombie thing, and she's going to be fast and she's going to want to eat my face, because I'm the cutest, and the cutest always get their faces eaten off first."

"You know, he might have a point," Dawson said, one eyebrow raised. "I like to consider myself a zombie expert."

Luc turned to him. "A zombie expert?"

He nodded. "Yeah, and I'm sure I've seen this in—"

Sarah rose.

Like, lifted straight up off the floor without standing as if a hidden puppeteer pulled her strings. Within a second, she was on her feet, and then she was *off* the floor.

Holy crap, she *hovered* off the floor, and yeah, Coop hadn't done that.

My mouth dropped open, and I blinked once and then twice, thinking I was seeing things, but nope, the chick was suspended in air.

"That is not a zombie," Grayson said, the pupils of his eyes turning white. "I don't know what in the hell that is, but *that* is also not a human."

Curiosity etched into Luc's face as he stared up at the girl. "This is . . . different. Unexpected."

My heart was pounding against my ribs like it was going to beat its way out while Luc was staring at her like she were an interesting science fair project.

Sarah lifted her head. Her eyes—whoa, her eyes were black orbs with a center that was . . .

I looked at Grayson.

Sarah's pupils were like that of a Luxen's, like Grayson's, when they were about to take on their true form. Her pupils were like two stars in a dark night.

Dawson and Luc had just said she was human, and while I might not be a doctor or scientist, I knew they weren't human eyes and that humans didn't levitate.

The fine hair all along my arms stood up.

She came back to the floor, those weird eyes scanning the room. Her lips peeled back when Luc moved forward. A low snarl reverberated.

Was she growling at Luc?

Her head turned sharply, and I sucked in a breath as our gazes connected. Her nostrils flared as she sniffed the air. She took a step toward me. Her head cocked to the side, and a low, eerie trilling sound came from her.

I pressed back against the wall, flattening myself. I had no idea what was going on, but I so did not want to be the center of her attention.

Luc sidestepped, blocking me once more. "Easy there, Sarah. I don't want to hurt you." The smell of burned ozone filled the air as a faint whitish hue surrounded his body. "But I will."

Sarah's head jerked toward Luc. A moment passed, and then she moved—and she moved *fast*. She darted past Luc, rushing past the bed and the chair that had been sitting there, toward the square window.

She didn't stop.

I tensed. "She's going—"

Racing across the room, she jumped. Glass shattered, sending shards to the floor. A curtain came down, and then Sarah was gone—gone out the window and down to the alley below.

All of us were stuck in place, standing in silence until Luc sighed heavily and said, "Well, I was thinking about replacing that window, anyway."

14

So, we're just going to pretend like that didn't happen?" I asked, sitting in one of the common rooms on the third floor. Luc had left with Grayson and Dawson, who were also joined by Zoe . . . in her Wonder Woman outfit . . . to try to locate the girl since she wasn't sprawled in the alley, a mess of broken bones and tissues like a normal human would've been if they'd pitched themselves out the window.

Kent placed a fresh Coke on the coffee table in front of me. "Welcome to my world. Just a regular Halloween here at Foretoken."

I stared at him.

"You said she . . . levitated?" Emery asked, drawing my attention back to where she sat across from me. Emery was dressed like Catwoman, head to toe, deep blue leather. Heidi was in her red, white, and blue outfit, and Kent was still dressed as Pennywise, so it was really weird to be having this conversation right now.

I picked up the drink with shaky hands, welcoming the splash of carbonated bubbles against my dry throat. "She totally levitated off the floor."

"And this occurred after she spewed black swamp water everywhere." Kent sat on the arm of my chair. "And something blue. I have no idea what the blue stuff was."

Heidi shuddered as she tucked a strand of crimson-colored hair back. "What could've made that happen?"

"Zombie bite?" Kent suggested helpfully. "Because I really think she turned into a zombie. Maybe a vegetarian one since she didn't try to eat us, but definitely a zombie."

I blinked once and then twice.

"I checked in on her earlier, before you got here." Emery glanced at Heidi. "She had a pretty high fever, but I really thought it was just a flu. I figured she'd caught it somewhere on her travels, and with everything that happened to her boyfriend, she had to be emotionally and physically drained."

"That was definitely not the flu," Kent commented. "Unless a flu now causes your veins to turn black under your skin."

"I don't know anything that causes that," Heidi said.

I sat back as my gaze fell to my Coke. That heavy, uncomfortable feeling from before resurfaced. Sarah had said something that kept cycling over and over in my head.

They did something to me.

"It was a lot like what happened with Coop," I said. "But also not the same. Like, he didn't levitate or have black veins, but he was superstrong."

"Whether it was like what happened to that Coop kid or not, I've never seen anything like that." Kent kicked a striped leg up on the couch beside us.

That was saying something, because I had a feeling he'd seen a lot of things. It was also telling that I wasn't more freaked out—like running from the building screaming and flailing kind of freaked out. Three months ago? I totally would've been. Now? I was disturbed by what I'd seen, but I'd also seen a lot of weird, disturbing stuff since Luc had come . . . back into my life.

"Her bones . . . I could hear them breaking," I said, almost afraid to close my eyes for any period of time because I was sure I would see her. "How in the world did she jump up and run after that?"

Kent lifted a shoulder.

"And she survived the fall, which is insane." Heidi tucked her legs to her chest. "Are you guys sure she's human?"

Emery nodded. "Definitely human."

"But we don't do that," Heidi replied. "We don't get sick like that, survive what her body did, launch ourselves out of the window, and survive a fall from five stories to then just scamper off."

I wasn't quite sure Sarah *scampered,* but that image was now stuck in my head. "But look at Coop. He was completely human, too."

Kent crossed his arms. "She was as human as I am, despite what Grayson might claim about me."

"I know you guys say mutations don't look like that, but maybe that's what it is," Heidi said. "And no one knows for sure if those serums the Daedalus used are still out there."

"We would've seen the trace on her." Emery stretched out her legs. "Just like Zoe would've seen the trace on that guy you all went to school with."

"Maybe there's a whole different serum that removes the trace," Kent tossed out there. "Anything is possible."

"Sarah did say something." I glanced at Kent, tapping my foot on the floor. "You heard her, right? She said, 'They did something to me.'"

A frown tugged at his mouth. "I didn't hear that."

"What?" I stared up at him. "She said it right after she vomited and before she turned into something straight from a horror movie. She said it twice."

His reddish-brown eyebrows lifted. "I didn't hear her say anything like that."

"How . . . ?" I looked over at the girls, who were staring back at me. How in the world had Kent not heard her?

Kent's brow creased. "She did make these weird trilling sounds, though. I heard that."

I'd heard them, too, but I'd heard her speak. It had been a little slurred, but she'd spoken. A lot had been going on, so I guessed I couldn't be that surprised that Kent hadn't heard her in between the vomiting and snapping bones.

"What do you think they'll do with the girl if they find her?" Heidi asked, twisting toward her girlfriend.

Emery glanced over at Kent, and a long moment passed before she answered. "It'll depend on what she does. He's not going to let her hurt anyone, and he's not going to let her expose what we're doing here. If it comes down to something like that, Luc will take care of it." Emery's tone was blunt. "That's what he does."

That's what he does.

I swallowed hard as those words replaced what Sarah had said. Luc would . . . *take care* of her, just like he'd had to take care of those Origins the Daedalus had created, those *kids* that had been more dangerous than any adult Luxen could ever be to humans. He'd take care of Sarah just like Micah had forced him to do that night in the woods.

He would have to kill this girl if she proved a risk to people or to what they did here.

My mouth dried, and the drink of soda didn't help.

Luc was . . . he was a guy who, a little over an hour ago, had danced with me and told me I only had to be who I was, not who I used to be. He could make me laugh with his ridiculous surprises or terrible pickup lines, distract me when I got lost in the past I couldn't remember or the leftover fear from Micah's attack. He was a guy who wore absurd shirts and took in Luxen and humans alike who were in need, collecting people around him like one would take in and care for stray animals. He helped get Emery clean. Luc was *kind.*

And Luc was also a killer.

I'd seen it with my own eyes, when three Luxen had shown up and one of them had attacked me. I'd seen it when he'd finally ended Micah's murderous reign. I'd seen the brutally cold precision of his kills, and I'd also seen the haunted look in those stunning amethyst eyes afterward. He hadn't killed Brandon, but he'd broken the guy's hand with absolutely no remorse.

A shudder racked me.

The contrast of who he was and what he could be, his unending gentleness and unyielding hardness, was startling even though I'd seen both sides of him before, knew exactly what he'd do and how far he'd go to protect others.

And hearing it now still rattled me.

"Hey." Kent nudged my shoulder with his elbow. "He'll do what's right, honeybuns. He always does."

Surprised that Kent had followed my thoughts, I forced a brittle smile as I placed my glass on the end table. Needing something to do with my hands, I started working out the tangles in my hair with my fingers.

"And she might've just been scared. Who knows what happened to her or why she's sick," Kent reasoned. "It doesn't have to end in the worst possible way. Not always."

But didn't it?

"I'd do it," Emery spoke up, drawing my attention. Our gazes met and held. "All of us would do exactly what Luc has to. I'd kill to protect those I care about and those I love without hesitation. I'd do the same to protect this place and what we do here. So would

Kent. So would Grayson. It's not something we want to do; it's something we have to do. None of us would hesitate. All of us have to live with that."

I tried to swallow again, but my throat was like a desert as I nodded in understanding. Daemon had said the same . . . and then some.

Heidi leaned into Emery and whispered something to her, then kissed her olive-tone cheek before pulling back.

"I don't think what Luc has had to do is wrong. You all talk about killing like it's nothing, though, but I know it is to Luc—to all of you—and that it's an everyday part of your lives." I stopped messing with my hair. "To be honest, I don't know what to think about it because . . . all of this is new to me."

"And to me." Heidi threaded her arm through Emery's as her stare connected with mine. "This isn't a world we've been a part of."

This was a world I used to be a part of, back when I'd been Nadia. I had no idea if I'd easily accepted the ruthless nature of survival or if it had distressed me then, too.

Or if I'd just had a better understanding of it.

But I'd just demanded of Luc to let me in, to involve me in this world. I didn't think I wasn't cut out for it. I just wasn't expecting this.

Emery brushed her lips over Heidi's forehead, and I closed my eyes, rubbing my fingers along my temple. Had I offended Emery? I hoped I hadn't, but she had to understand that none of this was a normal Halloween to me or to Heidi.

We normally bought candy and had a scary movie marathon. We didn't generally witness some girl turning into God knows what before tossing herself out a window.

"Well." Kent drew the word out. "This has taken a turn for the awkward."

I snorted.

The door opened behind us, ending the strained silence. I twisted at the waist, heart skipping a beat when Luc strolled into the room with Dawson behind him. The door swung shut as I clutched the back of the couch. Luc's gaze immediately connected with mine. There was nothing to be gained from his expression. His features were shut down.

"Did you find zombie girl?" Kent asked.

"She's not a zombie," Luc said with a sigh as he walked around the couch. I followed his progress, straightening when he sat beside me, close enough that his thigh rested against mine.

"That's what people keep saying until someone crashes through a door and starts eating your nose off," Kent retorted.

Heidi's lips curled as she blinked rapidly.

"We didn't find her." Dawson leaned against the wall, crossing his arms. "And we scoured this entire city."

"How is that possible?" Heidi's voice pitched as she bent forward. "The condition she was in, how is she even alive?"

"Good question." Luc leaned back, tossing an arm over the couch, behind me. "If she's still in this city, she's hiding somewhere. Grayson and Zoe are checking a few places."

"Do you think whatever happened to her is the same thing that happened to Coop?" I asked.

"I don't know, Peaches." His gaze slid toward me, and I felt his fingers sifting through the strands of my hair, finding the center of my shoulders. Luc was always . . . touchy, whether it be how close he sat, brushing his hand over mine, or playing with my hair. The act seemed almost unconscious, as if he were unaware of his need to prove that I was, in fact, sitting beside him. I didn't mind it. If I had, I wouldn't have let him. To be honest, I liked it because there was this part hidden deep inside me that needed the reminder that he was also there.

I thought about what Emery and Kent had said. "She said something was done to her."

His eyes met mine. "What?"

No way.

Luc hadn't heard her, either?

I glanced at Dawson, and he looked as if he didn't know what I was talking about either. "I thought I heard her say something."

"Say what?" His fingers dragged over the nape of my neck.

"I thought she said, 'They did something to me,' but you all didn't hear her?"

Dawson shook his head.

Luc's gaze searched mine intently. "No, Peaches. We didn't hear that."

What the hell? Had I imagined that? My shoulders slumped. Maybe it was an auditory hallucination? Or I thought the sounds she was making were words? The mind could do that, take sounds and turn them into something familiar.

Luc still watched me, brows pinched.

"You know, it kind of reminded me a little bit of the people that the Daedalus mutated with those newer serums." Dawson's jaw worked as he stared at the floor. "I saw enough of it with my own eyes while I was . . . with them."

Air lodged in my throat. Dawson had been with the Daedalus at some point? I remembered what Luc had said about the Luxen that had been held by the Daedalus and all the terrible things the organization had forced them to take part in. Unspeakable things.

"It's like what some of those subjects went through, but not. The ones I saw were a lot . . . bloodier." Dawson exhaled heavily. "And the Daedalus is no more, so it can't be that."

"But that doesn't mean that someone didn't get their hands on leftover serums or injections, just like we already suspected." Luc now had my hair between his thumb and forefinger. No one in the room could see it, but it felt like everyone knew because I was so hyperaware of what he was doing. There was something soothing about his touch and the gentle tug on my scalp every time he ran his thumb over the strands of hair. "It's possible that's what happened to her."

"Or maybe—God, I can't believe I'm saying this—but maybe it is some kind of sickness," Emery said, exhaling heavily. "We don't think there's anything we can pass to humans, but things evolve, right? Or maybe it's something human we haven't seen yet. You all saw the news about the people that got sick with something that resembled the flu, right? Killed them quickly and supposedly had symptoms that none of the doctors had seen before. You guys had someone already die at the school, and then the other guy got sick."

"Can we all just acknowledge that a flu doesn't do that?" Kent was still perched on the arm of the couch. "Unless it's, you guessed it, a zombie flu."

Dawson cracked a grin.

"She levitated," Luc reminded Emery. "Straight up left the floor. That's more supernatural than viral."

Emery exhaled heavily. "We need to find her, because that's the only way we're going to figure this out."

Actually, I had an idea. A good one. A smart one. A *helpful* one.

Excitement thrummed through me. For once, I could actually be useful when it came to their problems instead of being a part of their problem. "I can talk to, um, my mom. I mean, if anyone knows anything about the Dae—"

"No," Luc cut me off. "Absolutely not."

I stiffened. "Why not?"

His eyes flicked to mine, and those jewel-tone eyes were as hard as granite. "I don't want you discussing anything you see here with Sylvia Dasher."

My skin prickled like an army of fire ants had descended on me. "That makes no sense. She already knows about Ryan and Coop, and if anyone knows—"

"Wait." Dawson pushed off the wall, arms unfolding as he stared at me, his eyes slightly wide. "You're the daughter of the Dashers? I thought you were—"

"Kind of," I said. "She's kind of my mom."

A whitish glow began to surround Dawson's body as he moved toward me. The center of his pupils turned white, encompassing the irises until his eyes shone like hard diamonds.

I didn't see or feel Luc move.

One moment he was lounging next to me, and a heartbeat later, he was directly in front of Dawson, eye to eye. "You need to calm down," Luc said, his voice as soft as it had been when he'd spoken to Sarah. "Evie has nothing to do with the Daedalus."

Dawson didn't respond, but Emery had removed her arm from Heidi, her entire body tensed and ready. Meanwhile, Kent looked like he was missing a bucket of popcorn to go along with what he obviously found entertaining.

The whitish glow pulsed around Dawson, and Luc stepped into him, forcing the Luxen a step back. "She's not his daughter. She's had nothing to do with them, man. You need to calm down or I'll have to make you calm down. You feel me? I'm hoping you do, because I really don't want to make Bethany a widow and little Ash fatherless."

"Luc!" I gasped, scooting to the edge of the couch as Daemon's warning surfaced once more. "Jesus. That's a bit much."

"No, it's not." His reply came on a low growl. "Not nearly enough."

I gaped at him. "Yes, it is."

The faint light around Dawson faded as a long, tense moment passed. "I feel you, Luc."

"Good."

Neither moved for a long moment, and then Dawson returned to where he'd been standing against the wall, his jaw thrumming as his emerald gaze flicked from Luc to me. "Sorry, I'm just a little confused."

"Welcome to the club." Kent grinned as Luc returned to the spot beside me.

Heidi eyed me, her nose pinched like it always was when she was trying to figure something out, and my stomach sank. Since she didn't know the truth about me, I knew none of this made sense to her.

Dawson's entire body was taut and stretched as if he were trying to hold himself back.

Luc smirked.

I glared at him until the twist to his lips faded. "That was totally unnecessary."

"If you knew what they did to him and what he'd give for just a tablespoon of retribution, you'd understand just how necessary that was."

Blood drained from my face as I glanced at Dawson. He didn't deny what Luc had said as his eyes met mine. If I had been Jason Dasher's real daughter or if Luc hadn't been here, would Dawson have hurt me?

"I don't want you saying anything to Sylvia," Luc repeated. "Nothing, Peaches. Absolutely nothing."

The corners of my lips tugged down. "She works with infectious diseases, and she—"

"And she worked for the Daedalus," he cut me off, pulling his arm off the back of the couch. "She is the absolute last person that needs to know about what happened here."

"She worked for them in the *past* tense," I reminded him as Kent drew his leg off the chair and straightened. "And she wasn't a part of the horrible stuff they did."

"That's what she says, Peaches. That doesn't mean that's the truth."

Every muscle in my back locked up. "You don't believe her?"

Luc didn't respond.

The dark-haired Luxen in the corner did. "I never met this Sylvia, but I knew her husband well, and I also know that maybe, in the very beginning, the Daedalus had good intentions. They wanted to eradicate disease and to better human life, but there wasn't a single person within that organization that did not know what they turned into. Everyone in the Daedalus was fully aware of what they were doing and how they were developing their serums."

I pressed my hands between my knees. "She didn't. I swear. I know she worked for them, but you don't understand."

Could I tell Dawson who she really was and what she had done to ensure Jason Dasher wouldn't hurt another person?

"She can help us at least figure out what happened to Sarah," I repeated. "And it's not like tonight was an isolated case."

"Not going to happen." Luc rose to his feet once more. "What happened at school is not the same as what is happening here."

Whatever grip I had on my patience was lost as I glared up at him. "Last time I checked, bud, you don't get to tell me what I can and cannot do. You don't get to tell me to do *anything*."

Emery's eyes widened as Luc pivoted fluidly, facing me. "I do get a say in who knows about what happens here, Peaches. That's not the same thing as telling you what to do."

"That is the exact same thing as telling me what to do," I snapped.

"Not in my world," he replied.

"In my world, which is everyone's world, it is." I shot to my feet, throwing my arms wide. "There is no reason why I can't tell her, especially when she is probably the only person in this entire city that could figure out what happened to that girl—who is still out there, by the way, running around with black snake veins and hopefully not eating someone's face!"

"For God's sake, the girl is not a zombie, because zombies aren't real."

"But aliens are?"

He shot me a bland look.

"You don't trust her at all, do you?"

Luc dipped his chin toward me, voice low. "Not even remotely. I wouldn't trust her with a lab mouse," he said, and I gasped, because that seemed excessive. "I wouldn't even trust her with Diesel."

"Diesel is a damn rock!"

"Exactly," he retorted smugly.

I shook my head. "You're being ridiculous."

"I'm being smart. You should try it."

"I am!" I shouted. "And maybe you should try not being a demeaning asshole."

"I'm not being—"

"Think really hard before you finish that statement, because you just said I was being stupid," I cut him off.

His chest rose with a deep breath. "You're right. That was wrong. I'm sorry," he said, eyes flaring an intense purple. "I shouldn't have said that, and acknowledging that doesn't change who she is. You might have forgotten that she lied to you and what she took from you, but I haven't."

My fingers curled inward, pressing into my palms. "You lied to me, too, Luc, or are you conveniently forgetting that?"

"I haven't forgotten *anything*." His features were set, lips pressed into a thin, hard line. "She took the life you knew from you."

"You took it from me, too." I rose onto the tips of my toes, and Luc flinched. "You cannot put it all on her." A voice I barely recognized as mine left me. "You made the choice to give me to them. You—"

"How in the hell can you say that? I didn't *give* you to them, Evie." His eyes were storm clouds now, churning and dangerous. "Do I need to remind you of that? I did the only thing I could do to save your life. You were dying, and that bastard Jason Dasher had a cure. It was Sylvia who demanded that I stay away from you afterward. That was a deal she forced me to make, because if I didn't agree, you would've died. I didn't abandon you. It *killed* me to walk away."

Shuddering at his words, I quickly realized I shouldn't have said that. "I know you didn't just give me to them. I'm sorry. I shouldn't have said that, but that doesn't change the fact that you also kept huge secrets from me."

"Yeah, because you would've definitely believed me if I'd told you right away."

"That's still no excuse for lying by omission." Truth was, I wouldn't have believed him. Who would? But that wasn't the point, because this whole situation made me realize something very important. Luc kept me in the dark about a lot of things, and I'd thought it was to keep me at a safe distance from the dangerous and illegal things they did here, but now I was beginning to think that wasn't the only reason. There was a good chance he was keeping me in the dark because of Mom. "You still don't tell me everything, Luc. You keep stuff from me now."

"Like what?"

"You didn't tell me about Sarah or what happened with the other Luxen. You don't tell me 99 percent of the things you do here even though you have officers randomly showing up, and I bet that happens a lot even though I only know of that one time."

Luc looked away.

"Answer this—do you go on these runs? Help move Luxen out?"

His jaw clenched. "Sometimes I do when you're at school. Quick trips where Archer or Daemon are coming up to meet me."

The breath of air I took went nowhere. "And you never told me about this." My heart started pounding in my chest. "What if something happened to you on one of these runs? I wouldn't even know, Luc. I'd have no idea. You'd just be *gone*."

His gaze shot to mine. "I don't tell you because I don't want you to worry."

I blurted out the truth. "Do you think I don't already worry, Luc? What you do here is crazy dangerous. Hell, your very existence is dangerous. Not telling me is not going to make me worry less."

The line of his jaw softened, as did the glint to his eyes. "You don't need to worry about me, Peaches. I'm always going to come back to you. That's a promise."

Warmth flushed my face. *I'm always going to come back to you.* That promise excited and angered me, left me feeling hopeful and full of dread.

And then the strangest sensation hit me. I'd heard him make that promise before, hadn't I?

"I don't tell you where I go with those Luxen or where they're taken because knowledge like that puts you in danger, and it also makes you dangerous."

"Makes me dangerous?" It took me a moment to realize what he meant, and I couldn't believe it. "Do you really think I'd tell anyone what goes on here? That I'd do that?"

He didn't respond for a long moment. "I don't think you'd say anything to be malicious, but the fact that you trust Sylvia means there are things I cannot trust you with."

Luc and I stood toe to toe, and I realized that everyone had bounced out of the room like rubber balls. We were alone, and I hadn't even noticed up until that point.

"I have to trust her. She's my mom—"

"Sylvia is not your mother."

I sucked in a sharp breath, feeling as if I'd been smacked right in the face, because what he said came close to what I was feeling and thoughts that already left me reeling with guilt and confusion.

Mother. Daughter. Just words and labels, but powerful words—words that went beyond blood.

It struck me then as I blinked back the uncomfortable burn behind my eyes. She had told her fair share of lies and kept even more secrets, just like Zoe had and just like Luc still did. Things were a little awkward between Zoe and me, and I was just beginning to find my way with Luc, but it wasn't fair to give them passes and not give one to her.

Because at the end of the day, she was my mother. She kept a roof over my head and my belly full. She showered me with love and encouragement, and she was my mother in every sense of the word.

"She's the only mom I remember," I said, voice thick. "I love her."

"Shit." Luc thrust his hand through his hair. "Evie, I—"

"She didn't have to care for me or provide for me over these years. You know that." I stepped back from him. "Maybe you're right. Maybe she can't be trusted completely, but she's still my mother, and I'm still her daughter. And I don't believe for one second she'd ever do anything that would put me in danger or hurt me. And I just realized that you don't trust me, and I don't even know what to say about that."

Luc moved toward me, but I held up my hand as I backed toward the door. He held himself still. "Where are you going?"

"Home." I stalked across the room. "You know, where *my mom* lives."

"Evie," he called out, and I stopped, turning back to him. "I'm serious. Don't say anything to your mother."

My hand tightened on the knob, and if I could tear it off the door, there was a good chance I would've thrown it at him. "You don't have to repeat yourself, Luc. I get it. Peace out."

Then I slammed the door behind me with enough force I was sure everyone in the club could hear it.

My lungs were burning as I shoved through the exterior doors of Foretoken, keys in hand, stepping out in the cool October night. Taking in deep breaths of the chilly air, I welcomed the breeze that washed over my stinging skin.

I couldn't believe Luc had said that to me.

I couldn't believe what I'd said to him.

And I really hoped Sarah didn't pop out of nowhere and try to eat my face off.

Anger buzzed through my veins as I forced myself to keep walking, my free hand open and closing. Part of me totally understood why Luc had trust issues when it came to Mom. That didn't surprise me at all. Look at what happened during #grilledcheesegate. But she'd apologized, and so had he, and he wasn't even giving her a chance. Worse yet, he didn't trust me, and that was a shock.

Heading down the block to where I was parked, I passed several closed-up shops, many of them with HUMANS ONLY signs. I shook my head as I stomped down the sidewalk. What a—

The streetlamp flickered above me, and then the one across the street did the same. My steps slowed and then stopped as the lamp at the end of the block, near where my car was parked, also flickered.

That wasn't normal.

And the last time the streetlamps had done that, I'd found the dead body of a classmate.

Nope. Not about to repeat that traumatic event.

Spinning on my heel, I found myself standing eye to chest. I gasped as I jerked back a step. A man stood before me, so close that I could feel the . . . *iciness* radiating off him.

He was older, maybe in his late twenties. His hair was a deep black, blending into the starless sky above, and his skin was the color of alabaster. His eyes . . .

They were the palest shade of blue I'd ever seen, as if the irises had almost been leached of all color.

A chill invaded my skin. "Excuse me." I stepped back, heart racing.

The man cocked his head to the side, his slash of a mouth thinning even further as he *sniffed* the air.

Oh no.

Oh hell no.

When people started smelling the air, I didn't want anything to do with that. Muscles in my legs tensed as I prepared to run back to the club just in case—

The chest, covered in a dark button-down shirt, *scattered*. His entire body broke apart in a puff of inky-black smoke that rose several feet off the ground. Thick tendrils of midnight mist pulsed as the thing drew back several feet.

Pure terror exploded in my stomach as my mouth opened but no sound came out. I stared up at the creature.

Oh my God, I knew what this was. Emery and Kent had described this to me before.

An Arum stood in front of me.

They were archenemies of the Luxen, another alien race that had battled Luxen for eons before both of their planets were destroyed in their war, forcing them to seek shelter on Earth. They were just as deadly as Luxen could be, but for very different reasons.

I'd never seen one, but I knew this was what I was staring up at, and that meant I needed to get the hell out of here.

The shadowy mass pieced back together, rapidly taking the shape and form of a man. For the briefest second, he was nothing but sleek obsidian, an opaque darkness, and then he looked like a man once more.

He took a step, lips peeling back to reveal straight, oddly sharp-looking teeth. "What are you?"

15

Did he seriously ask me what I was when he'd just turned into a freaking blob of pulsing smoke?

"I'm human," I said, clenching my keys. I was prepared to shove them deep into his face if he moved one inch toward me.

The Arum's pale gaze flickered over me. "Are you sure?"

I gaped at him. Was I sure? "Yes, I'm totally, 100 percent . . ."

Wait.

I wasn't 100 percent human, now was I? I did have a little bit of alien DNA in me, thanks to the Andromeda serum. Could the Arum sense that? That kind of made sense since I'd been told that they could sense the Luxen, and there was a teeny, tiny bit of that in me.

But if he could pick that up in me, wouldn't the RAC drone have hit on the DNA? Or were the Arum more sensitive?

"Hey," Grayson called out from the direction of the club, and the Arum turned around. "Is that you, Lore?"

Lore?

That was a name?

"Yeah," Lore responded, stepping to the side.

"Who are you talking—?" Grayson appeared a few feet behind the Arum, the Blow Pop's white stick poking out from the corner of his mouth. "Oh, it's *you*."

He said *you* like it was a brand-new STD.

My eyes narrowed at him. I was guessing he hadn't found Sarah since he was out here lollygagging around.

"You know her?" Lore looked over his shoulder at me.

"Unfortunately," Grayson replied. "She belongs to Luc."

"Excuse me?" I blinked once, twice. "I do not belong to anyone."

Lore lifted his hands, taking another wide step away from me.

"I didn't touch a single hair on her head. All I did was startle her. Accidentally. Not on purpose. I am on my best behavior."

My eyes narrowed.

Grayson snorted. "If you're looking for him, he's inside. Let Clyde know, and he'll call Luc down."

I had so many questions, starting with what the hell were a Luxen and an Arum doing talking all amicable-like when they were, like, mortal enemies? And why in this world did Grayson say I belonged to Luc?

"I'll meet you in there," Grayson said, speaking to the Arum.

Lore nodded and turned to continue to the club, stopping to briefly look over his shoulder at me, his pale face marked with uncertainty.

I was still standing there under streetlamps that were no longer flickering, thinking of the night I'd found Andy's body. It had been after I'd learned that I wasn't Evie. I'd gone to Coop's party and hung out with James just to get some distance from everything that had been falling apart. And that was when I'd learned that Zoe was also an Origin. It was when I was leaving the party that I stumbled across Andy. I hadn't been close to him, and he had been bullying the younger Luxen Daniel, but the way he died . . .

Slowly, I lifted my gaze to the buttery yellow light. Lights had flickered and gone out, and the temperature had dropped significantly the night of Coop's party, just like it had done now. I thought once again about how Micah had denied killing Andy and that family.

What if it had been an Arum?

But I didn't think an Arum could kill like that, making it look like the person had been struck by lightning or burned from the inside.

Shivering, I lowered my chin and glanced around the dark, empty street. What if Micah had been telling the truth and there was another killer among us?

Those thoughts faded to the background as I realized I wasn't exactly alone. "Did you find Sarah?"

Grayson faced me. We were several feet away, and he stood outside the reach of the streetlamp, but when he spoke, I could hear the smile in his voice. "Does it look like I did?"

My hand curled so tightly the keys dug into my palm. "You're such an asshole."

"Been called worse."

"Oh, I'm sure you have."

Grayson was suddenly right in front of me. He was nearly as tall as Luc, and he towered over me. Every instinct I possessed screamed at me to take a step back, and I think he sensed that based on his smirk.

I held my ground. "I'm not afraid of you."

"Now, you and I both know that's not true. Well, unless I overestimated your intelligence, which is possible."

My entire being burned with the desire to smack that smirk all the way back to whatever galaxy he came from.

"Humans should be afraid of us even if we come in peace and mean no harm." Derision dripped from his tone. "After all, we are the higher life-form on this planet."

"Wow," I said. "And here I thought no one could ever surpass Luc's ego."

"And here I am wondering why in the hell he's so obsessed with you," he retorted. "You remind him of someone he used to know. I get that."

My heart stuttered. Grayson didn't know who I was, but he knew about Nadia?

"But I've spent an ungodly amount of time over the last three years or so keeping an eye on you. You're so boringly and pathetically human, it's actually laughable to think that Luc would be interested in you," he continued, and I fought the urge to roll my eyes. "And while there are humans who are surprisingly interesting, there's nothing unique or special about you."

His words stung like a hornet, more than they should have, but I refused to show it. "Tell me how you really feel, Grayson. Don't hold back."

The smirk on his face faded. "You're a risk to Luc and to what we're doing here. We're saving lives, Evie. You know what will happen if your president gets his way? Wholesale genocide of my people. That's what we're trying to prevent here while you're running around, doing what? Going to school? Parties? Taking photos or hanging out with your friends and maybe, every once in a while, standing up for some poor, helpless Luxen? You do nothing but put us at risk."

I flinched at the harsh truth in what he said. What was I doing? Big fat nothing most days.

Grayson wasn't done. "You're not just a threat because of who

Sylvia Dasher is but because you're the weakest link that can and will be exploited," he said, and each word he spoke was like a slap. "Despite popular opinion, Luc is not indestructible. The longer you're in his life, the more likely you're going to get him killed . . . or worse."

"Brunch is kind of stupid when you think about it," I muttered as I watched Zoe pick a chunk of walnut out of her chocolate muffin. "Like, why not just have lunch? And why don't you just order a plain chocolate muffin like me instead of sitting there, picking out the nuts?"

Zoe looked up, grinning. "You're in a wonderful mood this morning."

I was in a terrible, no good, really bad mood.

I didn't even know why I'd agreed to meet Zoe late Sunday morning. I was not fit for company. Obviously. Grayson's words still burned through me like a wildfire. What he'd said to me the night before had been harsh, but it also had been true. I wasn't . . . strong. Not like Zoe. Not like any of them. Even if I were a badass with a katana, which I wasn't, I'd still be the weakest link among them. That was a bitter pill to swallow.

And as much as I hated to admit it, I'd lain awake last night after returning home, expecting Luc to show up at my bedroom window, and he hadn't. No visit. No text.

Not even after I managed to fall asleep and woke up, gasping for air from a nightmare.

I was guessing he was still ticked off, and I didn't know how to feel about that. I was also still mad, but I wasn't used to Luc being mad at me. Not at all. I'd always gotten the impression that even when he was getting irritated with me, he was happy to be able to be irritated with me, which was kind of weird but, given our history, also made sense.

"And I like just a sprinkling of walnuts in my muffins. Not chunks. It's just too much nut." She dropped the nut on a napkin while I wrinkled my nose. "Are you not feeling well? Usually you've already swallowed your muffin whole by this point. I hope you're not getting sick." Her eyes widened. "Or coming down with what that girl had."

"Well if I am, I can at least throw myself out of windows and survive, so there's that."

"Look at you, being positive and stuff."

I snorted as I toyed with a straw. "I can't believe she's just missing. Like, where in the hell did she go?"

"I don't know." Zoe sighed as she shook her head. "She could be anywhere. Maybe she went somewhere and died."

Heaviness settled on me. "God, I know there was something very badly wrong with her, but I hate the idea of anyone dying by themselves like that. She was scared, Zoe. She had no idea what was happening to her."

"I know."

"Emery seemed to think that she caught that weird virus that we saw on TV, but if Luxen can't make humans sick, and even if it were some unrelated thing—"

"It doesn't make y'all do that." Zoe nodded. "Unless it's something totally crazy. I mean, something that someone created, but with the Daedalus being gone, that doesn't make sense."

Which meant all we had was a lot of questions and absolutely no answers.

I flicked my muffin onto its side. "I saw the strangest thing when I left last night—not as strange as what happened to Sarah, but weird."

"Since you were around Foretoken, that could literally be anything."

"True, but I saw an Arum. Actually, I talked to him."

"Lore? You ran into him?"

I blinked as my fingers stilled around the straw. "You know him?"

"Not really well or anything, but I've seen him and his brother a time or two—his brother Hunter. Not the legit psychotic other brother," she explained. "He was there when I got back."

"I'm a little confused. I thought Arum were, like, the bad guys. The Luxen's archnemesis."

"Most are, but not all Arum are out to murder people and feed off unwilling Luxen. Some are just like the Luxen, trying to find a place in this world and eke out an existence."

"There are Luxen willing to be fed off of? That sounds . . . kinky. And Lore is one of them?"

"If he weren't, he wouldn't be alive right now." Zoe smiled tightly. "Luc wouldn't tolerate him if he harmed people."

All righty then.

"Lore helps us every so often," she explained. "Moving *packages* and stuff. He was there to help Dawson move the rest of the group, since they ran into problems."

I took a quick sip. "Do you help them move packages, or are you just on Evie duty all the time?"

"I'm not on Evie duty. More like best friend duty," she said, resting her arms on the table. "But I have helped them in the past."

"Does that . . . scare you?" I asked, keeping my voice low. "I mean, people think you're human, but if you get caught moving unregistered Luxen, it wouldn't matter even if you were."

"It's . . . worrisome, but doing nothing to help these people is worse," she said. "Here's the thing, Evie. No one really knows where these unregistered Luxen go when they're captured. Are they locked up somewhere? Kept in facilities? Killed? We don't know, but what we do know is they're not registered and released back into society. They're never seen again."

There was a naïve part of me that wanted to believe that the Luxen who'd been captured were out there, somewhere safe, because that was easier to live with. But naïveté didn't equal stupidity. After all that I'd learned, I knew better.

I sat back, glancing over at the glass case of baked goodies as a man with two small kids entered. *You do nothing but put us at risk.* I squeezed my eyes shut briefly as Grayson's words haunted me. "Can I help? I mean, with the packages?"

Zoe smiled at me as a curl fell across her cheek. "You already are helping."

"How?"

"By being my best friend."

"That is not helping." Sighing, I tucked my hair back behind my ear. "I'm sure I can actually do something."

Zoe leaned forward. "Being my best friend is helping. You have no idea what it means to be normal."

Actually, I knew exactly what it was like to be normal.

"I grew up in a lab, Evie. My classrooms were white rooms with kids who were bred and designed to be the perfect soldiers. No family to speak of. I didn't have friends to go to brunch with, because we couldn't be friends—not when we had to fight against one another to prove that we were the best. And you had to be the best. If not, the consequences were . . . extreme."

"Zoe," I whispered, chest aching for her, for *all* of them.

"When Luc freed me, my life began, but I really didn't know what life was until I met you and Heidi and James," she said. Tears pricked my eyes as she continued, "When I'm at school or hanging out with you guys, I feel normal. I feel like I'm more than just whatever the hell I was created to be. You have no idea how much that helps."

I reached across the oval table and placed my hand on her arm. "I know, and I'm glad I can give you that. It's just that I don't want to be a risk or useless, you know? I just want to be useful."

Her gaze searched mine. "Why would you think you were useless or a risk? You're one of the strongest people I know."

"I appreciate the sentiment, but there is no way I'm one of the strongest people you know."

"You found out the truth about who you are, your mother and me—*and* Luc. You dealt with a psychotic Origin, and you picked yourself up, dusted off your ass, and dealt with it. Most people, including my kind, would be rocking in the corner somewhere. Not only that, when you thought I could be hurt, you didn't think twice before making sure I got out of harm's way," she reminded me. "You don't give yourself enough credit. You know why? Let me tell you."

Oh no. Zoe was about to rant.

"It's all the bullshit ideals of strength being shoved in our faces. Movies. Books. Television. Magazines. You'd think that after the world almost ended, people would've gotten their lives right, but oh no. We still operate by the broke-ass ideology of girl power, but it's only girl power if you're an assassin."

I sat back.

"What is that teaching us ladies? That if you're not physically strong, if you can't kick ass, you're weak? That if you feel overwhelmed or emotional, you're not strong? Or that if you aren't emotional, something is wrong with you? That's bullshit, and it's unrealistic." Her shoulders tensed. "Real strength does not exist in muscles or deadly skill. It exists in your ability to pick yourself up and keep going after the shit hits the fan. That's strength."

"It's okay, Zoe. I completely agree."

She exhaled heavily. "God, I'm superhuman, and even I'm like, can I just read a book or watch a movie where the girl is actually, I don't know, a normal human being? And don't even get me started on the whole 'boy crazy' or 'girl crazy' shit, because I will rant until the day I die about the internalized misogyny behind all of that."

"Okay. Simmer down." I patted her arm and then picked up my soda, taking a huge gulp. "People are starting to look at us."

"Whatever." She leaned back in her chair. "I just can't stand the idea of you feeling this way about yourself."

"I'm sorry. It's just that . . . I don't know." I smiled tightly. "There's nothing we can do to figure out what happened to Coop, and how can I help look for Sarah? I guess . . . I'm just in a weird mood, so you shouldn't pay attention to me right now."

Zoe watched me as she knocked a stray curl out of her face. "Does your strange mood have anything to do with you and Luc having an epic throwdown last night?"

I shrugged half-heartedly.

"I heard you wanted to go to Sylvia about Sarah." She continued picking at her muffin. "And Luc was none too pleased about that."

"That would be the understatement of the year," I replied dryly.

"A little." She picked up her muffin. "You do understand why, though? Right?"

A *whooshing* motion filled my stomach. The why behind Luc's demand was all I'd thought about the night before. "I do understand, and at the same time I don't."

"What do you mean?"

My gazed dropped to my own chocolate goodness. "I get why Luc wouldn't trust her. I do. But I have to believe what she told me, Zoe. That she wasn't a part of the horrible things the Daedalus did."

Zoe said nothing as she popped a piece of the muffin into her mouth, chewing slowly.

"What?" I said, reading the hesitation in her features. I tipped forward, lowering my voice. "You know Luc said she wasn't my mother."

"And he was a dick for saying that. Totally."

"You know she's the one who killed Jason, right? It was her. Not Luc. Their entire marriage fell apart when she learned what he was a part of."

She was slow to respond. "I know all of that, Evie, but . . ."

"But what?"

Zoe shoved about half her muffin into her mouth. "But what if she isn't telling the truth?"

I opened my mouth.

"Hear me out, Evie. We don't know. Neither do you, and what Luc does is too much of a risk."

"I know that." Irritation pricked at my skin.

"Here's the thing. She could have been knee deep in all things Daedalus and had a change of heart. Or she could've had nothing to do with the horrible experiments. We just don't know."

Zoe had a point. "I get it, but I have to believe her. She's done nothing to show me that what she has told me is a lie. And why would it be? Why would she take me in, heal me—"

"And give you false memories of the real Evie?" Her voice was low, but her words clapped through me like thunder. "Why did she do that?"

Ice replaced the heat, drenching my veins. That was a question I'd asked myself way too often, even after I was given an answer. "I think . . . she just missed the real Evie."

Zoe was quiet for a long moment. "I can understand that . . . to a point. I do, don't get me wrong. But you had a life before you met her. You had friends—friends who were your family. People who loved and missed you. Why did she not heal you and give you back your life by letting Luc in four years ago?"

I thought I might vomit.

What Zoe was saying was something that crept into my mind late at night, but it was something I almost couldn't afford to entertain.

"Why did she make that deal?" Zoe continued, rolling up her napkin. "I'm not trying to upset you, but I just never understood why she insisted you become someone else."

The sharp slice across my chest felt too real as I lifted a hand, dragging my fingers through my hair.

"It's not the only thing I don't understand."

"There's more?" A shaky laugh left me.

Zoe stared at me for a long moment. "Where were you between the time Luc took you to Sylvia and when you enrolled in school?"

I blinked. "What? What do you mean?"

Her brows lifted. "Luc never asked you? Talked about it?"

"No. I mean, he told me that he took me to them and that he made the deal, but I didn't have a time line of events or anything."

Her jaw worked as she looked away. "Luc took you to Sylvia in June, about a month or so after the invasion ended, and no one saw you again until you started school that following November. It was the first day schools were open after the invasion."

My brows pinched. "What are you saying?"

"I don't know." She lifted her hands. "Do you remember that summer? I mean, beyond vague recollections?"

I started to say yes, but was that true? Memories after the invasion were brief and vague. I remembered . . . staying inside a lot, holed up with books and . . . watching the television when it started running again. The harder I thought about those memories, though, the thinner they became. Holes appeared, large gaps of time where I couldn't exactly say what I'd been doing. Just glimpses of sitting in front of a window or on the couch with a book and the feeling of . . . waiting.

Before I found out who I was, I'd remembered enough that I didn't question the vagueness of my memories, but now?

Now I knew too much to not question.

"I don't remember anything that feels . . . concrete." I lifted my gaze to Zoe's. "Are you saying I was just missing during that time?"

"I don't know if *missing* is the right word, but Luc had eyes on that house from the beginning. He didn't see you. That's not saying that you weren't there or that you didn't leave, but it's strange." She sat back, crossing her arms. "Her choices were just . . . strange."

Suddenly, I thought about what Mom had said to me before she'd shown me the missing photos of the real Evie.

I just wish I'd made different choices so that you could have made different ones.

I'd thought she'd been talking about Luc.

But what if she was talking about something entirely different? And if Luc had eyes on that house those months between when he took me there and when I went to school, why in the hell hadn't he brought this up?

What did he know?

16

When I left Zoe, I didn't go home. I just . . . I couldn't at that moment, so I drove out to Centennial Lake and did something I hadn't done in a while.

With my camera in hand, I started snapping pictures of all the reds and golds of autumn. My camera was sort of my shield, and it was once again in front of me, keeping a barrier between the world and me and forming a barrier within myself. I needed that, because what Zoe said was tattooing my skin, drilling into my bones.

Why did Mom give me Evie's life?

I spent most of the afternoon there, leaving just as dusk crept across the sky. Getting out there, doing something that I loved, helped calm the itchy restlessness. I didn't have a better understanding of everything or sudden clarity, but I felt more like me than I had for weeks.

Whoever *me* was.

When I got home, Mom wasn't there, and I ended up standing in the kitchen, dragging my fingers along the cool granite of the kitchen island, feeling like I should be doing something . . . else. Something more.

Something with a purpose.

Like going out there and searching for the still-missing, possibly zombified Sarah, but where would I even begin to look? If Luc, Grayson, and Dawson couldn't find her, why would I be able to?

Skin too tight and itchy, I turned slowly in the kitchen. Mom had finally gotten new candles to replace the damaged ones. They were positioned in the center—thick, white pillars on distressed gray wooden candleholders. The downstairs finally looked like it had before Micah showed up.

I picked up my phone from where I'd left it on the counter and opened up my text messages. My finger hovered over the last text Luc had sent Friday afternoon, which had been another weird rant about how raccoons don't get enough love.

My fingers flew over the keyboard, typing out the words *Why did she give me Evie's life?*

I didn't hit send.

Because I wasn't sure what was worse—Luc not knowing or . . . Luc knowing exactly why.

Sighing, I deleted the text and then headed into the living room, picking up the camera from the back of the couch. I made my way to my bedroom, placing my phone on the nightstand beside Diesel. My history textbook lay open on my bed. Knowing that I had an exam coming up, I should have been studying, but I was too restless for that.

Instead, I sat down and clicked on my camera. I hadn't looked at any of the pictures I'd taken in the last several weeks, not even the ones of Luc, and what was better than mindlessly clicking through pictures?

At this moment, there was nothing.

Scrolling back to the pictures I'd taken of Luc, I realized immediately that I'd been right when I'd taken the photos. All those striking lines of his face had communicated through the lens.

The black-and-white photograph of him was my favorite. There was something about the monochromatic colors that gave it a raw, brutal edge. The corners of my lips turned up as I kept thumbing through the photos. It had been ages since I'd uploaded them or even looked at them on the camera, but I was still surprised when I came upon the pictures I'd taken the day my classmate Colleen had been found dead in a school bathroom.

Goodness, I'd forgotten I'd taken them.

I continued flipping through them as a knot of emotion swelled in my throat. Seeing these pictures was like being back in that moment, swallowed up by confusion and fear. The faces in the photos were blurs to me as I blinked rapidly to clear my vision. The images of their shadows on the pavement hit me hard.

That was how I felt.

I was the shadow and not the person.

God.

That was a depressing thought and a bit overdramatic.

Squeezing my eyes shut, I exhaled roughly. I needed to get my life together. Seriously. I was alive. It could be way worse. Like, I could be dead.

I started to flip past the pictures of that day when something weird caught my attention. "What the hell?" I whispered.

The last picture was of a small group. One of them was Andy. God. My chest twisted. There was an unreal quality about seeing a picture of someone days before they died and thinking about how they had no idea their days were numbered, but that wasn't what caught my attention. It was who was standing next to him.

April Collins, and there was something wrong with her picture.

Frowning, I zoomed in. It was like there were two Aprils. One was normal—well, as normal as April could be. Tall. Slender. Long blond hair pulled back in a high ponytail. And then one standing directly behind her like a shadowy overlay. I flipped back through the pictures and saw nothing like that in any other photos I'd taken that day, and that was beyond weird.

This wasn't the first time I'd seen a picture like this of her. Clicking back to the picture I'd snapped of her in the park, I stared down at the picture of April by the swings, with her little sister.

Same thing. It looked like a shadow stood behind her.

"So weird," I muttered, flipping back to the picture at school. I remembered that I had taken another photograph of her, when she'd been protesting in the parking lot.

Hurrying through the photos, I found the picture. There was April, hair pulled back, face twisted, as I'd caught her in the middle of yelling something. The anger practically vibrated through the photograph. Her anger wasn't the only thing I'd captured.

The weird shadow, almost like an overlay, was also visible.

This was freaking bizarre.

I thought about what I'd seen outside of Coop's party, right before I'd found Andy's ruined body, and what I'd seen when Lore appeared outside the club. Arum were like shadows—shadows that burned, a darkness that was threaded with light. Everyone else was convinced I'd seen Micah the night I'd found Andy or had mistaken what I'd seen, but . . .

"Holy shit," I whispered. "Is April an . . . Arum?"

I swallowed a rather nervous laugh. I knew it sounded ridiculous, but April hated the Luxen. And she was kind of evil incarnate.

I blew a strand of hair out of my face as I stared at the weird image of April. There were a lot of holes in my theory, though. If April was an Arum, wouldn't Zoe sense that? The other Luxen? Also, I'd thought Emery had said that Arum didn't often mingle with the human populace, that they kept their distance.

But if it wasn't just some random, weird photo fail, then what could this be?

An idea sparked somewhere between English and chem the next morning, while I was doing my best not to stress over the whole argument with Luc or obsess over what Zoe had said. Which meant I was in a super-weird mood, but a somewhat productive one.

I needed another picture of April, one preferably taken inside to see if there was that weird overlay effect, and I knew exactly where to find one.

Yearbooks.

I had no idea if I'd actually bought one last year, but the school library had a metric crap ton of them.

At lunch, I made a detour. Making my way into the cold and musky-scented library, I headed to the left, near the main desk, to where all the annual yearbooks were kept.

In the back of my mind, I knew my sudden obsession with April had more to do with me than with her. That tiny, annoying voice in the back of my head told me that I was focusing on her because it was so much easier than focusing on everything else.

But whatever.

Thumbing through the glossy pictures, I quickly found where April's picture would've been squeezed in between Janelle Cole and Denny Collinsworth.

There was no picture of April in our junior year.

Closing the yearbook, I shoved it back in place and then picked up the one from our sophomore year. A few seconds later, I was staring down at a picture of April, taken almost two years ago, and it was definitely her. Her name was under the picture. Her blond hair was pulled back extremely tightly, and the familiar red lips curved into a wide smile.

That photograph of April was normal. No weird shadow effect. Then I checked our freshman year and found another normal one.

Two normal photographs and then a missing one. Did that mean anything? I really had no idea, but I knew enough about photography to know that the weird effect only happening on pictures of April was super-bizarre.

Instead of heading to the cafeteria, I found a seat by the windows that overlooked the quad and pulled my camera out of my backpack. The low hum of the computers and overhead lights was broken only by the occasional sneeze or laugh. There was something relaxing about the stillness of the library, and after getting only about two hours of sleep the night before, it was probably a good thing that I was sitting there and not with my friends.

Not that I was avoiding them, but I needed, I don't know, silence.

Finding a bag of chips stowed away in my backpack, I munched on them as I turned on my camera and started flipping through the photos from the lake. I hadn't looked at them the day before.

They were pretty good, I thought. Not that it took a lot of talent to take pictures of trees. The pictures of Luc, though? They were amazing. I wanted to print them out and frame them, but yeah, that seemed creepy. I kept thumbing through my photos and found myself all the way back to the first weird picture of April.

Slinking down in my seat, I popped another chip in my mouth as I stared at it. All three pictures were taken outside. The only two indoor pictures of April were from over a year ago. Did that mean anything? Maybe. Probably not. Another chip went into my mouth as I thought about how April had always reacted rather strongly to the idea of her picture being taken, even when we were on friendlier terms. The girl had reacted a bit excessively in the parking lot. Like she had some—

"Yo."

Jumping at the sound of Heidi's voice, I almost dropped the camera as I looked up and saw her braided crimson hair. "Hey."

She lifted her brows. "Is that all you have to say to me?"

"Um." I looked around. "Good afternoon?" I paused. "Would you like a chip?"

She shot me a bland look as she dropped into the seat beside me. "What are you doing in here?"

"I was looking at something." I shrugged. "And I'm not really hungry."

"That's BS. First off, you're always hungry."

That was actually true, but I muttered, "Geez. Thanks."

"You never hang out in the library during lunch." She propped her chin onto her palm. "I'm worried about you."

"Why? You shouldn't be."

"I shouldn't be?" The look on her face said I should know better. "Things got really weird Saturday night and then a little ugly. And I know you've been through a lot lately, especially with the whole Micah thing."

I opened my mouth but closed it. She might know about Micah, but that was only the tip of the iceberg. "You shouldn't be worried."

"Really? You and Luc still mad at each other?"

I shook my head, sighing as I fiddled with the camera. "Everything is fine with Luc." Not exactly true. "I'm just being a little antisocial right now."

"It's okay to be a little antisocial every once in a while." She paused. "Luc said some strange stuff Saturday night about your mom."

Crap.

I'd forgotten that she'd borne witness to some of that.

Looking away, I struggled to not have an impressive amount of word vomit and tell her everything—that I wasn't Evie Dasher, that I had feelings for Luc, and there was a good chance the only woman I knew as my mother hadn't been entirely honest with me, and that I . . . felt *useless*.

And as I sat there, I had that sudden sense of clarity that I'd been hoping would come the day before at the lake. I'd felt this way long before I'd learned the truth and before Luc came back into my life. Like I was going through the motions every day, existing but not really living, restless and without direction.

Could it have been because I'd been shoved into someone else's life?

Well, duh. Now it sort of seemed obvious.

Either way, Heidi deserved to know the truth. "It's a really long story."

"We got time."

"I don't think we got enough time for all of it, but Mom . . . I found out she isn't my birth mom," I said, keeping my voice low.

"Did she adopt you or something?"

"Kind of?"

She was frowning when I glanced over at her. "Are you not telling me what's going on because I didn't tell you Emery was a Luxen?"

"No. No, not at all. It's just . . . it's really kind of messed up, but . . . I'm not . . . I don't know how to say this." My hands tightened on my camera. "Okay. I'm not Evelyn Dasher."

Even though I didn't look over at her, I could tell she was staring at me. "Come again?"

Drawing in a deep breath, I told her the . . . truth. That I used to be called Nadia Holliday and that I had lived with Luc until I'd gotten sick. It took almost all of lunch for me to explain to her what the Andromeda serum was and how I became Evie.

By the time I was done, Heidi was staring at me, her mouth gaping. "Holy shit, Evie—I mean, Nadia. What am I supposed to call you?"

"Evie. I guess. I mean, Nadia feels weird. I'm not her—well, I am, but I'm Evie."

"Yeah. You're Evie." She slowly shook her head. "I don't know what to say."

I laughed under my breath. "Welcome to the club."

"It's crazy," she said, her gaze flicking over me as if she were looking for some sign that I wasn't who she thought I was. "What the Daedalus was able to do, you know? Some of the stuff is nothing short of miraculous. They were able to save your life, but then they did all these horrible things. It's just . . . it's a lot."

It was. "I've been thinking about it. Like, I think everything has a good and bad side, and the Daedalus was no different. They probably saved a lot of lives, but none of that makes up for the terrible things they did. Maybe that was why Mom worked for them, because of the good she was doing—they were doing at one point."

"I can't believe she's a Luxen. Damn." Heidi suddenly laughed. "Is that why Zoe never went over to your place when your mom was home?"

I nodded. "Yeah, Mom would've known what she was. Zoe steered clear."

"Damn." She smoothed a hand over the fine wisps of hair framing her forehead. "Damn, Evie."

My lips twitched. "I know."

"It kind of makes sense—at least the whole Luc part. How he was with you. Emery couldn't figure it out. As long as she's known him, he's never been the way he is around you with anyone else."

Pressing my lips together, I took a tiny breath and then closed my eyes, saying something I didn't really even let myself think. "I like him, Heidi."

"I know."

I shook my head, keeping my eyes closed. "Things with him are complicated. I like him. I can feel it in here." I raised my hand to the center of my chest. "I like Luc and his stupid shirts and his really dumb pickup lines, Heidi. They're so bad, you have no idea. And I like the way he looks at me like—" My voice caught. "He looks at me like you look at Emery. And I like the way he makes me feel special. I like that he's funny and that he's super-smart. I even like how . . . unrepentant he can be, even though that's wrong. I don't even care. I know that I like Luc, and now he's mad at me."

"That's all good, Evie. Not the Luc being mad at you part, but everything else."

Slowly, I opened my eyes. "I know I like him for who he *is,* but he likes me for who I *was.*"

Understanding crept into her eyes. "Evie, you don't know that."

"But I do. Maybe that will change? Or maybe that doesn't matter, because I am her, but it terrifies me, because what if I don't ever hold up to her? You know?"

"Oh, Evie. I didn't know you—Nadia, whatever—back then, but you're cooler than shit now, and you do not give yourself enough credit."

I smiled at her. "You have to say that."

"No. I don't. I could just pretend like I have a phone call and leave this conversation."

A laugh burst out of me. "That's terrible." Exhaling heavily, I straightened. "I'm glad you know the truth now."

"So am I." She took a deep breath. "Okay. So, what are you doing with the camera?"

Welcoming the distraction so I didn't break down in tears, I decided to show her the picture of April. "The last picture she was in was like this, too. See? Nothing else about the photo is weird except her."

She frowned. "And you have another pic of her like that?"

"Yes." I told her about checking out the yearbook. "It's so freaking weird. I've never seen anything like that, and you know what I was thinking?" I lowered my voice as I looked around the library to make sure no one was near us. "I couldn't help but think about the Arum, but wouldn't Zoe know if she was one?"

"I think so. At least, that's what Emery has said. They can kind of sense one another, even the Origins and hybrids." She brushed a thin wisp of red hair back from her face. "Maybe she's got one of those ghosts from that old movie—you know? What was it called? Aha! *The Grudge*. Maybe the grudge ghost is attached to her," she said, frowning at the screen of my camera. "You know what I'm talking about? The creepy ghost girl—"

"I know what you're talking about." I stared at her, eyebrow raised. "I don't think that's what this is."

"Then what is it?"

"I don't know." I studied the weird shadowy outline. "I wish I had another picture of her, one indoors to see if it's just some kind of weird exposure issue outside versus . . ."

"Versus her being haunted by a revenge ghost?" she suggested.

I shrugged. A revenge ghost sounded just as plausible as April being . . . who knows what.

"I mean, that would make sense, you know? Maybe that's why she's so bitter and mean." She sat up straight. "Let's go get a picture of her."

I laughed. "April is really not a fan of mine."

She rolled her eyes. "Like April is a fan of anyone. I like seeing April get mad. It brings me an indescribable amount of joy."

"Whenever April gets mad, you literally disappear!" I whisper-yelled at her. "Like, there one second and gone the next."

She grinned, and I felt my lips start to curve in return. "That's true, but if you take the picture, then she'll get mad at you and not me, and I can just witness it."

"That's messed up."

"Come on. Let's do it. She was in the hall when I came down here, doing her stupid 'No Luxen, no fear' stuff,'" she said.

I groaned. "I thought they were banned from doing that inside the school."

"Me, too, but they were doing it when I came to find you. You can snap a pic of her and post it on the internet. Name and shame, baby."

Heidi didn't really give me much of a choice. Picking up my camera, she started walking toward the front of the library.

Crap.

I grabbed my stuff and hurried to catch up with her. She was already at the exit while I was zipping up my bag. "Give me my camera."

"Only if you promise to take a picture of April." She held it up too high for me to reach.

"This is stupid." It really was, because I was almost positive that the photo would come out normal, but I was smiling, and I wasn't thinking about how I was a mess, and I knew that was why Heidi was doing this. "Okay. Give me the camera."

"Do you promise?"

"Yes. I promise."

"Score." Heidi handed over the camera, and we made our way to the hallway near the cafeteria.

"I don't hear any chanting." We rounded the corner, finding about a dozen students standing near the trophy case, holding their stupid posters. Brandon was among them. Ugh. His hand was in a cast, and a rather cruel grin tugged at my lips as I scanned the group. There was a teacher standing in front of them, arms crossed. I hoped that meant they were all in trouble. "And I don't see April."

"Hey." She stepped in front of me, waving her hands at one of the girls holding a poster. "Where's your ringleader?"

"Who?" a girl responded snottily.

Heidi let out a sigh that would've made Grayson proud. "April. Where's April?"

"In the bathroom."

Turning to me, Heidi grabbed my hand. "Perfect."

"You seriously want me to bust up in the bathroom and take a pic of her? Pretty sure that's against the law."

"You don't have to take a picture of her when she's in the stall." She dragged me back down the hall, around the corner, and toward the bathrooms. Our steps slowed as we both came to the same realization. April was in the bathroom that Colleen had been found in.

I stopped walking, like I'd hit a brick wall. "I'm not going in there."

Heidi stood beside me. "Well, I'm not, either."

There was only us in the hall, and I had to think it was because no one in their right mind wanted to be anywhere near where Colleen was found. The whole area just gave bad vibes. I started to turn away, but the bathroom door opened, and out stepped April, hair slicked back into her standard ponytail and wearing a fresh coat of red lipstick.

She drew up short when she spotted us.

"Do it," Heidi whispered, and then she elbowed me so hard in my arm, she almost knocked me over.

April began to frown. "Do what?"

Feeling goofy, I lifted the camera and chirped, "Merry Christmas!"

"What? It's not even Thanksgiving—" April sucked in a shrill breath as the flash on my camera went off. "What the hell?" she exploded.

Heidi giggled, reminding me of a hyena, as I lowered the camera and switched the screen to the images taken. "Sorry," I murmured, not at all sorry as I stepped back. "I just wanted to check something out."

"Did you seriously just take a picture of me?" April demanded.

"No," I lied, clicking on the image I just took. There was April. Eyes narrowed and lips pursed. I was unsure of what the hell I was looking at, because there it was again, the weird shadow outline all around April's form. "There it is."

"Again?" Some of the humor faded from Heidi's voice.

"Yeah." I lifted my gaze.

April looked completely normal standing in front of me. Maybe it was a revenge ghost.

"What?" April demanded. "Let me see."

Before I could respond, April snatched the camera out of my hand. I half expected her to throw it against the wall, but all she did was stare at the image, her lips thinning until nothing was left but a slash of red.

"Well," Heidi said, drawing the word out. "This is really—"

I turned to Heidi as she made this weird choking sound. Her mouth was moving, but no words were coming out. Her entire body jerked like something had grabbed her.

Heidi blinked as her bag slid off her arm and hit the floor.

Time stopped.

Something red leaked out of the corner of her mouth. Confusion swamped me. What was that red? My gaze dropped. There was—oh my God—her shirt was ripped open over her right shoulder, and red—red was everywhere. Horror seized every part of me in its icy grip.

"Heidi?"

She fell—folded like an accordion—and I shot forward, trying to catch her, but my feet slipped under me, and her sudden weight was too much. I went down, my knees cracking off the floor, and I tried to hold her, but she slipped out of my arms, rolling onto her back.

"Heidi," I whispered, grabbing at her shirt. "*Heidi.*"

Her eyes were open, and her face was so pale, too pale. She started to speak, but the only sound that came out of her was a wet, *bloody* cough as she clutched at my arm.

Slowly, I looked up at April.

She held my camera in one hand, and her other . . . wasn't right. Her hand looked almost see-through, but her forearm was covered with blood . . . and tissue. Pressure clamped down on my chest.

Smoke wafted from my camera. The smell of burned plastic mingled with the overwhelming scent of blood. April's gaze met mine, and I shrank back. Her eyes—oh my God, her eyes.

The entirety of her eyes was as black as obsidian, but her pupils shone like white diamonds.

I'd seen eyes like that once before.

Sarah.

The girl Kent strongly believed had turned into a zombie and launched herself out the window.

April dropped the ruined, smoking camera. "Look at what you made me do."

17

Every muscle in my body locked up as I stared at April.

She laughed as if someone had just told a joke. "You should see your face right now. It reminds me of Andy before, well, you know. He died."

I jerked, my gaze swinging back to Heidi. The deaths Micah had said he hadn't caused. Andy. Those families . . .

"You," I whispered. "It was you."

April's mouth twisted into a semblance of a smile. "Guilty."

Heidi's hand slipped off my arm. Rage rolled over the horror, and I wanted to dig into April, rip into her with my nails and teeth like an animal, but the logical part of my brain was in control. Heidi was the priority. I knew I needed to get her out of here fast. Luc could heal her—fix her like he'd fixed me before, because Heidi was not going to die.

I would not allow that to happen.

April reached for me, and my heart seized as I threw my arm out but didn't make contact. Her ponytail lifted off her shoulder as she stumbled back several steps. She caught herself before she went down.

Her chin dipped as she bared her perfect, straight teeth in a growl that did not remotely sound human.

Holy crap.

Springing into action, I scrambled backward. I shot to my feet and turned, running toward the wall behind me—to the red metal square. Wrapping my fingers around the white lever, I pulled the fire alarm.

The high, shrill buzz of the alarm was immediate. I spun as the small bright lights flashed up and down the hall.

April stepped back, her head swiveling toward the increasing sound of voices and footsteps. She whirled on me, letting out an unnerving trilling sound that sent a chill down my spine.

It was the same sound Sarah had made.

April blew me a kiss, smirking as she spun away. She was gone in a heartbeat, nothing but a blur.

I didn't give her a second thought. Not right then. I rushed to Heidi's side and gripped her right arm. "You've got to get up, Heidi. Please. You have to help me get you out of here. *Please.*"

Heidi groaned as I pulled her upright. She didn't speak.

Panic blossomed in my chest. "Heidi. Please." My voice broke. "Oh God, please get up."

Shoving my arm around her waist, I used every ounce of strength I had in me to lift her up onto her feet. Her entire body was trembling as I guided her down the hall to the nearest exit. "It'll be okay. I promise. I'm getting you help."

Even though Luc and I hadn't spoken since our argument, I needed him. I didn't know if Zoe could heal Heidi. I knew it wasn't something all Origins or even Luxen could do, but I knew Luc could. "I promise. Please hang in there."

Using my hip, I pushed open the door, and we tripped onto the gravel part of the back parking lot. Reaching into my back pocket, I found Luc's number through the haze of tears. *Please, answer the phone. Please.*

Heidi whimpered as I forced her up the small grass hill, toward the line of cars. Her breath was coming out in shallow pants and strange wheezes. "Evie, I . . . I don't . . ."

"Just hold on. Please." The phone rang once in my ear, and then there was Luc's voice. "I need your help. Right now."

"Where are you?" he demanded immediately.

"Heidi is hurt—she's hurt really badly." My grip started to slip as we reached the second row of cars. "It was April. She's . . . I don't know what she is, but she attacked Heidi. It's—"

"You at school? Where are you?"

"In the parking lot—Heidi!" I screamed, nearly dropping the phone.

Her knees gave out, and I eased her down the best I could. "Please, hurry. Oh God, please tell me you can get here *now.*"

"I'll be right there."

I dropped the phone and pressed my hand down on Heidi's shoulder. The skin felt wrong under my palm, uneven and too soft to be right. "It's going to be okay. Luc's coming."

Her wide-eyed stare kept darting from me to the sky. "That . . . that was . . . a dumb . . . idea. The . . . whole picture thing."

"Stop." Tears tracked down my face. Blood was seeping through my fingers. How could she lose so much blood and have any left? Her face was even paler, the skin starting to turn blue around her lips. Was calling Luc the right choice? "It's okay." I kept saying that. "It's okay."

"I want . . ." She coughed, spraying fine droplets of blood. "I want to see . . . Emery."

"You will." I leaned down, kissing her forehead. "You will totally see her."

Suddenly, Zoe was there, her face obscured by a wealth of curls. "Luc called. He's on his way."

"Can you heal her?" Blood ran down my arm, under the sleeves of my shirt.

Zoe shook her head as she scrambled to Heidi's side. With a shocking display of strength, she lifted Heidi into her arms. "My car is the closest."

Grabbing my phone and bag, I lurched to my feet, following Zoe as she raced two rows down. Everything at this point was a blur. Zoe put Heidi in the back seat, and I had a terrible sense of déjà vu, but it was me who was now holding on to Heidi. Her head was in my lap as I kept my hand on her shoulder. Zoe climbed into the driver's seat. She'd just turned the car on when the passenger door across from me opened.

It wasn't Luc.

Emery climbed through, her expression stricken. "Oh, God—oh no, Heidi." She brushed my hand aside, placing hers where mine had been. "Open those eyes for me, babe. Open those beautiful eyes for me, Heidi. Come on, *please* open your eyes for me."

"I'm sorry," I whispered, my hands hovering over Heidi. "I'm sorry—"

The door opened behind me, and the moment arms circled my waist, I knew it was Luc. He hauled me out of the car, keeping one arm around my waist as he leaned around me. "Get them to the club."

He closed the door just as I saw Emery slip into her true form. The entire back seat of the car filled with brilliant white light.

"I have to go with them." I pulled at his arm, reaching for the back door. "I have to—"

Gravel kicked up as Zoe tore out of the parking spot, flying down the narrow opening. I twisted, my blood-soaked hands slipping off Luc's arm. "No. I need—"

"There's nothing more you can do." He whipped me around, keeping an arm secured around my waist as he cupped my chin. "Are you okay?"

"Emery said before she wasn't good at healing. That's why I called you—"

"She's in the best possible hands. Evie, I need to know if you're—"

"I'm okay!" I shrieked, trying to pull away, but Luc held on. "Emery said—"

"Emery loves her." Luc pulled me against him as his hand slipped around the back of my neck. "Listen to me. You do not get between a Luxen and who they love, no matter what."

"What?" None of that mattered to me at the moment. "Heidi can't die, Luc. She can't—"

"She won't. Emery will not allow that." He dropped his arm and took my hand. "Give me your keys. I'll drive us to the club."

"She'll be okay?" I reached around, grabbing my keys out of my bag as I heard the fire trucks wailing. "She'll be okay?"

Luc took my keys. "Emery won't let her die."

"I don't understand," I said, hands shaking as we hurried to my car. "Emery said she wasn't good at healing."

Luc opened the driver's door. "Remember how I told you that all Luxen have the ability to heal? Some are better at it than others, but I'm telling you, when it's someone they love, there is no one else better to heal them."

"That makes no sense." I sat in the front seat as Luc slammed the door shut behind him. "You healed me . . ."

Luc's intense gaze found mine as he turned the car on.

My heart lurched against my ribs as I looked away and swallowed hard, my throat too dry. I couldn't even think about that at this moment or even the fact that we hadn't spoken since our argument Saturday night. All I could think about was Heidi.

He pulled out of the parking spot. "You know that Luxen and

some Origins can heal and that not all are good at it, especially when it comes to someone they . . . don't feel strongly about. But when it's someone they do care about, no matter how poor their skills are any other time, they can bring that person back from the brink of death. The Daedalus studied it extensively. There is a science to how we can heal a human."

That much I remembered. The energy inside them could repair tissues and damage done to the body. It's how they could heal themselves, but none of that explained how Emery, who couldn't heal my broken arm, could then heal a giant, gaping hole in Heidi's shoulder and chest.

"There is also mysticism to it," Luc continued. "A part that not even the greatest of researchers or doctors can explain." There was a pause. "Please put your seat belt on."

I laughed, and it came out sounding choked. Hands shaking, I clasped myself in. My hands . . . they were caked with blood—Heidi's blood. If she died . . .

I smashed my lips together, vaguely aware of my body slowly rocking back and forth. A numbness settled over me as Luc drove. I stared at my hands.

"You need to tell me what happened," he said after what felt like an eternity.

I drew in a deep breath, but it went nowhere. "It was April. It was her."

"I need a little more detail."

A shudder worked its way through me, and I squeezed my eyes shut. I needed to pull it together. Luc needed to know what I saw. I took another breath and started at the beginning, with April's pictures and the weird effect I'd seen. "I showed Heidi the pictures. I think I was focusing on it, because then I wasn't thinking about everything else and Heidi . . . she knew that." My voice cracked as a wave of hot tears crawled up my throat. "She suggested we go get a picture of April to see if it was some weird outdoor effect. It was stupid, but she was just trying to distract me."

Luc listened as he turned onto the street that led to the back of Foretoken.

"We found her, and I took a picture of her. That . . . that was all." Lifting my right hand, I wiped at my cheek. "The effect was the same. She had this shadow around her. April took my camera and saw the picture, and I don't even know how it happened. All I knew was I had to get Heidi out of there, that I needed to call you, because it was bad. I pulled the fire alarm."

"Smart. You did good."

The next breath I took was steadier, but I didn't feel like I did well. If I hadn't had my head up my butt and Heidi hadn't sought me out none of this would've happened. "It was like April put her hand *through* Heidi's shoulder. Through it, and April's hand . . . it was almost transparent. And her eyes . . . they were just like that girl's—Sarah's. Pure black with white pupils."

Luc pulled into a narrow space by the back entrance, and I could feel his gaze on me. "Are you sure?"

"Yes." I looked at him. "Her eyes were all black except for the pupils. They were white. Like a Luxen. And she was fast like a Luxen. Just like Sarah was, but neither of them are Luxen."

"No."

"And they aren't Arum or Origins?"

He shook his head.

"Sarah got sick. We saw that with our own eyes, and even though I've never seen a human mutate and you guys said that wasn't what it looked like, I think we need to reexamine the whole mutation thing," I said, and Luc looked away, his jaw tight. "Because whatever the hell April is, it's what Sarah is, and I know you guys didn't hear Sarah, but I did. She said someone did that to her."

His gaze found mine as his head turned toward me. "I believe you."

"If that was done to Sarah and to April, then who did it?"

Luc rested his head back against the seat. "There's only one group of people that can . . . do something like that."

I thought I might already know. "The Daedalus?"

"Yes."

I sat side by side with Zoe in silence as we waited for an update. Luc had brought me up here when we arrived and then had left to check in on Emery and Heidi. We hadn't seen him since.

Kent had shown up at some point, and he was abnormally quiet as he stood by the window, looking out to the ground below, his blue hair pulled back in a small ponytail.

Letting out a shaky breath, I rested my cheek on Zoe's shoulder. Things were suddenly clear in those long, silent moments. There was a lot about the world I didn't know. A lot about me I still had to figure out, but there was one damn thing I knew.

I was going to straight-up kill April.

And I knew Zoe would be right there with me when I did.

I don't know how much time had passed when the door opened and Luc entered. I lifted my head from Zoe's shoulder, and she grabbed my hand as we stood together.

"Is she . . . ?" I couldn't bring myself to finish the question.

"Come on." Luc held the door open for us.

Zoe squeezed my hand as we walked out into the hall and followed Luc down a flight of stairs and then to a room three doors from the entrance. Grayson stood outside, and for once, he wasn't staring at me like he wanted to zap me through a wall.

The door opened, and I was no longer thinking of Grayson. I felt sick as we walked through a dimly lit room and into another, my gaze bouncing around until it settled on a bed.

I saw Heidi and Emery.

They lay in the center. Heidi was on her back, and Emery was on her side, curled around her. Both were incredibly still. A blanket was tucked under Heidi's arms. Her shoulders were bare, and I could see the angry, puckered skin of her right shoulder. It was a decent-size scar, but it looked like something that had happened weeks earlier, not hours.

I pulled my hand free from Zoe's. "Are they . . . ?"

"They're okay," Luc answered.

Zoe moved first, walking around to the side of Heidi's bed. She knelt, placing her hands on the bed. She didn't speak, but Emery lifted her head slightly. Dark smudges marred the olive-tone skin under her eyes.

I couldn't move, rooted to the spot I stood on.

Just then, Heidi's lashes fluttered and her eyes opened. Her nose pinched as she looked at Zoe. "Hey," she whispered.

"Hi." Zoe's voice cracked. "How are you feeling?"

"Like . . . someone had their hand *inside* me." Heidi turned her head toward me. She wet her lips. "I had . . . possibly . . . the worst idea ever, didn't I?"

I let out a hoarse laugh that ended in a sob. My legs started moving, and I went to the bed, sitting carefully beside her. "I'm so sorry. I'm so—"

"It wasn't . . . your fault." Heidi drew in a shallow breath as her lashes lowered.

I wasn't sure I could agree with that.

Heidi swallowed as she glanced at Emery. "I always . . . thought April was . . . an epic freak."

Emery brushed a limp strand of red hair back from Heidi's face. "I'm going to kill her. It's going to be slow and extremely painful."

"You're going to have to get in line for that," Zoe said.

I couldn't believe Heidi was lying there, alive and talking—and joking. Awe filled me as I looked at Emery. When Luc healed me, I'd been amazed but somehow detached from it at the same time. Probably as a coping mechanism, but this was extraordinary.

"Thank you," I said.

Emery didn't pull her gaze from Heidi. "You don't have to thank me."

"Where . . . is she?" Heidi asked. "April?"

"I don't know." I swallowed and then glanced back at Luc. "But we'll find her."

Heidi's eyes drifted shut again. "It's so strange."

"What?" Zoe asked, and I felt like there were a million things that were strange right now.

"She hated Luxen. Right? She was leading protests and . . . she's obviously not human."

Zoe's jaw hardened as she met Emery's gaze. "It's awfully ironic."

"Yeah," breathed Heidi.

She fell asleep after that. It was hard leaving them, but it was evident that Emery was also exhausted. They needed to rest. Out in the hall, I leaned against the wall, nearly dizzy with relief.

"I thought . . ." I shook my head. "I thought she was going to die."

"She would've if you hadn't acted quickly." Zoe rested her shoulder against the wall next to me. "You saved her."

"No, I didn't. Emery did."

Luc and Grayson joined us, closing the door to Emery's apartment behind us. Taking a deep breath for what felt like the first time in hours, I lifted my head.

"You ready?" Grayson said to Zoe.

Nodding, she pushed off the wall. "Yes."

"Ready for what?" I asked, straightening.

"We're going to go check out April's house," Zoe explained. "See if she's there."

"What?" Concern exploded. "You're going there? I saw what she was capable of, Zoe."

"We're not going to engage," Grayson interjected. "Not that you're worried about *my* well-being or anything."

I shot him a look. I really wasn't. "She put her hand *through* Heidi's shoulder—"

"And I'll put my hand through her chest," Zoe said, smirking. "Not that we're engaging, but if I happen to get close enough and I accidentally kill her, then oops."

"You guys don't even know what April is," I argued. "April is not a Luxen, an Arum, a hybrid, an Origin, or a magical unicorn. She's something even Luc hasn't seen before."

"Really?" Grayson slid a long look in Luc's direction. "That would be a first."

One side of Luc's lips kicked up. "There is a first time for everyone."

My hands balled into fists. Nothing about this was remotely funny. "The RAC drones never hit on April," I reminded all of them. "God only knows what she is, and you're going to go looking for her. I don't want you getting hurt."

"If we don't try to find her, then who?" Grayson challenged. "Do we call the police? We don't know if their weapons will stop her."

"But you guys can?" I demanded.

Grayson lifted his brows. "Do you doubt our extreme awesomeness?"

I stared at him a moment and then shook my head. "I'm not suggesting calling the police. I'm not an idiot."

"That's good to know," Grayson replied blandly. "I was beginning to worry."

Whatever tedious hold I had on my self-control snapped. "That is my friend who almost died in there, and that is my friend," I said, pointing to Zoe, "who will be risking her life. So, if you don't have anything of value to add, how about you shut the hell up?"

Zoe had her lower lip sucked between her teeth. I knew that look. She was doing everything not to burst into laughter.

"Well, now that we got that out of the way, I think it's time for everyone to hit the road," Luc announced.

Lead filled my stomach as I twisted toward Zoe. "I don't want you to get hurt."

"I won't."

"Neither will I," added Grayson with a sigh. "But you don't care."

"Nope," I remarked, hating that I couldn't do anything. I may have a tiny bit of alien DNA in me, but it did nothing to make me useful in these situations . . . unless there was a random fire alarm to pull.

Snapping forward, I hugged Zoe, squeezing her tight enough that there was a good chance I'd crack her ribs. I'd seen what Luc was capable of, but that didn't mean I wouldn't worry about her . . . or even him. Or any of them . . . even Grayson, contrary to what I'd just said. "Be careful."

"I will."

I glanced at Grayson. "Don't get yourself killed, either. It might traumatize Zoe."

He rolled his eyes.

Only then did I look at Luc, and there was an amused glint to his eyes. "Are you going with them?"

"No, you and I have something to do."

We did?

"Come with me." Luc took my hand, not really giving me a choice. Probably a good thing, because there was a good chance I was going to run after Zoe and tackle her, preventing her from leaving.

Luc didn't speak as he led me upstairs to his apartment, nor did he say a word as he sat me on his wide, fluffy couch.

Rubbing my palms over my knees, I looked behind me as he stepped up onto the raised platform of what was his bedroom.

An image of me and him formed immediately. Us dancing and then us on the couch, so close to kissing.

Damn, that felt like an eternity ago.

I heard the water turn on while I thought about how fast everything could change.

Luc walked back into the room, carrying a wet cloth. He knelt in front of me. My breath hitched as he picked up my hand and began to wipe away the dark stains. I'd forgotten that I was covered in blood.

"Do you still have your stun gun?" Luc asked.

It took me a moment to realize what he was talking about. "No. I, um, I haven't seen it since that night with Micah." I watched him for a moment. "Why didn't you go with them?"

"I was needed here." He went on before I could respond. "I'm going to take you home, but I need to get you cleaned up first. Once I'm done, I'll get a clean shirt for you. Then we'll get out of here."

"What about Heidi?"

"She's going to be weak for a little while." Luc dragged the damp cloth over my hand. "Then she'll probably feel like a million bucks."

"Like I did?"

"Yes, but she has a trace on her. So, she's about to come down with a nasty case of mono."

Heidi had a trace like a human was supposed to. I didn't have one after Luc healed me because of the Andromeda serum.

"So, she'll stay at home where no Arum can see her?"

Arum tracked Luxen and those close to them by the traces left behind that could only be seen by the aliens and Origins.

Luc nodded. "Until it fades."

I thought of Lore. "Is that Arum still here?"

His lashes lifted, and violet eyes pierced mine. "He left with Dawson, but she would be safe with Lore."

I had to take his word for it. "Will she . . . mutate?"

He scrubbed gently between my fingers. "We don't know yet. Probably not since this is the first time she's been healed by a Luxen, but it was pretty substantial. It's a wait-and-see kind of thing."

My stomach plummeted. "But if she does mutate, she could die, right?"

"We won't let that happen." Placing my hand back down, he picked up the other. "We have the stuff necessary to aid in the mutation, to make sure it holds, if it comes to that."

"Stuff taken from the Daedalus?"

He nodded.

A long moment passed as I tried to make sense of everything, but then my attention got snagged. I finally read the front of his black shirt.

There was a spaceship beaming up dogs, and it said WE'RE HERE FOR THE DOGS BECAUSE HUMANS ARE GROSS. A wild-sounding laugh erupted out of me.

The corners of his lips tipped up. "What?"

"Your shirt." I blinked back tears—tears of laughter or stress, I had no idea. "It's funny."

"Oh." He glanced down at himself. "Kind of ironic, isn't it?"

I nodded.

Luc studied me quietly for a few moments. "You okay?"

Yes. No. Maybe? I didn't know what I felt, so I said nothing.

"Have you called Sylvia?" he asked.

"She won't even be home, but I texted her to let her know that I was with Zoe and Heidi. I didn't tell her what happened."

"Part of me doesn't want to even bring this up because of how things ended the last time, but I need to say this. Sylvia cannot know about this. Even if I trusted her, she's in a very precarious position. There's no way that everyone she works with and works for doesn't realize what she is. For some reason, they're okay with her pretending to be human, but if she started poking around . . ." His hand stilled. "She doesn't need to know about this, and we need to be careful of who we trust and who we put in danger."

His gaze met and held mine. "It could put you in danger. Even with the Daedalus being no more, there are still people out there that would kill to discover how you were cured. They'd come for you."

A shudder worked its way through me.

"They'd try to take you. Do you understand that?"

I did. His gaze dropped as he seemed to focus on what he was doing. "Luc?"

"Peaches?"

That was the first time he'd used that nickname since he'd shown up in the parking lot. "I know things got . . . heated between us Saturday night, and I know you don't trust her, but she can't be involved in what happened to Sarah or whatever the hell April is."

"She was involved in healing you. She worked within the Daedalus in some capacity up until four years ago." He stilled. "All I do know for sure when it comes to Sylvia is that she loves you very much and that she wishes you never walked into this club."

I gripped my knee with my free hand, unable to even fathom where I'd be if I hadn't walked into Foretoken that night with Heidi.

Luc looked up at me again. "I can count on one hand how many people I irrevocably trust, and she is not one of them. I've learned that people, no matter how much we love them or how much we think we know them, are truly capable of doing anything and everything."

The back of my throat burned. "If that's true, then how do you trust anyone?"

He lifted one shoulder as his gaze lowered. "You prepare for the worst and hope for the best, Peaches."

"Do you trust me?" The question burst out of me like a volcano erupting.

A muscle popped along his jaw. "I used to."

Used to. Total past tense there, and that hurt like a kick to the chest. Looking away, I stared at the guitar I'd never seen or heard him play. "Is it because I don't remember . . . everything or because of my mom?"

"Yes. No. All of the above and none of it," he answered.

"You're mad at me," I said. "You're still mad at me."

Luc didn't answer. A flicker of emotion shot across his face, gone before I could read what it was.

"Because of Halloween. Because I—" I stopped, feeling like my tongue was glued to the roof of my mouth. I screwed my eyes shut. "I walked out of here on Saturday, pissed off. I was angry at you. You're obviously still angry at me, but you came the moment I called you. You didn't hesitate and . . ."

He was staring up at me. "Sometimes I want to shake you."

"Excuse me?"

"What would you think I'd do? You needed me, and I was there. There is no other option." Something fierce flashed in those amethyst eyes. "How do you not know that yet? Yes, I'm mad; I'm in a constant state of being angry, Evie. I just hide it well."

My heart thundered in my chest.

His gaze pierced mine. "I'm mad at what you've had to experience. I'm mad that you have nightmares, and I'm pissed over the situation we're in. I'm furious at what happened to Heidi and to innocent Luxen who want nothing more than to just live their lives. I'm enraged that I thought I was saving—" He cut himself off, his chest rising with a deep breath. He shook his head. "There's a lot that I'm angry over, but I'm never angry *with* you."

My entire body jolted.

Luc threaded his fingers through mine. "Was I annoyed Saturday night? Yes. Irritated that you're surprised that I would come when you needed me? Hell yes. But I'm never mad at you," he repeated. "I was trying to give you some space after everything. Figured you needed it. Figured we both needed it."

I didn't know what to say, and I realized in that moment that even though words were powerful, they weren't always necessary.

Springing forward, I wrapped my arms around Luc before I could give myself time to think about what I was doing. The action obviously surprised him, because he froze but didn't topple backward. That lasted only for about a second before his arms swept around me, holding me tightly.

My face was planted against his chest. "Thank you," I said, and I wasn't sure I even knew what I was thanking him for.

Everything?

That sounded about right.

His hand folded around the back of my head, fingers tangling in my hair. "Peaches . . ."

I squeezed him tighter.

His chin brushed over the top of my head. "One of these days, you're going to realize that I've never left and I never will."

18

Before Luc and I left, I peeked in on Heidi. Both of the girls were asleep, and I didn't want to wake them, so I crept away, telling myself I'd come back the next day.

Once I was in the car, with Luc behind the wheel, we grabbed burgers and I answered James's string of texts. He wanted to know where everyone had disappeared to after the fire alarm, and I hated being evasive.

"I know I can't tell James the truth, but this sucks." I put my phone back in my bag and let it rest next to my feet. "It's like having an alternate life."

He arched a brow. "It'll get easier."

"Really?" I stared out at the dark stretch of trees. The subdivision I lived in was surrounded by thick woods on either side of the road, and I used to like that. Now it seemed dark and full of nightmares. "I'm not sure if that's a good thing."

He glanced over at me. "Depends on how you look at it."

I wasn't sure how else I could look at it, but whether it was good or bad, it was now my life and I was going to have to deal with it.

When we pulled into the driveway, I immediately knew Mom still wasn't home. It wasn't all that late, but the only light on was in the upstairs hallway, signaling she hadn't returned from Frederick yet.

I glanced over at Luc as he killed the engine. "Thank you again—"

"Don't thank me for this."

"I just did."

"I don't accept it." Opening the driver's side door, he unfolded his long body and stepped out.

I hurried out of the car, almost forgetting my backpack. Snatching it up, I darted over the grass, causing the motion detectors to come on. Luc was waiting on the front porch. "What are you doing?"

His face was shadowed under the porch light. "Waiting for you to unlock the door."

I cocked my head. "I figured that, but you're coming in?"

"I don't want you here alone. Not when April is out there and we have no clue where she is." He paused. "If you don't want me here, I can call Zoe back or—"

"No, it's okay." Digging out my house keys, I unlocked the front door, hoping he didn't notice how my fingers trembled. "We just have to be careful."

"Sylvia will freak if she comes home and finds me?" He chuckled under his breath as he followed me. "She won't know I'm here."

Even though Mom hadn't said anything about Luc's last late-night visit, I wasn't sure that meant she had no idea he'd been here.

Standing in the foyer, I shifted my bag up my arm. "I need to take a quick shower." Even though I was wearing one of Luc's thermals that smelled like him, I knew there was blood in places where Luc had not cleaned. "If you're still hungry or want a drink, help yourself."

His gaze flicked to me and he nodded, hands in his pockets.

I hesitated and then spun on my heel, dashing up the stairs. Once in my bedroom, I closed the door and dropped my bag by my desk. Snatching up a pair of sleep bottoms, I quickly undressed, rolling my jeans into a ball and tossing them into the hamper. I started to grab a shirt but decided to bring Luc's borrowed shirt with me.

After pulling a brush through my hair, tearing out God knows how many strands in the process, I pulled it up in a topknot and then stepped into the shower.

The hot water stung my chest and stomach, causing me to flinch as I stood under the spray. I took a deep breath, but it went nowhere. Slowly, I lifted my hands, placing them over my face.

Something cracked inside me. A wall I never knew was there, and it wasn't a small fissure but a gaping fracture that rattled every bone in my body. Tears raced up my throat and welled behind my closed eyes. There was no keeping them back, and I let them out, clamping my jaw tightly so I didn't make a sound.

I cried for Heidi and how close she'd come to dying today. I cried for the panic Emery must've felt when she saw her. I cried for how scared Zoe and I had been waiting to hear if Heidi was going to be okay. And I cried because I didn't want Luc to be angry all the time. I cried because I had Luc's affection, his loyalty, but I didn't have his trust and, truth was, I doubted him, over and over.

Pull it together.

Put it back together.

I pulled my shaking hands away from my face and picked up my pink loofah, focusing on scrubbing at my skin until it turned pink and the water circling the drain was clear. By the time I dried off and changed into my sleep shorts and Luc's thermal, steam had covered the mirror and I had pulled it together. I opened the door, and my heart launched itself into my throat.

Luc was in my bedroom, standing in front of the corkboard of pictures. He looked over his shoulder, his gaze roaming from the tips of my toes—toes that I still needed to either take the polish off of or redo—to the damp tendrils of hair curling around my cheeks. A soft smile appeared. "Sorry," he said, turning back to the tacked photos. "I figured I should wait up here just in case Sylvia comes home."

"Makes sense." Fingering the hem of the gray thermal, I walked over to the bed and sat. "I hope you don't mind that I'm wearing your shirt."

Luc turned to me. "Actually, it's the exact opposite."

I didn't know what to say to that.

He faced the corkboard again. "Grayson called while you were in the shower. They just checked out April's house. She wasn't there, and it didn't look like anyone else has been there for a while. No parents."

"That's really weird. April has a little sister."

"Grayson said Zoe pointed that out, too, but no one was there."

Dread formed like a weed in the pit of my stomach. "That update couldn't be good whatsoever."

"Probably not."

He walked over to the nightstand, reaching into the pocket of his pants. I immediately recognized the small, black object. A stun gun.

"I grabbed some stuff before we came here. Keep this on you. Who knows if it will work against April, but it's worth having."

I nodded.

"And I also brought you this." In his palm was a long, shiny, pendant-shaped black object that was chiseled to a fine point. It was secured to a silver chain. "This is obsidian. Remember what that does?"

"Yeah, it's deadly against Arum."

"Again, no idea if it will work against April, but I want you to keep this on you at all times. Even when you're showering." He held up the necklace, and I leaned over, heart thumping heavily as he draped the necklace over my shoulders, securing it behind my neck. The tips of his fingers brushed over my skin as he straightened the chain. "Okay?"

"Okay." I picked up the piece of obsidian. The necklace wasn't as heavy as I'd thought it would be. The volcanic glass was about three inches long, and the silver chain was delicate, spiraling over the top of the obsidian. "This would stop an Arum? I was picturing something . . . bigger and thicker."

"That's what she said."

Lifting my head, I stared at him. "Really?"

"I mean, you kind of set that one up perfectly," he replied with a sly grin. "A very small piece of obsidian can do major damage to an Arum. Stab them anywhere with that, and they're going down. And the end is wickedly sharp, so please try not to stab yourself."

That was a promise I wasn't sure I could keep.

I let the obsidian go, and it came to rest between my breasts, on the outside of Luc's borrowed shirt.

Luc roamed back over to the corkboard. "Can I admit something to you and you not get mad?"

Pulling my legs up and crossing them, I picked up my pillow, planting it in my lap. "Depends on what it is."

"I've seen some of these photos before, and I'm not talking about when I was here before."

"What do you mean?"

Angling his body sideways, he placed a blunt fingertip against a picture. It was of Zoe and me, freshman homecoming. "I saw this nearly four years ago. It had only been a few months, maybe four, since . . . since you'd become Evie. I'd never seen you in a dress before then. I thought . . . you were so pretty."

I'd been wearing a deep purple dress with an empire waist, and I wasn't sure if I'd looked pretty in it. However, I did look like someone had thrown glitter up all over me.

But Luc had thought I looked pretty, and despite everything, that brought a small smile to my lips.

"And this one? Halloween. Three years ago." He pointed to a picture of me with Heidi and Zoe as my breath caught. He knew the exact year. We were dressed as the Heathers from the movie *Heathers*. "Such a dark costume. I loved it. And this one? The first time I saw you in a pic with James, I . . ."

"What?"

Luc shook his head. "I thought he was your boyfriend."

"James? What?" I laughed softly. "It's not like that; it's never been like that with us."

"I know. Zoe said the same thing."

Something occurred to me. "Did you see pictures of Brandon and me?"

"I did. You could've done better."

I swallowed another laugh, mainly because that was true considering his anti-Luxen rhetoric. God, if he only knew what April was.

Luc's back was to me again. "Did you love him?"

My eyes widened as I felt my cheeks flush. "I . . . I think I did at first. I mean, he was my first real boyfriend."

His shoulders seemed to tense. "You think? Then that means you didn't?"

"I thought I did for, like, a hot second, but I didn't." Talking about my ex with Luc was weird. "I liked him, but it always felt like it should've been more." I clutched the pillow. "So, you saw most of them in real time?"

"I got to watch you grow up without you ever knowing." His arms folded across his chest. "That sounded creepier than I intended."

"It's not." And it wasn't—not for me, not for us. Out of context, sure. But I knew how he'd seen those photos. Only two other people had copies of them. "Zoe?"

He nodded absently. "I didn't ask to see them. It felt wrong to do so, and it was already creepy that I was having Zoe keep an eye on you. But I wanted to see them. I wanted to see you, and Zoe sensed that, and she'd periodically show them or make sure they were obviously displayed at her house. Please don't be mad at her."

"I won't." I probably would've done the same thing.

I watched him for a few moments, knowing he had none of his own photos. "Did you ever want that?"

"What?"

"A normal teenage life? Halloween parties and friends? Pictures on corkboards? Instagram accounts?" I laughed a little, and the sound quickly faded. "Going to school. Hating it. Wanting to go to college, but . . . being afraid of growing up. Did you ever want any of that?"

Luc gradually faced me. "Honest?"

I nodded.

"My answer might . . . bother you."

"I've seen a lot recently that has bothered me, so I doubt your answer is going to be worse."

Luc walked over to the other side of the bed and sat. "I never wanted any of that until you had it." He leaned against the headboard. "There was never a part of me that wanted to go to school or parties until I saw those pictures. Then I did."

An ache pierced my chest. "You'd be so bored in school."

"Not if you had been there." A lopsided grin appeared. "I even considered it once, you know? Enrolling to be close to you. But I couldn't risk it. So, I stayed in the city, and once they started registering Luxen, forcing them to wear Disablers, I opened Foretoken."

"And that's it? You never wanted to do something else?"

"Like what?" He lifted his hand, and the remote flew from the dresser to his hand. "Live like I was a normal teenager?" He handed the remote to me. "No."

"I meant be someone else. Someone who doesn't have to worry about people figuring out you're not exactly human."

"I don't worry about that," he remarked with a lift of his shoulder. "And why would I want to be someone else? I'm awesome."

"Wow," I murmured, thinking that he wasn't exactly being truthful. How could he be when he'd admitted earlier that he was angry all the time?

He grinned, but it quickly faded. "I didn't mean to make you cry."

"What?" I almost dropped the remote.

The hue of his eyes deepened. "I know you were crying earlier."

"How—" I shook my head. "I was in the shower. You could hear me?"

His gaze flickered over me. "I didn't hear you, Peaches. I could tell when you came out. Your eyes."

"Oh." That made sense. "You didn't make me cry. It's been a . . ."

"Rough day? I know it has been, and I know what I said about not completely trusting you didn't help. I didn't . . . mean to do that. And I do trust you, Evie. It's just that your relationship with Sylvia complicates things. We just have to figure out a way to work with that."

A knot formed in my throat. If I was being honest with myself, his lack of trust wasn't so much to do with me but came into play when my mom was involved. "I know. It's just . . . today was scary, and there's a lot going on in my head. All day, actually. It's why I was in the library. It's why I was trying to distract myself."

"From what?"

Dragging the remote over the comforter, I thought about what Zoe had told me on Sunday as I placed my head back against the headboard. Words I needed to speak crowded my throat, but I didn't want to give voice to them. I felt like once I gave life to the creeping thoughts and suspicions, I couldn't take them back.

But I needed to.

"I talked to Zoe yesterday, and she said some stuff that made sense."

"Zoe making sense? Never."

My smile was brief and my stomach full of knots. "Like, it's weird that Mom gave me Evie Dasher's life," I whispered, staring at the slowly churning ceiling fan. "I think she did it because she just missed Evie—the real one—but what she did wasn't fair."

Luc was so quiet, so still, I had to look at him. He was staring at me, pupils slightly dilated.

"It wasn't fair to me at all. I had a life. I had friends," I said, thinking how what Zoe had said was so full of truth it hurt. "I had friends that were my family. I had *memories,* and it just wasn't right."

His eyes closed, thick lashes fanning his skin. "No. It wasn't."

I swallowed hard. "Why didn't she just let me become me? Why make me become someone else?"

He turned his head away, throat working. "I don't know, Peaches."

"I started to text you yesterday, because what if that wasn't her reason? What if I'm just being willfully naïve? You don't trust her.

She did work for the Daedalus. What if there was a different reason?" The knot in my throat swelled, threatening to choke me. "Zoe told me something I can't get out of my head. She said that you took me to the Dashers around June and I wasn't seen again until I went to school, which was in November. And I don't know why that's bothering me so much, but it is."

Luc's eyes opened and his lips parted, but he didn't say anything.

"Is it true?" Wetness gathered on my lashes as I stared at his profile. "No one saw me during that time? Not once?"

He dragged his teeth over his lower lip, and unease built as several moments passed. "I didn't see you. No one did. I . . ." He looked over at me, placing the tips of his fingers against my cheek. "I don't think you stressing yourself out about this is going to do you any good."

"But—"

"There are a lot of things that are unexplained. Things I don't know the answers to, but right now, don't go down that road."

My gaze searched his. "What if I want to go down that road? Like, I want to run down that road?"

"If you want to, you'd have to go down it with her, but I want to be there if you do. Okay?" Luc asked, voice soft as his thumb moved along the line of my jaw. "I need to be there."

"Okay," I whispered, unsettled.

Feeling him lean in, I tensed and then, a heartbeat later, I felt his lips brush the center of my forehead. "Now, let's just try to relax and see what's on the TV."

I wasn't sure how I could ever relax again, but I nodded, watching him pull away, and then I picked up the remote. I turned on the TV and started mindlessly flipping through the blurry channels.

"Stop," he said. "It's Dee."

Luc was right.

She was on the screen, along with Senator Freeman, who looked seconds from blowing a major blood vessel along his temple. "President McHugh is within every right to repeal the Twenty-eighth Amendment."

"You're saying he's empowered to strip the rights of citizens of America?" Dee challenged. "Once he starts with the Luxen, who's to say it stops there?"

"Luxen are not American citizens."

"The Twenty-eighth Amendment says differently," Dee corrected him. "What the president wants to do is unconscionable—"

"What the Luxen have done to our planet is unconscionable, *Ms.* Black." The senator shook his head. "Luxen have killed indiscriminately, and now there is evidence suggesting that your kind is carrying some possible virus that's not only infecting but killing humans. What do you have to say about that?"

There was a crack in Dee's composure, a flushing of olive skin tone. "There is no way a Luxen is responsible for any virus or sickness. None whatsoever."

"So, you're suggesting that not only are our local governments lying but so is the CDC?"

"It wouldn't be the first time, now would it?" Dee replied. "If any report is claiming that Luxen are making humans sick, it's a lie, one that is biologically impossible. So, what you need to do and what all the viewers at home need to do is ask yourselves why anyone would lie about that."

19

What Dee said clicked things into place for me. I thought about how Heidi had questioned April's hate of Luxen and fierce defense of human rights. How ironic it was, considering April was obviously not human.

April had killed Andy and the family that had been local to the area, and while she hadn't admitted to a motive, it became rather obvious to me as I listened to the senator continue to rant about how violent and scary Luxen were.

"She wanted people to think it was a Luxen," I blurted out.

"What?" Luc looked over at me, brows raised.

"April! She killed Andy and that family in a way that would make you think a Luxen did it. Or an Origin. But no one knows you guys exist, so whatever," I continued. "Anyway, she was also out there, turning people against Luxen at school. I mean, she's amassed quite a following. None of this is coincidental, Luc. She was killing and making people think it was a Luxen. Why?"

Luc glanced at the TV to where Senator Freeman was now arguing with one of the human Luxen rights advocates.

"What if that family that the senator was talking about wasn't killed by a Luxen but by something that can make it look like it was? April can't be doing this alone. Murdering people and making it look like the Luxen were responsible. Getting people to hate and fear them. More people have to be involved, maybe even her parents."

"There are always more people involved."

"Then there has to be evidence of that. Maybe there is some evidence at her house. There might be something there that could point us toward whoever is responsible for those murders and maybe tell us what the hell April is."

He stared at me. "You're probably right, but you used the royal *we,* and *we* aren't doing anything. You're not going anywhere near April's house."

Irritation pricked at my skin. "Luc—"

"It's too risky."

"Everything is risky!" I nearly shouted as I shifted, rising onto my knees beside him. "Me being alive is freaking risky."

"Peaches . . ."

"It is! Just like you've said before, I'm a walking miracle. A rare example of the serums working for humans without mutating them. I live with an unregistered Luxen and I'm friends with them and you—and Zoe! Every single day is a risk."

"You're right, so let's not add to those risks." Those violet eyes flared.

I smacked my hands down on my thighs. "You just want me to do what? Stay closeted away in my house or school?"

"Uh." He frowned. "Yes."

"That's not fair. All of you are out there taking risks while I'm either sitting around doing nothing or getting people hurt—"

"You didn't get Heidi hurt."

I ignored that. "And I get that there isn't much I can do. You guys have superpowers. I'm pretty useless nine times out of ten—"

The frown deepened. "You're never useless."

I also ignored that. "But I can help here. I can look through stuff. This I can do."

Shaking his head, he looked away. A muscle along his jaw thrummed.

"I need to be able to do something," I reasoned, my gaze searching his face as I reached between us, placing my hand on his arm. "Please understand that I have to do something and help me instead of trying to stop me."

Luc tipped his head back, eyes closed as he pressed his lips together. Then he did the oddest thing. He laughed a deep, rumbling laugh.

Now it was my turn to frown. "What?"

He shook his head and then opened his eyes, sliding me a long look. "You want to know something about . . . Nadia?"

I tensed, not expecting him to say that.

"She was the only person who could get me to do something I didn't want to or didn't think was a good idea. No matter how much

I feared it was going to go sideways, she'd get me to do it. In reality, she had me wrapped around her pinkie." Thick lashes lowered. "We'll go to April's house tomorrow, after school."

My lips parted on a sharp inhale. Once again, Luc was saying so much while saying so little. I bit down on my lip, but there was really no stopping it.

I smiled.

A scream lodged in my throat as I shot up, gasping for air, my eyes peeling wide open. For a moment, I didn't understand where I was as the soft glow from the television shone light on the foot of my bed.

My heart hammered against its cage as I scanned my surroundings. I was in my bedroom, not in the woods outside the house, this time face-to-face with a bloody April instead of Micah. I was home. Safe. Heidi was safe. Micah was dead, and April . . . she was somewhere out there, God only—

"Evie?" The sleep-rough voice came from beside me.

In bed.

In my bedroom.

My head jerked to my left, and I saw the shape of Luc raising up on his elbow. He was still here? My mind was still clogged with sleep and images of April ripping apart—

"Hey." Luc sat up swiftly. His face was inches from mine as his hand moved in a slow, soothing circle along my lower back. "You okay?"

I swallowed the rise of nausea and croaked out, "Yeah."

His other hand came to my cheek. Even though I could barely see his eyes, I could feel his gaze inching over my face. He then carefully eased me back down so that my cheek was resting on his shoulder. There was space between our bodies—several inches, to be exact—but his arm was still around me, his hand balled in a loose fist, resting just above my hip, and my heart was still racing.

I kept my hands in the space between us. "You're still here."

"Yeah. Sylvia got home a little after midnight, I think. Then I fell asleep. Sorry."

"It's okay."

His other hand was resting low on his stomach. "Is it?"

Was it? I'd never hear the end of it if he were caught in my bedroom, sleeping beside me. Not like this was the first time, but neither of us knew where we stood with each other, and sleeping side by side surely wouldn't help anything.

Still, I nodded as my heart finally began to slow down.

Luc was silent for several long moments. "Nightmares?"

"Yeah," I whispered.

"Want to talk about it?"

I shook my head.

"Want me to stay?"

My legs curled under the soft blanket, pressing against Luc's leg. The blanket was usually on the floor somewhere, but he must've draped it over me at some point. I didn't speak. I couldn't.

I nodded.

The arm around my waist tightened, and the only sound was the low hum of conversation coming from the television. Luc didn't speak, but I saw his fingers moving. They were tapping in a slow rhythm against his lower stomach, and as my eyes adjusted to the dimly lit room, I could see that his shirt had ridden up when he'd lain back down, exposing a thin sliver of skin above the jeans he wore. I stared at those long fingers as they continued to move, thinking of the power those fingers could wield.

Slowly, my gaze lifted, traveling over his stomach to where his chest rose and fell steadily, almost as if he'd fallen back to sleep. I knew he was awake.

I wondered how many times we'd lain like this that I didn't remember, side by side with just the tiniest space between us—space that could easily become nonexistent if I just inched closer to him or lifted a hand.

Warmth flooded my skin, and I had the sudden urge to kick the blanket off. The thermal wasn't the greatest piece of clothing to wear to bed, but I knew the heat burning through my veins had little to do with the shirt I wore.

It had everything to do with who was lying beside me and what I felt for him. A confusing mix of yearning and trepidation.

My gaze found its way to his profile. His eyes were closed, but there was a tenseness to the line of his jaw. Was he as wide awake as I was? Every part of me became hyperaware of him—of each breath he took, how deep his chest sank and then rose, of the rhythm of his fingers. Was he as aware of me as I was of him in this moment?

I imagined it was countless times we'd lain like this, but I doubted I'd been thinking what I was thinking now. We'd been too young to harbor the images that were flipping through my mind. Memories of the night in his bed, our hands and mouths frantic and greedy. The quick kiss of thanks I'd bestowed upon him after seeing the framed photograph of Harpers Ferry. Us dancing hip to hip on Halloween and then him hovering over me, touching me, his mouth inches from mine.

If Dawson hadn't knocked on that door, Luc would've kissed me, and I would have *reveled* in it.

My pulse picked up, thrumming heavily as my fingers curled into the blanket between us. I needed to push these thoughts aside. It was late, and I'd just woken from a nightmare. Some really horrific stuff had gone down, so my mind wasn't exactly functioning at its best, but in the wake of a blood-soaked nightmare, there was a sudden sense of clarity that had eluded me at the lake on Sunday, that had eluded me since the first time I'd walked into Foretoken.

I was still trying to figure out who I was—if I was Nadia or Evie, and if that even mattered at the end of the day. I was struggling to find my place in Luc's world, to feel useful and less like a burden that needed to be protected. I was wary that after all that Luc had said and promised, he was still in love with who I used to be and not who I was today.

But knowing all of that didn't change that I remembered what it felt like to be held by him, or the sense that I was the only person in the entire world he'd move the universe for if need be. The uncertainty I felt didn't lessen the sweetness of him lying awake and watching funny videos with me or distracting me with terrible pickup lines. The wariness didn't overshadow his fierce protectiveness or how he understood when I needed space or when I needed to do something that didn't involve me staying behind. The confusion I felt over my past wasn't more powerful than how I'd felt the day he had held my hand and shown me Jefferson Rock.

All those things were when I was *Peaches* to him. Not Nadia. And what I felt had nothing to do with who I used to be or who I'd become. It had everything to do with who I was right now.

I wanted Luc.

I wanted his hands and his mouth on me.

I wanted to feel his body against mine.

I wanted to be his.

I wanted him to be mine.

I wanted his *trust*.

Closing my eyes, I shivered as the realization swept through me like a physical blow. I kept shivering, hands trembling, and as I inhaled deeply, the scent of him, fresh and outdoorsy, caused my breath to hitch. The shivers only increased because I knew what I was feeling, what I was wanting and I knew it was *me* wanting those things.

It was like suddenly waking up after years of a deep sleep. There was a swelling in my chest that felt like it could lift me straight to the ceiling were it not for his arm around me. The shivers didn't go away.

"Cold?" Luc murmured, his voice breaking the silence.

"Yes," I lied. Truthfully, I was burning up so badly that I might have spontaneously combusted.

In the shadows, I thought I saw him grin as if he knew better. Maybe he did. Maybe he'd been listening in on my thoughts this entire time, but I didn't care, because the arm around my waist curled, and then the front of my body was pressed against his side and my right leg tangled with his.

The contact fried my nerve endings. My chest became tight, heavy, and aching, and that fullness, that throbbing, slipped lower, between my legs, centering exactly where his thigh now rested against me.

The fist at my hip unfolded, and his palm flattened. Under the blanket, the heat of his hand burned through my thin sleep shorts. Then his thumb began to move, a slow circle that was a lot like he'd done against my back when I woke up, but there was nothing soothing about each pass of his thumb.

It was starting a fire in my blood, and there was a power in what I realized, what I was letting myself feel. Much like dancing on Halloween had made me feel.

Free.

I shifted my hips closer, hoping that his hand would move, would wander, but it stayed where it was, the circles getting smaller and smaller.

Whatever air I was managing to get into my lungs wasn't nearly enough as I placed my hand on his chest, just below his heart.

Luc became incredibly still. His thumb stopped, and his fingers were pressing into the flesh of my hip.

I didn't even feel his chest move as I dragged my hand down the flat surface of his stomach, to where his fingers had stopped tapping.

My fingers found his, tracing the elegant lines of his bones and tendons, over his knuckles and then the fine dusting of hair over his forearm.

"Peaches," he murmured. "You should be asleep."

In the darkness, my hand wandered up his arm, under the sleeve of his shirt. His skin was the most interesting combination of steel and satin. "I'm not sleepy."

Then his chest moved, deep and unsteady. "You should try to go to sleep. You have class in the morning. Try to be responsible."

The teasing in his tone brought a smile to my lips. "What if I don't want to be responsible?"

He shifted just the slightest, pressing his hard thigh against the softest part of me. I closed my eyes as he said, "Then you're a bad influence."

"I don't think anyone can influence you." I barely recognized my voice.

His head turned toward me, and when he spoke, I felt his breath on my forehead. "You are so very wrong about that."

I dragged my hand back over to his chest, to where I could feel his heart pounding. "Prove it."

Luc made this deep, throaty sound that curled my toes. "Evie . . ."

I bit down on my lip as I rose up on my elbow and stared down at him. Moving my hand from his chest, I placed my fingers against his jaw. The bristle of hair teased my fingertips as his hand slipped to my lower back. "I'm not sleepy," I repeated. "Are you?"

He looked up at me, and I saw a pinprick of white light where his pupils were. "Not even remotely at the moment."

"Sorry?"

One side of his mouth hitched. "There isn't a tiny part of you that is actually sorry."

He was right. "I was thinking . . ."

"About?" His hand trailed up my spine, tangling in the strands of hair that had come free during sleep.

"About something you said to me on Halloween." I drew my finger over his chin and then up, touching the center of his bottom lip. The hand in my hair formed a fist.

The pinprick of light grew brighter and wider. "What did I say to you?"

"You said it . . . it was only me. That it could only ever be me," I reminded him.

"Did I?"

My head cocked to the side as the corners of my lips started to turn down. "You don't remember?"

The hand in my hair loosened. "I do."

"Jerk." My eyes narrowed.

He responded with a quick nip to the tip of my finger, causing me to gasp as the bite sent a jolt straight through me. Those eyes held mine as I felt his lips close over my finger and the flick of his tongue.

My entire body tensed.

He gazed up at me. "What did I say to you? Can you repeat it? I have an incredibly short-term memory right now."

"You said it has only ever been me." Breaths coming out in short, shallow pants, I slid my damp finger on his lower lip. Smugness filled me when he gripped my hair again. "You said there's been no one else."

Those eyes took on a heavy, hooded quality. "I did say that."

I lowered my head, stopping inches from his mouth. "Is it true?"

"Yes." His voice was deeper, thicker.

The bridge of my nose brushed his. "Does it mean what I think it does?"

His other hand lifted from his stomach and landed on my hip. "What do you think it means?"

He was going to make me say it. "Does it mean you haven't been with someone?"

"There have been . . . others that I've had a few moments of . . . enjoyment with. Kissing," he said, gently tugging my head back, exposing my neck. "Touching. Learning. Some level of pleasure." His mouth found the center of my neck, and I shuddered. "But are you asking if I've ever been *with* someone?"

I flushed from the tips of my ears all the way to my toes. "Yes." My voice sounded coarse. "That's what I'm asking."

He pressed a tiny kiss to where my pulse beat. "Then the answer is no."

My eyes drifted shut.

"I could never be," he continued, tone raspy. "I never wanted to. Not with the memories of you and what we could've been."

The swelling feeling in my chest returned, and I thought if I had memories of him, it would've been the same with me.

But that wasn't the case. I lowered my chin, opening my eyes. Those pupils were all white now, bright as the sun. "I was with Brandon. We—"

"I don't care," he said. "That changed nothing for me. *Changes* nothing for me."

The next breath I took was shaky as I dropped my forehead to his. I didn't know what to do with the knowledge that he'd never been with anyone because of me. There was an absurd amount of possessive glee at that knowledge, and part of me knew I should feel bad about that, but I didn't.

"I'm still not sleepy," I whispered.

"I know."

I didn't respond. I didn't get a chance, because Luc shifted—moving faster than I could track. He rolled me onto my back, and then he was beside me, one hand on my hip and the other holding himself up. My heart about came out of my chest as he lowered his head to mine.

"Tell me what you want." His lips brushed mine in the darkness. "You need to say the words, Evie."

"You," I whispered into the space between our mouths, while my heart beat so fast I didn't understand how it could keep going. "I want you."

He shook his head, and a lock of his hair brushed my forehead. "You already have me. So, that can't be what you want now."

My heart clenched as the breath I held puffed out in a heady gasp. I lifted my hands, placing them on his shoulders.

"I think I know." His nose grazed mine. "You want my mouth." Those lips touched my cheek. "You want my hands." The hand at my hip squeezed. "You want my lips on yours."

He *had* been listening to my thoughts.

I tilted my body toward his, willing his hand to move, his lips to touch mine. Something.

Luc growled low in his throat as his hand pressed my hips back into the mattress. "No."

"No?" I repeated dumbly.

He nodded. "There's something you need to fully understand first."

I wasn't sure I was capable of understanding anything at this point, but I would try. "What?"

Those bright pupils latched on to mine, refusing to let me look away. "You have no idea how long I've waited for us to get to this point. I've fantasized about it. Dreamed about it. Had nightmares over it. There were times that I believed we would never get to this moment, but I never, *ever* gave up wanting this—wanting you. I never gave up hoping we'd find our way back to each other and that eventually we would be here, that you would find me and want me. That I would be worthy of you."

Worthy of me? How could he think that he wasn't?

"I want you so badly it hurts to breathe sometimes." His voice grew softer, but his words became more powerful. "There is nothing I want more than to lose every part of me in you. *Nothing.* And yeah, that's not an exaggeration. Screw world peace and fucking harmony for all species on this planet. You are all I've wanted for what has felt like forever."

Hearing his words was like being struck by lightning, and he wasn't finished.

"If I give you what you want, there's no going back. Are you ready for that?" His hand slid up my waist, stopping just below my breast. "Because I've already waited forever for this—*for you*. I've done nothing but watch and wait, and I am not walking away again. If I kiss you, if I touch you again, I will not be able to go back to the way things are now." The next breath he took trembled as much as I was. "I won't be able to pretend that you aren't my *everything*."

I couldn't breathe.

"That you'll always have me. That you'll always be mine," he continued, his words fast and heated. "Are you ready for that? Because it's intense, I know. I'm a lot to deal with. You think I'm a handful now? You haven't seen anything yet, Peaches. I'm needy when it comes to affection—your affection—and I've been *starving* for it."

And I was starving for *him*.

"So, tell me, *please,* did you really have a moment of clarity, Evie, or is this just a moment of need born out of a desire to distract yourself?"

I touched his cheek with trembling fingers, feeling his skin hum under my fingertips. I felt like I was about to step off a cliff. "I want you to kiss me."

A snarl of satisfaction left him, and then his mouth was on mine. No time was wasted. His lips parted mine in a deep, powerful kiss that left me shaken. His tongue slipped against mine as I pulled at his shoulders, dragging him to me, and for a moment, we were chest to chest as he tilted his head, his hand cradling my jaw.

Luc kissed like he *was* starving, like he could devour me with his lips, his tongue, and I wanted to be devoured whole. I tried to move, but the blanket had somehow tangled in our legs, keeping mine pinned. A groan of frustration broke our kiss, and Luc's thick laugh lifted the tiny hairs all over my body.

"Is that all that you wanted?" he asked.

I tried to shake my head, but his hand held my chin in place. I had to speak. I did. "No."

"What else?"

"You," I repeated. My hands slid down his sides, finding the bare skin underneath.

His head kicked back, and he groaned as my fingertips skated over the skin of his back. His chin snapped down, and he was kissing me once more, but he shifted off and onto his side. I didn't get a chance to protest.

Luc's hand left my chin and made its way down my throat. I moved with the path of his hand, arching as his palm grazed over the top of my breast. He didn't stop there, and disappointment flared.

"Later," he promised, and then his palm was trailing a lazy circle down my stomach, fingers slipping over my navel. His hand reached the band of my shorts.

I might've stopped breathing.

Luc's gaze was pure fire as his eyes lifted to mine. Just the tips of his fingers slipped under the soft material. "This? Is this what you wanted?"

I was beyond the ability to speak, my pulse pounding. All I could do was nod.

Electricity danced over his hand as it slipped fully under the band, and I bit down hard on my lip to keep from crying out. I tasted blood, and I didn't care. I reared off the bed as his fingers unerringly found their way.

"Yeah." His voice was thick as he stared down at his hand. "I think I know, but I just want to be sure. You know? What do you want now?"

I dragged in a deep breath as I vaguely realized he was going to make me say it.

One of his fingers moved, coming so close, a strangled sound came out of me. "Anything you want. Always. You just have to tell me."

"Touch me," I gritted out. "Please."

Those glowing eyes shot to mine. "Of course."

And then he touched me, and my hips bucked and my head fell back. I thought I heard him curse over the pounding of my blood. He might've said my name, but I couldn't be sure.

I was moving against his hand, hips lifting and twisting while he watched me, his eyes fixed to my face, soaking in every response. With anyone else, I would've been too uncomfortable, too self-aware to fully let go, but with him . . .

With Luc, anything seemed possible.

He swore again, and then he was leaning over me, taking from my lips as I clutched at him, my fingers digging into the taut skin of his side. He didn't let up. He didn't stop. My back arched off the bed, and he followed me, the tip of his tongue tasting the gasps parting my lips.

"I'm going to have to remember that," he murmured against my mouth. "You seem to really like it."

I did.

I so did.

Picking up my thoughts, Luc chuckled and then nudged my head back. His mouth blazed a hot path down my throat. "I know you're going to like this more."

My entire body jolted, legs curling, hips lifting. I grasped his wrist as a low moan escaped me. Not to pull his hand away but to keep it there.

"Knew it." He nipped my neck, eliciting a sharp cry from me.

His mouth closed over mine again, and I lost all sense of time, lost to the darkness of the room, to Luc. Breathing heavy against my parted lips, Luc cursed under his breath—

It was all too much.

The tension broke, and my cry was silenced by his mouth, by a kiss that was as fierce as the pleasure pounding through my body.

There was a good chance my heart stopped at some point, and the only reason I knew I was still alive was because I could feel the soft kisses Luc dropped along my damp brow, my closed eyes, the tip of my nose, and across my cheeks.

"Evie."

The way he said my name forced my eyes open, as if he were begging and cursing me in the same instant. There was a faint whitish glow surrounding him. His face was inches above me, and the need to shower him with the same attention powered through me. I wanted him to feel what I'd just felt, to share—

I reached for him, slipping my hand down his stomach, farther. My heart about stopped again.

Luc caught my wrist. "Peaches."

"What?" I strained against his hold. "I want to tou—"

"God," he groaned. "Don't finish that sentence. You're killing me."

"I don't have to finish the sentence. Just let me finish what I want to do."

His laugh was strangled. "You have no idea how much I would love to let you finish me."

My cheeks flushed.

"But not here." He lifted my hand to his mouth and he kissed the center of my palm. "We'll wake Sylvia."

I stared up at him. "Now you're worried about her?"

"Yeah. Trust me. I'll definitely wake her," he replied, and my brows lifted. "You want to give me something I want?"

"Yes." I did. I really did.

"Just let me hold you." He threaded his fingers through mine. "That's what I would like right now."

Based on what I'd felt seconds before, I doubted that was what he wanted, but I had forgotten that we weren't home alone, and we were pushing our luck.

"Later, then?" I felt my face burning. "We have later."

A soft smile played over his lips. "We do."

"Okay." I squeezed his hand. "I guess we can be responsible now and sleep."

He chuckled as he rose over me, kissing me quickly before settling beside me. A moment later, he had one arm underneath me and the other around me. My back was to his front, and he held me so close that there was no mistaking he was being responsible.

More so than I was.

I wiggled a little, grinning when he groaned in my ear. "Behave," he warned, squeezing the hand he still held. "And go to sleep."

"Okay." My grin grew into a smile and several moments passed. "Luc?"

"Yeah?" He sighed.

"Tha—"

"Please do not thank me for that," he cut in. "I know it was amazing. I could tell. I watched you the whole time. But it was my pleasure."

My eyes opened wide as I looked over my shoulder at him. "Wow, Luc. I was going to say that was something special."

"Oh, yeah, that, too."

"I wasn't going to thank you, because that would sound weird and those two words sound nothing alike." I placed my cheek back on the pillow. "You're so arrogant."

"You love it."

My breath caught in my throat. I did love his annoying arrogance. It made me laugh when it didn't tick me off. And I also loved how he was holding me, so tight there was no space between us, and with his fingers still threaded through mine. I loved what we'd just shared, because he found pleasure in giving me pleasure. I loved—

"Go to sleep, Evie."

Drawing in a shallow breath, I closed my damp eyes. I did go to sleep, faster than I thought possible, and I slept deeper than I had in months, maybe even years.

20

Luc was gone by the time the first rays of dawn began to creep through the window. I rolled over and took a deep breath. The pillow beside me smelled like him.

Closing my eyes, I shifted onto my back once more. Last night felt like a dream, but I knew it was real. Everything that I realized, everything that he said, and everything that we did.

I didn't regret a moment of it, not a single second, but that didn't stop the nervous flutter that forced me from the bed and into the shower.

Things had changed.

In me.

In Luc.

Between us.

I had all day to fixate over what exactly that meant and where it would lead, but right now there was another reason why I was rushing through getting ready an hour before I normally would be up.

I wanted to talk to Mom before she left.

Hair still damp, I hurried downstairs, greeted by the rich aroma of coffee. Mom was in the kitchen, pulling her travel mug out from the dishwasher. The cap of blond hair was tucked behind her ears, and she wore a black blouse and trousers. Her lab coat was next to her purse and briefcase.

"You're up early," she said, turning to me, and there was no mistaking the dark shadows under her eyes. "Is Luc upstairs?"

"What?" I stumbled to a halt, a whole different type of horror seizing my insides. Did she know . . . about last night?

She lifted a blond eyebrow. "Do you really think I don't know he hasn't broken his habit of knocking on your bedroom window like a thief in the middle of the night?"

Oh my word.

The centers of my cheeks heated. "A thief wouldn't knock on a bedroom window."

"Luc is the kind of thief that would."

I had no idea how to reply to that.

"I haven't said anything about Luc being here, because I know you're a smart girl," Mom began, and my eyes widened. This was not the conversation I was expecting nor wanting. Ever. "I also know after everything that's happened and after everything you've learned, you've needed the support, and I don't want to get in the way of that, so I've been very lenient with these visits, but he needs to start using the front door like a normal human being."

"He's not a normal human being," I pointed out, unable to stop myself.

That eyebrow stretched even higher. "He needs to start behaving like one."

"Okay. I'll tell him." I shifted my weight from foot to foot. "You got home late last night."

"Yeah, a lot of stuff has been going on at work." She walked over to the coffee maker.

"What's been going on at work? You've been working late a lot."

"I know." Pouring the coffee, she gave a little shake of her head. "It's the whole Luxen virus thing. We're basically chasing rumors and impossibilities to see if we've possibly missed some disease that was transmittable."

I went to the fridge and grabbed the OJ. I couldn't talk about Sarah, but that didn't mean I couldn't ask about her in a roundabout way. "Have there been more cases?"

"Just a few sporadic ones."

"Anything like what happened to Coop?" I asked.

Mom shook her head as she shoved the pot back into the coffeemaker. "Not that I'm aware of. Just more cases of people getting sick and some dying." She reached up, grabbing a glass and handing it to me. "Is this why you're up so early?"

No, it wasn't, and even though I wanted to prod her further on these cases, there was something else I needed to talk to her about before I had to go to school and she had to go to work.

I took my glass and juice to the island. "Actually, there's something I've been wanting to talk to you about."

She faced me, screwing the lid onto her mug. "Okay. I'm all ears for . . ." She glanced at the watch on her wrist. "For about fifteen minutes."

Fifteen minutes should be enough to go down the road that Luc wanted to be here for. He'd be ticked off if he found out what I was about to do, but I thought this was a conversation Mom and I would best have alone.

"I was thinking about after you gave me the serum that healed me."

"Oh." Surprise flickered across her face. "What about it?"

I poured my juice. "Luc brought me to you in June?"

Brows knitted, she nodded. "Yeah. Around the end of the month."

"How long . . . did it take for the serum to work?" I took a sip to wash away the dryness in my mouth and throat.

"It took a couple of days for the fever to break and then a week or so for you to completely heal," she said. "That's when I told you about . . . Evie."

"And then what?" I asked, my grip slippery on my glass. "I've been trying to remember that summer before I started school, and all I have are these vague recollections of reading books and watching TV, but nothing concrete. It's like when I try to think of who I was before I was given the serum."

"It was the fever and most likely a side effect of the serum." She placed her travel mug on a coaster. "It did some damage to your short-term memory."

She'd never mentioned that before, but I wasn't sure if that meant anything. "What did I do that summer? Was I just out of it?"

Mom placed her hands on the granite as her gaze seemed to sharpen. "What did—?" She wet her lips. "What did Luc say you did?"

Ice dripped down my spine, stiffening my body. "Luc didn't say anything." That part wasn't really a lie.

"Then why are you asking about this?"

"Because Zoe just pointed out that no one saw me until I showed up at school, and I remember that day. I remember the days leading up to that—back-to-school shopping and stuff—but I . . ." I swallowed hard. "I can't grasp on anything before that."

Was that relief that I saw loosen the features of her face or was I just being overly suspicious? I wasn't sure, but she sighed heavily as she tucked back the hair that had fallen forward. "You were recovering, Evie. You weren't really out of it, but you needed time to recoup and time—"

"For me to become someone else?"

She flinched, and I was torn between feeling bad and not feeling guilty at all. "Yes. There were days when you were perfect, but then you'd have no idea who you were. You weren't Nadia. You weren't Evie. You were just a shell of a girl. You needed time, so I kept you here."

I stared at her, my juice neglected. That made sense. Sort of. I doubted that after such an intense fever, I would be up and about, fully turned into the carbon copy of Evie, but . . .

"Is that what's bothering you?" she asked, her gaze searching mine. "I know Zoe probably didn't mean anything by talking to you about this, but I really wish she were more careful."

"About what?"

"About making you worry about things that don't really matter." She came around the island, stopping before me. "And you've obviously been worrying about it if you're up this early to talk about it with me."

I looked away. "Why?"

"Why what?" She cupped my cheek with her cool hand, guiding my gaze back to hers—to brown eyes that were familiar but weren't real. Contacts that hid who she truly was.

"Why did you give me Evie's memories?" I asked. "Why did you do that to me? Why didn't you just let me become me again?"

"I told you. I've asked myself that a million times, and I—"

"You missed the real Evie." I pulled away from her. "That wasn't fair to me." My lower lip trembled as I took a step back. "At all."

"I know." Pain sliced across her features. "Trust me, I know."

All day Tuesday, I kept expecting April to pop up at school, but she didn't, and no one seemed to be talking about her absence. Yet. Zoe and I both knew that wasn't going to last long.

And neither was keeping James in the dark.

"All I'm saying is just that y'all have been acting so weird," he was telling us as we trudged up the short hill that led to the parking lot.

"Who has been acting weird?" Zoe squinted as she dug around her bag for her sunglasses.

"All of you. Every last one of you." James pointed at me and then at Zoe and then in front of him. "That's me pointing at Heidi, who supposedly has mono."

"What do you mean *supposedly*?" I shared a look with Zoe. "You sound like people don't come down with mono."

"I have literally never met someone who has had mono at our age."

Zoe snorted. "That doesn't mean people don't get it all the time. She got it from Emery," she said, and I raised my brows. "Those two make out all the time."

"I don't care what any of you say. Each of you has been acting strange since . . ."

"Since when?" I asked.

"Since . . . *him*." James stopped, and Zoe and I did the same, following his gaze.

Luc was lounging against my car, long legs crossed at the ankles and arms folded over his chest. His eyes were hidden by silver aviators, and he wore the slouchy, gray knit beanie. He was dressed in dark denim jeans and a navy-blue Henley.

He looked good. Really good.

And just by looking at him, I immediately thought about last night—er, this morning—whatever. My entire body flushed, and even from where I was, I saw his lips curve up in a small, smug smile.

Egomaniac.

Nervous energy had buzzed around in my veins all day, partly because of the conversation with Mom, partly expecting April to show up, and partly due to what we were going to be doing tonight, but also because of Luc—because of us.

There was definitely an *us* now.

That smile of his kicked up on the other side, and I knew right then, the bastard was peeping in on my thoughts.

Then he tilted his head toward James, and that smile became downright predatory. He was like a large cat seconds before snatching up a mouse.

James and Luc had met briefly. It hadn't gone all that well. Not at all surprising—Luc didn't people well.

"Hey." Luc nodded at James.

"Hi," he grumbled, eyeing Luc like he wanted to ask for his ID, last known address, and possible aliases. "What are you doing here?"

"James." I smacked his arm.

Luc only chuckled as he pushed away from my car, approaching us. "I'm taking Evie to the movies," he said, and my brows rose as he dropped his arm over my shoulders. "Right, Peaches?"

We were so not going to the movies, but it wasn't like I could tell James the truth. I shot Luc a sharp look. "Something like that."

James's gaze bounced between us. "Can I go with you guys?"

"Actually, you're coming with me." Zoe, who knew what Luc and I were up to, looped her arm around James's.

"I am?" Surprise colored his tone as Luc's arm tightened around me.

"Yep." Zoe started tugging James away. "We're going to go to the store to get Heidi a get-well present. Something with chocolate and maybe some grapes."

"Chocolate and grapes?" Luc murmured, lip curling.

"Heidi loves to eat them together," I explained as Zoe waved back at us.

"That's gross."

I started to dip out from under Luc's arm, but he caught me and tugged me against him, front to front. I saw my eyes widen in the reflection of his sunglasses.

"Remember what I said last night?" he asked.

"You said a lot of things last night."

"I did, but I did warn you."

"Warn me about—"

Luc kissed me, and it wasn't like the fierce, starved kisses from last night. This was slow and sensual, a brushing of his lips over mine, once, twice, and then he urged the seam of my mouth apart. He deepened the kiss, and I tasted chocolate on his tongue as I sank into him.

When he finally lifted his mouth from mine, I was nearly panting for breath. "I warned you that I am needy."

"You did." That was about all I could say.

"Very needy."

I opened my eyes. "I can tell."

"Too much?"

"No," I whispered, and it wasn't.

"Good." Chuckling, he kissed my forehead and then stepped back. I stood there for a good minute trying to figure out what I was doing before I opened my back door and started to toss my bag in, but stopped, staring at the empty back seat.

Luc came up behind me. "What are you doing?"

Blinking, I shook my head. "I don't know. It just seems weird to not have my camera on my back seat or in my bag. April destroyed it. But it's not important. Ready?"

"Yeah." Luc walked over to the passenger side. "You sure James isn't into you?"

"Positive. And it wouldn't matter if he was, because I'm not into him like that." I opened the driver's door. "He just doesn't like you."

Luc rested his forearms on the roof of the car. "How can someone not like me? I'm awesome."

I narrowed my eyes.

"Actually, I'm adorable and well loved by the masses." He flashed a wide, way-too-charming grin. "Your friend has to like me."

My lips twitched. "Get in the car, Luc."

"I like it when you order me around. Especially last night when you were like, 'Kiss—'"

"Get in the car, Luc."

"Yes, ma'am." He gave me a jaunty salute.

Rolling my eyes, I got behind the wheel and closed the door. Hitting the ignition button, I glanced over at him.

"Wait." Luc leaned over, smoothing his thumb over my lower lip, sending a sharp thrill through my veins. Every part of my being became wholly aware of the pad of his finger. The contact was unexpected and brief, nothing like a kiss, but it still dazed me. "Got it."

"What?" I blinked.

"A piece of fuzz." A secretive little smile graced his lips as he settled back in his seat. "I thought we'd go to the club first. Give you time to visit with Heidi, get some food in you, and then we'll wait until the sun goes down. Sneaking around someone else's house is easier when it's dark."

That made sense, and it made me think that Luc had a lot of experience sneaking around places he shouldn't be. And I wanted to see Heidi something fierce. We'd texted throughout the day, and she sounded like her normal self, but I needed to see her with my own eyes. "Sounds like a plan."

Backing out of the parking spot, I kept my eyes on the busy parking lot.

"Anything interesting happen today at school?"

I shook my head as I lowered the window, letting the cool autumn air roll through the car. "Not really. No one seemed to think anything about April not being at school. Her group was protesting this morning."

He stared out the passenger window, hands resting on his bent knees. His profile was striking, especially in the bright autumn sun. It was criminal to wear a knit beanie so damn well.

"Hopefully they'll find a new hobby," he said.

"One would hope, but I doubt it. It's like April woke something up in them, gave them something to blame all their problems on."

Luc nodded slowly. "I was trying to be optimistic."

I snorted. "Well, I'm just being realistic."

"Peaches?"

My heart skipped. "Yeah?"

"The light is green, so . . ." He looked over at me, lips turned up at the corners. "You're going to need to stop staring at me and drive."

I blinked, flushing. "Oh. Yeah. You're right."

Luc chuckled.

Heidi had looked like she'd spent a month at a spa, skin glowing and her appetite utterly staggering. Even compared to mine. She'd downed the burger Kent had brought up from the kitchen and three cupcakes that had come from one of the nearby bakeries.

I'd eaten two cupcakes, and probably would've had more if Kent hadn't swiped the last two on his way out.

I spent the better part of the afternoon with Heidi and Emery, and it wasn't until the sun began to set that there was a knock on Emery's door. Figuring it was Luc and he was ready to engage in a little breaking and entering, my stomach was twisted in knots as I gave Heidi a kiss on the cheek and hugged Emery, the latter returning the gesture with the awkwardness of all non-huggers in the world.

Then I stepped out into the hallway. Luc had ditched the knit beanie and sunglasses, and his bronze, messy waves were adorably sticking up in every direction.

"Hey." I felt weirdly shy as I clasped my hands together.

His gaze trekked over my face. "How was Heidi?"

"Perfect. Like she's been on a monthlong vacation. Even Emery doesn't look exhausted."

One side of his mouth kicked up. "That's what love will do."

My gaze lifted to his, and he pushed off the wall. I didn't know exactly what to do as he closed the distance between us. The night before, I'd been brazen and confident, but a timidness crept into me as he stopped in front of me. It was like I'd never been in a relationship before, and even though we hadn't bestowed labels on each other, I knew that was what we were trying to do.

Maybe it was because now I was in a relationship that mattered and that was why this felt different? Like it was the first *everything*?

His gaze caught mine, and I looked away, letting out a shaky laugh. "I'm sorry. I'm being weird. It's just that I don't know how to act now."

"Just be yourself," he said, catching a strand of hair and tucking it back behind my ear. "Or be a unicorn. One of the two."

I laughed again. "You're bizarre."

"Bizarrely charming," he corrected, his hand lingering behind my ear. "Ready?"

I started to nod but stopped. "You and me. We're doing this, right? The together thing? Like boyfriend and girlfriend?" Warmth crept into my cheeks. "I haven't said anything to Zoe or Heidi, because I just . . . I don't know. Wanted to make sure that's what we are?"

Luc stared at me so long I began to get a little worried. Then he leaned in, bringing his mouth close to my ear. "If you have to ask that, then maybe I wasn't clear enough last night. There is only you and me. Boyfriend. Girlfriend. Mates. Lovers," he said, and muscles low in my stomach curled tight. "I don't care what you call me as long as you call me yours."

God.

God.

I melted right there, dropping my forehead to his chest. His hand slipped around to the nape of my neck.

"Okay?" he said. "Am I clear now?"

"Yes," I said to his chest.

"You ready, then?"

"Yeah."

"You've got to lift your face off my chest first."

"Right."

He chuckled, and then I lifted my head.

"It's okay," he said.

"What is?"

"To be nervous."

My gaze found his. "About what we're going to do tonight?"

"Well, yeah, about that, but I'm saying it's okay to be nervous or not know how to act because of us," he said. "I'm nervous, too."

"Really?" I said doubtfully.

"Really." His gaze searched mine. "You are the only person whose opinion I ever cared about."

The next breath I took hitched somewhere around my racing heart.

"I worry that I am *too* much, because I know that I am." His head tilted to the side. "I worry that what I want is going to rush you into wanting it. I worry that I . . . that I could never be good enough for you."

I stared at him, shocked. "How could you . . . ?" I shook my head. "You are good enough, Luc, and you aren't too much."

His brows lifted.

"Well, okay, you are a lot, but it's a lot that I like, and that's why it's okay." I placed my hands on his chest, and under my palm, I could feel his heart thrumming as fast as mine. "I can't believe you're nervous or that you think you're not enough."

"Just because I don't show it doesn't mean I don't feel it." He swallowed then, and his voice lowered. "I haven't done this at all, Peaches. I've never been in a relationship or held a hand before I held yours. I've done things with others, but you are my first . . . my first in a lot of things. How could I not be nervous?"

I didn't know what to say, because I knew inherently that words wouldn't matter in this moment. Not after what he'd admitted in a hushed voice.

Stretching up, I cupped his cheeks and brought his mouth down to mine. I kissed him, and in that kiss, I hoped he could feel what his words meant to me, what they did for me.

And I thought he did, because when I settled on my feet again and slid my hands back down his chest, his chest was rising and falling heavily.

The smile that tugged at Luc's lips warmed as he took my hand. Now knowing it wasn't just me that was nervous and worried, I felt the shyness seep away as he led me downstairs and out the back entrance to the alley. Kent was waiting for us there, behind the wheel of a black SUV, and by then, I'd pulled it together.

"Whose car is this?" I asked as I opened the back passenger door.

Luc smiled at me, and I decided that I probably didn't want to know who this vehicle belonged to and how they came to acquire it. "I figured it was best to not be in your car in case things go sideways," he said as he closed the door.

The knots in my stomach tightened as I leaned forward, gripping the back of his seat. "Do you think things will go south?"

"I don't think so, but it's better to be prepared."

"And if things start to go badly, that's why I'm here, honeybuns." Kent waved at me, and I frowned, having no idea why he called me that. His mohawk touched the ceiling of the SUV. "I'm one hell of a getaway driver."

"Is that something you have to do a lot?"

He smirked at the rearview mirror. "If you only knew."

My gaze swung to the back of Luc's head. How often did they need a getaway driver? Was it when they were moving unregistered Luxen? I sat back, clasping my hands together in my lap as I thought about all the things Luc and his crew did that I had no idea about.

That was going to need to change.

But right now, I needed to focus on my blossoming felonious aspirations.

It didn't take too long to get to April's place. She lived just outside the city, off a long stretch of road. The subdivision was smaller, houses spaced farther apart. Kent parked on a different block, remaining in the car as Luc and I climbed out. The streets were empty and quiet with the exception of the random car or distant, barking dog.

I was desperately trying not to think about what we were doing. While this had been my idea, I'd never broken into anyone's house, especially the house of a psychotic creature.

Then again, who knew? Maybe when I was Nadia, I'd been a badass burglar on the prowl.

My hands were trembling, so I shoved them in the pockets of my jeans as we crossed onto April's street and stepped up on the sidewalk.

"You doing okay over there?" Luc asked.

"I'm nervous," I admitted. "And I am not talking about us."

He glanced over at me. "That's expected. Not like you engage in a little bit of breaking and entering on a daily basis."

"Do you?"

He chuckled under his breath as April's two-story, colonial-style home came into view. "I have been known to break into a house or . . . twenty."

I shot him a look. "Nice."

"You don't have to do this. You can wait with Kent, and that would be okay. Actually, I'd prefer it."

"No," I immediately responded. "I can do this."

Luc nodded as he cut toward the side of the house, passing numerous dark windows. The backyard was fenced, but the gate was open, framed by overgrown butterfly bushes. I could see the outline of a large, outdoor play set. A swing swayed in the breeze, making a soft creaking sound. A wave of goose bumps rose along my arms, under my sweater.

I stopped.

So did Luc.

Instinct roared to life, screaming that we were being watched. No sooner had that thought finished, a shadow peeled away from the back of the house, stepping underneath the faint glow of a solar light.

Grayson.

God.

Relief nearly doubled me over as the tall Luxen said, "No one is inside. At least not alive."

My hand fluttered to my stomach. "Is someone . . . dead inside?"

"If there is, I haven't seen them."

"Then why would you . . . ?" I trailed off, immediately deciding it wasn't worth the time or energy to understand why he'd phrased it like he had.

Luc walked up the short set of steps and onto the porch. "Did you guys check out anything yesterday?"

He shook his head. "We just looked around to see if April was here, and that was about it. Then Zoe and I went to several of her known friends' houses. The house is unlocked, and no one has been here as far as I can tell."

"Perfect." Luc glanced back to where I stood. "Want to head in?"

Throat dry, I nodded as I came up the small set of steps, aware of Grayson watching me.

"You sure this is a good idea?" Grayson asked. "Her?"

I stopped and looked at the Luxen.

"Gray." Luc sighed.

"What? She has no experience in these kinds of things." Grayson had a point, the jerk. "She shouldn't even be here."

"I didn't know we needed your opinion," I snapped, and I could practically feel Grayson's laser-like gaze narrowing on me.

"We don't." Luc's tone was even. "Go keep Kent company."

Grayson stiffened. "Shouldn't I be keeping you guys company?"

"Are you going to be able to keep your mouth shut?" Luc returned.

The Luxen seemed to mull that over and then groused, "No."

I rolled my eyes.

"Then peace out."

Sending me one last wrathful look, Grayson was nothing but a blur as he left the porch, off to find Kent.

"Why does he hate me?" I asked when I was sure he was gone.

Luc paused in the entryway. "He doesn't hate you, Peaches."

I laughed at that. "Oh, come on. He totally hates me."

Shaking his head, Luc drifted into a dark mudroom. "You're reading it wrong."

"Pretty sure I'm reading him exactly right."

A whitish glow surrounded Luc's hand as he proceeded into the kitchen, guiding our way. "Once we close some of these curtains and blinds, we can probably turn on a few of the lamps."

I nodded as I crept behind him, scanning the area. A wooden bowl sat in the middle of the island. There were bananas in it, still fresh. I passed a fridge cluttered with random magnets. There were letters, but not pieced into any kind of word I recognized. Luc moved ahead, systematically closing blinds and curtains, using the Source to guide his way.

The kitchen flowed into a dining room and then a living room with fluffy pillows everywhere. There were magazines on the coffee table, coasters from a local bar on the end tables. The room smelled like apples, and everything about it seemed normal.

Turning, I spied the steps and made my way to them. I'd been to April's house a few times over the years, so I knew where her bedroom was upstairs. Luc and I went up the carpet-covered stairs, our steps silent, and entered a long hallway.

It was strange being here now, wondering if everything about April had been a performance she'd wanted us to see. Had she always been this . . . whatever this was? Was her hatred of Luxen real or an act? Did she know what Zoe was, and when we'd been friends, had any of that been real?

"There's something odd about this house," Luc said as he opened a door and found the linen closet.

"What makes you say that?" I moved along the other side of the wall.

"There's not a single sound here. No fan. No bumps or bangs of air kicking on and off." Now that he pointed it out, I realized he was right. "It's like walking through a graveyard—a haunted graveyard."

I shuddered as I opened the door to what appeared to be a guest bedroom. "Thanks for putting that in my head."

"You're welcome." A door opened, and then Luc said, "You said she had a little sister, right?"

"Yeah."

"This must be her room." He stepped inside. "There's some clothing laid out on the bed. Looks like something that belongs to a child."

My fingers curled over the cool handle, heart thumping. Where was April's family? Were they whatever she was, including her little sister? I moved ahead, pushing open the door to April's bedroom with one hand while I fiddled with the obsidian hanging from my necklace, rubbing my thumb along the smooth rock. The blinds in this room were already drawn, and I hurried over to a bed, turning on the lamp. I saw the makeup vanity first, where several tubes of red lipstick were neatly stacked in a little cubby.

"Jackpot," I heard Luc say from somewhere out in the hallway. "Found an office."

Her room was impeccably neat, much . . . like Mom's. Everything had its own place. A small bookshelf with books lined up in . . . *alphabetical order?* I squinted. Yep. Wow. Scarves rolled up in a basket on top, makeup stacked in cubbies, and her desk free and clear of clutter. It was like I remembered.

On the center of her perfectly made bed was a stuffed unicorn.

I knew that unicorn.

During the summer after school started back up, the summer I remembered, we'd gone to the county fair. Zoe had won that stuffed unicorn and had given it to her.

I don't know how long I stared at the unicorn, but I finally tore my gaze from it and approached her desk, opening the drawers. Nothing but staplers and an assortment of colorful paper clips. Her walls were bare. No pictures. No paintings or posters, and I thought she'd had photos before. I turned to her dresser, letting go of the obsidian.

I really didn't know what I was looking for. Not like there would be a diary April kept, explaining everything.

Though that would be helpful.

Opening the first drawer, I saw a bunch of undies and winced. Was I really going to go—

Luc suddenly appeared behind me, folding his arm around my waist, drawing me back against his chest. "Someone is here."

21

My heart jumped into my throat as I whispered, "What?"

"Just came through the front door."

"Shit," I hissed, stomach hollowing.

"I want to see who it is and what they're up to."

I nodded, hoping that meant no one was killing anyone tonight. Unless it was April. I was totally down with killing her.

A grin flashed across Luc's face. "Bloodthirsty. I like it."

There was no time to be annoyed with him reading my thoughts. Luc, obviously way more skilled at this kind of stuff, launched into action. Moving fast, he picked me up as if I were nothing more than a stunned kitten. The dresser drawer closed, and the lamp flipped off without him touching it, pitching the room into darkness as he spun toward the closet door.

Footsteps pounded up the stairs, nowhere near as quiet as we'd been. My body flashed hot and cold. A second later, I was pressed back among shirts and sweaters as Luc quietly and quickly closed the closet door behind him.

Hangers swayed, clacking off one another and sending a plume of dust into the air. My hand snaked out, and I caught them, stilling the little bastards a handful of seconds before April's bedroom light came on.

My heart was speeding so fast I thought I might be sick as Luc reached behind him, placing his hand on my hip. There was no space between us as he stepped back, keeping me against the wall.

The last time we'd been in a closet, it had ended with a stolen kiss and flying ART officers.

I was really hoping there were no ART officers involved this time.

Through the tiny gaps in the slats of the closet door, I saw a woman wearing black trousers stride into the room.

I gripped the back of Luc's shirt, pressing my lips together. He squeezed my hip in return. Whoever was in the room opened the dresser I'd been at—

My nose suddenly tickled and itched. The dust! The tickling grew until my eyes watered. Oh no. I could feel it. A sneeze building in the back of my nose.

Oh no. Oh no. Oh no.

This was a terrible idea. Horrible idea. I was going to spin-kick myself in the face for coming up with this.

I squeezed my eyes shut as my fingers dug into Luc's back. He turned his head toward me, and I planted my face into his back, praying to God I could stop the sneeze, because I knew if we were exposed, Luc would react first and think later, and we had no idea who was out there, if they were bad or good . . . or human.

The drawer closed, clicking into place. A shiver of electricity danced over my skin, radiating from Luc. Tension poured from his body, electrifying the small space. Could he tell I was about to sneeze? Was he reading my—

It happened.

My entire body jerked as the sneeze came out as a small *achew.*

"Shit," Luc muttered.

Eyes wide, I jerked my head back just in time to see the woman in front of the dresser spin toward the closet doors.

Everything happened so fast.

Luc shoved me back as the closet door swung open, slamming into the wall. A whitish, snapping energy powered down his arm, spitting sparks into the air around us as the woman lifted her arm. A bolt of Source left Luc's outstretched hand.

Pop. Pop. Pop.

The woman screamed as her body spun around, arms pinwheeling. A gun. She'd been holding a gun before it flew into the air along with something white, and then both fell to the carpet as she hit the bed, clutching her shoulder.

Luc staggered into me, and my arms went around him, trying to catch him, but it was no use. He was too large and heavy. I was hit with a wicked sense of déjà vu as Luc went down onto one knee, his grunt of pain sending a jolt of pure terror through me as his weight dragged me down to the space between the closet and the bed.

No.

No way.

Red, nickel-sized holes appeared in the front of Luc's shirt, and those holes quickly started to leak, running down the front of his stomach.

"No!" I shouted as I gripped his shoulder. This wasn't possible. This was Luc. He couldn't be shot. "*No.*"

That word didn't change reality. Luc—oh God—Luc had been *shot*. Three times. Horror gripped me with icy talons.

I can't do this without him.

The voice that entered my thoughts sounded like mine but wasn't and carried a heaviness that felt like years in the making.

Panic exploded as Luc rolled onto his back, eyes screwed tightly shut and lips thinned. The glow of the Source flickered around his arm and then went out as the veins under his eyes filled with brilliant white light, becoming visible under the skin. Those holes—those wounds—seemed to be spreading. I placed my hands over them, trying to staunch the flow of . . . reddish-blue blood.

"Luc," I whispered. He was powerful. He was a freaking superhuman, but he had been shot in the chest three times, and he had a heart in that wrecked chest. I'd felt it beating, and one of the holes—oh God—

I cut those thoughts off.

Luc was going to be okay. He had to, because I could not lose him. Not like this. *Not ever again*—

The woman rolled off the bed onto the other side. My wide gaze swung around the room, spotting the gun lying a few feet in front of me.

Scrambling forward on my knees, I snatched the gun up as the woman rose, swaying unsteadily. The metal pressed into my palm as I leaped to my feet and I got my first real good look at her. She was older, with dark hair pulled back in a ponytail. I'd never seen April's mom. This woman didn't look like her, except for the ghoulish red lips, but who else could it be? One hand was pressed into her shoulder. Blood poured down her arm.

She screamed, rushing me, and I . . .

Instinct roared to the surface, taking over. My brain clicked off as I leveled the gun and pulled the trigger. I didn't hear the crack of the gun firing, but the bullet struck true. The woman jerked backward, arms going limp as she fell onto the bed, sliding about an inch or so before stopping. Her chest didn't move. Her eyes were open, wide and unseeing. Her forehead . . .

A haze of familiarity crept along the edges of my thoughts, just out of reach of me grasping it and making sense of it. There was this sense of being here before—having done this before? That couldn't be right, though. I'd never even held a gun before.

I sure as hell had never shot anyone before, but a voice whispered at the edge of my subconscious. *You pick up a gun, you aim to kill. Not to wound. To kill.* That voice . . . it was familiar . . .

Slowly, I lowered the gun.

"Evie," Luc groaned, and I jerked as his pained voice snapped me into action.

"Luc!" Whipping around, I dropped to the floor beside him, placing the gun on the floor next to me. I reached for him, pulling up his shirt. A slice of panic cut through me as I saw the three wounds. One on the left side of his chest, entirely too close to where his heart was. One on the right. Another just below. Blood trailed down his stomach, glimmering blue in the light.

His eyes were open, those pupils a brilliant white as he lifted his head off the floor. "This was . . . my favorite shirt."

"What?" I laughed, but it came out as a strangled sob. I touched his forehead, brushing his hair back and leaving a smudge of blood behind—his blood. "It's just a stupid shirt, Luc. You're bleeding badly. You've been—"

"Poked full of holes. I know."

"Tell me what I need to do," I begged, because I knew it wasn't like I could call 911. "Because this can't be good."

"Get my phone out of my pocket. The right one. It'll be unlocked. And call Grayson. It's not that bad, so he can fix this."

"Not that bad? You have three bullet holes in your chest!" I shouted at him as I reached into his right pocket, pulling out his phone and quickly finding Grayson's number.

The Luxen answered on the first ring. "Yo."

"Luc's been shot," I said.

"So? Wouldn't be the first time."

Wouldn't be the first time? *What?* My gaze swung to Luc's pale face. "He's been shot multiple times in the chest, you asshole!"

Luc's chuckle ended in a groan. "Ouch."

"You should've said that first." Grayson hung up.

"I *think* he's coming." I slipped his phone into my back pocket.

"He's coming. With his help, I'll heal . . . faster, but . . ." Lifting one arm, his brow pinched as the whitish-blue light swallowed his hand. "You may want to look away, because this is . . . gonna be gross."

There was no way I was going to even blink, because I feared if I did, he would stop talking, stop breathing, and I couldn't risk that.

"I've got to get these bullets out. There's something . . . off about them." Luc's jaw clenched, and his head kicked back against the carpet as his hand trembled and the light of the Source pulsed. A heartbeat later, his back arched and then three bullets tore free from his chest, hovering under his palm.

My mouth dropped open as I fell back on my ass. "Holy shit."

I couldn't even believe what I was seeing, and I'd seen Luc do some crazy stuff before. Rip up trees from the roots. Throw Micah several feet through the ground. Recover from injuries that would kill a human in under a nanosecond. But this . . .

Luc collapsed back, breathing heavily. "Fun times."

"How?" I pitched forward, grasping his hand. "How did you do that?"

"Special," he gasped, his pupils ultra-white as he looked at me. "I'm not a . . . weapons expert, but they don't look like normal bullets to you, do they?"

The bloodied, small, cylindrical bullets were . . . odd. The rounded tips were clear, and inside was something that looked like blue light or water.

"No." I watched his hand close around them. "Shouldn't they look more . . . used?"

"I think so. Something must've gone wrong with them." A trickle of blood seeped out the corner of his lip. "I'm sorry."

I shook my head as I quickly wiped away the smear of blood along his mouth. "For what?"

"You having to shoot her. I should've taken her out."

Muscles along my back locked up as I brought his hand to my chest. "It's not your fault. I sneezed like an idiot, and I had to do it. Right? She shot at you immediately, before she could even see who you were. She had to be bad, right?"

"Right."

His eyes closed, and my heart stopped.

"Luc! Open your eyes. *Please*."

When he did, his pupils were black once more, and all the blood seemed to have drained from his face.

"I've seen you get impaled with branches and get back up, but—"

"Something is up with the bullets."

"What—"

"Well, this is a freaking mess," Grayson announced from the doorway, and then he was beside Luc, checking out his chest. "Can it wait until we get you out of here?"

"He can't wait." I squeezed Luc's hand. "Fix him."

Piercing blue eyes met mine. "You're a curse, you know that?" Grayson spat. "Heidi yesterday. Luc today. Who's the lucky SOB going to be tomorrow?"

I sucked in a shrill breath, unable to respond, because I *was* beginning to feel like a curse.

"Shut up," Luc groaned, "and get me out of here."

Grayson shook his head as he got an arm under Luc's shoulders, helping him sit up and then stand. I rose, legs shaky as I let go of Luc's hand. I turned to the bed—

"Don't," Luc groaned. "Don't look at her, Peaches. No good will come from that."

Luc was probably right. As I started to avert my gaze, I saw it on the carpet: the item the woman must've pulled out of the dresser. It was a small white zippered pouch about the size of a hardcover book. I grabbed it, and then I followed Luc and Grayson through the house and out the back door. The fact that Luc was upright was nothing short of a miracle.

Thank God Kent was pulling up to the curb as we burst out from around the side of the house.

Barely able to catch my breath, I looked back at April's house. There was a sedan in the driveway that hadn't been there before.

Everything looked normal, but the neighbors had to have heard something.

"Peaches," Luc said, tone urgent.

The back door of the SUV was open, and I climbed in, scooting over as Grayson helped Luc into the seat beside me. Immediately, I reached out to grab Luc's hand.

"How can I help?" I asked, placing the white pouch beside me.

He rested his head back against the seat, jaw working. "Just be here."

"I can do that," I promised, heart squeezing as the back of my throat burned. "I can definitely do that."

"Are you going to bleed all over the inside of this car?" Kent was leaning between the two front seats. "Because I'm, like, an Uber driver. Blood or vomit, I'm going to hit you with a fine." Kent gave me a look. "Would you like water?"

I stared back at him.

"He likes to pretend that he's an Uber driver sometimes." Luc's grin was weaker than normal. "And he doesn't have water."

Kent rolled his dark eyes. "I wanted to run out and get water, but someone—Grayson—said we didn't have time. It's like no one understands my dreams and aspirations."

"No one understands anything about you, Kent."

I yelped as the door behind me suddenly opened. Zoe climbed in, startling me. "How . . . ?"

"Our Uber driver Kent called." She closed the door behind her. "Figured you guys could use an extra hand."

"Luc's been shot," I told her as Grayson climbed into the front passenger seat. "Like, three times."

"I can see." She winced as she leaned around me. "Can't believe you let yourself get shot. Again."

"You guys are so sympathetic," Luc muttered as Kent pulled away from the curb.

"Why do you all keep acting like this happens often?" I twisted toward Luc. "Does this happen often?" My voice pitched. "Do you get shot a lot?"

Luc fell quiet.

I turned to Zoe, who was studiously staring out the window. "Does he get shot a lot?"

"Don't answer that," Luc ordered.

"What?" I shrieked.

"You know, I just want to remind everyone in this vehicle what a bad idea I thought going into that house was," Grayson announced. "But no one ever listens to me."

"Is there a point to your statement, Grayson?" Luc asked.

"Not really."

Half of Luc's face was in the shadows, but I thought I saw a hint of a smile. "You didn't have to come here."

Shaking his head, Grayson turned around as we passed a set of headlights heading toward the subdivision. "Like I had a choice."

"You can't see me," Luc said. "But I just rolled my eyes so hard that they fell out of the back of my head."

"Can you two just not right now?" Zoe snapped, and I 100 percent agreed with her. "Pretty sure you look like you're going to pass out, Luc."

He did.

"Really?" Grayson twisted toward us. "I can heal you now, because I'm sure as hell not carrying you."

"I think you should definitely heal him now," I told Grayson.

He ignored me.

"I'm not going to pass out," Luc grumbled. "I never pass out."

"You'd better not, because you're heavy," Grayson muttered. "And that's not how I want to close out my evening."

"Sometimes you have to do things you don't want to do," Luc retorted.

"Like right now?" Grayson shot me a look.

"Well, now I want to pass out, just so you have to carry me." Luc's hand spasmed around mine.

"Zoe can carry you," Grayson replied.

"Yeah, I could. Why? Because we Origins are nowhere near as whiny as Luxen."

"You sound like you just realized that." Luc's chuckle ended in a wet-sounding cough. "Come on, everyone knows that. *Luxen* means . . . 'over-entitled crybaby' in Latin."

"No," Grayson said, peering into the back seat. "It doesn't."

Zoe snickered. "Actually, I think *Luxen* means 'lack of personality' in Latin."

"Yeah, that sounds about right." Luc nodded.

"Hey, guys . . ." Kent had one hand on the steering wheel as the SUV picked up speed. "Behind us."

I twisted in the seat at the same time Zoe and Luc did. The car that had passed us going the other way had pulled a U-turn and was catching up to us. High beams came on, causing me to wince.

"Here we go." Luc tipped his head back and let out a wild laugh, the kind of laugh that might've been infectious in any other situation. "Things are about to get really interesting."

Things were *about* to get interesting? Were all of them out of their minds? I was pretty sure that the answer was *yes*, and I had a really bad feeling about Luc's laugh.

"Is it just one car?" Grayson asked.

Luc nodded. "Appears to be."

The headlights were getting closer, and my head was suddenly filled with images of epic car chases that ended with flesh mangled with metal.

"You need to put your seat belt on." Luc lurched forward, patting around the crease of the seat, looking for the belt.

I stared at him like he'd grown a hand in the center of his forehead and was flipping me off. "You're worried about a seat belt?"

"Yes. I don't want you to go through a windshield or something." He couldn't find the belt. There was a good chance I was sitting on it. "Can you move? I think it's behind you or Zoe."

As I leaned forward, Luc spoke directly in my ear. "We'll be fine."

Before I could respond, Grayson's veins lit up. My breath caught. It didn't matter how many times I saw a Luxen take their true form, it was still a shock to see them do it and be this close.

A white sheen filled the inside of the SUV as the light in his veins seeped into his skin, replacing bone and tissue. Heat flared as if the hot air had been kicked on, and I shrank back, pressing into the seat. The glow was so intense, like staring into the sun, and I had to shield my eyes. I had no idea how Kent was able to drive.

Within moments, Grayson was encased in light, and he was beautiful—like I imagined an angel looked. All he was missing was the wings.

"I think we need some music." Kent hit a button on the steering wheel, and music blasted out of the speakers, startling me.

Music? Now was a good time to turn on *music*? Was he for real?

He was.

At first, I didn't recognize the fast tempo of the drums or the words. Maybe under difference circumstances, I would've, but it was just noise—loud noise that made everything feel more surreal, so much more out of control. My heart rate kicked into overdrive as the white pouch slid from the seat, landing near my feet.

Tires screeched as Kent slammed on the brakes, pitching me forward. I would've ended up on the dashboard if Luc hadn't thrown his arm out, clotheslining me. He grunted as the music flowed, "*Oh! I see a man in the back—as a matter of fact his eyes are as red as the sun. And the girl—*"

Zoe grabbed my flailing arm, pulling me back as the SUV suddenly careened, going up on two wheels as we spun in the middle of the road, skidding across asphalt.

"Oh my God! Oh my God!" I yelled.

"Seat belt!" Luc shouted.

Grayson threw open the passenger door as the lyrics screamed, "*And the man in the back said, 'Everyone attack,' and it turned into a ballroom blitz.*"

Grayson exploded from the vehicle, holding on to the swinging door. For a split second, I was sure he had to be roadkill, but then he shot past our SUV, a blur of light shaped like a human.

"What's he doing?" I shouted, twisting around as the SUV fishtailed, spinning like a top. My stomach heaved, and I smacked my hand over my mouth. Beside me, Luc hummed along with the music, his fingers tapping off his knee as the entire world spun, completely unaffected as he continued to look for my seat belt while bleeding from *three bullet wounds*.

In his true form, Grayson appeared between the SUV and the car. His light pulsed, flaring with a reddish tint.

The window beside Zoe shattered, spraying shards of glass everywhere—at my face, in my hair. Someone—Zoe or Luc—pushed on the back of my head.

A bolt of light shot out from Grayson, hitting the front tires of the vehicle.

Sparks flew out from under the front of the car, and it went completely airborne, flying right into the air as the speakers screamed.

The car flew over the SUV, flipping like a cartwheel, hood over trunk. My mouth dropped open.

The car slammed down on its roof on the other side of us, shaking our SUV.

"I'm going to be sick," I moaned, not fighting when my head was shoved down again. "I'm going to be so sick."

"And the girl in the corner said, 'Boy, I want to warn you . . .'"

I jumped as I heard Grayson slam the front passenger door shut.

The SUV lurched into motion, tires spinning out as I was thrown up and back. My butt came off the seat as the SUV turned sharply. Zoe threw an arm out to brace herself, and I thought someone—maybe Luc—tried to catch me, but it was too late.

My head smacked into the ceiling of the SUV. Pain exploded and powered down my spine, knocking the air out of my lungs as starbursts erupted behind my eyes. There was a flash of blinding white and then a quiet, blissful nothing.

22

I was surrounded by the scent of pine and citrus and enveloped in humming warmth, lying in plush, warm grass as the hot summer sun beat down on me—on us.

I could stay here forever.

Whatever you want.

The memory dissipated like smoke at the sound of another voice. "You need to be careful, Luc."

Grayson. He was here, not in my memory, but here, and I was . . . lying next to Luc? Yes. I was curled up beside him, my head in the crook of his shoulder. How I ended up here was a weird blur.

"I'm always careful," Luc replied, his voice sounding weary but strong. Surprise flickered through me, because he'd been shot. Three times, and—

Everything came rushing back. April's house. Luc being shot. Weird bullets. Me . . . me killing the woman, and then the car chase. I'd hit my head, but I felt fine. Rested. Warm, even.

Someone had healed me.

"Yeah, I'm going to have to disagree with that statement," Grayson responded. "You got shot three times, Luc. You were distracted because of—"

"I may be lying on this bed, but if you blame her for this, I'm going to throw you *through* a wall. Not against one, but through one." Luc's voice was soft, too soft. "And that's going to piss me off, because I like my apartment and really don't want to get a wall replaced."

I did not doubt for one second that Luc could do exactly as he warned.

That didn't seem to stop Grayson. "I'd rather not be thrown through a wall, but that doesn't change the fact that you were distracted because of her. What would you have done if I hadn't been nearby to heal you?" he challenged, and fear coiled deep inside me. "If I hadn't been able to heal her?"

Wait. What? Grayson healed me? Did someone hold a gun to his head and make him do it?

"And while we're on the subject of healing her, why in the hell does she not have a trace yet again?" Grayson demanded. "She didn't have one when you healed her broken arm or after things went down with that Origin. That's not normal."

"What it is, is none of your business."

Grayson laughed, but it was cold. "What the hell is she, Luc? Because she's not human."

Tension crept into my muscles. I was human. I just had some alien DNA in me, but Grayson didn't know that.

"It doesn't matter if she's a human or a freaking chupacabra. If I have to repeat myself one more time, you're not going to like it." There was a terse pause. "You feel me?"

Grayson was silent for a moment. "Yeah, I feel you, Luc."

"Good." Luc sighed. "Now get out of my face."

"Whatever, boss."

"Gray?" Luc called after a moment. "Thank you for taking care of us."

"Of course." There wasn't an ounce of sarcasm in his response. "I'll let you know if Kent figures out what's up with those bullets."

"Perfect," Luc responded, and then I heard the door close. A moment passed. "You can stop pretending you're asleep now."

I shot up so fast it was like I had springs under me, and I twisted toward him, my gaze soaking in every detail of him. The tone of his skin had improved. No longer ghastly pale, he stared back at me with heavily hooded eyes. My gaze dipped to his bare shoulders, and then I snatched the blanket, pulling it away and exposing his chest.

My mouth gaped as shock roared through me even though I knew he was obviously healed. I still couldn't believe what I saw beyond the dusting of brown hair. A bruise above the rosy-pink skin of his left nipple. Another faint bluish mark low in the center of his chest, and one purplish bruise on his right shoulder, near where my head had been resting.

I moved without thinking.

Clasping his cheeks, I brought my mouth to his, and every moment of fear and uncertainty poured into that kiss. There was nothing skilled about the way my lips pressed to his or the desperate way I sought his breath on my tongue. There was a panicked edge to the kiss, one that told me that even though I hadn't allowed the thought of not being able to kiss him again to enter my head, it had been there.

Luc broke contact, breathing heavily. "You keep kissing me like that and I'm going to end up engaging in activities I'm probably not physically fit for at the moment," he drawled, his hands a light touch at my waist.

I lifted up. "They're just bruises. I mean, I shouldn't be surprised, but . . ." Gently, I placed my fingers near the bruise that was so close to his heart. "You were hurt."

"I'm okay." He placed his hand over mine. "Just a little worn out. In a couple of hours, I'll be as good as new."

I heard him. I did. And I saw that he was okay. I saw this with my own eyes, but I also kept seeing the blood trickling from his chest and his pale, drawn face. My lip trembled. "You could've died."

"Not that easily."

"That wasn't easy." I looked up at him, shaking my head. "You were bleeding, and you needed help. I've never seen you need help before."

Something flickered over his face. "I'm okay, Peaches. You don't need to worry."

"But I am worrying!" I sat back, withdrawing my hand. "You were shot because I sneezed, and then everyone talks like you've been shot a dozen times and it's no big deal."

"I wouldn't say a dozen times."

"Luc!" I wanted to smack him. "I'm being serious."

"So am I." He turned his head toward me. "I've been shot three times. Twice when we were moving Luxen, and once when I turned my back to the wrong person. Contrary to what the others will say, it's not something I make a habit of doing."

I gaped at him. "You do realize that most people go their entire lives without being even shot at, Luc?"

"I'm not most people." His lips hitched on one side.

"This isn't funny!" Shaking my head, I tried to swallow the rise of emotion clogging my throat. "Yesterday, it was Heidi. I thought I was going to lose her. Today, it was you, and I thought I was going to lose you. And I can't do this without you."

The laziness vanished from his features as his gaze sharpened. "You're not going to do this without me."

Stupid tears crowded the backs of my eyes. "What would've happened if her aim was a little better? A few centimeters to the left? Or if she—"

Luc sat up swiftly with only a quick grimace. "Evie—"

"You shouldn't be sitting up!" I cried out. "You should be lying down and getting better and—"

"I'm okay." He clasped my cheeks in his warm hands. "I promise you. I'm not going anywhere. I'm not leaving you."

"You can't make that promise again! You told me you were never going to leave me, and you broke it!" The moment those words came out my mouth, I sucked in a shrill breath. A wave of dizziness swept over me.

"What?" whispered Luc, his eyes searching mine as he held my face close to him. "What did you just say?"

"I . . . I don't know." I screwed my eyes shut. "I don't know why I said that. You didn't make that promise to me before."

"But I did."

My eyes opened. "What?"

"I promised that before I took you to the Dashers." His thumbs slid over my cheeks. "I told you that I was never going to leave you."

"I . . . I don't remember that," I said, confused. "I mean, I said it, but I don't remember it."

He nodded slowly as he slid a hand into my hair. "I didn't break that promise, either. I stayed close. I never left you, but I could see where you would've thought that at the time."

"But that doesn't make sense that she—I mean, that I would think that. The fever took my memories, so I wouldn't have remembered you. Like, I wouldn't have thought that you broke a promise at the time." I tried working that out in my head. "This is so confusing."

"Yeah, it is." He curled his fingers in my hair. "You feeling okay?"

"Yes. My head doesn't even hurt," I told him. "I can't believe Grayson healed me. Did you threaten him?"

A half grin appeared. "No. I didn't."

I wasn't sure I believed that.

"But I wasn't talking about hitting your head," he continued. "More like what's inside it. These last two days have been . . . a lot."

"I'm fine." I blinked back the tears. "You are fine. So is Heidi."

"Yes."

Closing my eyes, I leaned in, pressing my forehead to his. A long moment passed. "I was scared. I didn't know what to do. I felt totally useless seeing you bleeding."

His lips brushed mine, and a shudder worked its way through me. "You weren't useless."

"I . . ." He was right. For once, I wasn't useless. I'd shot someone in the head, and I wasn't sure if that was better or worse.

"Better," he whispered, his grip in my hair tightening as his lips ghosted over mine again. "Because the alternative was you getting hurt, and that is unacceptable."

"Did I . . . ?" I drew in a shallow breath. "Did I kill someone before?"

"What?" He drew back.

I opened my eyes. "I shot that woman in the head like it was nothing. I picked up the gun, aimed it, and pulled the trigger, and I . . ."

He dropped his hands to my knees. "Adrenaline can make people do what seems impossible. It can heighten the senses, even feel like it's slowing things down."

"Maybe, but I . . . afterward, I heard a voice in my head."

Luc became very still. "Heard what?"

"A man's voice saying something like, '*You pick up a gun, you aim to kill.*' The voice was familiar, but I don't know who I heard say that or . . . if I maybe heard it on TV or something." I shook my head. "I'm not even sure it's real or what it could mean."

"We'll figure it out." His hands went to my arms, and then he pulled me down beside him, so we were lying face-to-face. "You also did something else."

"What?" I asked, distracted.

He kissed my brow. "You took something from the house. The thing the woman grabbed from the dresser."

The white pouch. I'd forgotten. "What was in it?"

"Syringes," he answered. "Syringes full of what appear to be serums."

About an hour later, Luc was up and moving about like nothing had ever happened. We were in one of the common rooms on the third floor.

The whole crew was there, and I was sitting next to a now fully dressed Luc. His arm was resting on the back of the couch.

I'd texted Mom letting her know I was studying with Zoe. I didn't get a response, so I figured that meant she was still at work.

"They were some kind of law enforcement officers. Well, I'm assuming," Kent was saying from where he stood behind Emery and Heidi. His arms were crossed over his chest. "They weren't in uniform, but since they gave chase, we're going to say they were definitely with some level of the government."

"What happened with the car and the people that were in it?" Heidi asked.

"Poof," Kent replied. "Chas and I made sure no one will find the wreckage. He lit it up."

Zoe smiled, and it was downright creepy. "He used the Source, burned it and everything in it until nothing but ashes remained."

Dear God.

"And the woman in April's house?" I asked.

"I've heard there was a gas explosion there," Kent offered, and the grin on his face was just as disturbing as Zoe's.

"So, no evidence of anything?" Heidi surmised, and as I glanced over at her, I wondered what the trace looked like to those who could see it. "You guys are all in the clear?"

"We're in the clear, but we do have evidence." Grayson walked forward, placing several cylindrical objects on the coffee table. The bullets that Luc had removed. I tensed. Grayson wasn't done with his show-and-tell. He then pulled four guns out of thin air, it seemed, and laid them on the table. "These were taken from the occupants of the car before their untimely cremation."

I briefly closed my eyes.

Luc stretched forward, picking up one gun. He unloaded the

Glock like a pro. "Bullets are the same." He showed them to me, and he was right. Their tips were full of something that looked like blue light. He glanced at Kent. "Are they what I think they are?"

"A newly weaponized form of an EMP? Yes. They are," he answered, and my stomach dropped.

EMP stood for *electromagnetic pulse,* a weapon deadly to Luxen. They had been used over cities during the invasions on a mass scale, frying the electrical grids of those cities and killing the Luxen inside. The ART team used some form of the weapon, but that was more like a Taser.

"Not just Luxen, Peaches. That will take out a hybrid and an Origin." Luc picked up my thoughts. "But these bullets are different." He placed the Glock and chamber on the table. "Something new."

"They weren't designed to kill but to wound." Grayson picked one up, his brow knitting as he studied it. "Which is fairly interesting, don't you think?"

"Yeah." Luc sat back, tossing his arm behind me once more. "Why would they have a weapon that injures instead of killing?"

"That sounds like a good thing," Heidi commented, looking at Emery. "Right?"

"Not necessarily. We don't know what would have happened if Luc hadn't been able to get them out." She was staring at the bizarre display on the table. "Regular ART teams aren't armed with these. They have the good old-fashioned, kill-on-sight EMP weapons and tasers, and they don't go for the tasers often. They go for a kill shot. This group, however, has something we'd never seen before."

Damn.

I folded my arms across my waist, feeling like I'd slipped into an old episode of *The X-Files*. "What about the white pouch? Any idea what kind of serum is in it?"

Kent shook his head as he sat on the arm of the chair Zoe was sitting in. "No idea. None of us really have a way of figuring that out beyond looking at it, so there's no way for us to tell if it has anything to do with Sarah or that guy you all went to school with."

"Most of the serums looked similar." Luc threaded his fingers through my hair. "When Dawson or Archer come back around, which should be soon, we'll give it over to them."

"Why?" I asked, toying with the obsidian pendant.

"They have someone who'd know what it is," he answered.

So did I.

Mom.

But I knew better than to suggest that. "So, here are the facts. We still have no idea what April is, but she's obviously working with the woman who was in her house, who had a case full of some kind of serum that may or may not have caused what happened to Sarah and possibly Coop, and whoever you guys . . . cremated—people who happened to have specially designed EMP weapons."

Luc grinned. "Sounds about right."

"Which brings us to the question of who these people could be," Emery said.

"It has to be the Daedalus." A muscle flexed in Luc's jaw as he looked over at me.

"How?" Zoe's eyes widened. "You destroyed—"

"I did destroy every location I could find, and I thought that was the end of them, but obviously I was wrong."

No one in the room cracked a joke about Luc being wrong. That was how serious the mere thought of the Daedalus being active was.

Rising from her chair, Zoe cursed as she stalked toward the window. "They can't be back. They just can't."

Luc drew his arm off the back of the couch. "I don't think they're back," he said. "I'm beginning to think they never went away."

Act normal.

That was what Luc had said last night, before he fell asleep with my cheek resting on his chest, close to one of the healing bullet wounds. He'd come home with me and stayed the night even though there was a good chance Mom would figure out he'd been there.

But he did use the front door, and there'd been no shenanigans between us, nothing like the night before. He'd kissed me. A lot. Brief brushes of his lips against mine or my cheek or temple. But he'd fallen asleep before I did.

I thought those modified bullets might've taken more out of him than he was letting on, and that terrified me. Which was probably why I lay awake half the night, listening to him breathe.

Act normal while I was at school. Act normal at home. Act as if I hadn't shot a woman in the head, that an entire carful of possible officers hadn't been cremated, and that it wasn't possible that one of the most powerful and evil government organizations known to man was still functioning.

And that they wouldn't love to get their hands on me.

We were all supposed to lie low. Do nothing that would draw unwanted attention while we figured out what was truly in those syringes and if the Daedalus was really still active.

That was easier said than done, because every time someone even glanced in my direction, I became confident that they knew everything.

Like right now.

Brandon and his group of anti-Luxen bigots were sitting at their table, rather subdued without their ringleader, over there eating their lunch like normal people instead of protesting.

Except Brandon kept glaring at me about every five seconds. It was probably because of the massive blue-and-white cast on his hand, but what if he knew what April was?

What if that whole table knew?

I sounded paranoid.

Coughing into his elbow, James picked up his water and took a drink. "Ugh. I think I'm getting mono now."

Zoe lifted her brows. "Really? Didn't you say yesterday that mono was fake news?"

"Apparently, God is proving me wrong." He sniffled. "I feel like crap."

"I don't think it's mono," I told him, resisting the urge to scoot away from him at the same time concern blossomed. "Unless you were making out with Heidi or Emery."

"I wish." He reached over with germ-covered fingers and stole a chip from me. "Just a cold."

"You just got your funk on my chips." I picked the bag up and dropped it on his plate.

James slid me a grin as he snatched up the bag. "Thanks."

My eyes narrowed. "You did that on purpose."

"Maybe." He drew the word out.

"You're evil."

Zoe's laugh sounded forced to me, and I looked over at her and saw that she was watching James with concern, too. "But also clever."

It was unlikely that James was sick in the same way Coop and Sarah were, or even Ryan, but I worried nonetheless. "Do you have a fever or anything?"

He shook his head. "Not at all. I don't know why either of you would be worried about catching something. I can't remember either of you getting sick," James said, munching away on my chips. "Even when Heidi and I got the flu last year, you two were completely fine."

I knew why Zoe hadn't gotten sick. Origins didn't catch flus or viruses. Was that the same for me because of the Andromeda serum? Come to think of it, I couldn't remember being sick at all.

Huh.

I checked out the clock on the wall and saw that we had only a few minutes before lunch ended. Rolling up my napkin, I slung my bag over my shoulder and rose.

"Where are you going?" Zoe asked.

"To the bathroom." I picked up my tray. "Want to come?"

She shot me a look as she picked up her fork. Wiggling my fingers at them, I walked over to the trash and dumped my tray before heading out into the hall. I veered left, making my way toward the bathroom at the front of the school. It was out of the way, but the only other option nearby was the bathroom Colleen had been found in—the one where the confrontation with April had gone down.

Even knowing that April was something other than human, I couldn't imagine how she'd used that bathroom.

Ugh.

As I walked, I rooted around in the front pocket of my backpack until I found my phone. Pulling it out, I saw I had a text from Luc.

Meet you in school parking lot after school. I have a surprise for you.

A smile tugged at my lips as I typed back, *Is it a Chia Pet?*

You wish, was the response.

I laughed as I pushed open the door to the bathroom. The scent of disinfectant about knocked me over, and my smile faded. It felt weird to have a moment of normalcy after . . . after everything, but it also felt good.

It really was like an alternate life, I supposed as I went into the stall, and maybe I was getting used to it—used to it quicker than I ever thought I would.

Or maybe I was really good at compartmentalization.

I hadn't told Zoe or Heidi about my change in relationship status yet. Mainly because there really hadn't been time, and it also felt super-unimportant in the midst of the possible reappearance of the Daedalus and everything else.

But I wanted to tell them.

There was a silly part of me that wanted to shout it from the rooftops.

Flushing the toilet, I slung my backpack over my shoulder and opened the stall door, coming face-to-face with April.

23

My skin turned to ice as I stared at April, shocked into immobility. The strangest thought occurred to me as the stall door swung shut behind me.

She looked so . . . normal, so April.

Blond hair pulled back in a sharp, tight ponytail. Lips as red as fresh blood. Her white sweater had these little fluttering cap sleeves. The pale blue gaze locked with mine looked human.

Did she know I quite possibly killed her mother?

"Are you going to wash your hands, Evie?" she asked.

Tiny goose bumps rose over my flesh. "Are you going to let me?"

"Of course." She stepped back and to the side. "You and I need to chat, and I'd rather do that hygienically."

Unsure if this was some kind of trick, I watched her as I walked over to the sink closest to the window—a window too small to climb out of.

Not like I'd have a chance if I made a run for it. I'd seen how fast she was.

"You seem surprised to see me."

Hands shaking, I turned on the water as I found her reflection in the water-spotted mirror. "Yeah. I am."

"You shouldn't be."

My mind was racing a million miles a second as I struggled to stay calm. I had my Taser in the front pocket of my backpack and the obsidian necklace under my sweater. I wasn't weaponless. I just had to get to them. Then what? Could I stab April?

Hell yeah, after what she did to Heidi? I could. But would I get the chance?

"Why wouldn't I be?" I asked, forcing my voice to remain level. "You almost killed Heidi."

"Almost?" She sighed as she crossed her arms. "That's disappointing. I was hoping she was dead."

Fury swamped me as I slowly washed my hands under the warm water. My gaze shot over to the door.

"No one is coming in. Not until I want them to. It's just you and me. And I have a question. Heidi shouldn't have survived that. That means she's got a Luxen wrapped around her pretty little finger, doesn't she?"

I said nothing, swallowing hard.

"Or an Origin?"

My heart stopped.

"You think I don't know about them—about *him*. Luc. I know enough to stay away from him. For now," she continued. "And you think I don't know what Zoe is? I've always known. Was it her that healed Heidi?"

Like hell I was telling her anything.

April huffed, smiling. "It doesn't matter. I'll find out all your secrets very, very soon."

I was going to shove the obsidian blade into her eyeballs very, very soon. "What are you?" I asked, turning off the water.

"We are the alpha and the omega." Her smile spread, flashing her teeth. "We are the beginning and the end."

"Okay. Well, that answered the question of whether or not you're clinically insane." I reached for the paper towel. "You're also a murderous, stupid bit—"

"Now, now. You don't want to make me mad, Evie. I have to play nice."

Drying my hands, I faced her. "Why do you *have* to play nice?"

"Rules." She rolled her eyes. "Even I have to follow them."

Tossing the paper towel into the trash, I shifted my backpack to the front and reached for the front pocket.

April stepped forward. "What do you think you're doing?"

"I'm just getting my hand sanitizer," I told her, slowly unzipping the front pocket. "Who are you working with?"

Her head cocked to the side.

"The Daedalus?"

If she was surprised to hear those words, she didn't show it.

"I mean, you were killing people and making it look like the

Luxen are doing it. You were turning people against them, and you're clearly not human."

"Of course I'm not human. I mean, duh." She laughed as if I'd suggested the most ridiculous thing ever. "You know, I first thought it was Heidi."

My brows snapped together as my finger stilled on the zipper. "What?"

"Who I was looking for." April flipped her ponytail over her shoulder. "Obviously, I was wrong."

My fingers curled around the cool plastic of the stun gun. "I don't know what the hell you're talking about."

"You will. Really soon. I'm not supposed—"

Pulling the stun gun out as I jerked forward, I swung my arm toward her.

Her hand shot out, as fast as a cobra striking. She caught me by the wrist and twisted sharply, putting the right amount of pressure to cause a spike of pain. I gasped. "Drop it," she cooed as if she were talking to a puppy. "Bad girl. Drop it."

I held on.

"A stun gun?" She twisted my wrist again, and that was it. My fingers sprang open. I had no control. She quickly snatched it up. "The only thing that would do is really piss me off." Letting go of my wrist, she stepped back and tossed the stun gun into the trash. "Here I am, being polite and patient, and you—"

Snapping the chain of my necklace, I ripped the obsidian pendant free as I launched myself at her. The move must have caught her off guard, because she didn't move and took the brunt of my weight as I crashed into her, slamming the obsidian into her chest. Skin gave way with a sickening suction sound. Wet warmth met my fist as April started to topple backward—

Suddenly, I was in the air.

Flying backward, I slammed into the wall beside the window. Air punched out of my lungs as I fell forward, my knees cracking off the tile. I caught myself a second before face-planting on the dirty, nasty-as-hell floor. Panting, I lifted my head and stared through the strands of hair.

The obsidian pendant was stuck in her upper-left chest, too high to have hit her heart. Dammit.

Dark, inky blood spotted her white sweater as she reached up and gripped the obsidian. "Really? Obsidian?" She dropped it on the floor. "Do you think I'm an Arum? Because if so, that's kind of insulting."

I pushed down the panic crawling up my chest, threatening to choke me. "What the hell are you?"

April moved so fast.

One second she was standing by the sinks and the next she was kneeling in front of me, her fingers curled around my chin, forcing my head back. "I'll give you one good hint."

Her fingers dug into my chin as she reached around to her back pocket and pulled something out. For a moment, I almost didn't recognize what she was holding between her slim fingers.

It was a picture.

A photo of a little blond girl with a man—a man I'd been told these last four years was my father—and a woman I knew as my mother.

It was one of the missing pictures from the photo album.

Holy crap. "You were in the house—you took the photos."

"Yeah, it was me." April flicked the picture at me, and I flinched as it smacked me in the face and then fluttered to the floor. "I suspected it was you after you started defending the Luxen, so then I helped myself to your house and found these photos. Interesting. That girl looks a little like you, so I thought maybe it was you. Weirder shit has happened, you know? But then you started hanging out with that Origin. Luc."

My heart was racing so fast as she leaned in. Her lips brushed the corners of mine as she spoke. "I wasn't supposed to be exposed yet. I had my purpose. You've already figured out what that is, but you went ahead and ruined it with that stupid camera of yours." Her grip tightened, causing me to cry out. "You have no idea how much trouble I got in for that."

There was no way I could speak with her fingers digging into my jaw, holding me in place. I threw everything I felt into my glare. Every ounce of hate and fury poured out of me.

"So, what do I call you? You're obviously not Evie Dasher. That's what I can't figure out," she continued, and I had no idea what she was babbling about. "Who the hell are you? That makes you very,

very interesting to me." She laughed. "But we'll know soon. Everything that I've done, that *we're* doing, is the price of the greater good. A war is coming, Evie. The great war—the only war—and we will level the playing field."

April sounded *insane.*

"We are going to make the world a better place." April let go of my chin, and I fell back. "You and me."

"The only thing I'm going to do is straight up kill you."

April cocked her head to the side. "*You aren't killing anyone.*"

"I killed your mother," I spat, barely recognizing the voice inside me. "Shot her right in the head."

She snorted. "That wasn't my mother. That was my handler. And I didn't say that out loud."

A chill swept down my spine. "What?"

Smiling at me as if we were gossiping about a juicy secret, she rose, and her eyes turned pitch-black, all except for her pupils. They glowed white as she pulled something out of her front pocket. What she held in her hand looked like a key fob.

I lurched to my feet, ignoring the flare of pain that shot down my back.

"Time to wake up." She pressed her finger on the key fob. "Whoever you are."

My world exploded.

24

Sharp, stinging pain exploded along the base of my skull, stealing the next breath I took and knocking my legs out from underneath me.

Clutching my head, I went down, but I didn't feel the impact with the floor.

Pressure built inside my skull, and I opened my mouth to scream, but no sound came out. The pain came in waves and waves, sparking through my brain and starting fires along the synapses. My brain was on fire. I could feel it burning through my skull as I rolled onto my side, curling into a ball.

The pain—oh God—

The pain was so severe that I could be run over by a dump truck and I wouldn't care.

Hell, I'd welcome it.

My entire body went rigid, legs painfully straight as my hands jerked away from my head. *I can't take this.* I couldn't. My brain was turning to mush. I could feel it. Everything was being scrambled.

"They call it the Cassio Wave, because obviously, someone is obsessed with Greek mythology. It's a sonic sound wave. Can't hear it, but it's in your brain, doing its thing." April's voice cut through the slicing pain. "Kind of works like a jammer, or so I've been told. Gets in there, scrambles all the neurotransmitters and *stuff.* Kind of messed up, if you think about it. Apparently, there are much larger-scale weapons in development, but none like this. This has no impact on humans. Did you hear that, Evie? This little thing is kind of like a dog whistle."

I thought she might have toed me with her shoe, but I wasn't sure. Nausea churned as my vision went white and panic ripped through me, twisting with the stabbing, blinding pain. I couldn't see. I was going to—

Bright images began flashing *inside* me. Golden sand. Blue-green water. Sea foam. I'd never been to the beach, but I saw it and felt the warm sun on my skin, the heated sand under my feet—under my bare toes. Another image replaced it. A man I'd never seen before, scrawny, with greasy blond hair. Strung out and passed out on a couch that smelled like cat urine and stale food. Then a boy running along the bank of the Potomac. He was laughing, and the sun turned his hair bronze. He was running too fast, and I couldn't catch up to him.

It's going to be okay now. That's what he'd said. I remembered. *Just like I promised.*

But he'd lied. He'd promised to never leave me, and he'd lied about that, too. He'd left me, and I hadn't even wanted to go to *them.* I didn't trust *them,* but he insisted, and it was all a lie. Everything about them, about what they offered, it was a lie, and I paid for the lie in sweat and tears, blood and *death*—

Fire swept through, erasing him, erasing us, and it was forever, his face and voice shattering into pieces. I was dying—no, I had died at the hands of a needle and a woman who promised me everything would be okay.

Truth.

It was the truth wrapped in lies.

"The Cassio Wave only affects people with a certain genetic code that comes from the Andromeda serum," April was saying, and I heard her, but the words weren't connecting or making sense. "The serum is a code waiting to be accessed."

I saw myself. I saw a younger version of myself. Thirteen or so? It was me with my hair pulled back in a ponytail. Me in black pants, black shirt. A gun—a gun in my hand and a voice in my ear.

His words. Dark brown eyes focused on mine. *You're not like them.* I was a miracle that wasn't. I knew that. He knew that.

You know what you have to do.

I knew what—

Another voice intruded, one that I thought I recognized. *They're going to come for you. And when they do, they're not going to know what hit them.*

No. No, they—

Nothing.

Suddenly, there was just nothing in my head. Just cool, vast emptiness. Vacant. The pain was gone, leaving nothing but a sweet, blissful void behind. Slowly, the rigidity leaked out of my muscles, and my legs curled. Sweat coursed down the side of my face as I pried my eyes open and saw denim-clad legs.

Where was I?

I lifted my gaze to see a girl standing before me, her eyes all black and her pupils white.

Who was she?

I knew her. I thought I did, but my head was full of fuzz and cotton, as was my mouth and throat.

The girl lifted her arm and offered her hand. "A life—"

"For a life," I croaked.

"Perfect." Her red lips curled into a smile. "Come. He's waiting for us."

Lifting my hand, I placed mine in hers. I took her hand, and then I took *her.*

Planting my other hand on the floor, I kicked out, sweeping her legs out from underneath her. Her eyes widened with surprise before she went down, her hip cracking off the floor.

I rose to my feet.

"What are you doing?" she sputtered, pushing up. "This isn't right. You're not supposed—"

Snapping forward, I gripped her by her ponytail and yanked her onto her feet. Icy air blew off her, and her lower half began to lose some of its solidness.

I whirled around, bringing her with me. With my hand along the back of her head, I dragged her forward. She tried to catch herself by grabbing the sink.

Not going to happen.

Muscles flexed, and her arms gave out. I slammed her into the mirror face-first.

"Not cool." She spit blood as I jerked her back. "You're making a mistake. Huge mis—"

She kicked back, catching me in the stomach. I stumbled back a step, catching myself. She spun toward me, her body lifting off the floor as red-tinged light-laced shadows spilled out from her, wrapping around her legs, climbing up the length of her body.

She became a shadow—a shadow that burned.

Springing forward, I snatched the obsidian blade off the floor. The stone was red-hot in my hand as I jumped up onto the sink behind her. I pivoted and grabbed her ponytail, yanking her head back.

"How—?" she gasped, the shadows over her chest.

"I'm not like you."

Then I slammed the blade into the center of her head, piercing tissue and bone.

Her mouth dropped open, but no sound came out as she fell forward, her body flickering between smoke and light.

She was dead before she hit the floor, a pale, sunken body in a pool of inky darkness.

I hopped down from the sink, wiping the blood off the blade onto my jeans. Then I lifted my other hand, running my fingers through my hair, smoothing the strands as I turned to the shattered mirror.

I saw myself.

I saw my eyes, and the irises were black, the pupils were white. I saw—

Like being sucked back in, I slammed back into myself. My consciousness finally woke up and took hold.

Gasping, I jerked back from the mirror and dropped the piece of obsidian. "Oh my God, what did I—?"

I spun around and saw her—saw April with a hole in her head. "Oh God."

I did that.

I completely recalled doing that. Wasn't quite sure how, but I totally kicked her ass . . . and shoved a blade into her head.

And I didn't feel at all bad about that part.

A logical part of my brain took over. April was dead, and no one could come in here and find me with her. Or possibly find her at all, because that would be bad, really bad.

Because I legit just murdered her and wiped her blood on my jeans. I was swimming in evidence.

Springing into action, I rushed over to the bathroom door and nearly cried out with relief when I saw that it had a lock on the interior. I made sure it was still locked and then raced back to my backpack. I had no idea how much time I had before someone tried to come in here.

Grabbing my phone, I tried Zoe first. She was here and could get to me the fastest, but as the phone rang and she didn't answer, I realized she probably had it on silent.

"Shit." I hung up and called Luc as I glanced behind me to where April lay sprawled. Bile crept up the back of my throat. The phone rang once.

"Shouldn't you be in class?" Luc answered. "Or are you just that excited about my surprise? It's not a Chia Pet, Peaches."

My knees nearly buckled at the sound of his voice. I held myself up, but I doubled at the waist. "Something bad has happened."

All traces of humor vanished from his voice. "Are you okay?"

"Yes, but I . . . I totally just killed April in the school bathroom, and I don't know what to do. I called Zoe, but she's in class and not answering," I told him in a rush. "And I really killed her, Luc. She's super-dead, and I can't leave the bathroom."

"Why can't you leave?"

I glanced at the mirror and shuddered. "Something is wrong with me."

"Tell me which bathroom you're in."

I told him where to find me. "Luc, please . . . please hurry."

"I'll be right there."

Holding the phone to my chest, I squeezed my eyes shut as I leaned against the sink. Luc was fast. He'd be here in minutes, if that, and everything would be okay.

Like he's always promised.

A sharp burst of pain sliced across my temple, and I almost dropped my phone. Fragmented memories tried to surface—the images I'd seen after April had . . . What had she done? Opening my eyes, I drew in a shallow breath. She'd hit a button on a key fob.

What had she called them? Cassio Waves? I winced as the throbbing pain stabbed me behind the eyes. Wetness gathered under my nose, and I reached up with a trembling hand to wipe. Red smeared my fingers. My nose was bleeding. I turned back to the mirror, half afraid to see my eyes.

They were normal, plain old brown. Not creepy black and white.

Not at all like Sarah's and April's. Maybe I'd just imagined it. Something had been—

I saw April's body in the mirror, lying there.

"Okay," I whispered, and I swallowed hard. "You did not imagine jack. You jumped on this sink like an assassin and stabbed her in the head."

Turning around, I saw April's open hand. The key fob rested in her palm. I dipped down, swiping it out of her hand, and slid it into my pocket.

Clutching the phone, I inched around the sink, keeping clear of April's legs. I probably shouldn't have killed her. I had questions—lots of them—but then again, I hadn't exactly been in control of myself. As soon as her hand touched mine, I reacted with . . . rather deadly precision. I wanted to kill her. Needed to take her out, and while at no point in time had I been joking about wanting to kill her after what she did to Heidi, I didn't really think I was capable of it.

I also hadn't thought I was capable of picking up a gun and shooting someone in the head.

His voice came again, thready and weak, but there, in the back of my mind. *You have to be faster and stronger than he is.*

It was the same voice I'd heard after I shot the woman in April's house—her handler.

"Evie?" came a muffled voice from the other side of the bathroom door. "Can you let us in?"

Darting to the door, I quickly threw the lock and swung the door open. The minute I saw Luc in the doorway, I launched myself at him, wrapping my arms and legs around him. He caught me easily, walking forward as he threaded his hand through my hair.

"Peaches," he murmured against the side of my head. "If it takes a murder to get you to greet me like this, I'm not going to complain."

A hysterical-sounding giggle rose through me as I buried my face in his neck. "That's not funny."

"I'm not joking." There was a pause. "Are you hurt? I saw blood on your face."

"Just a nosebleed." My head was thumping something fierce, and my back hurt like hell, but I was okay.

"You sure?"

I murmured a *yes* against his warm skin.

"Wow." Grayson's voice filled the bathroom. "You really did kill her."

I nodded, wondering if he wore contacts to get past the RAC drones.

"Impressed," he added reluctantly.

"Is that a hole in her head?" That was Emery, and I started to lift my head, but Luc kept my face buried. "And . . . is it just me, or does her blood look super-weird?"

"I need you guys to get this bathroom cleaned up before anyone realizes what happened here," Luc ordered. "Hand me her bag, Gray." A second later, I felt Luc shift my bag on his shoulder. I started to wiggle to get free, but the arm around me tightened. "Nope. I like you right where you are."

Someone sighed heavily. Sounded like Grayson.

"I need to get down," I told him.

"No, you don't." Luc started backing up. "What I need you to do is to hold on."

"What—"

Luc turned, and then he was taking off, and I knew he was running, moving so fast that he'd be nothing but a blur to anyone who might see him. The moment I felt cool air, I knew we were outside, and it was only a few seconds later that he was slowing down, stopping, and opening a door.

"We're at your car." He wasn't even out of breath as he lowered me into the passenger seat, and then his hands were on my cheeks, tilting my head back. "Your nose is still bleeding."

"It's okay." I felt his palm start to warm, but I gripped his wrist, pulling his hand away. "I don't think you should do that anymore."

"I can fix whatever has your nose bleeding—"

"I don't think you can," I whispered.

"I think you know me better than that."

He wasn't getting it. I rocked toward him, my fingers digging into the skin of his wrist. "Something happened to me."

"What?" Luc's eyes searched mine as he flattened his palm against my cheek.

"I think I turned into the Terminator."

His brows raised. "You what?"

"Yeah. I kicked her legs out from under her like I know jujitsu, and then I vaulted, Luc, I *vaulted* onto the sink and pivoted like a ballerina. I grabbed her head and stabbed her through it with the obsidian blade."

He cocked his head to the side. "That's . . . kind of hot."

"Luc, I'm being serious."

His violet eyes flared. "And again, I'm not joking."

"Neither am I. I did something that was impossible for me, and it's more than that. Way more than that." My nails were digging into the skin of his wrist. I could feel it, but he didn't so much as flinch. "I think—oh God—I think I'm like them—like April and Sarah."

His lips parted. "Evie—"

"You don't understand. There's something in me that April unlocked." I shuddered. "It was me, but it wasn't."

His intense gaze searched mine. "Okay. I'm going to need you to tell me everything."

I did just that as Luc drove us to the club and led me up to his apartment, where he put a cold Coke in my hand. I drank the whole thing like I'd just crawled out of the desert, dying of thirst.

"You said she hit a button on a key fob?" He stood before me.

Placing the empty can on the end table, I leaned to the side and pulled out the key fob. It was black with a small red button in the center. "It's this." I handed it over. "She said . . . I think she said it was some kind of sound wave called the Cassio Wave? And that it only affected people with the Andromeda serum, unscrambling some kind of code in the serum. Do I have a code in my head?"

"Like a computer code?" He turned the key fob over. "I don't think you have a computer code in your head."

"Duh," I snapped, rubbing my palms over my knees. "But there's something in there, because besides the brain-killing pain, I had images, Luc. Like glimpses of memories. I saw a man; he looked strung out, and there was this smell of cat pee . . . and mold."

Luc had become very still. "I think you saw your father—your real father."

I jerked, somehow not surprised and yet . . . disturbed. "And I saw you—you as a young boy. Running by the river—by the

Potomac. We were barefoot and muddy. I think . . . I think we were laughing. Did we do that?"

Luc took a step forward but stopped himself. "Yes. A lot."

I let out a shaky breath. "When the pain stopped, she started to say something to me, and I finished the sentence for her. 'A life for a life,' and that sounds like some Stephen King stuff right there."

His brows climbed up his forehead.

"I knew what she was saying then—what it meant—but now I have no idea how or why I knew that. Then she said to me, 'Come. He's waiting for us.'"

White light appeared in his pupils. "He?"

I nodded. "I have no idea who he is, but I did hear a man's voice when my head felt like it was being pulled apart. It was the same voice I heard after I shot April's handler. He said something like, 'You're not like them,' and then I had a memory of being dressed in black pants and a shirt, holding a gun. I didn't see him, but I heard his voice."

His fingers curled over the fob. "And that's when this voice said you aren't like the others?"

"Yes, and he said something else. Like I needed to be faster and stronger. I don't remember exactly." I winced as a burst of pain lanced through my skull.

"Are you okay?" Luc was immediately by my side, his hand on my cheek.

"Yeah." I breathed slowly as the pain receded. "Whenever I try to remember what was said, it makes my head hurt."

"Then don't. Stop—"

"I can't stop. None of this makes sense, and I'm sure as hell not going to figure it out if I don't try." I pulled away, dragging my hands through my hair, holding the strands back from my face. "April acted like once she hit the button, I would be different, that I would willingly go with her or something. I thought . . ."

Placing the key fob in his pocket, he placed his hands over mine and gently removed my fingers from my hair. "What?"

I drew in a shallow breath. "I thought I was going to die. The pain was that bad, Luc. It felt like nothing was going to be left of me by the time it ended. I thought—" My voice cracked. "It was so bad. I don't know how I'm alive . . ."

"Peaches." He leaned in, resting his forehead against mine. "Stop.

I can't . . . I hear you saying this, and I want to blow something up knowing you felt that kind of pain and there was nothing I could do to stop it. That I didn't even know it was happening—that I should've been there."

Shuddering, I closed my eyes. "I don't know what she did, but she did something, Luc. That Cassio Wave or whatever it is, it unlocked something in me, and I saw it, Luc."

"What do you mean?" He pulled my head back, and when my gaze met his, I could see the worry etched into the striking lines of his face. "Besides turning into the Terminator?"

Clasping his wrists, I nodded and whispered, "I'm almost too afraid to say it out loud."

"Don't be afraid." The tips of his fingers touched my cheek. "Never with me."

Never with me. Those words gave me the courage to speak what was terrifying to even acknowledge. "I saw my eyes. They were like Sarah's—like April's. They were black, and my pupils were white. That's why I couldn't leave the bathroom. They went back to normal after a couple of minutes, but I saw them."

His brows knitted. "That's not possible."

"I know." I swallowed hard. "But I saw them. I didn't imagine it. I saw my eyes, and that's what they looked like."

A tremor coursed through his hands. "You're human, Evie. You're human except for—"

"Except for the Andromeda serum, and April said that there was some kind of code in that serum. Maybe not a computer code, but she hit that button and my brain shorted out, and then I kicked ass, Luc. I can't walk a straight line sober most days, but I kicked her ass in like a nanosecond. But it's more than that," I said, heart thumping. "That guy's voice? I heard it before, and then James mentioned something randomly today. He's got a cold, and he said I've never gotten sick—neither Zoe nor I, and you know what? He's right."

"That doesn't mean you're not human." He let go of my cheeks and rose.

"But what I did today wasn't something someone like me could do." I wet my lips. "Maybe that's why I don't have a trace. It's not so much the serum but what was in that serum, and now . . . What is going to happen? What if I start to mutate like Sarah or Coop?

Because let's just accept the fact that Coop was probably going through some version of whatever was happening to Sarah. What if—" I sucked in a shrill breath. When Sarah got sick, she'd run off like she had no idea who she was, like she was running toward someone. "What if I lose myself again? What if I mutate and I don't remember any of this—"

"Nothing is going to happen to you. *Nothing.* I'm not going to let anything happen to you."

"Stop saying that!" I shot to my feet, heart pounding. "You can't control everything that happens. No one can."

"I beg to differ." His lips thinned as he turned from me. Tension tightened his shoulders, and the air became charged with static. "I am always in control—"

"Not when it comes to this," I reasoned, shaking my head. "Why do you think it's impossible? All the evidence points to there—"

"Because I would know!" he roared, spinning back to me. A charge of energy ripped through the room. The bulb exploded inside the lampshade of the lamp on the end table, causing me to jump. His voice lowered as his chin dipped. "I *should* know if you weren't human—if that serum had done more than give you back your life."

"You can't know everything, Luc."

He shook his head as he stepped forward. "I know *you.*"

I sucked in an unsteady breath. "Just a few days ago, you told me you knew Nadia, but you didn't know me. Did that change?"

"*Yes.* I was wrong." In a blink of an eye, he was right in front of me. "I realized I was the moment you told me you wanted me."

My heart stuttered and then skipped a beat. "That doesn't mean you know what is happening to me, and something is."

Luc's chest rose with a deep breath, and then he turned from me, walking to the window. The blinds were up, and the overcast November sky was gray and gloomy. "I don't like this, because I always know what is going on. I always have answers." He thrust a hand through his hair. "And I have no idea what is going on here. It reminds me of . . ."

I took a step toward him. "Of what?"

"Of when you first got sick." His voice had gone so low that I barely heard him. "I didn't have the answers then. I couldn't fix you.

I couldn't do anything, but . . ." His head tipped back and he exhaled heavily. "It's the only time I've ever been scared."

I wanted to go to him, but I was rooted to where I stood. "Are you scared now?"

Another ripple of energy coasted through the room, sending static dancing over my skin. "I am."

25

If Luc was afraid, then I should be terrified. I was scared, but at the same time, I felt . . . detached from it. I knew it was happening to me, but I felt normal as I watched Luc turn from the window and face me.

I felt like Evie, whatever the hell that meant.

"You never struck me as the type to ever be afraid," I said, being honest.

"Usually I'm not, but when it comes to you . . ." He trailed off, looking away. A muscle flexed along his jaw. He inhaled deeply. "We'll figure this out."

"Will we?"

"We will." He came over to me and took my hand. He sat, pulling me onto his lap, and I went, pulling my legs up and draping them over his. His sharp gaze flickered over my face. "There's a lot we need to talk about. Things are going to change now."

Air lodged in my throat. Things *had* to change now. I knew that. Huge things. Tiny knots formed in the pit of my stomach as I lowered my gaze. Dread and uncertainty took root. I didn't have to ask to know that those things were life-changing.

Two fingers pressed against my chin, tilting it up. "But there are two things we need to take care of first that are more important."

"What could be more important than this?"

"This."

The fingers under my chin curled as he brought my mouth to his, stopping just an inch from his lips touching mine. The hand along my chin slid to the nape of my neck. A heartbeat passed, and then he kissed me. There was an undeniable spark that passed between us the moment our lips met. The kiss started out slowly, just a brushing of his lips, but as soon as mine parted, he made this sound that caused a curl low in my stomach. He kissed me harder and then harder still, and I had to think that only Luc had the power to kiss away the fear and uncertainty, the tainted knowledge that there was something drastically wrong about me.

All those problems were still there, but for a little while, they couldn't touch us. When he lifted his head again, I was a little dazed.

"There's still one more thing."

"Mmm." My lips were still tingling, parts of my body were still throbbing in tune with the beat of my heart.

"My surprise."

I'd forgotten about that. "Are you sure it's not a Chia Pet?"

He chuckled as he lifted his hand. A moment later, a box appeared in his hand, coming from somewhere outside the line of my vision. It was wrapped in paper that eerily matched his eyes. He handed it over.

I looked at it and then at him. "What is this?"

"Open it."

None of the surprises were wrapped before. I slid my finger along the gap and tore the shiny paper aside.

"Oh my God," I whispered, staring down at a brand-new camera—an expensive-as-hell camera. A Canon T6 Rebel with all the accessories—accessories I'd never had the spare cash to buy or use. "*Luc*."

"Your old one was ruined, and I know how much you love to take pictures."

Tears blurred my vision as I stared down at the camera.

"Plus, you need to retake those pictures of my stunningly handsome face."

"Luc," I whispered, clutching the box.

He was silent for a moment. "Are you going to cry? Please don't cry. I don't like it when you cry. It makes me want to fry stuff, and I'm already down two lamps today—"

Laughing, I lunged toward him and kissed him. "You didn't have to do this, but I'm keeping it. Forever."

He grinned as he scrunched his fingers through his hair. "Glad you like it."

"I love it." I ran my hand over the box, and then I laughed.

"I turned into a master assassin today and killed April. I may or may not be some kind of Lord knows what, but I . . . I feel okay. It's not the camera or the kissing—though both helped," I added when he raised his brows. "But it was you. Thank you."

Grinning, he looked away and dropped his hand. "It's nothing . . ." His phone went off, and he reached into his pocket to check it. "They're back . . . with April's body."

Part of me didn't want to know why they'd brought back April's body, and yet I was morbidly curious as I followed Luc down to the main club floor, where everyone was waiting.

Zoe made a beeline for me, quickly followed by Heidi. They both hugged me, and when Zoe pulled back, she said, "I can't believe you did it, and I have questions. I'm kind of pissed that I didn't get to do it."

"Join the club," Emery commented as she strode by, heading toward the hall we just came from.

"How did you kill her?" Heidi demanded, practically hopping from one foot to the other. "Okay. That came out kind of wrong, but how did any of this happen? I have so many questions."

I glanced at Luc. "Well, that's kind of a long story . . ."

"Show me your hand," Grayson said, appearing out of freaking nowhere.

Half afraid that he was going to drop a tarantula in my hand, I did as he asked.

Grayson dropped my obsidian pendant into my palm, clean of blood and chain replaced. Before I could thank him or ask how he replaced the chain that quickly, he was already walking away from me, heading into the kitchen.

My gaze met Luc's, and there was a secretive little smile on his lips as he inclined his head. I curled my fingers around the pendant. That was nice of Grayson.

I still didn't like him.

"Where is everyone going?" I asked.

"An autopsy," Luc answered.

"What?" Heidi and I demanded at once, and then Heidi spun, taking off after Emery.

Luc strolled past me, stopping to place a brief, unexpected kiss on the corner of my lips. He murmured, "Don't forget. I'm needy."

My eyes widened, and I felt my cheeks flush as Luc walked off.

Zoe turned to me. "You and I really need to have a long conversation. And I'm not talking about just April."

I glanced at the hallway everyone had disappeared down. "Luc and I . . . well, we're together, I guess. I mean, no. I don't guess. I know." My face was burning. "We're totally together—"

She smacked my arm. "And you haven't told me?"

"Ouch." I rubbed my arm. "It just kind of happened a couple of days ago, and everything has been so crazy, I just haven't had a chance."

"You can always make time to tell me that you have a boyfriend, especially when that boyfriend is Luc. Geez, Evie."

"I should've told you in between Heidi nearly dying and Luc getting shot," I retorted. "Maybe work in a mani and a pedi."

"I would've loved a mani and a pedi." Her smile was wide and fast. "Seriously, though. I'm happy to hear this. You both have been through a lot to get here."

Nodding, I toyed with the pendant in my hand as I looked down the hall. "He's . . . he's Luc."

Zoe laughed. "That's all you need to say for me to understand."

I grinned. "We should probably see what they're up to, and then I can tell you what happened."

She agreed, so we went down the hall and through the swinging doors and into the kitchen as I put the necklace on. Wearing it after I'd used it to stab April in the head was—

We both skidded to a stop.

Lying on a prep table, underneath stainless-steel pots and pans, was April. Her skin had taken on a waxy pallor, and her forehead . . .

I quickly looked away from her to where Heidi and Emery stood, the former's head cocked to the side as she stared at the dead girl.

Luc was standing with his back to the door, arms crossed, and Grayson stood at the foot of the table, face impassive.

It was Clyde, the tattooed and pierced bouncer, and the Luxen, Chas, that I was focused on. Clyde was dressed like a butcher from a horror movie, wearing thick gloves that reached his elbows and some kind of rubber apron that covered his overalls. A pair of small, black-rimmed glasses were perched on his nose.

"You guys weren't joking," I whispered, horrified and somewhat morbidly interested.

Chas handed what appeared to be a scalpel to Clyde, who said, "I'm going to do my first autopsy."

"In the kitchen?" Kent rushed into the room, skidding to a stop. "Where I make myself fritas in the morning?"

Clyde arched a pierced brow. "Well, yeah, I mean, it's the perfect place."

"No," Kent argued. "It's the exact opposite of the perfect place."

"It's a clean, flat surface that offers privacy and many bowls," Clyde responded.

"I do not want to know what you plan to put in the bowls I use for my salad and cereal!" Kent exclaimed, and I had to agree with him.

"Why are we doing an autopsy?" Emery asked, looking a little pale around the mouth. "I mean, is it really going to tell us what she is?"

Luc shrugged as he slowly shook his head.

"I want to see what her insides look like," Clyde responded calmly.

My eyes peeled wide. "I'm pretty sure that's the first statement every serial killer makes when caught."

Clyde gave me a toothy grin.

All righty then.

"In another life, Clyde was a doctor." Luc looked at me over his shoulder. "He's actually pretty skilled at all things cutting and slicing."

That last statement wasn't particularly reassuring.

"When Luxen and Arum die, they revert back to their true forms. Both look like . . . shells. Their skin becomes translucent; one is light, the other is dark." Luc tilted his head to the side. "Hybrids look like humans when they die. The same for Origins. We already know that she's none of these things."

I held my breath.

"But we do know that whatever she is, in death, it is not like an Origin or a hybrid," Luc continued as he gestured at Clyde.

"Her body is still rather warm," Clyde explained, and I was going to have to take his word on that. With a gloved hand, he lifted her limp arm. "See these marks, looks like bruises? That's blood pooling. It's too soon for that to be this noticeable. Usually takes a couple of hours." He laid her arm back down and then lifted her sweater, revealing about an inch of her stomach. There were blackish-blue pools there, too. "That's not all."

Heidi swallowed thickly and squeaked, "It's not?"

"No." Clyde pulled the hem of her sweater back down. "She's . . . disintegrating."

"What?" I said.

"Her skin is beginning to flake off and turn to what reminds me of ash or dust." He lifted his hand and turned it over so it was palm up. There was a dusting of something pinkish white on the gloved fingertips. It looked like powder. "She appears to be rapidly decomposing."

"Plus her blood is different," Grayson said. "It was almost black with a tint of blue. Looked like what Sarah vomited up and what you all said Coop's looked like."

Was my blood black?

No. My blood was red and normal looking. I'd seen it enough times to know that. But if I were like April in some way, was I going to disintegrate when I died? My skin would just . . . flake off? Pressure clamped down on my chest as I folded my arms across my stomach.

"There's a chance that there may be other things that are different about her," Clyde continued as Luc turned, walking back to where I stood. "Tissue. Organs. So on and so forth. I got a trusted friend who's a pathologist that can run some tests. Got to get the samples, though."

"Can we talk about this?" Kent asked, hands on his hips. "Because I am not happy with this happening in the kitchen. I know damn well that one of you is going to expect me to clean up, and this isn't the America I was promised."

Zoe's lips quirked as Clyde lifted the scalpel once more.

"Nope." I backed up, raising my hands. This was all too surreal. "I can't be in here while you do this. I know I'll see things I can't unsee. I don't need any part of this."

Grayson smirked, but I didn't care. I wheeled around and walked out of the kitchen into the quiet, dimly lit hall.

"Peaches?" Luc was right behind me, and I kept walking. I wasn't sure where I was going, but I was near the bar when he appeared in front of me, moving too fast for me to track. "Hey," he said, placing his hands on my shoulders. "Where's your head right now?"

"Right now?" I laughed. "Um, I'm just hoping I don't flake away when I die, but then again, I'd be dead, so I guess I wouldn't care."

"You're not going to flake away."

"Well, we really don't know that, do we?"

His hands drifted to my hips. "Look, there is something going on with you. I'm not denying that, but things don't add up right now." His hands tightened, and then he lifted me onto the bar. "We don't know anything at this point, so let's not focus on the whole death thing."

Swallowing, I nodded as I heard the doors open from the hallway. A few moments later, we were joined by Heidi and Zoe and Grayson.

Noting how Luc was standing between my legs, his hands on my hips, Heidi lifted a brow and pursed her lips.

I was so going to be having a conversation with her later, too.

"So, what's the deal?" Zoe asked, leaning against the bar. "What happened in the bathroom with April?"

Luc looked up at me, his eyes searching mine. "You want to talk about this now?"

I nodded, knowing this was something that needed to be said now rather than later. So I started to tell them everything, and while I talked, Luc stayed by my side, his presence oddly comforting.

"She had pictures of the real Evie—the ones that were taken from my mom's photo album. I thought Micah had done it, but it was April," I explained, rubbing my hands over my knees. "But she doesn't know that I'm really . . . Nadia."

"Wait. *What?*" Everything about Grayson turned rock solid.

I cut a quick glance to Luc. He was watching his friend closely. "I'm really Nadia Holliday. I was given the Andromeda serum and, well, it's a long freaking story, but I don't have memories of my time as Nadia."

"You're *the* Nadia?" he demanded, unfolding his arms.

"She is," Luc answered.

Luc spoke only two words, but they seemed to blast through

Grayson like a cannonball. The Luxen took a step back as he stared at Luc. "How could you not tell me?"

"Zoe knew because she knew Evie before." Luc's voice was low, calm. "The only other people who knew were the ones who'd met her before. Daemon and Dawson. Archer. Clyde. No one else needed to know. It would be too much of a risk. Still is a risk."

Grayson blinked as if something had come too close to his face. He looked like he was going to say something, but closed his mouth, shaking his head.

A long moment passed, and then Grayson said, "I should've known."

Luc inclined his head. "Would it have changed anything?"

I wasn't sure what Luc meant by that question, but if he meant if Grayson knowing I was Nadia would've made him nicer to me, I was going to go with a big, fat no. Grayson didn't answer, though. He looked away, a muscle spasming along his jaw.

Luc turned to me and said softly, "Go on."

I told them the rest, leaving nothing out, but the Luxen kept snagging my attention. Grayson looked *furious.* Sapphire eyes narrowing with each passing second, lips thinning and jaw hardening.

Part of me couldn't blame him for being angry.

He'd watched me for years on Luc's orders, and I thought he might hate me for that, but he never knew I was Nadia—*the* Nadia.

Still didn't give him a pass for saying I was useless.

When I finished, Zoe and Heidi stared at me like I'd grown a third eye in the center of my forehead and was winking at them with it.

"I know all this sounds impossible, but it's true," I finished. "Everything is."

Zoe shoved a hand over her head, gathering curls and pulling them back. "I don't think anything is impossible. Not after seeing firsthand what the Daedalus is capable of. But this is really out there."

Grayson still looked pissed, but he asked, "You have this key fob thing?"

"I do." Luc reached into his pocket and pulled it out. "Haven't seen anything like this that can do what it did to Evie. I'm hoping maybe Daemon or one of the others has some insight. I'll get a message to them."

I glanced at the fob in his hand, easily recalling the pain. "She pressed that button, and that was it. Pain—and then I turned into the Terminator."

"What happens if you push it again?" Grayson asked.

My gaze shot to him, eyes narrowing. "Besides it feeling like I'm being stabbed over and over in the head?"

"Yeah, besides that." Dryness seeped into his tone.

"We're not hitting it again," Luc replied, his fingers curling over the fob.

"What if hitting it again does something? Gives her back more memories and turns her into the Terminator again?" Grayson shot back.

"And what if it causes her more pain? Hurts her?" Luc lowered his hand, fingers still closed around the fob.

"Or what if it does nothing?" Grayson challenged. "Knowing that tells us something."

"No." Luc shook his head.

"How could pressing it and it doing nothing to Evie tell us something?" Zoe asked.

"I don't know why we're still having this conversation." Luc crossed his arms.

"Well, it could tell us that whatever that thing did—the Cassio Wave—it's unlocked whatever code April claims was in the serum. It would tell us that at least we don't have to worry about someone else hitting the button again and doing God knows what to her."

Zoe looked thoughtful, and . . .

Dammit.

"He has a point," I said. "If it does something or not, it does give us some answers."

Luc turned to me, his expression stark. "Not going to happen."

"Luc—"

"There is no way anyone is pushing a button that could possibly cause you debilitating pain."

"Maybe it won't, though." I gripped the edge of the bar top. "Look, I don't want to feel the pain again, but it's a risk—"

"That I'm not willing to let you take."

Irritation pricked along my skin. "But I'm willing to take it."

He cocked his head. "Is there anything about my words or my

stance that gives you the impression that this is going to happen? So, let's change the subject."

"It's my choice, Luc."

"And it's also my choice to stop you from making stupid choices," he retorted.

I hopped off the bar top. "You do not get to make a choice over what I do and do not do with my body."

"Oh no. Don't even try that argument." He faced me. "That's apples and oranges. This isn't about your right to do as you damn please. This is about me stopping you from potentially hurting yourself."

"I agree with Luc. We could find something out by hitting the button, but we also don't know what it will do," Heidi spoke up. "Because we also don't know if hitting that button will strip your memories on a more long-term basis. So, I don't think we should do it."

I crossed my arms. "Not helping."

"Sorry," Heidi muttered. "But that's my two cents."

Taking a long, slow breath, I tried a different route. "What if it gives me back more memories—memories of who I used to be? That's worth the risk. Do it. Hit the button. It's the only way."

"Nothing is worth the risk of seeing you hurt. Not even you remembering every damn second of what it was like to be Nadia." His chin dipped, and his voice lowered. "I know you want to feel useful. That you want to prove that you can help us—help yourself—but this is not the way."

I stilled.

Grayson cursed under his breath. "Forget it," he said. "It was a shit idea."

"Yeah." Luc slipped the fob in his pocket. "It was."

"No, it wasn't!" Shaking my head, I turned around and leaned against the bar. "I get that you don't want to see me hurt—"

"Or worse," he interjected. "We don't even know what the Cassio Wave truly is. What it really means when it gets in there and scrambles shit around in your head. Until we learn more about what it is and what it does, we need to hold off on randomly pushing buttons."

"Going to also have to side with Luc here." Zoe rested her elbows on the bar. "I think we should wait until we know more."

Of course, they also had a point. Frustrated, I folded my arms. "And what am I supposed to do while we wait?" All those important things Luc and I needed to discuss, but I had pushed to the side earlier, came to the surface. "Can I go to school? Do I even go home? If April was with the Daedalus or some other group, they're going to realize she's missing, maybe dead, and then what? She talked like they knew I existed."

"I'm not sure you're ready for this conversation, Peaches."

I wasn't, but that didn't mean we shouldn't have it. "I need to get ready, because tomorrow is going to be here sooner than later, and then what?"

"You can't go near a RAC drone. Not until we can test one out. So, school is out of the question until then."

I think I'd already known that the moment I saw my black-and-white eyes in the mirror, but still, it was a gut punch. What if I couldn't go back? Ever? What if I couldn't graduate?

"You know, we could just put her in contacts," Grayson said, and my gaze shot to him. "No one would know the difference."

"He's right, but it's not safe there for you," Luc said, taking a step toward me. "Not until we know more."

I knew what *more* meant. If it really was the Daedalus behind everything. If they were now going to come for me. But if school wasn't safe, was my home?

Was my mom?

A shudder racked me, because all afternoon I'd been trying not to think about her—think about whether she knew that there was something in that serum, if she had been lying all along. I looked up and found Luc's gaze fastened to mine.

"None of this . . . this doesn't make sense," Heidi said, twisting a strand of red hair. "You're human—I mean, yeah, the whole serum thing, but you're human. The RAC drone has never hit on you—"

"And it's never hit on April," Zoe cut in, her brows furrowed.

"Could April have been wearing contacts then?" Heidi suggested.

"I guess we'll find out if Clyde pops her eyeballs out," Grayson answered.

I curled my upper lip. "I saw her eyes change."

"April wearing contacts before or not doesn't explain anything. You've bled red. You haven't turned into a half-smoke creature,"

Heidi pointed out, and I nodded, because both were true. "I just don't get it. How in the world did you go from tripping over air to taking April out like a trained hit man?"

I pursed my lips. "That's a good question."

"Can a serum do all of that?" Heidi turned to Luc.

"None that I know of. Serums can mutate, but they don't turn you into a martial arts specialist five seconds later," Luc answered.

Zoe pushed away from the bar top, and as her gaze met mine, I had to think she was considering the same thing I was.

Those missing summer months I had no real memory of. What if I hadn't been in the house? I thought about how I'd handled that gun in April's house. The male voice I'd heard. What if? . . .

I couldn't even bring myself to finish the thought, because how could it be possible? How could I be trained and then all memory of that be wiped? How could a sound wave unlock that?

And how in the hell was my mother not involved?

"You asked me . . . if I knew why Sylvia gave you Evie's life, and I told you I didn't," Luc said into the silence.

I stiffened. He didn't know I'd talked to her about this. I hadn't a chance to tell him with everything that had happened.

"I wanted to believe it was because she missed this other girl. The heart, even a Luxen's, can make people do crazy things. But I never could make myself believe it," he went on, his purplish gaze latching on to mine. "When you asked me if I knew where you were the summer after you were healed, I didn't lie. I wanted to believe that you were there, inside those walls, being taken care of. I had to believe that at the time."

A chill swept through me, and I felt all the eyes on us.

"You want to know why I don't trust her? It's because of this. Right here. Right now. I may not know what was done to you, but there's one person who has to. That's Sylvia."

26

My house was empty when Luc and I showed up an hour later, which made sense since school had just gotten out. Mom wouldn't be back for at least three more hours, and that was if she came home on time.

"Did you text her?" Luc asked as he followed me in, carrying my backpack and my new camera.

I nodded. "I tried calling, but it went straight to voice mail." Nervous energy buzzed through me as I went into the kitchen. "That's normal, but I texted her, telling her I needed to talk to her and that it was an emergency."

"Perfect."

"You know, I haven't seen her since . . . the day before yesterday," I realized as I opened the fridge and grabbed a bottle of water. "Want one?"

Luc stood in the doorway, shaking his head.

"I mean, she's been working so late. You know that, so that's not all that suspicious, but . . ." I shut the door, turning to him. "You're going to be mad at me."

"Doubtful."

I shuffled over to him. "I talked to her the morning after Heidi was hurt, about . . . about the summer before I started school. I know you said that you wanted to be there, but I . . ."

"Couldn't wait?" He started walking backward. Shaking my head, I gave him a bashful smile as I followed him. "What did she say?"

"Not much. She thought you said something to me and then asked what you told me."

His gaze sharpened as we reached the stairs. "Of course she did."

I started up the steps. "I told her it was something that came up in conversation with Zoe, and she told me that I was here, but I wasn't suitable for going out in public. That some days I didn't remember anything, not even that I was Evie, and others I was fine. And I asked her why she did it—giving me Evie's memories." We rounded the landing, and I knew Luc was substantially slowing his steps so I could keep up with him. "She said what she'd told me before. That she missed the real Evie."

Luc was quiet as we walked into my bedroom, placing my bag by the desk and the camera on it. Then he spoke. "Do you believe her?"

Not ready to speak those words, I walked over to the bedside table and put the bottle on the stand, next to Diesel. Picking up the remote, I turned on the TV, keeping the volume low. "I . . ."

"You don't have to answer the question." He sat on the bed, resting his arms on his thighs.

"Why? Because you already know the answer?"

Luc didn't respond, and he didn't look smug about it, either. Instead, he changed the subject. "I know you were upset with me earlier."

"What gave that away?"

A half smile appeared. "I think you're brave—"

I laughed outright at that. "I'm not brave."

He lifted his brows. "You say that even though a handful of hours ago you were dealt another life-changing blow."

"Oh, I may seem like I'm dealing with that, but I'm probably going to need years of intensive therapy." I paused. "If there's such a thing for possible alien experiments."

Experiment.

That's what I was, wasn't I?

God, that was just as hard to process as learning the truth of who I was.

Luc was undaunted. "Not only that, you had to defend yourself. You took a life today, and you had to do that, but I know that's not something easy to process."

He would know, wouldn't he? A shiver coursed through me. Truth was, I couldn't let myself think about the fact that I had killed someone . . . or the fact that I felt no guilt. Did that mean something was wrong with me? Like, shouldn't I feel—

"Nothing is wrong with you," Luc answered, eavesdropping on my thoughts. "You did what you needed to do."

I was pacing in front of him, fiddling with the piece of obsidian. "Like you do?"

Luc nodded. "There are times I feel no guilt. None. It's not always like that."

I thought about the young Origins. "You're brave, Luc. You do things no one else would want to do so that others are protected."

"And you volunteered to possibly go through what sounds like the worst pain possible again," he insisted. "And you're ready to face Sylvia, knowing what that could mean."

She could tell us nothing or she could tell us everything, and if it were the latter, I didn't know what I would do.

But it definitely wouldn't be pretty.

"If that doesn't make you brave, I don't know what does."

It made me . . . desperate to know what the hell I was and what could happen.

"No." Luc reached out, catching my hand. He tugged me down onto his lap. His gaze caught mine.

"You're so much like who I knew you as. You have no idea. You've always been brave. You've always been strong."

I relaxed into him.

"You faced the cancer diagnosis the same way. Just dealt with it. Did you get upset? Yes. Did you break down a time or two? Yes." Letting go of my hand, he splayed his fingers along my cheek. "But you got up every day, and you faced it. Just like you've gotten up every day since you learned who you really are. That's strength, Peaches. The real kind."

That was what Zoe had said. "I just feel like I have no control over anything. Neither of us knows what is going to happen." My voice dropped as if I was worried about being overheard. "I could mutate. I could . . . Anything is possible."

Sliding his hand to the back of my head, he drew my forehead to his. "If something like that happens, I'm going to be here. I won't let you run off. I won't let you forget."

"Promise?" I whispered.

"Never again," he swore, his nose brushing mine. "And I know you will get through it. Not because of me, not because of your friends, but because of *you*."

The next breath I took was shaky. Maybe . . . just maybe both of them were right. Perhaps I was brave in my own way. I was strong, and if that was true, if what he said was right, then I could face what was to come . . . whatever it was.

Letting myself believe in that loosened some, not all, of the tension in my shoulders, and I wasn't sure if he knew how much that meant to me.

I closed the tiny distance between us and kissed him, hoping that he could feel what I did even if I didn't have the courage to say it, or think it, because even though I could be as brave as he said I was, there were still some things that terrified me.

What I knew I was beginning to feel for him was one of them.

His gaze snapped over my shoulder, to the television. "Oh, hell."

"What?" I followed his gaze to the TV. The volume rose, and unless the TV had become self-aware, I figured I knew who was responsible for it. "Him again."

A wry grin twisted his lips. "He's on TV a lot."

"Seriously. I don't think there's ever been a president on TV as much as President McHugh," I commented.

Luc snorted.

The president was giving some kind of briefing outside, in what I guessed was the White House Rose Garden. Along the bottom there was yet another BREAKING NEWS banner, announcing that the House had not passed the bill that would change the Alien Registration Program, or the Twenty-eighth Amendment that recognized and afforded the Luxen the same rights as humans.

The president was obviously not happy about it.

"When I campaigned to be the president of these great states, I did so on the promise that I would make America safe once more, and today's vote is a disappointment." He stared directly into the camera, doing that creepy non-blinky stare thing. "These changes to the ARP are both necessary and inevitable. Within the last forty-eight hours alone, there was an attack in Cincinnati by two unregistered Luxen terrorists—and make no mistake, that is what they are. Terrorists."

A muscle flexed along Luc's jaw as his fingers made quick work of the tiny buttons on my sweater.

Nothing knocked you out of the mood quicker than seeing the president on TV.

"There are Luxen who want to play by the rules—the changes to the ARP will keep them safe. There are Luxen who don't want to play by the rules and who want to hurt us," President McHugh continued. "And that is why I cannot in good conscience stand by and do nothing to protect the people I was voted to protect. I am issuing an executive order that will implement these changes into the Alien Registration Program."

I slid off Luc's lap and onto the bed.

"Not only that, I am issuing an executive order to reinstate the Patriot Act and the Luxen Act, allowing all branches of the government, including the military, to take unprecedented action."

Could he do this? I had no idea. I mean, I knew how basic levels of the government worked. The whole checks and balances thing. The House. The Senate. The judicial branch. Could the president just issue an order and it be followed?

The president was still looking directly into the camera when he said, "These changes will go into effect immediately and will have the full force of the law, under the Constitution of the United States of America."

Luc stiffened as he murmured, "So it begins."

"Evie, wake up."

Groaning, I rolled onto my belly and planted my face in the pillow. It couldn't be morning yet. I hadn't heard my alarm go off.

Mom's hand landed on my shoulder, shaking me. "I need you to wake up."

I shook her hand off, thrusting my arm under my pillow.

Mom shook me again. "Honey, I need you to get up. Now."

Something about her tone reached through the cobwebs of sleep, and everything that had happened earlier slammed into me. April. The questions. The president on TV and then Luc getting a call from Grayson an hour later. The officer was back—Officer Bromberg, enforcing a mixture of the Luxen Act and the Patriot Act.

He'd demanded access to the club, and he wanted to see Luc. I'd wanted to go with him, but Luc didn't want me there until he knew what Bromberg was up to.

He'd promised to come back, and I waited all evening for him and for Mom, eventually changing into my pajamas and then falling asleep. Part of me couldn't believe that I had, after everything.

Had something happened?

My heart kicked against my chest as I rolled onto my side. The room was dark, but I could make out Mom's outline. She was leaning over me, one of her hands planted on the bed next to me. Some of the cobwebs of sleep cleared. Clearly, it was still night.

"Is it Luc?" I asked, scrubbing my hand down my face.

"No," she answered. "I need you to get up."

"What time is it?"

"It's a little after two." Mom backed away from the bed as I dropped my hand. "I need you to get up," she repeated.

A second later, the ceiling light came on, flooding the room with a stark white glow. Wincing, I threw my arm up to shield my eyes from the bright glare. Mom hurried over to my dresser and crouched in front of it, grabbing what appeared to be my undies.

What the . . . ?

"What are you doing?" I rose onto my elbows. "Did you get my message—"

"There's not a lot of time to explain," she said without looking at me. "And I need you to do exactly what I tell you, Evie, because they're coming for you."

27

Icy fear paralyzed me. Some kind of primal instinct told me who *they* were, and I knew, I just knew.

"The Daedalus?" I asked.

Mom rose swiftly from the dresser and hurried to my side. Kneeling down, she clasped my hand in her cold ones. I stared at her, my chest rising and falling heavily. "I'm sorry," she said, her face pale. The thin lines at the corners of her eyes seemed deeper than normal, more noticeable. "I'm so sorry."

"What's going on? Where's—?"

"Oh, Evie." Mom closed her mouth and shook her head before she squeezed my hand. "Things at work have gotten out of hand."

"You know what happened today?" I asked.

Her eyes searched mine as she clasped my cheeks. Her hands were like blocks of ice. "Things are about to start happening, and when they do, it's all going to happen fast. Do you understand?" Letting go, she rose. "People won't even realize until it's too late."

"People won't realize what?"

She let out a shaky breath as she swallowed hard. "It was a part of the plan. From the beginning. They let all of this happen, but they lost control, and we need to leave."

"What plan? What are you talking about?" Nausea twisted my stomach. "Do you know what—?"

"Yes. I know. So do they."

I stared at her from where I sat. If she knew and they knew, then that meant she'd *always* known. And then she'd lied.

"I'll explain what I can, but I need you to get up and get ready." Mom turned to my desk. I saw my purple weekender bag sitting there, the cute one with the blue polka dots. It looked packed full. "Just do what I'm asking. Please."

Rising on shaky legs, I watched her walk over to my closet. She snatched a pair of dark-rinse jeans off the shelf. "Here. Put these on."

Feeling way out of it, I took the jeans from her and dropped them on the bed. She grabbed a sweater. The hanger spun and fell to the bottom of the closet. The fact that she didn't pick up the hanger or comment on how messy my closet was freaked me out more than anything. She'd lied—she'd been lying, but the way she was acting . . .

Something bad was going down.

She handed the sweater over to me. "Evie, I really need you to get dressed now."

For a few seconds, I couldn't move, and then I took the sweater. Mom's hands were shaking as she smoothed the flyaway hair back from her face. She was dressed like she'd just gotten home from work. Dark slacks and a white blouse. She was even wearing what she called her sensible pumps, black shoes with a low heel. She'd obviously come straight from Fort Detrick.

Mom stopped in front of me again, cupping my cheek with one hand and brushing my hair back with the other. "God, Evie, I never wanted this day to come."

Air hitched in my throat as I dropped my shirt on the bed and clasped her wrists. "You know what happened to me?"

"Please, Evie. There's no time." Her eyes, those brown contacts, met mine. They were watery. "It'll be okay, I promise you, but I need you to get ready."

I didn't believe her for one second.

Even if everything that happened today never had, being woken up like this in the middle of the night did not mean things were going to be okay.

Leaning down, Mom pressed her lips to the center of my forehead. "I know you have questions, but I need you to trust me."

My lower lip trembled as I took a step back. "But I don't."

She flinched as if I'd smacked her, lowering her hands. "I deserve that. I do. But please, get ready."

Suddenly wanting to cry and scream all at once, I forced myself to nod as my stomach flipped and flopped. Shimmying out of my bottoms, I grabbed the jeans and pulled them on.

Where was Luc?

Mom walked to the foot of the bed as she pulled out her cell phone and glanced down at it. "Come on," she murmured, pressing her lips together as her finger tapped on the screen. "Come on."

Keeping an eye on her, I grabbed a bra from my dresser and hooked the tiny clasp in the front.

I knew without a doubt, I was not going anywhere with her.

My foot, the left one, started tapping nervously as I pulled the sweater that was more of a heavy shirt on over my head, unease forming like balls of lead in my stomach. Everything felt surreal as I straightened the worn cotton.

Walking over to where my flats were by the desk, I toed them on. There was a thick envelope next to the bag. I picked it up and opened it. "Holy crap."

Hundred-dollar bills were neatly lined up in the envelope. There had to be over a thousand dollars there. Probably even a couple of thousand. A dark green billfold was at the end of the wad of cash. A passport. I pulled it out and almost fell over.

A picture of me smiled back. The same picture from my driver's license, but the name under it was not Evie Dasher.

It wasn't even Nadia's name.

The unease spread like a noxious weed. "Who the hell is Stephanie Brown?" I turned to her. "It's a fake ID and money."

"Just get ready," she repeated, taking the money from me and placing it by the bag. "Now."

I stared at her. "You need to tell me what the hell is going on right now."

"Evie—"

"You've been lying to me since the beginning!" I shouted at her, heart racing. "If you know what happened to me today, then you've always known that there is . . . there is *something* inside me."

"Please, I'll explain—"

"You took my life from me, and you just expect me to trust you?"

"And I'm trying to give your life back to you—"

Glass exploded.

Mom's body jerked as if someone had pushed her. She stumbled forward. The cell phone bounced off the carpet. She opened her mouth as her chin dropped.

Everything seemed to slow down.

I saw the broken window and the billowing curtains behind her, and then I followed her gaze. She was looking at the front of her pretty white blouse—the pretty white blouse with a quarter-size red splotch in the center.

She took a step, and her knees gave out. She folded like a sack, falling onto her back before I could draw in another breath.

The red stain spread so rapidly that her entire chest was covered in seconds.

I was rooted to where I stood, and then every muscle reacted. I sprang forward. "Mom! Oh my God, Mom!" I dropped onto my knees beside her. "Mom!"

She opened her mouth as she blinked rapidly, her hands fluttering in the air. That wasn't a stain on her blouse. It was blood, so much blood. "Evie . . ."

Horror swamped me as I pressed my hands down on her chest, a horrific sense of history stuck in a vicious cycle overwhelming me. Heidi. Luc. Mom. Blood soaked my palms.

"No. No, this isn't happening." A knot swelled in my throat, threatening to choke me. "This isn't happening!"

Mom's slim body spasmed as she grabbed at me. Her fingers dragged over my arm. Her eyes widened.

No. No. No. No.

I pushed on her chest, but it didn't help. I thought I might've made it worse, because wet warmth poured through my fingers. A tremble took hold, making it hard for me to keep my hands steady.

"You're going to be okay," I told her, voice thick. Phone! I needed to call Luc. He could heal her. "It's going to be okay. I need to call—"

She gripped my wrist as I lifted my hands and reached for the phone she'd dropped. "I tried." A thin streak of blood trickled out from the corner of her mouth, and I knew, oh God, I knew that was bad. I'd watched enough *Life in the ER* reruns to know that. "No matter . . . what, Evie." Her breath rattled as she drew in air that didn't appear to go anywhere, didn't seem to help at all. "I love you . . . I've loved you like you were mine, and I . . . I tried to make this . . . right, but it's . . . it's too late. He's coming . . . for you. I'm sorry."

"No," I whispered, and I didn't know what I was saying no to.

She let go of my wrist, and her hand fell to the floor. Her chest rose, but that was it, and her stare fixed on me, but I knew she wasn't seeing me.

A prickly sensation danced over my skin. It was like being split in two. One part of me was logical and knew what was happening. Mom had just been shot through my bedroom window and she was gone, the bullet striking her somewhere not even a Luxen could survive, or it was a bullet designed to take out a Luxen. I wasn't sure, but I knew she was past saving, and yet I didn't because I couldn't accept it.

I grabbed her shoulder, shaking her slightly. My fingers smeared blood over the neck of her blouse. "Mom?"

There was no response.

"Mom!" This wasn't happening. Oh my God, this wasn't happening. Tears streamed down my cheeks as I leaned over her. My bloodstained hands hovered uselessly over her. "Don't do this. I'm not mad at you. I'm not. I'm sorry. I trust you. I—"

A faint light flickered under her blouse, like a flashlight going on and off. My gaze flew to her face, and from her mouth, liquid radiance spilled. Jerking back, I fell onto my butt as a dull light replaced her pale skin, and her body . . . wasn't *hers*. I saw the shape of hands and features of her face, but there were silvery veins under semitransparent skin.

No.

I shook my head as I stared at what had been my mom, in her true form. I knew what that meant. I already knew, because her chest wasn't moving, and she wasn't breathing, and I couldn't take back anything I said to her. I couldn't change any of it.

I curled my fingers into my palms, digging my nails in as I briefly squeezed my eyes shut. My mouth ripped open, but I didn't make a sound. I couldn't. Rage and terror choked me. I screamed—screamed from deep inside, jangling my skull and jarring my insides.

The floor rattled underneath me. The bed shook beside me. The dresser trembled, and the entire house shook—

"Back door open. Left rear window open."

I sucked in a sharp gasp.

That was the house alarm. My gaze flew from my mother's translucent face to the open bedroom door. Icy fingers of fear dragged down my spine. That wasn't Luc. He came to the window. Granted, someone just shot through said window, but if Luc were here, he wouldn't trigger an alarm.

"System disarmed. Ready to arm."

Air punched out of my lungs. The house alarm had just been turned off. No one besides Mom and I had the code . . .

Someone was in the house. Instinct screamed at me to get up and get moving.

Body shaking, I rose and backed away from Mom. Her body blurred as my vision swam. I couldn't even think about what her body looked like right now, what that could mean. *What do I do? What do I do?* Turning around, I saw the bag and wad of cash.

Get out of the house and call Luc. Hiding was stupid. I'd seen *Taken* enough times to know that never ended well. Fighting back wasn't an option unless I miraculously turned into the Terminator again, and I didn't feel like a badass at the moment.

Moving as if I were caught in a dream, I grabbed the envelope and shoved it into my bag, wincing when I left bloody fingerprints behind.

I wiped my palms along my hips and then darted back to the bed, grabbing my cell phone. I started to turn, but then stopped, snatching up Diesel. I spun, having no idea where my charger was. Maybe in my book bag? There was no time. I ran back to the bag as I dialed Luc's number. It rang . . . and rang, and that was bad, because Luc always answered on the first or second ring.

What if they'd come for him, too?

Pressure clamped down on my chest as I hung up the phone and dropped it in my bag. I couldn't think of that right now. I couldn't think of . . . of *Mom*. Grabbing the strap, I draped it over my shoulder.

Inhaling deeply, I crept toward the open door. I didn't look back. I couldn't look back. I had to focus. That's what Luc would tell me. To focus. But it was hard, because as I stepped out onto the hardwood, every step I took sounded like a herd of cows stomping their feet. Tremors racked every limb of my body. I inched out into the hall, keeping close to the wall.

The foyer light was off, but there was a soft glow coming from the sitting room. I didn't hear anything, but I knew someone had to be in the house. The only way out was going downstairs.

I didn't want to look.

I didn't want to move.

But I had to.

Peeling away from the wall, I held my breath as I made my way to the railing. Sweat dampened my forehead as I looked down. At first, I didn't see anything.

Then I saw a rifle.

Like the assault rifle the ART officers carried. Whoever was carrying the rifle was dressed all in black. His face was covered. Not by one of those SWAT-like helmets but by a black ski mask I imagined murderers wore.

Murdery Dude wasn't alone.

Another man or woman was behind him, and then I saw another. I stopped counting as I saw four, because they were heading for the stairs.

Shit.

I stumbled back from the railing and pressed against the wall. If I was going to turn into a badass assassin, now was the time. Now was—

I opened my mouth but couldn't get in enough air. Panic clawed its way through me. They were here for me. My chest compressed. *Don't think about this. Not right now.* My wild gaze swung around the hallway, landing on my mom's bedroom door. I started to move, because all I could do at this point was hide.

The doorknob on my mom's bedroom door turned.

My heart stopped.

Oh no.

I could hear boots on the steps. The edges of my vision darkened as the bedroom door opened soundlessly. Muscles locked up as I prepared to be riddled with bullets.

Terror consumed me like a rising tide. Without warning, the ligaments and muscles in my knees just stopped working. My body slid down the wall. They were coming from both sides. I was screwed every which way from Sunday, and whatever was inside me earlier when I'd faced April wasn't there anymore. I was going to die.

I was going to die before I even had a chance to tell Luc—

A form stepped out from Mom's bedroom, long legs quickly eating up the distance between us. I shrank back, trying to make myself invisible, but it was no use.

Death strode forward, and my eyes adjusted to the darkness, picking out features—familiar features. Full lips quirked in a smirk. On his gray shirt was one of those red-and-white stick-on name tags that said HI MY NAME IS and written in black marker in the white space was TERMINATOR.

Terminator?

He extended his hand toward me when he was a few feet from me. "*Come with me if you want to live.*"

I opened my mouth, and a harsh, low laugh barked out of me as I dragged my gaze up to his. The pressure clamped down harder on my chest.

Luc stood before me.

His gaze moved from his hand to my face. "You're supposed to take my hand, and I'm supposed to pull you to your feet."

I stared up at him, breathing heavily.

"Then I save you like a total badass." He cocked his head to the side. "This is not panning out like I'd anticipated." Closing his hand, he lowered his arm. "And this is getting kind of awkward."

"What?" I breathed. That was the only word I could get out.

His gaze flickered to the stairwell. "*Terminator 2.* Peaches, if you haven't seen the movie, we're going to have problems." Those deep violet eyes shot back to me. "Please tell me you're an Arnold fan? If not, I might cry."

My blood-covered fingers dug into the strap of my bag. "Are you seriously asking me—"

He moved unbelievably fast.

Luc grasped my arm. One second I was half crouched against the wall, and the next I was stumbling backward. I bumped into the wall as he walked to the center of the hallway, just as a ski mask–covered face cleared the top of the steps.

"Are you an Arnold fan?" Luc asked again, this time addressing the guy.

The commando-looking dude swung the rifle toward Luc. A red dot skated off the wall, landing on the center of Luc's chest. My breath caught as I pushed off the wall. Not again—

"I'm going to take that as a no." Luc shot to the side, grabbing me as the man fired. The bullet slammed into the wall.

Luc was a blur as he let go of my arm and darted forward, whipping the rifle out of the guy's hand. "Already been shot this week. Not looking for a repeat."

A heartbeat later, the commando went flying over the railing. His shout of surprise ended in a grunt and fleshy thud.

Two seconds.

That was maybe how many seconds passed.

Holy crap.

Backing up, I spun around, prepared to run, but I stumbled as I saw Zoe—

Downstairs, the front door blew open and ripped right off the hinges, crashing into one of the men in the foyer. He was pinned to the floor like a squashed bug. Standing in the doorway was Grayson, who looked normal for all of about five seconds, but then he lit up from the inside. A network of bright white veins appeared under his skin. Static filled the air.

"Evie . . ." Zoe didn't look at me as she strode forward. "You need to run."

I ran.

I went straight for my mom's bedroom, the heavy bag thumping off my thigh. Someone shouted out in pain behind me, but I didn't look as I barreled into the bedroom, catching the door and slamming it shut.

Tripping over my own feet, I turned as I shoved my hair back from my face. Mom's room was dark—too dark. I smacked along the wall, hitting the switch. Light flooded the room. The curtain in front of the window swayed in the breeze.

I knew I wasn't thinking straight. Later, I would hate that I ran, but at the moment, nothing was making sense in my head. Nothing—

"Oh God," I whispered, swallowing hard as I scanned Mom's room. Her sneakers were tucked under the bench at the foot of the bed. Next to them were her fuzzy kitten slippers that were just so ridiculous. She'd bought them for herself on her last birthday.

My throat constricted as tears filled my eyes. Oh God, she was lying on my bedroom floor dead, and I couldn't do this. The bitter bite of loss was all consuming, sucking out energy and—

Cutting those thoughts off, I told myself I needed to get it together. I had to, because there were only two roads in front of me. Survive or give up, and I didn't want to die. I didn't want to hide. I wanted to fight.

That's what you are trained for . . .

The voice doubled me over as dull pain flared behind my eyes. It was him, the male.

The bedroom door swung open, and Luc's intense gaze swept over my face and then down, lingering on my arms and hands. "Are you hurt?"

"No." My hands were shaking. "The blood isn't . . . it isn't mine."

"Then who—?" Understanding flared in his face, and he cursed swiftly. "Evie . . ."

The way he said my name, full of sorrow, nearly broke me, because it was heavy and genuine, and he knew.

"She said . . . she said they were coming for me."

A thump hit the wall outside of the bedroom as he stared at me.

"How did you know to come? I called you, but you didn't answer."

Luc moved before I could track him. It felt like a heartbeat had passed, and then he was right in front of me, clasping my cheeks. "We don't have time for any of that right now."

He was right.

I slipped free, putting distance between us. "But—"

"Sylvia called me about an hour ago, but I was . . . occupied. I came as soon as I got the message, apparently with either the best or the worst timing, depending on who you ask."

That was literally the last thing I expected him to say.

"Now, I need you to be brave, Evie, like I know you can be, because we need to get the hell out of here. We're almost out of time."

Body trembling, I nodded. "I'm ready."

Something loud crashed outside the bedroom, and I jumped, half expecting someone or something to break down the door.

Luc pivoted, stalking toward the window. With a wave of his hand, the curtains flew across the room. "This is our only way out."

"The window? How am I supposed to get out of the house through that window?"

He looked over his shoulder. "You jump."

My mouth dropped open. "I know I went badass on April, but I don't think I can jump out of this window."

He twisted at the waist and extended his hand to me. "I'll make sure you land safely."

My gaze flicked from his face to his hand. I knew he'd make sure I didn't break my neck, but jumping out of a window . . . "What about Zoe?"

"She'll be fine," he said. "Give me your bag."

Lifting it off my shoulder, I handed it over. Luc took it. "What do you have in this? A baby?"

"I don't know. Mom—" My breath caught. "She packed it."

He didn't respond to that and dropped the bag out the window. I didn't even hear it hit the patio below—the hard, cement patio a neck-breaking distance below. He was crouched in the windowsill in less than a nanosecond, perched there like he had all the room in the world. "Hop up."

My gaze bounced from him to the window and then to his hand. In a daze, I placed my hand in his.

Because I trusted him.

Irrevocably.

Luc's fingers were warm as they wrapped around mine. I got one leg up as I gripped the window frame. I peered down into the darkness, feeling like I couldn't catch my breath.

Luc shifted, circling an arm around my waist. His lips brushed the curve of my cheek. "You're going to be okay."

Then he moved.

There was no time to react. He pushed out from the window. A second later, we were in the air. There wasn't even a moment to scream. The night reached up and swallowed us whole, dragging us down so fast the wind caught my hair, plastering it to my face.

The impact was jarring.

Landing on his feet, Luc took the brunt of the fall—a fall that would've snapped the legs of a human in half. He didn't even stumble. Straightening, he still had ahold of my hand as he picked up my bag. "We've got to go."

Luc started running, and I went with him, not given a real chance to think about the fact I'd just jumped out of a two-story window and survived. Dogs barked as we crossed several more yards. I was panting as he cut down the side of one of the houses several down from mine, racing toward the street. Sweat poured, and my heart felt like it was going to claw its way out of my chest.

A dark SUV waited on the curb. Luc let go of my hand and opened the back door, and I didn't hesitate. Scrambling into the back seat, I was relieved to be greeted with Kent's blue mohawk.

But something was wrong.

Under the glow of the dome light, I could see that his lip was busted. There was a dark, ugly bruise on his face, above his left cheekbone.

I gripped the back of his seat as Luc tossed my bag in beside me. "Are you okay?"

"Seen better days, honeybuns."

Luc was next to me, slamming the door shut. "Go."

I twisted toward him. "What about Zoe? Grayson?"

"They know where to meet us." He immediately found the seat belt, dragging it across me and hooking it. "We're not having a repeat of last time."

Kent tore away from the curb, gunning it as I looked behind us, half expecting to see cars giving chase. The street was empty and dark.

"What happened?" I turned to Luc, thinking of Kent's face, the call that sent him to the club. Knots crowded my stomach. "Something happened. What?"

Luc leaned back, exhaling heavily in the silence. There were no arguments. No music blaring. This was bad. "It wasn't just Officer Bromberg who came. It was him and a damn near army of ART officers."

My hands slipped off the back of Kent's seat.

"The executive order," he continued, staring out the window. "They didn't just raid Foretoken, they razed it. Took everyone before I even got there, and those that didn't go willingly . . ."

No.

"Who?" I whispered.

"Chas." Luc's voice was flat. "Clyde. They're . . . gone. Dead."

No.

"Kent got out. So did Grayson."

But—there was always a *but*.

"They took Emery and Heidi," he said, voice razor sharp while I felt my insides start to cave. "That's why I was occupied. Not at the club but at a holding area. I got them out. It was rather . . . explosive, and I'm sure it will be headline news in the morning."

Relief swept through me, but it didn't last long. Headlines tomorrow? Clyde? Chas? I didn't know them well, at least not as Evie, but their loss . . .

And Mom's . . .

I sucked in a shaky breath. "Where are they? Emery and Heidi."

"Somewhere safe for the time being. We can't worry about them right now." Luc looked over at me, and I wasn't sure how I was not supposed to worry about them—about Zoe. Even Grayson. "They knew. They made sure I was occupied, and then they made their move for you. This was a setup, Evie."

28

They failed.

This was a setup, a massive one, targeting Luc's place and mine, but they failed to capture or kill me.

I tried to sort through it all. "The club? You said it was razed?"

"Nothing but smoke and embers now," Kent answered from the front. "But that was Luc."

Luc wasn't looking at me anymore. He was focused on the darkness outside the window. "Once I got there, saw what was going down, and I made sure no one was left, I got a little angry. Needed to get rid of it, though. We were careful, but that doesn't mean there wasn't evidence."

Like April's body?

I reached over, placing my hand on his arm. "I'm . . . I'm sorry about Chas and Clyde. About everything."

He moved his arm to his leg, and my fingers curled around empty air. "It wasn't until I got to the facility they were holding Emery and Heidi in that I knew what was going down at your place."

"How?" I pulled my hand back, holding it to my chest.

"Radio transmissions." Kent's laugh was without humor. "Stupid commandos. We overheard them talking. Heard your address."

"And then I saw Sylvia's message," Luc added. "She said that I needed to come and get you out. That they were coming for you."

I jerked. "Just get me and not her?"

Luc's silence was answer enough, and I wondered if she'd even planned to leave that house. If she knew . . .

Pulling myself away from those thoughts, I rubbed my hands on my legs. "It was the Daedalus?"

"Yes," Luc growled, and white light flickered over his knuckles. "It was the Daedalus."

The drive was a blur of shadowy trees and then homes. All I knew was that when the SUV pulled into a narrow alley behind a row of dark homes, we were outside of Columbia.

I followed Luc out of the back seat, gasping and stumbling back into the side of the SUV when Grayson suddenly appeared beside Luc—alone.

I tasted fear on my tongue. "Where's Zoe?"

"She's okay," he answered, and I wanted to hear more than that. I needed to see it.

Luc placed a hand on my shoulder, guiding me away from the SUV a few seconds before Kent drove off. "Where is he going?" I asked.

"To meet up with Zoe to grab supplies," Luc answered, turning me around. "He'll be back. Both of them."

Would they?

"Yes," Luc answered, picking up on my thoughts as he led me across a gravel driveway and then into a small yard.

Grayson was up ahead, unlocking and opening a door. We followed in silence, entering a small kitchen that smelled like spiced apples. They moved ahead. A lamp came on, casting buttery light over well-worn furniture sporadically placed throughout the closed-in room.

Grayson went to the window, stopping to stand with his back to us. He was as still as a statue, almost as if he were a part of the room, a piece of furniture.

"Why don't you sit?" Luc offered.

For once, I didn't argue. I sat and then realized how weak my legs felt. I looked down at my hands. Covered with blood. Again.

Mom's blood.

I squeezed my eyes shut. "Where are we?"

"We're in a safe house for the time being."

"A safe house . . ." Opening my eyes, I let my gaze sweep the room again. My brain was full of fuzzies, like it had rubbed up against a towel. "What are Kent and Zoe getting?"

Grayson sighed so heavily it could've rattled the walls, and then he finally faced us. "Hopefully some really strong alcohol."

I wasn't sure if I wanted to see a drunk Grayson.

My gaze snagged on a framed photo on the end table next to me. Reaching over, I picked it up. It was a picture of a family—a mom and dad, and two little kids smiling with their cherub faces.

Safe house? Or did we just break into someone's home?

"I need to know what, if anything, Sylvia said to you." Luc sat in front of me on the edge of a scratched, wooden coffee table. "Can you tell me?"

The back of my throat burned, but I nodded. "I waited up for you to get back. I was worried and all, but I ended up falling asleep. The next thing I knew, she was there, shaking me awake. It was a little after two."

"So, probably not even thirty minutes before we got there," Grayson stated.

"Then what?" Luc rubbed the heel of his palm against his chest.

I stared up him, breath catching. "She told me that we needed to go, that they were coming, and that she was sorry. That things had gotten out of hand."

His gaze collided with mine, and then he knelt so we were eye level. "Did she say what had gotten out of hand?"

I shook my head. "No, but she said that this has been the plan all along. She was kind of rambling. I've never seen her like that. She was scared." I noticed that Grayson had turned to us. "She said that they let this happen, but they lost control. She never said who 'they' were, and I told her I . . ."

I saw my hands again. They were more rust-colored than pink. So much blood. The next breath I took got stuck as I lowered my hands to my lap. Luc's gaze followed my movements. I was vaguely aware of him standing and walking away, leaving me in the room with Grayson.

Which was like being left alone.

Grayson was back to staring out the window again, and he looked calm at the moment, laid-back, but tension poured from him. Air sawed in and out of my lungs. I half expected the family that owned this house to walk in any minute and freak out. They'd call the cops, and then Grayson would turn into an alien lightbulb and people would get hurt again.

People would die.

More people would die tonight.

I squeezed my eyes shut, squeezed them until I started to see white flecks of light. Maybe this was some kind of nightmare.

I was still in bed, and I was going to wake up. Life would be the *new* normal. Mom would be downstairs, getting ready for work in her goofy slippers, and I would ask about the serum and the Cassio Wave, and she would have a logical explanation for it. She always did.

But this wasn't a nightmare, and it was foolish to even entertain the thought, because reality was coming fast, in the amount of time it took to pull a trigger on an unseen gun.

There would be no waking up from this.

This was life.

It was happening.

Too many thoughts were racing, all of them competing for attention. Slowly, I opened my eyes. The room blurred a little as Mom's words came back to me.

She'd apologized to me.

The last thing she ever said to me was that she was sorry. My chest constricted.

I tried to empty my head, because I needed to prove that what Luc had said earlier was right. I was strong. I was brave. I would deal. But a horrible thought occurred to me, stealing my breath. Was Mom still lying on the bedroom floor? Had anyone found her? I had no idea how much time had passed. Or did no one know, no one care yet?

I shut down.

Right there.

Right then.

It was like a cord connected to my emotions had been snipped in two. My shoulders slumped, and the breath parting my lips was empty.

"Here."

Dumbly, I looked up. Luc had returned, and he held a damp washcloth.

A muscle thrummed along his jaw, and then he sat down on the edge of a coffee table. He was directly in front of me, close enough that our knees touched.

"We've got to stop doing this," I said, motioning to the towel. "It's becoming a habit."

He arched a brow.

I don't know why I said what I did next. The words just blurted out of me. "I should've listened to her. She told me to get up and get dressed, but I took too long. I asked too many questions. Maybe if I hadn't, we would've gotten out of the house before—"

"I don't think so, Peaches." The cloth dangled from his fingers. "I think if you hadn't stalled, they would've captured you outside, before we could get to you."

"Before she . . ." I took a deep, slow breath to ease the suffocating weight in my chest and throat. "She said she tried, but he was coming for me. She didn't get to say who it was."

Luc took my hand, folding the warm cloth over my fingers as he lifted his gaze to mine. "No one is going to take you. No one, Evie."

I believed him.

I did.

"You said she called you. I think she was talking about you," I said, and that made sense, that she was trying to assure me. "I can do it myself—clean my hands."

Several long moments passed as we stared at each other.

"I know you can, but I need to do this."

Letting out a shaky breath, I nodded. Brief silence fell between us. "Luc?"

Those thick lashes lifted as his hand stilled over mine.

"I told her I didn't trust her," I whispered. "When she asked for me to just trust her, I said I didn't."

He leaned in, getting eye level with me again. "Don't do this to yourself." His voice was just as low as mine.

"I said to her . . ." My gaze strayed from his face, back to my hands. My hands were clean, spotless except for under my fingernails. I swallowed the knot in my throat, but it got stuck. "I told her she took my life from me."

His forehead came to rest against mine. "Evie—"

"And she said she was trying to give me back my life. That's what she said before she was shot."

The towel disappeared in a flicker of Source and ash, then he was moving and pulling me toward him, and we ended up tangled together on the couch. The strange, curt distance in the SUV was no longer there. He held me, and I held him, because we'd both lost tonight.

We'd lost a lot.

Some time passed before Grayson spoke. "She said things were getting out of hand? At Fort Detrick?"

"She didn't say that, but I know she'd just come from work," I said, and Grayson turned from the window. "She said things were going to start happening and that they would happen fast. I don't know if she was talking about the people who came to the house or something else."

Rubbing my hands over my thighs, I tried to remember her words more clearly, but the panic and confusion of those moments made it hard. "She'd packed a bag with this fake ID and money—" I realized it was still in the SUV. "She had a lot of money. Thousands, probably."

"She was prepared," Luc said, sliding his arm away from my waist. "Unless she normally has thousands lying around, she was prepared."

"Which means she knew this could happen," I whispered. "This whole time . . ."

Luc looked away for a moment, and then his eyes found mine. "I'm sorry, Evie, for what happened to her, for what you had to witness."

Now I was the one who couldn't look at him. I dipped my chin, weary. "Thank you," I whispered, clearing my throat. "Do you know why they killed her? Like, they had to know she was unregistered. She worked for them."

"Seems to me that she was trying to get you out. She knew they were coming, and she wasn't going to let them take you." Sliding his hands over his face, he shook his head. "Which leaves us with a hell of a lot of questions."

I sucked in a shaky breath. "She knew what happened to me at school—with April and the Cassio Wave—but if she was in on whatever was given to me, then why would she try to stop them from taking me?"

"There's no way she didn't know what was given to you," Luc said, his gaze sweeping over my face. "She's the one who administered the serum."

"That doesn't mean she knew exactly what was in it," I reasoned desperately.

A muscle flexed in Luc's jaw as he focused on the scratches along the surface of the coffee table.

"Either way, she was trying to get you out of there before they got there," Grayson said. "They must have known that."

"And the Daedalus would see that as a betrayal," Luc added. "It wouldn't matter what she did for them in the past or the present; they would see her as a traitor, and they do not tolerate those they see as an enemy."

I closed my eyes. Could it be that she knew what was given to me, had gone along with it, but then had a change of heart? And if that were the case, did it make what she did any less horrible? If she knew at any point what was done to me, did that make her death any less hard to process?

No.

It didn't.

I pressed my palms into my eyes. "I tried to . . . I don't know, summon whatever happened to me earlier with April. I wanted to fight back, but I didn't feel any different. Not like I did when I went after April."

"Maybe that was a one-time-only thing," Grayson suggested.

"Or maybe you just don't know how to use . . . whatever is in you," Luc said, and when I lowered my hands, he'd stood. I hadn't even heard him move.

I lowered my gaze. "I can't believe she called you."

Luc faced me. "Because she hated me?"

The breath I took got stuck. "I don't think she hated you."

"She didn't like me. It's okay." A wry grin appeared. "When she pulled a shotgun on me, it was a good indication of where we stood with each other."

"She pulled a *shotgun* on you?" Grayson demanded.

"Yes."

The Luxen laughed. "Wow. I wish I could've met her."

I stared at him and then shook my head. "After the whole grilled cheese—" My voice cracked. "I think she was trying to trust you."

"She had no reason not to trust me," he said, and I recoiled at the truth in that and what it meant. We had no reason to trust *her*. "Sylvia knew if you were in danger, I would come. No matter how we felt about each other, she knew that."

Minutes ticked by as we waited for Zoe and Kent to return, and each minute felt like an hour in that living room. Grayson had returned to staring out the window, and he didn't speak. Neither did Luc.

But at some point, Luc returned to where I sat on the couch, and he was quiet as he pulled me over into his lap and folded his arms around me. There were no words as he guided my cheek to his chest and rested his chin on top of my head.

All that he could offer me in these moments were the same things I could offer him. To be there. Comfort. Closeness. It didn't change anything that happened, didn't lessen the raw grief or the confusion or anger coursing through my veins like battery acid, but it helped. I wasn't alone. Neither was he.

A tremor coursed through me, rolling from my fingertips to my toes. My throat seemed to shrink. *Keep it together.* I repeated that over and over until I felt like I could breathe again. I needed to prioritize and focus. Things had to be done.

The breath I took felt as frail as glass. "We have to call someone to take care of Mom." I lifted my cheek. "I can't just leave her there. We have to call someone."

"Okay." Grayson's hands were on his hips. "This is probably a rhetorical question, but are you an idiot?"

"Careful," Luc warned, his gaze narrowing on the Luxen. "I am not in the mood to explain how unwise it would be for you to irritate me right now."

Grayson's nostrils flared.

"I'm not an idiot." I twisted toward him. "I cannot leave my mother just lying there. I know it sounds insane, but you don't understand. She was—"

"You think I don't understand what it's like to leave the bodies of my loved ones behind to rot?" A whitish glow surrounded Grayson, and I sucked in a breath. "That you're the only one to have ever had to live knowing that you could do nothing to give your family the barest of respects? Hate to break it to you, but you're not the first or the last to go through that."

"That's enough." Within a second, I was dumped on the couch, and Luc was in front of me. "You know firsthand what it is like to watch the light go out. She *just* went through that."

I couldn't see Grayson, but I knew he turned from Luc, because he was by the window again, and I shook my head. "I'm sorry," I whispered. "I didn't know."

Silence greeted me.

Straightening out my hands, I pressed the tips of my fingers into my knees. I was going to have to leave her there. No one who loved her to take care of her. No funeral. Nothing. That was a lot to deal with. Even for me.

"It is." Luc was by my side again. "But think of it this way. Sylvia wanted you safe. She wouldn't want you to do anything to jeopardize that."

Before I could respond, Luc turned, eyeing the back of the house. Grayson stepped forward. I tensed as I heard a door close and relaxed when I saw it was Zoe and Kent.

"How are you feeling?" She immediately came to where I sat while Kent went to Luc, speaking to him in a voice that was too low for me to hear. Concern filled her expression as she placed her hands on my shoulders. "Evie?"

I could feel it, this *crumbling* inside me. I caught it in time, putting all those pieces back together. "I'm okay."

She didn't look like she believed that at all.

"Are you?" I asked. "Were you hurt when they showed up at the club?"

Zoe shook her head. "No. I'm okay. I got out, but . . ."

"Have you seen Heidi? Emery? They're okay?"

"Yes. They are. Heidi's scared, but she's okay." She glanced over at Grayson, who had returned to staring out the window like a dog waiting on the mailman. "I went into your bedroom . . ."

Air lodged in my throat.

"I am so sorry, Evie. If we had gotten there quicker . . ."

If they had gotten there sooner, would anything have changed? I didn't know. I would never know.

"Where are we going now?" I asked, looking around the room. Kent sat on the arm of the couch.

"We're going to Zone 3," Zoe answered, and honestly, if she'd said we were going to the moon, I wouldn't have been more surprised.

A dry laugh escaped me. "What?"

"We're going to Houston." Luc stepped forward. "That is the safest place I know. There are people there that can help us figure out what has happened."

Confusion took hold. "Zone 3 is nothing. It's a wasteland," I said. Houston was one of the cities absolutely destroyed by the nonnuclear pulse bombs. They were evacuated and walled up. "Why in the hell would we be going there?"

"You have no idea what is beyond the walls, in those cities." Luc tilted his head. "It's where we take the unregistered Luxen. Well, one of the places. It's also where Daemon and Dawson live."

I didn't understand. "How? They said—"

The entire front room window exploded, sending glass shards flying. Zoe yelped as she was knocked backward.

Blinding terror roared through me as I shot forward. "Zoe!"

Out of nowhere, an arm snagged me around the waist and hauled me back against a hard chest. *Luc.* I hadn't even seen him move.

I strained, gripping his arm. "Let me go! Zoe's been—"

"She's okay," he said, holding me tightly to him. "Look, she's okay."

I was looking, but it took me long seconds for everything to visually make sense. Zoe was crouched down. Grayson was holding something in his hand. She was peering over the coffee table, rubbing her shoulder.

"A rock," Grayson said, sounding bewildered. "*A rock?*"

Kent was on his belly, on the floor. His gaze darted from Grayson to us. "I'm so confused."

"That stung," Zoe said, and my legs almost gave out.

"Well . . ." Luc's arm was like a steel band around my waist. His thumb moved along the side of my rib in a slow, calming circle. "That's unexpected."

I was still gripping his arm. "You think?"

Grayson stood slowly, and then he was nothing more than a blur. He ended up at the front door, most of his body hidden as he peered out the small window. "I don't see any— Oh, shit!" He slipped into his Luxen form, becoming a human-shaped lightbulb at the exact moment the door exploded off its hinges.

Luc cursed as he grabbed me, pressing me down to the floor. A second later, another blast rocked the house—the *entire* house. A burst of heated air slammed into us. I felt my feet leave the floor as a scream got stuck in my throat. Walls shook. Dust plumed into the air. Windows blew out, and I could no longer feel Luc behind me.

I hit the floor on my knees. Instinct flared to life. I threw my arms up, over my head, just as something came down on me. Pieces of the wall? Drywall. I grunted as it hit my back, knocking me down. The air immediately became thick, coating my throat and making it hard to breathe.

Were we just *bombed*?

Ears ringing, I peeked through the space between my arms. White smoke poured into the living room, and I couldn't see more than a foot in front of my face. Heart pounding, I started to call out, but my lungs seized. Deep, body-rattling coughs consumed me as I shifted onto my side. Debris slipped off me. Eyes watering and body spasming, I cleared my throat. "Zoe? Luc?" I thought I called out, but the ringing was still so loud.

Scanning the destroyed room, I saw where the coffee table had been. It was in pieces, legs snapped right off it. Zoe was nowhere to be found. I looked to the right, and I thought I saw someone stumbling to their feet. It was just a shape.

Panic dug in with razor-sharp claws as I scrambled across the floor, looking for Luc. There! Something was sprawled along the floor near the stairs. It couldn't be him—no way.

"Luc," I croaked out, starting, trying to rise.

Out of the thick, cloudy smoke, a tall figure came toward me. I thought at first it was Grayson, maybe even Kent, but as the shape grew closer, parting the smoke, I saw what was held in its hand, pointed right at me.

The barrel of a gun.

29

The man wore a black ski mask, shielding the entirety of his face. My entire being focused on the tip of the barrel as my heart seemed to grind to a halt in my chest.

I was going to die, and people lied.

I didn't see my life flash before my eyes. There was no mental photo album, highlighting all the best moments. All I saw was the barrel of the gun. The gloved hand that held said gun. That hand did not shake. Not even a tremor. He held it like he'd pointed a gun at a teenage girl a hundred times.

A shiver of energy rushed over my skin as I saw his forefinger twitch, pulling back on the trigger as he lowered the gun, so it was pointed at the center of my chest. The shot sounded like a crack of thunder. I threw my arm up out of instinct, as if my hand could somehow deflect the bullet.

I waited for the pain—the blinding, final pain.

It didn't come.

The man was staring down at the gun. Had it misfired?

"What the hell?" his muffled voice asked.

I didn't question my good luck.

Gripping the heavy piece of drywall that had landed on me, I sprang to my feet and swung the piece of the wall as hard as I could. It connected with his arm, breaking in half. The man grunted, and the gun fired again, this time the bullet drilling through the floor next to me.

I took a step back as the smoke and dust settled, empty-handed. My wild gaze darted around for another weapon. His hand whipped out, and I didn't even see the blow coming.

Red-hot pain erupted along the side of my head. Stars burst

behind my eyes. Crying out, I stumbled to the side, dizzy and nauseous. My knees smacked off the floor.

Holy crap, the man punched like a pro boxer.

A roaring sound invaded my senses, and for a second, I thought maybe a tank was coming through the house. At this point, anything was possible, but the sound . . . it was part animal, part human. A sound of pure, primal rage letting loose. Electricity filled the air, popping and crackling.

I lifted my head, wincing as the room seemed to shift and whirl. Without warning, a figure appeared in front of me, standing before me like a wrathful sentry, shoulders broad and legs widespread.

It was *Luc*.

He was the source of the sound—the source of the growling fury. The house began to tremble again. Gasping, I fell back against the destroyed wall.

"*That* was a huge mistake," Luc growled.

Floorboards rattled. Particles of dust lifted into the air, broken chunks of wall following. White, luminous light filled the veins along Luc's forearms. Static charged the air. Pieces of furniture rose, sucked right up to the ceiling.

That was Luc, all Luc, and that kind of power was unfathomable.

Masked Man had a death wish. He swung the gun toward Luc, and Luc . . . laughed. A deep, challenging laugh that raised the hairs all over my body. Micah's words came back to me in a rush.

We were all dark stars, but Luc was the darkest.

The gun flew out of Masked Man's hand, landing in Luc's. Muscles flexed along his back and shoulders. Metal ground together. "I don't think you'll be needing this."

Then Luc opened his hand.

Nothing but dust sifted through his long fingers, falling silently to the floor.

"Christ." Masked Man shuffled back a step.

I echoed the sentiment.

White light flickered over Luc's knuckles, snaking out and spitting electricity. Pitching forward, I pushed up with my hands and stood.

Luc lifted his arm. A powerful bolt of energy erupted from his palm, smacking into the chest of the man. The blast lifted him into the air, sending him spinning back down to the floor several feet away.

Masked Man landed in a boneless, smoking heap.

No twitching. No moaning. The man was dead the moment the light hit him.

Luc started to turn toward me, but I heard Zoe shout his name. He stopped just as several men, over half a dozen, filed in from where the front door had once stood and spread out across the room.

These men looked like the ones who had entered my house—dressed all in black, carrying the same long-barreled rifles.

Zoe came out of nowhere, vaulting over the overturned couch like a damn Olympic gymnast. She was fast, nothing but a blur of curls and long limbs as she appeared in front of the closest killer dude. Snatching the rifle out of the man's startled hands, she whipped it back around like a baseball bat, catching the masked gunman upside the head. The man went down, and I doubted he was getting up again.

Like a strike of lightning, she dipped low as another fired. Her hand shot out, gripping the man's calf. He screamed, dropping the rifle. His knees buckled as he turned into a living x-ray. His bones lit up underneath his skin.

A bolt of pure energy shot across the room, slamming into another gunman. It came from Grayson. He was on his feet, in full Luxen mode, but Luc . . .

He rose off the floor by several feet. I tripped over broken drywall, my mouth hanging open. He was suspended in the air, hovering several feet off the floor.

I'd never seen him do *that*.

"Have you guys seen the first X-Men movie?" Luc asked, speaking as if he were discussing the weather. "It's an old one, but a favorite. If you ask me, one of the best cinematic scenes in all of movie history was in that film."

They stared at him, slowly backing up as somewhere, off in the distance, sirens screamed to life.

I could hear the smile in Luc's voice when he said, "I'm going to do you a solid and re-create it."

Luc lifted his hands.

All the rifles flew out of the hands of the attackers, then stopped in midair. The rifles flipped around, turning on their owners.

I'd *seen* this movie.

I *knew* this scene.

I so doubted there was a Professor X to step in here.

"Zoe?" Luc clipped out.

A warm hand curled around mine, and I looked over. Zoe now stood behind me, her face and hair covered in chalky dust. She spoke, but I didn't hear the words over the pounding of blood. When she started moving, started pulling me forward, I went.

Dodging fallen furniture and crumbling walls, we entered what was left of a kitchen. The cabinet doors were open, and even in here, items had risen to the ceiling. Pots and pans. Utensils. All the metal was bent in half, as if it were trying to be sucked through the ceiling.

"We've got to go." Kent appeared, throwing open the screen door. It came off its hinges, hanging crooked. Blood marred the skin under his lower lip, and I wasn't sure if that was from earlier or not. I was just glad to see him still standing.

Zoe rushed out of the kitchen, holding tightly to my hand. I dug in, though, looking back through the mess. "What about Luc?"

"He'll be fine." Zoe stepped out into the cool, night air, but I dug my feet in.

"I'm not leaving him," I said.

"He'll be okay. I swear—Christ," she gasped as I jerked my arm free from her grasp, causing her to stumble.

I spun around and was halfway back through the door when I heard a series of what sounded like fireworks going off, a quick succession of *pops* and then fleshy thumps, one after another.

I didn't know what to feel as I stood there. Sympathy for these men? Empathy? No. I felt nothing like that. They were here to kill us.

Luc was suddenly in front of me, appearing out of the dust. The pupils of his eyes burned brightly as his gaze fixed on mine.

Heart thumping, I lifted my hand, palm up.

His hand folded over mine, and then we were running through a narrow backyard, pushing through overgrown grass and weeds. We passed a run-down shed, bursting out into an alley.

Zoe stopped suddenly up ahead. An oversize SUV was parked out back, running. Painted white and definitely big enough it could nearly seat a baseball team, I knew this was not the one I'd gotten into earlier. This was a Yukon. I didn't know a lot about cars, but I knew these things were super-freaking expensive.

"How did you get this car?" I asked.

"I used skills and my amazing credit score." Kent climbed into the driver's seat, rubbing his hand under his lip. "Get in."

"Is your skill grand theft auto?"

Zoe opened the back door, motioning me to climb in. "Among other things."

At the moment, stealing a car was definitely the least of my concerns. I climbed in, and seconds later, Zoe was beside me, slamming the door shut, and Luc was coming through the other as Grayson got situated in the front seat.

No one said anything as the SUV coasted out of the alley and onto the main road, slowing down as several police cars raced past us, heading to the poor, destroyed home. We left the silent, sleeping neighborhoods behind and hit the highway, picking up speed.

I stared at Luc. He was looking out the window, his profile as if it were cut out of stone. Tension radiated from him.

"Should've kept one of them alive," Grayson grumbled, shifting in the seat. "I imagine we could've made one of them talk."

My head snapped in Grayson's direction. "I don't think we had the time for that."

Luc slowly looked at me. In the darkness of the SUV, his gaze swept over my face. My heart stuttered as he gently placed his hand along my jaw, his cool fingers brushing my temple, right where pain flared from the blow I'd taken.

The touch was barely there, not exactly unwanted but definitely eliciting a riot of responses throughout me. I drew in a shallow breath, and then felt *it.* Warmth radiated from his fingertips, and I jerked back, bumping into Zoe. He was healing me, and it wasn't necessary. I was okay, but he was thinking of me, always thinking of me, and I leaned over, placing my fingers along his jaw. A moment passed, and then his fingers were gone from my cheek. I pulled back, scanning his face. Shadows crept across Luc's features as he withdrew, staring out the window once more, and there was nothing but quiet for miles and miles.

It was Kent who broke the silence, first by attempting to play a game of I Spy with Grayson, which was impossible for two reasons. One, it was pitch-black outside and we couldn't see anything, and two, Grayson was not interested. Not even remotely. I was pretty sure I heard Grayson threaten to punch Kent in an area that would ensure Kent would have some difficulty going to the bathroom.

Then Kent turned on the radio.

Much to everyone's dismay, he settled on a station that played country music.

Huh. Never would've guessed that.

An argument ensued, ending when Grayson threatened to zap him, and so the radio went off, and it was silent again while I tried not to focus on four things:

My mom.

Luc's abnormal, stony silence.

Heidi and Emery's whereabouts.

The nearly overwhelming need to visit a bathroom.

I looked over at Luc, wishing we were somewhere private where we could talk. Something was wrong with him, and I knew it had to do with what had happened back in the house and in his club. He'd killed those men. He'd had to, but I could tell it was bothering him, as was the loss he'd suffered tonight. He'd told me that some deaths didn't get to him, but others did, and I knew which way these were falling.

Unease warred with the need to find a potty. They had been living, breathing people.

People who probably had families. People, I imagined, who got up every morning, maybe drank coffee and checked out the news. People who probably liked chocolate cake and steak. People who wanted to end my life.

People who had ended my mom's life before I had a chance to really know her, because as I sat in the Yukon, wedged between Zoe and Luc, I realized I never knew her.

Not really.

I only ever knew what Mom had shown me.

And it was far past the time to admit that most of what Mom had shown me was a lie, just like April. What had April called the woman I'd thought had been her mom? Her handler. Was that what my mom was, too? A handler?

Thickness crept into my throat and made the next breath I took hard as I stared at Luc's profile, pushing aside my own problems. These deaths were cutting into him, and those people . . . they hadn't been good. I believed that in my heart.

Clearing my throat, I rubbed my hands on my knees. "So . . . um, where are we going? I mean, I know you said Houston, but how long will that take?"

"Driving nonstop would take a little over twenty hours." Zoe drew one leg up, resting it against the door. She yawned, and I guessed catching a flight was totally out of the question. "Give or take a few hours, depending on traffic."

"We'll be hitting rush hour in a few of the big cities," Kent chimed in from the steering wheel.

"We're not going straight through," Luc said, and it was probably the first time he'd spoken in well over an hour. "We can't."

I peeked over at him. "Are you going to elaborate?"

He didn't look over, and I thought his eyes were closed. "We can't just roll up to Zone 3 and knock on a door."

Kent chuckled. "Is there even a door to knock on?"

"You've been there?" I asked.

"I come from there."

So many questions rose to the surface, but Luc jumped back in. "We need to make a few . . . calls. Make sure our arrival is known. We're going to have to lie low for a couple of days."

"We're going to the ATL." Kent's Mohawk bobbed and weaved. "To Hot-lanta, which rhymes with Mylanta. And Santa. Oh, and Fanta." He paused. "God, I'd do dirty, nasty things for some Fanta right now. What about you, Evie? I've never asked. Do you like Fanta?"

I stared at him. "I haven't had it."

"What? That's the first thing we're going to do when we get to the Peachtree City. Gonna get you some Fanta. It's like carbonated fruit orgasming in your mouth."

My eyes widened. The imagery that painted . . .

"God," Zoe muttered under her breath. "We aren't actually going to Atlanta, but one of the suburbs."

My stomach took that moment to remind me that there were actually five things I was trying to ignore. It rumbled loudly.

Luc lifted his head off the window, angling his body toward mine. "Hungry?"

No point in lying. "Yeah."

"Stop at the next gas station or rest stop," he ordered.

"Yes, sir." Kent saluted him.

"You sure that's a good idea?" Grayson pulled his legs off the dashboard. "We're only in Virginia. Not that far."

"We make it a quick stop and get back on the road." Luc leaned forward, resting his arms on his thighs. "We should be fine."

Should be wasn't exactly reassuring.

"We'll *make* it fine," Zoe said.

From that point on, the conversation circled around the different types of Fanta that Kent insisted I had to try, and honest to God, I'd only thought there was one kind. About fifteen minutes later, he took an exit near Richmond, and we ended up in the parking lot of a large, open-all-night Exxon. There was only one other car in the parking lot.

Zoe lightly touched my arm, drawing my attention. She'd already gotten out and was leaning across the seat. "Your bag is in the back. You might want to grab a clean shirt before you head in there."

At first I didn't get why, but then I glanced down at myself. It was dark, but I could see the shadowy stains on my stomach and chest. Blood.

Yeah. That would draw unwanted attention.

Suppressing a shudder, I nodded and scooted out. Looking up, I saw that Grayson and Kent were already cutting across the parking lot, heading inside. Zoe lingered on the other side, her back to me as she watched the road. My legs felt wobbly as I walked around to the back of the Yukon. The hatch was already open, and my purple bag was sitting right there.

The bag Mom had packed.

I blinked rapidly, fighting the wetness gathering in my eyes as I carefully tugged the zipper open and spread the sides. The envelope of money was still there, as was the passport . . . and Diesel.

Trying not to think about the smudges along the envelope or how everything got into this bag, I pulled out the first shirt I saw. After making sure the coast was clear, I quickly yanked off the ruined shirt, planning to toss it in the nearest garbage can or maybe light it on fire. One of the two. I pulled on the new shirt, breathing in the scent of detergent.

Pain squeezed down on my chest, so real and so tight. Home. My shirt smelled like home, like Mom—

I cut those thoughts off and started to zip the bag up, stopping suddenly when I thought of my phone. Hadn't I dropped it in my bag?

"You won't find your phone," Luc said.

Gasping, I spun around, placing a hand against my chest. "Christ, you're going to give me a heart attack."

"I wouldn't want that to happen. Seriously." He came around the rear of the SUV. "We destroyed your phone when we got to the house in Columbia. Probably not soon enough. After all, our location was ferreted out with a quickness that was impressive."

Months ago, I would've flipped out if my phone had been destroyed. I mean, my phone had everything on it. Even a game of Candy Crush that I'd been playing for about two years straight, reaching a level of 935. But today?

I just sighed. "Okay."

Luc leaned a hip against the SUV. He was quiet as I pushed the clothing back down. "I had to," he said finally.

Zipping up my bag, I faced him. I knew exactly what he was talking about. "I know you did. I know that sounds harsh, but it had to happen. They were going to kill us—"

"The man who had his gun on you didn't have bullets loaded into his gun." His arms crossed over his chest. "It was some kind of tranquilizer. They weren't planning to kill you."

Shock rippled through me. "Why does that feel worse than them wanting to kill me?"

"Because it is."

A shudder worked its way through me. The Daedalus didn't want me dead. They just wanted me, and knowing what I did, that would be worse than death. I pushed those thoughts aside, because what could I do about it right now? Nothing. I stepped toward Luc. "Are you okay?"

Luc didn't answer for a long moment. "It's not their deaths that are bothering me, Evie. The moment they came for you, that was it for them. They weren't going to walk out of there. It's not even what happened at Foretoken. Losing Chas and Clyde is going to eat at me, no mistake there, but what is happening to you now is my fault."

My stomach *whoosh*ed.

"I did this to you," he said. "I did this to you to save you, and all I've done is put you in the crosshairs of the Daedalus."

30

I tried to get Luc to talk to me after what he'd said, but he wasn't having it, and we really didn't get the chance. There was no privacy, and we didn't have time.

I'd let it go for the time being.

After using the restroom and grabbing a buffet of chips and cookies from the gas station, we got back on the road. My full stomach told me that I'd successfully pigged out. There was even an orange Fanta soda involved, courtesy of Kent. At some point, Zoe climbed into the seats behind us, stretching out while I stared out the window, watching the tree-covered valleys blur by.

I didn't remember falling asleep, but I must've, because after some time, I found myself tucked against Luc's side. Daylight streamed in through the windows as all my senses fired up and started working again.

Luc's chest rose and fell deeply under my hand. Steady. The hand above my hip was still. He was asleep, and I didn't want to wake him. I didn't dare move or breathe too deeply. My gaze shifted from the back of the seat.

And right to the ultrabright blue eyes of Grayson.

I sucked in a startled breath but managed not to move.

Grayson was peering around his seat, staring at me—at us. Whoa. How long had he been doing that?

"Creepy," I mouthed.

He smiled, and my nose wrinkled. The wide, ear-to-ear smile was even more creeptastic. His gaze flicked up, and then he started to turn around, leaving me to plot how to sit up without waking Luc. I would just need to be stealthy, like a—

The thumb attached to the hand on my hip moved. Air hitched in my throat. The movement wasn't a twitch. Oh no, it was a very controlled, slow swipe of the thumb over the curve of my waist, eliciting a sharp series of tingles down my legs and up my side.

I was back to staring at the seat in front of me, my breathing now fast and shallow.

Luc was . . . he was drawing . . . *symbols*? An idle circle. A star. An . . . ampersand?

He was definitely awake.

Every part of my being focused on that thumb, leaving no room to think about why I was here, where we were heading, or what had happened. My brain had officially checked out, handing over control to my body, and my body was brimming with curiosity.

Luc drew a check mark.

A warm, heady tension swept over me, and inside my shoes, my toes curled. Luc was barely touching me, and my heart was still racing.

My eyes drifted shut, and I immediately saw her—my mother in her true form, lying dead on my bedroom floor. Sorrow punched through the pleasant haze. I stiffened as my thoughts wandered from that to another train wreck. After what happened with April, I knew it would be a while before my life returned to normal. If it ever would. I guessed I'd held some hope that I'd be able to return to school, see James, and graduate. That I could have those two lives. But as I lay there, nestled against Luc, escaping to a city I'd never been to and then to another I'd believed destroyed, I realized that maybe I knew why Luc hadn't wanted to include me in what he did at the club.

There was no straddling these two worlds. You were either in or out, and now there was no choice. I was in over my head.

His hand stilled.

Slowly dragging in a deep breath, I turned my head and looked up.

Amethyst eyes met mine. "Hey."

"Hi," I croaked out.

"Sorry," he whispered, and I knew he was talking about my loss of choice. Maybe he didn't even need to peek in on my thoughts to know where my thoughts went.

I sat up, pushing the hair out of my face, not at all surprised to find that it felt like a squirrel had nested in it.

Looking over my shoulder, I saw that Zoe was still out, curled up on the back seat. Turning back around, I clasped my hands together.

"Nice of you all to finally join us," muttered Kent from the driver's seat.

I couldn't believe he was still driving, but I realized the bruise and split lip were gone. I glanced at the passenger seat. Had Grayson healed him?

I looked out the window, squinting. I had no idea where we were. We were surrounded by thick, tall trees sporadically broken up by cute, old-looking homes. Kent turned down a narrow road, and those ancient oaks eventually blanketed the street, creating an eerie canopy that reminded me of steepled, bony fingers.

This was not how I imagined a suburb of Atlanta looked. "Where are we?"

"About five minutes out from where we need to be, Evie Beanie," answered Kent, and I frowned. "We're in Decatur."

Evie Beanie? I think I preferred *honeybuns*. "How far is it from Atlanta?"

"Not far at all. A handful of miles," he answered. "MARTA rail system runs from Atlanta to here. A lot of commuters. A lot of people that aren't going to pay attention to us."

My hands twisted together nervously. "The . . . trees are beautiful. Creepy but beautiful."

"Decatur is an old town, founded before the Civil War." Luc shifted on the seat beside me. A second later, he smacked his hand down on the back of the seat, making me jump.

"What the—?" Zoe shot up, stopping mere inches from hitting her head on the roof of the car. She swung toward Luc, eyes narrowing. "Asshole."

He grinned as he lifted his hand, dragging his fingers through the messy waves. "We're almost there."

"You know, you could have woken me up in a nice way," she shot back.

He chuckled under his breath. "You know me better than that."

"True," she muttered, sitting back. Her gaze flickered to mine. "How long have you been up?"

"Just a few moments."

"Bet he didn't wake you up like that." She sighed.

I grinned a little, and it felt weird as I faced the front. Letting out a shaky breath, I went back to staring out the window, because that was easier than, well, thinking about everything at the moment. The Yukon slowed and then hung a right, climbing a steep hill. Sunlight peered through the trees as some of the oaks cleared. A house came into view.

A large log-style house.

Two stories with a raised front porch, the place looked like a retreat. I leaned forward, my gaze skating over the many windows. "Whose house is this?"

"Mine," answered Luc.

Leaning back from the window, I looked over at him. "What?"

One side of his mouth kicked up. "I own many properties under a false identification with real money." He paused, scratching idly at his chest. "This is one of them."

Shock rendered me speechless, and I didn't know why, out of everything that had happened, him owning multiple properties surprised me so much. Maybe it was because he hadn't mentioned it. Then again, I couldn't fathom when that would've come up in conversation.

The Yukon halted outside of a wooden garage door. Grayson opened the passenger door. The engine was still rumbling when where we were really truly hit me.

I wasn't in Maryland anymore.

I was in Georgia, in a town I'd never heard of.

"What happens now?" I asked no one in particular.

It was Luc who answered. "We go inside."

Swallowing down the lump in my throat, I looked at him.

"We rest up. We wait," he said, his gaze holding mine. "That's what we do."

None of that sounded like enough. Not at all. We could rest. We could wait. But there was more. "We need to find out what the hell was done to me and why it led to this."

Admiration danced across his striking features. "We will."

The inside of the house was jaw-dropping, just as beautiful and spacious as it was on the outside. The lower level was completely open, the space dominated by a large living room with one of those sectional couches that were two wide cushions deep; the kind of couch that sucked you in and never let you out. There was a TV about the size of the Yukon mounted to the wall. There was a dining area and a kitchen worthy of a top chef. There were stairs that led to a second floor.

"Do people live here regularly?" I asked, thinking it was a waste of beautiful space for it to sit empty.

Luc walked ahead, toward the kitchen. "A lot of people are in and out, but no one stays here on the regular."

"It's my favorite place." Kent dived onto the couch, landing with a happy-sounding grunt. " 'Wake me up before you go-go . . .' "

I stopped behind the couch, frowning at him. He'd face-planted on one of the cushions, and all I could see was the limp, blue mohawk.

Grayson drifted into the kitchen, following Luc, who was now at the fridge. "We're going to need to stock up on some food and drinks," he said, head tilted as he eyed whatever was in the fridge.

"How long do you really think we'll be here?" I asked.

"As long as it takes for Daemon to know what went down." Closing the door, he straightened and walked behind a huge kitchen island. "That's what we're waiting on. See that door there?" He nodded at the two across the kitchen. "The one on the left is the pantry. The one on the right leads down into the basement. Don't go down into the basement."

"Well, that sounds like the start of every horror film," I replied.

He shot me a dry look.

I lifted my hands. "Okay. Whatever." Not like I was planning to. Basements were always full of spiders, cobwebs, and ghosts, but now I was super curious.

Zoe brushed past me. "I'm heading upstairs to pick out a room."

"Not fair!" came Kent's muffled voice, but he didn't move from his prone position on the couch.

Zoe shook her head as she started toward the stairs. Picking up my bag, I followed her. "There are two master suites," she explained when we reached the top. "One at the end of each hall."

"You've been here before?"

Zoe nodded, not looking at me.

"When?"

She walked toward a closed-up room with double doors. "The last time was this summer when I . . ."

My mind raced back in time. "When you said you were going

on vacation with your uncle? You told me you guys were going to Ocean City."

"I came here instead." Zoe pushed opened the door, and cool air that smelled faintly of woodsy teak greeted us. "I had to. Anyway, you take this bedroom. It has its own bath, like the one at the other end, which I am totally commandeering. The guys can have the other bedrooms and share the other bathroom." Flipping on a light, she stopped and turned to me. "Because I am so not sharing a bathroom with them." She paused. "But I'm guessing you'll be sharing one with Luc?"

I didn't know how to answer that. We were together. Boyfriend. Girlfriend. Sharing a bedroom, though, seemed . . . next level. So, I just shrugged.

Zoe arched a brow.

Walking into the spacious bedroom, I dropped my bag on the bed and then sat down. Zoe joined me after a few seconds. We said nothing as we sat there, staring at the closed door of the bathroom. I scanned the room, spying a guitar in the corner.

This was Luc's room.

She spoke first. "This wasn't how I was expecting my week to go."

My lips twitched, and then a rough laugh burst from me. "Same."

"We're going to be okay." She knocked her shoulder off mine. "We'll make our way to Zone 3, and there will be people there that can tell us what was . . . done to you. They'll have answers, and we'll be safe."

Swallowing hard, I nodded. "Will we see Emery and Heidi again?"

"Yes. Of course. They're heading there, but they're going to lie low for a while. They were spotted, so they just have to be careful."

"And then what?" I asked, looking over at her. "What happens once we get there? We find out what . . . was done to me, but then what?" I huffed out a dry laugh. "We live out our days there, in a city destroyed by EMP weapons? No school. No college. No job, I guess." I shook my head. "Is that the future?"

Zoe was quiet for a long moment. "I don't know, Evie. I really don't."

31

The first thing I did when Zoe left to commandeer her room was to take a shower. I felt sticky and gross, and I hoped once I was clean, my mind would be clearer.

Rooting around in the bag, I pulled out a pair of jeans and a shirt. Even though it was comfortable in the house and November, it was still sticky and humid outside. My hand brushed over a tube as I pulled out a pair of undies.

Peaches.

My breath wheezed.

Mom had packed my favorite moisturizer. I couldn't believe it. Crazy things had been going down, and my mom had packed my moisturizer.

Tears burned the backs of my eyes as I placed the tube on the bed and then took out Diesel, placing him on the nightstand. Blinking back tears, I backed away and headed to the bathroom.

Stripping off my shirt, I yanked off my jeans and stepped out of them, glancing down. I froze. Coppery brown smudges were on my stomach, my thighs . . .

My hands hung limply at my sides.

The blood had soaked through, drying on my skin. I hadn't noticed it because the jeans were dark rinse. Then again, I wasn't sure I would've noticed anyway. A twisting motion in my chest stole my breath. I looked up, catching my reflection in the mirror above the vanity.

I almost didn't recognize myself.

When I had stopped to use the restroom at the gas station, I hadn't looked at myself. I don't know why. I just couldn't. I didn't want to look at myself now, but I couldn't look away.

Faint shadows formed under plain brown eyes that looked tired.

My face was paler than normal, almost like I was about to get sick. Was I? I thought of Sarah and the black bile she'd spewed. It was possible. Who knew what would happen? The freckles were there, always there. My lips looked a little dry, and that was kind of gross.

I touched my cheek, where the man had struck me. There was no mark. Nothing.

I looked like I always did. How many times had I stood in front of my bathroom mirror, trying to figure out if I was more Evie or Nadia? How many times had I lain awake at night, struggling to come to terms with who I used to be and who I was now? Countless times.

Too many.

Because it now seemed so clear to me that it didn't matter. I was a mixture of both, and I was also neither of them.

I also looked like I hadn't slept in a week.

Maybe a month.

Pulling away from the mirror, I turned on the shower, and within moments, lovely warm steam was building. I peeled off the remaining clothes and stepped inside the stall, biting back a moan when the water hit my skin. Muscles I didn't even know I had screamed in relief as I turned around, letting the stream wash over me. I looked down at my feet, and a puff of air parted my lips.

Pinkish water ran between my toes, circling the drain. Blood. Mom's blood.

Smacking my hands over my face, I squeezed my eyes shut and pressed my lips together, holding my breath.

Mom.

Disbelief rippled through me, that part of my brain that still couldn't believe she was gone. It had only been sixteen or so hours since I'd last talked to her.

Sixteen hours. Maybe a little more, but just *hours* ago, she'd been alive . . .

Now she was gone.

And I was now gone, wasn't I?

Tiny white lights were forming behind my lids. A burn started in my lungs.

Were people looking for me right now? Did they leave Mom there to be found by police? The commotion had to have been reported.

Had anyone found my mother and begun to ask questions? Was I a missing person, assumed . . . dead? Or did the public not even know what happened? Maybe we'd been erased.

My head began to swim, and my body began to feel shattered. A tremble shook my arms and then my legs. I started to double over but caught myself. Yanking my hands away from my face, I opened my eyes and mouth, dragging in deep gulps of air, so deep that I choked and then heaved. Throwing out an arm, I slammed my hand on the tile wall and steadied myself.

Pull it together. That's what I needed to do. *Pull it together.* I could do this. I had to do this.

So I did.

I opened my eyes and straightened, removed my hand from the tile—the *cracked* tile. My head tilted to the side as I looked between it and my palm. Had I done that? Or had it been cracked before?

Unease slithered through me as I lifted my face to the pounding water, but I forced my mind blank, and then I stitched every broken part back together. I washed my hair twice, scrubbed my body down twice with the wonderful woodsy-scented body wash that I was sure belonged to a dude. I even scrubbed the bottoms of my feet and between my toes. By the time I finished with my shower, my body was pink from all the scrubbing, and I thought I had pulled it together.

I grabbed one of the big, fluffy towels and wrapped it around me, cinching the two halves above my breasts. Finding a comb, I got down to working out all the ridiculous tangles while staring at my feet, because avoiding the mirror felt like it would be counterproductive to keeping it together.

Satisfied with my hair, I opened the bathroom door, stepped out, and immediately came face to chest—a well-sculpted, golden, *damp* chest.

Luc's chest.

Gasping, I stumbled back a step as my hands flew to my towel, holding on to it for dear life. My gaze shot to his.

All the oxygen fled my lungs and my body and my brain at the sight of his *expression,* his *stare.*

His eyes were wide, and the purple hue was literally churning, swirling with a potent emotion that singed the tips of my ears. His features were stark and sharp, full of tension. Lips parted, he didn't seem like he was breathing at all as he stared at me, and he . . .

Luc looked . . . *hungry*.

A fine shiver skated over my skin. Demands rose to the tip of my tongue. *Hold me. Touch me. Kiss me. Be with me,* because then I wouldn't have to think about anything else, and I knew Luc could make that possible.

His gaze dipped—dropped to where my fingers clenched the towel and then lower. The towel was big, but it wasn't long. It barely covered all the lady bits, and his gaze was slow and heavy like a caress.

My heart started pounding in my chest, and those impossibly thick lashes rose as he dragged his gaze back up. I felt like I wasn't even wearing a towel.

I felt *bare*.

Our gazes collided, and I realized how close we were standing. Only a couple of feet separated us.

His chest rose. "You're . . ." He trailed off, but that one word was deep, raspy.

That one word felt *bare*.

A hand lifted from his side. One leg moved forward, toward me, and a warm flush spread across my skin. The pupils of his eyes turned to diamonds.

I dampened my lips as a nervous, edgy feeling swamped me, and a deep, throaty sound came from him, causing the muscles low in my stomach to tighten.

I knew if he touched me right now, I would be lost. He would be lost.

Luc blinked, and it was like a switch being thrown. He stepped back. His cheeks seemed to deepen in color. Was he blushing?

Oh my God, Luc *was* blushing.

"I'm sorry," he said, his voice rough and raw. "I just took a shower in the other room and was coming in here to grab the guitar. I was going to be in and out." He swallowed hard. "I didn't intend for this to happen."

I believed him, but confusion surfaced. "It's okay."

Luc opened his mouth but seemed to change his mind. For a second, he looked wholly unnerved. He pivoted around, movements stiffer than his normal fluid grace, and he left the room without looking back. And I stood in the same spot for several moments, wondering what in the hell had happened. What was going on with him?

I glanced over to where the guitar still sat.

Then I quickly got changed. Barefoot, I padded across the room and went out into the hall. I saw the open doorway to the bedroom across the hall. Somehow I knew he was in there.

I walked over and peered inside. Luc was standing in front of a narrow bed, all the long, lean muscles of his back on display as he pulled a shirt on over his head. As his head poked free of the collar, he stilled, letting the hem float down.

Luc knew I was there.

"You forgot the guitar."

"Yeah, I kind of did." He turned so slowly, and such relief flickered across his face when he saw me that I wondered if he'd thought I was still wearing only the towel.

Feeling unsure, I lingered in the doorway. "I saw that you had a guitar at your apartment. I'm guessing you play and it wasn't just for display."

That statement sounded as stupid out loud as it did in my head.

Luc nodded.

"Is that bedroom normally yours?"

"Yes, but the room is all yours." Luc faced me fully, his gaze roaming over my face. "You should probably get some rest. Grayson and Zoe headed out to the grocery store to pick up some food. They'll be gone for a little bit."

"I don't think I can sleep right now. Too much going on in my head." Tiny balls of uncertainty took root in my chest. I wanted to ask why he wasn't staying with me, but I couldn't get the words out. Maybe he just wanted to give me my space or have some space for himself. It wasn't a big deal.

"Understandable," he said.

Anxious energy buzzed through me as I clasped my hands together. "Is Kent still passed out on the couch?"

"Yeah. A nuclear bomb could be dropped and he wouldn't wake up."

"Must be nice." Right at that moment, I ran out of things to say—

well, things I had the courage to say. I started to leave. "Okay, um. I guess I'll try to get some rest—"

"My real name is Lucas."

Thinking I was hearing things, I turned around.

Luc sat on the edge of the bed. "Well, at least that's what I was called when I was with the Daedalus. I never had a last name. I was just Lucas."

Walking back to him, I stopped just short of touching him. Some innate instinct told me he wouldn't want that. "Last names are overrated."

"I guess so." A wry grin twisted his lips. "No one calls me that anymore. Hell, most don't even realize that Lucas is actually my name. Not even Zoe. Paris did, though. You . . ." He exhaled heavily. "You knew. I told you when we were younger." There was a pause. "I don't even know what made me start thinking about it, but I just wanted you to know again."

Sympathy rose as I watched him, even though I was now discovering that I'd been given something that had the possibility to further mutate me—something that had given me the ability briefly to fight and to kill. There were gaps of time that couldn't be accounted for, an entire summer that was just missing, and it made me sick to think too deeply about it. I was an experiment, but I still had no idea what it was like to grow up as he and Zoe had. At the end of the day, it didn't matter how powerful they were. They still had human emotions and thoughts, wants and needs, and everything had been stripped from them, even a last name.

My heart broke for him—for all of them and for us. "You could give yourself a last name, you know?"

"Seems a little late for that."

"Why?" I leaned against a dresser. "I don't think there's a time limit on picking a last name."

He inclined his head. "You know, you have a good point."

"Of course I do." I smiled faintly. "Pick one."

His brows lifted. "Right now?"

"Why not? Not like we have anything better to do."

Stretching out his long legs, he crossed them at the ankles. "We have to figure out what was done to you."

I tensed. "We do, but can we do that right now?"

One side of his mouth tipped up. "No. Only because there's not much we can find out while here. When we get to Zone 3, there will be people there who may know. Or will know where to go." He paused. "It's weird."

"What's weird?"

"That I don't know what was done to you," he replied, folding his arms over his chest. "I keep thinking about it. I know everything. Always. But this? I have no clue."

"Well, that's a crappy time for your all-knowing skills not to kick in."

"Truth." He eyed me.

"You also don't know what Sarah and April are—or were, which is probably what I am," I pointed out.

"Thanks for showcasing my flaws."

I smiled. "That's what I'm here for."

"That and telling me to pick a last name."

I nodded.

Luc's gaze lifted to mine. A moment passed, and then he patted the space beside him. "Sit. I need your help, and your closeness will give me inspiration."

"That makes no sense." But I pushed away from the dresser and went over, sitting on the bed. There wasn't much space, so our thighs were pressed against each other's. "Happy?"

He looked over at me, his smile mysterious. "Getting there. Okay." He crossed his ankles. "I think I know what I want my last name to be."

"What?" I said.

"I think it will be a fitting last name. You'll like it."

"Only the good Lord knows what this is going to be," I replied dryly.

"King."

"What?" I arched a brow.

"King. I'm going to give myself the last name King."

"Wow." I laughed. "I don't even know what to say about that."

"Luc King. I think it sounds amazing."

"I think it sounds like you should be a mob boss."

"Like I said, completely fitting."

Running my toes through the soft carpet, I grinned. "It does have a nice ring to it. Luc King, badass extraordinaire."

"What? You think I'm a badass?"

I shot him a sidelong glance. "You know you're a badass. I mean, come on. You can hover off the ground."

"Is that a requirement for being a badass?"

"I'm pretty sure that it is." Tucking my hair back behind my ear, I stopped moving my feet. "So, this whole Zone 3 thing. I really don't understand it. Those towns are basically useless, right? No electricity. Nothing. And they've all been evacuated."

Luc inhaled deeply. "The cities aren't empty. They never have been." He twisted toward me, planting a hand on the bed behind him. "The general public thinks that the nice, caring government went in there and evacuated everyone after the EMT bombs were dropped and all the Luxen were dead, right?"

My forehead creased. "They had to, right? Because nothing works there—no lights, no cooling or heating. No stoves or medical equipment. I could keep going, but I think you get the point."

He studied me closely. "They didn't."

Disbelief gave way to pure shock. "Are you seriously telling me that they left people there . . . walled up in those cities, and then told the world that they evacuated every human out of there?"

"Yes. That's what I'm telling you."

I gaped at him. I had no reason not to believe him, but this was huge and also horrific.

"There were people who couldn't evacuate. Those who were elderly or sick. Those who were too poor or had family they needed to take care of. People—human people—that the government decided were not worth saving. People they judged and decided wouldn't make tomorrow a safer, better day."

Horror rose. "Oh my God . . ."

His face was hard. "I don't think God had anything to do with that, but people did. Humans. Biggest assholes on Earth."

Couldn't argue that.

"Each of the zones had varying degrees of population in them. A lot of people have . . . well, let's say that their living conditions were so poor, many didn't make it past the first year of the walls. Many of them were dying inside those walls, in those barren cities being fed a lie that help was coming, and finally help did come. The Luxen."

"The . . . unregistered Luxen?"

"Yes. Those cities may be without electricity, but they are not without power."

So much disgust and anger filled me that I couldn't even think straight. How could they just leave people there? How could they be so damn *inhuman*?

How did the world not know this? The walls had gone up quickly, unbelievably so, but how could the world not know that there were people in those cities?

"The world only sees what it wants to see," Luc answered my unspoken question quietly. "They don't want to acknowledge just how inhuman humans can be. This isn't the first time people have been left behind when tragedy strikes."

"How could they hide it, though? Not everyone in the world is an uncaring douchebag."

"The pulse bombs. Airplanes can't fly within a hundred miles of those cities. Drones don't work, either. Satellite images are disrupted over the areas, as are cell phone signals. Experts say it'll be like that for at least another decade or so."

He was right. I'd dumbly forgotten about the fallout radius and how several major airports near those cities had had to relocate. "So these people are just stuck there?"

"For now," he said. "They are being taken care of."

"By the Luxen? By unregistered Luxen?"

"Registered and unregistered."

"When did you start helping Luxen go there?" I asked, hoping he wouldn't shut me out like he often did.

He didn't.

"When President McHugh starting campaigning. He said things that made a lot of Luxen uneasy. It started with wanting to move Luxen to their own communities." His lip curled in a sneer. "I think *communities* is code for another, less attractive C-word that history has never favorably looked upon."

A shudder worked its way through me. No, not for one second did I think anything good could come from Luxen-only communities.

"Zone 3 is one of our hideouts for those we're moving and if anyone needs to lie low. Obviously, transporting Luxen has its risks."

"Obviously," I murmured, once again awed by him, by all of them. "I don't know if I've ever told you this or not, but what you're doing is amazing."

He shrugged. "What I'm doing also means a lot of people owe me favors."

I eyed him closely. "I don't think collecting favors is the only reason you're helping the Luxen."

Luc didn't immediately reply. "And why would you think that?"

"Because I feel like I know you well enough to know that's not true," I told him.

His gaze flickered over my face, and I wished he'd touch me. Wished that he'd do more.

"I don't think you know me as well as you think you do," he said.

"Why would you say that?"

"Because you're giving me far too much credit." One shoulder lifted, and then he changed the subject before I could respond. "Obviously, a big issue with the zones is communication. Since cell phones don't work within about a hundred-mile radius of the cities, we set up hot spots outside that radius, places where messages can be left on burner phones."

"A Harry Potter owl would be cooler," I muttered.

"True."

Silence fell between us as my mind wandered over what I'd learned. There was a sense of awe and hopelessness, a weird mixture. The thing was, Luc and the gang couldn't move all the Luxen to safer areas. Many would be forced into these *communities*.

Something had to be done, because there was no way all the Luxen could be moved out.

"Hey." The back of his hand brushed over my cheek as he caught a piece of hair, tucking it back behind my ear.

I lifted my chin, and my gaze moved to his. Bright eyes the color of the most intense lilacs held mine. It seemed like he'd been about to say something, but words had fallen by the wayside.

His fingers lingered just below my ear. A spark flared to life, passing from his skin to mine, humming in the air. I took a breath, but it didn't go anywhere.

Please.

That was all I could think. *Please.* I wanted him to kiss me. I wanted to lose myself in him. I wanted to forget, and I wanted to remember.

Tension lined his mouth, and my heart sped up. His breath was a warm stroke along my cheek, moving closer and closer—

A swift curse carried up from the living room, and I jerked back, a little breathless as Kent's voice boomed. "Luc? Evie? I think you two need to come down here."

I could feel Luc's intense gaze as I rose, not really seeing the room. "I thought you said he was still passed out and a nuke wouldn't even wake him."

He cleared his throat, but when he spoke, there was this smoky quality to it. "Apparently, I was wrong."

Somewhat disappointed, and totally confused by why I hadn't just kissed him, I hurried out of the bedroom. Luc was right behind me, easily slipping past me and heading down the steps first.

I glared daggers into his back, and at the bottom of the stairs, he looked up and winked.

My eyes narrowed.

Kent was sitting up on the couch, his attention focused on the TV. His mohawk had given up on life and had flopped over to the side. "You guys need to see this."

"See what . . . ?" Luc trailed off, and then he cursed.

"What?" My gaze followed Luc's as I stepped down into the living room and looked up at the TV.

My jaw dropped.

There was a picture of my mom—my beautiful, happy mom. It was her Fort Detrick badge.

The floor swayed.

A hand—Luc's hand—wrapped around my upper arm just as the image on the TV changed.

"Oh my God," I whispered.

There was *my* face—my smiling yearbook photo, to be exact, and underneath my face and my name were words in capital letters that blurred together.

WANTED IN CONNECTION WITH THE MURDER OF COL. SYLVIA DASHER.

32

I'd laughed.

I'd sat down and listened to the Columbia chief of police's briefing while my mom's picture was on the left side of the screen and mine was underneath hers. The police chief said I was a suspect in an ambush-style killing.

I didn't even know what *ambush-style killing* meant. Like I'd hidden in a freaking bush somewhere and then jumped out?

The police chief also said I was considered armed and dangerous.

That's the exact moment when I laughed.

So that was my reaction to hearing I was suspected in my mother's murder. I *laughed,* and I felt like I was going to laugh more. Like in the never-stop-laughing kind of laugh.

Something was wrong with me.

It never crossed the minds of the law enforcement that perhaps something bad had happened to me? No one thought that I needed help? I was immediately implicated in an act where the evidence had to have proved otherwise. I wasn't a forensic pathologist, but I knew that it was obvious to see a bullet was fired from *outside* the house. Did they think I was an expert marksman? Besides the fact that the front door had been blown in?

Why was I even asking these questions? They weren't reporting what really happened, and I knew what that meant. The police were involved in what happened to my mom.

They were involved with the Daedalus.

Kent turned off the TV, tossing the remote onto a cushion. "Things just got really complicated. This is way bigger than we'd anticipated."

I pressed my lips together because I could feel a really inappropriate giggle bubbling up.

Luc crossed his arms over his chest. His jaw was clenched so hard I wondered if the lower half of his face was going to snap in half. "That's an understatement."

"This is what they do." Kent dragged his hand through his blue hair. "They twist what really happened to fit their agenda."

I stared at him, opened my mouth, and then closed it, utterly at a loss as to how to respond.

The garage door suddenly opened, and all three of us whirled. Grayson and Zoe walked in, carrying several bags straining with groceries. They stopped.

"What's going on?" Zoe asked, looking between the three of us.

Grayson sighed. "Do I even want to know?"

"Oh, nothing big," Kent said, plopping down on the couch. "Just that Evie was just implicated in her mother's murder on national television."

Zoe lowered the bag she was holding.

"Nothing like a little matricide to start your week off," I said, another near-hysterical laugh building in me. "Right?"

"Right," she murmured.

I stared at the ceiling, unable to sleep, unable to shut my brain down long enough to even doze.

It had been the same last night.

After Zoe and Grayson got back with groceries, dinner was made. Spaghetti. I'd eaten half a plate and then gone to my room and stayed there, pretending to be asleep when Zoe knocked on my door and called my name.

The moment Zoe had seen me in the morning, she'd tried to talk about what had been on the news, but I shut that down really quickly and tried to ignore the look of concern creeping into her expression.

Luc never knocked on the door, last night or tonight. He'd been gone this morning when I'd woken up, and according to Zoe, he was scouting the surrounding area to make sure there was no unusual activity that would indicate that someone had discovered our whereabouts.

I had no idea what was up with Luc. Something had shifted between us. Who he was in my bedroom the day before they came for Mom, for me, was not the same Luc I saw now. There were glimpses of him, when he'd washed my hands and held me at the safe house. He was the Luc I'd begun to fall really hard for while I'd slept against him in the car.

But there was a distance between us I didn't understand, and right now, when I needed him, he was gone, and I didn't know if it was because of what happened to his club, to Clyde and Chas, or if it was something else.

Moonlight stretched over the ceiling as I rolled onto my side. I thought about my mom, about how little I knew her. She could've been involved in the Daedalus up until the moment they took her life with a single gunshot. I had no idea, and it was unlikely that I'd ever know.

How could she, though? Treating me like I was her daughter, loving me and taking care of me—

Sucking in a sharp breath, I sat up and swung my legs off the bed as pressure clamped down on my chest. I couldn't lie here any longer.

The room suddenly constricted. My brain had clearly decided to really start messing with me, because it started throwing out more terrible, panic-inducing questions. Would I forget what my life was like before, well, before everything went to hell? Would I even survive—

"Stop it." My hands closed into fists.

Would I see Heidi again? Was she truly safe? What was I going to do once I got to Zone 3?

My throat clamped shut, and then I yanked off my tank top and slipped on my bra and button-down cardigan since I had no idea if anyone else was awake. I spun around, hurrying to the door. Wrenching it open, I quickly headed downstairs, my bare feet whispering on the steps. A small lamp had been left on beside the couch, casting a soft glow throughout the room.

Moving toward the kitchen, I stopped when I reached the back door that led out to a screened-in porch. "What am I doing?"

"Good question."

Gasping, I spun around and saw Grayson standing in the living room. "God." I swallowed hard, placing my hand on my stomach. "You scared me."

He arched a brow, staring at me.

All righty then. I glanced around. "I . . . I couldn't sleep."

He stared.

Silence stretched out between us as I shifted my weight from one foot to the other. This was getting awkward. "I'm guessing you couldn't sleep, either?"

"I was patrolling. Making sure no one is getting too close to the house without our knowledge."

"Oh." I twisted my fingers around the hem of my sleep shorts. "Is that something you normally do?"

He eyed me disinterestedly, which was an improvement from him looking at me like I was the legit worst. "Yes, it is something that all Luxen do and have done since the beginning of time."

Well, that sounded dramatic, but what did I know? "I had no idea."

"Of course you didn't. You fear tomorrow now, because you've now experienced something personal that shows you just how scary the world can be." His tone was hard. "We've always feared tomorrow."

I shifted uncomfortably. "I know what fear is."

He looked away, a muscle throbbing along his jaw. "I guess you do."

I had no idea how to respond to that.

Grayson inclined his head. "I didn't know you were her."

He was talking about Nadia.

"It makes sense now. I never understood why he was willing to risk everything for you." He paused, his gaze flickering over me. "I couldn't figure it out, but I'd heard about Nadia. He spoke about her—about you only a few times. It was obvious that he'd been in love. Now I understand why he is the way he is with you. If I'd known who you were, I never would have said you were useless."

I opened my mouth to point out that he shouldn't have said that to me no matter who I used to be or who he thought I was.

But Grayson was already gone.

He'd moved so fast the ends of my hair lifted, and I was left standing in the kitchen like I'd been talking to myself.

"What the hell?" I muttered.

Scrubbing my hands down my face, I turned and eyed the fridge. The idea of eating filled me with nausea, but I was stressed; therefore food was the only acceptable—

A low, creaking sound pierced the silence—the sound of unused hinges on the door rubbing together.

Lowering my hands, I twisted around slowly. The kitchen looked normal. No source of the sound—*there*. The door to either the pantry or the basement was open a couple of inches.

What in the world?

Inching toward it, I touched the cool knob and pulled the door open. Hinges *squawk*ed as musty air surrounded me. My heart bounced as I stepped forward, peering into the darkness. "Hello?"

Silence greeted me.

Frowning, I looked at the door. It was hanging sort of cockeyed. It probably hadn't been latched properly. I started to close the door and a chill skated over my skin. I exhaled, and my breath puffed a misty cloud in front of my lips. Tiny bumps rose as the temperature dropped.

My gaze swung back to the dark stairwell. It was pitch-black, so much so that I could only see the two steps in, and the light from the kitchen seemed to hit an invisible wall, not penetrating the depth of the darkness.

The inky blackness of the basement brushed over the second step, rolled over the old, worn wood like oil.

Well, that was strange.

Really strange.

Maybe-this-house-was-haunted kind of strange.

Still gripping the door, I took a step back. The darkness, the shadows rose, expanding and rippling over the wall. Smoky tendrils crept into the light, and the air turned frigid.

A scream built in my throat and died in the freezing air.

The thick shadow constricted, pulling back and swirling. Out of the blob of darkness, a shape took form. Two legs. A torso. Shoulders and arms. A head. An entire body that was as black and shiny as midnight oil.

An Arum—it was an Arum.

It rose up, reaching the top step. The head tilted, moving much like a cobra. A voice whispered. *What do we have here?*

Holy crap, the voice—the voice was in my head.

An arm extended. Fingertips formed, and a startled heartbeat later, the fingers drew back. *Sssomething not right.*

There was a moment in the back of my thoughts when I acknowledged that the voice reminded me of Sarah's—of the words only I had been able to hear in a roomful of people.

The shadow body pulsed and rippled, drifting closer. Fingers curled inward. A tugging motion swept over my body, and I slid an inch forward before I was able to stop myself.

The thing hissed as it reached out again. *Sssomething not right. Sssomething not natural—*

It made another sound, a cross between a growl and a moan. The thing shrank back, losing its form. In a puff of icy, black smoke, it faded into the shadows clinging to the cracked walls. The shadows in the stairwell of the basement returned to the normal level of acceptable creepiness.

I stood there, mouth hanging open. Did that just happen? Or was that just some really, really messed-up nightmare? Like, a long, extended nightmare.

"What in the hell are you doing?"

33

Jumping a good six inches off the floor, I let out a little shriek. "Luc."

He stood just inside the kitchen, his amethyst eyes churning. "I know you were told not to go into the basement."

Heart thundering, I struggled to catch my breath. "I didn't go into the basement. The door opened, and this Arum came up the steps. Holy crap, I thought this place was haunted at first."

A bland expression settled over his face. "The place isn't haunted."

"Yeah, I know that now. Why is there an Arum in the basement?"

Luc strode forward, brushing past me as he peered down the stairs. A moment passed. "The reason you were told to stay out of the basement is because there are tunnels that run underground, allowing the Arum to travel without notice. Sometimes they come up and say hi when they know I'm here."

My mouth dropped open. "Well, that sounds perfectly normal, Luc."

"They're not always in the basement, and it's not always a problem." He closed the door and faced me. "I didn't tell you because I didn't think anyone would be here, and I didn't want you to freak out."

I stared at him, pretty sure my expression summed up every *What in the hell?* thought I could possibly have.

"But of course, I should've figured that you'd be actively trying to get yourself killed and put a dead bolt on the door."

"Whoa. I'm not doing anything." I snapped out of my stupor. "The door opened by itself. I didn't touch it, and if you say that again to me, I'm going to start thinking you're actively trying to get yourself killed."

His eyes narrowed. "What are you even doing in the kitchen at two in the morning?"

"I couldn't sleep," I confessed, surprised when I saw his expression soften a bit. I ignored it. "And what are you doing in the kitchen at two in the morning?"

"Couldn't sleep, either."

I pushed my hair back from my face. "And what was an Arum doing in the basement at two in the morning?"

His lips twitched as he glanced at the closed basement door. "Probably stopping by to see who was here."

"Do you think maybe you could've told me about the Arum possibly creeping around in the basement instead of being all vague?"

Luc's jaw locked down.

"Yeah. I see that didn't cross your mind. Instead of '*Don't go into the basement,*' you could've been like, '*Hey, sometimes Arum creep around in the basement, so don't go in there.*'"

"I thought you didn't go into the basement."

Oh my God, I wanted to stomp my foot, like legitimately stomp my foot *in his face*. "I didn't go in there. I just opened the door the rest of the way, and it came up the stairs like something out of a freaking horror movie."

Luc arched a brow. "I think the Arum would find that description a bit offensive."

My mouth dropped open as anger simmered, mixing with frustration over *everything*. "Whatever. I'm not talking to you."

"Actually, you *are* talking to me."

Raising a hand, I flipped him off as I stormed past him. "Talk to that."

"That's really mature."

I lifted my other hand and extended that middle finger. "Two-for-one special."

"Now that doesn't even make sense."

Reaching the stairs, I looked over my shoulder at him. "Shut up."

He laughed—he actually laughed.

Doing my best to not stomp up the stairs because other people were sleeping, I stalked toward the bedroom, my hands curled into tight fists. I stepped inside.

"I can't believe you told me to shut up."

Whirling around, I glared at where he stood in the hall, right in front of my door. "I can't believe you think I care that you're surprised." Gripping the bedroom door, I launched it shut. "*Lucas*."

Like it hit an invisible wall, the door stopped mid-swing. Oh dear. Luc prowled into the room, his expression a mix of disbelief and anger.

Perhaps using his full first name was a mistake.

Without anyone touching the door, it closed behind Luc, clicking softly shut. When I looked at him, he appeared . . . awed. Like I imagined someone did the first time they saw a falling star. "I cannot think of the last time someone told me to shut up and didn't end up a burn mark on the ground."

"Oh, I haven't said it before to you? For some reason, I feel like I have, but just in case, let me say it again. Shut up. And let me add to that. Get out."

His lips parted. "You're . . ."

"What?"

He was quiet as his gaze flicked from me to the nightstand, and I wondered if he was looking at Diesel. "You're beautiful when you're angry."

"You know what? You can go— Wait." My entire system jolted. "What?"

Luc's head tilted to the side, sending several locks of hair toppling to the side. "I said you're beautiful when you're angry. And you're beautiful just standing there. You're even beautiful when you're sad. And when you're happy, you are breathtakingly beautiful."

I was stunned into absolute silence. My hands went limp. "I wasn't expecting you to say that," I said, my voice hoarse. The flutter was there, deep in my chest, but there was also this cracking motion in my chest. Like a sledgehammer was slamming down on my ribs. Raw, potent emotion slammed into me with the force of a speeding freight train. "Don't say that to me right now. It's bad timing."

"Bad timing? I like to think that there is no bad time to tell someone they're beautiful," he said quietly. "Especially when oftentimes people, no matter if they're human or not, tend to run out of time before telling someone that."

"God," I whispered.

The cracking sensation spread, cutting deep. I smacked my

hands over my face as the knot of emotion swelled, threatening to choke off all rational thought. Tears burned the back of my throat, and climbed into my eyes.

There was silence, and then Luc's warm fingers wrapped around my wrists. "I didn't say that to upset you."

It wasn't what he'd said that upset me.

It wasn't how he'd said it, either.

It was because it made me feel and it made me think, and right now, combining those two things was dangerous.

Luc gently tugged my hands from my face. He didn't let go, and when I opened my eyes, his searched mine intently. "You're going to need to let it out. You can't keep going not thinking or feeling."

Pressing my lips together, I shook my head.

"It'll burn you up from the inside like a fever. You've got to let it out."

A broken sound split the air, and it took a moment for me to realize it was me who'd made that sound. "You said I was brave and strong, and that's what I'm trying to be right now. I need to keep it together."

He dipped his chin. We weren't eye level, not with how tall he was, but we were close. "You are brave and strong, but I'm telling you not to be right now."

Panic took hold. I couldn't let it out, because I couldn't face what had happened to my mom, not right now, because then it would be true and it would be real.

I yanked my hands free from his. "I'm mad at you, so stop trying to be supportive. It's confusing."

Luc's brows arched. "What?"

"Yes! I'm mad and you are confusing me. First off, you were acting like a douche toward me downstairs. I didn't open that stupid basement door, and you've been acting weird, ever since my—since everything happened."

"Evie—"

"You've been distant, and I know you've gone through bad stuff. I'm trying to be understanding. You lost Clyde and Chas and the club, but I—" My voice cracked, and it took me a moment to speak again. "I watched my mom die right in front of me. Her blood soaked my hands and my clothing. And I don't care that she really wasn't my mom or if she had anything to do with what was done to me; she was still my mother! I have no idea what is really going on, what's going to even happen five minutes from now. And you lost people you care about, that you've protected and took care of, and I know it's hurting you whether you admit it or not. I want to be here for you, but you just shut me out, and I don't understand."

His mouth snapped closed as he looked away. He had no response, and that wasn't good enough. Not now. Not after everything.

I took a step toward him, hands shaking. "You told me that you weren't going to leave me. Not ever again."

His head snapped in my direction, eyes blazing a stunning violet. "And I haven't."

"But you have," I whispered. "Mentally and emotionally, you've totally left me, and I don't get what you want from me. You say that there can only ever be me. Like I'm the one—"

"You are." He was closer, a mere foot from me. "You are the *one* for me; you've always been. We were made for each other."

"Then why have you shut me out, Luc?"

He looked away, shaking his head once more.

Chest caving in, I shook my head. I didn't have space for this on top of everything else. "Just leave. Please. It's late, and I—"

"I did this to you," he said, his voice so low I wasn't sure I'd heard him right at first.

But I had.

I jerked. "What?"

"I did this. All of this, because I was selfish and weak and couldn't bear to think about living in a world you no longer existed in."

My heart stopped.

"When that bastard Jason Dasher made an offer to heal you in exchange for his life, I knew better. Deep down, I knew there had to be a catch, because there is *always* a catch, but I was desperate. I'd do anything, so I took you there and agreed to let them give you God knows what. Then I walked away. I held up my end of the deal and walked away while who knows what was being done to you. I did this, Evie."

Emotion clogged my throat. "Luc—"

"And now look. I ensured that you lived, and for what? For you to experience everything you thought you knew about your life being destroyed. For you to find dead bodies and be targeted by an Origin. For you to watch your mother die and for your entire future to be ripped away from you and for you to be hunted by pure, fucking evil, because that is what the Daedalus is. I did this, and people died. That's what I did. That's what I think about when I look at you, because I—"

"Gave me life," I whispered.

His entire body jerked.

"That's what you did. You made sure I lived. You didn't know this was going to happen."

"That doesn't matter." The pupils of his eyes turned white. "Because I should've known better. That I would be exchanging your death for—"

"For life!" I repeated. "Yeah, things are super messed-up right now, but if you didn't take that risk, we wouldn't be standing here. We wouldn't have this second chance, something so few people get. We have it because of you."

"And does that second chance overshadow everything? What has happened to Sylvia? To you? Does it—" Air shuddered out of him. "It doesn't matter. I don't think I'm worthy of you."

That stunned me, and it took me a moment to realize he'd said something similar before. "How can you think that?"

"I don't think," he responded, thick lashes lowering. "I just know."

"You're wrong." I crossed the distance between us. He stiffened, and I placed my hands on his cheeks. "You do deserve me, and I wish that all these bad things hadn't happened, but I don't blame you. I could never blame you, because I think I love you, and I don't want you to regret being here with me—"

Luc jerked out of my grasp, his chest rising and falling rapidly. "What? What did you say?"

I lowered my hands. "I said I don't want you to regret being here with me."

"Not that." His entire pupils now glowed. "What you said before that."

I raced back through my thoughts, and I . . . Oh my God, I'd said I'd loved him. Those words had come out of my mouth, an admission of what I wouldn't even let myself acknowledge. A proclamation I hadn't been ready to feel but I had been ready to speak.

Because it was the truth.

I'd fallen in love with Luc, and I didn't even know exactly when. Whether it was somewhere between the first terrible pickup line and the weird surprises that made no sense. Maybe it was the first time he'd kissed me in the closet at Foretoken or the first time he'd held my hand.

Or maybe I'd always been in love with him, because I was certain I had before, even if I couldn't remember.

"I love you," I said, trembling. "I'm in love with you, Luc."

34

Luc moved so fast I didn't see him. Only knew that he had when his mouth touched mine and his arms folded around me. The kiss took my breath and then my soul. The fierceness shattered me and it pieced me back together.

"It feels like I've waited my entire life to hear you say that," he said against my lips, his hands gliding down my back. "To see your lips move around those words. I may not deserve them, but I'm greedy. I'm still selfish. You can't take them back."

"I wouldn't." I gasped as he lifted me up and turned, bringing me down to the bed so that I was on his lap, straddling him. "And you do deserve me."

His hands came to my face. His fingers traced my lips and jaw, and for a long moment, he just stared at me, and then his lips were on mine. Our kisses took on a different life, became full of an urgency I'd never quite experienced before. I straightened in his arms, placing my hands on his shoulders. They drifted down his hard chest, becoming pinned between us when he tugged me closer. Something about the way he kissed me became desperate, panicked even. He was kissing me like we were running out of time.

The moment that thought crossed my mind, I felt the same desperate surge even though I told myself we weren't. I wiggled to free my hands, and Luc's groan turned the tips of my ears red.

I didn't slow down, even though I knew there was so much we needed to be focused on. We both needed these minutes amid the confusion and lack of answers, the blood . . . and death.

I don't know if it was him or me or both of us, but his hands were on my hips, open and closing, rocking them as he nipped at my lips, at my throat. Then the tiny buttons on my sweater came unclasped and the material was parted, but his hands never left my hands.

Stunned, I pulled away and looked down, seeing plain pink lace. "That's a nifty talent."

"Isn't it, though?" Pricks of white light filled his pupils as one side of his mouth kicked up.

His mouth returned to mine and then wandered away. The path of kisses blazed a trail down my throat, over the slope of my collarbone, and then lower, over a swell. I felt his fingers along my shoulder, hooking under a strap, guiding it down and down until the cup loosened and those fingers, those lips drifted over sensitive skin. The same thing happened to the other strap, to the other cup, and goose bumps spread over my cool, damp skin as my head fell back, my mouth opening in a sharp gasp.

Luc lifted his head and sat back. There was a wicked gleam to his eyes, a daring twist to his lips as he stared at me. I'd never been exposed like this before, and I didn't know what he thought when he looked at me, seeming to watch the flush spread from my neck and lower.

"You're beautiful, Evie," he said, voice husky and reverent. "I've told you that, but it doesn't matter. I already know I haven't told you enough. You're so beautiful it drives me to distraction. Perfect." Those eyes lifted to mine, and there was an awed look on his face.

I placed my hands on his cheeks and I kissed him, hoping that somehow he could feel what I thought of him when I knew words wouldn't suffice. Luc was worthy, and that had nothing to do with all that he'd done for me, but what he'd done for countless Luxen, for Emery and Grayson, for Kent and Zoe, and more.

I tugged at his shirt, and he obliged, leaning back and lifting his arms so I could tug it off over his head. I dropped it on the bed beside me and soaked in all the bare, hard skin.

No bruises in sight.

Luc was completely healed from being shot three times, but I still bent, kissing each spot that had been struck. I didn't need a bruise to know where he'd been hit; I'd remember those locations until I died. An inch below the right shoulder. The center, between the defined pecs. Centimeters to the left of his heart.

I heard his ragged inhale as my hands made their way down his stomach, to his navel and then to the button on his jeans, and lower still. I felt him straining against my hand. "Can I?"

"Yes. Y.E.S. Totally," he said. "Definitely."

A soft laugh left me as I reached for the button on his jeans and then his zipper, and when he didn't stop me, I was emboldened.

At the first touch of my fingers, his back bowed as if I'd burned him, and he broke the kiss as his entire body became impossibly taut. I opened my eyes, worried that I'd done something wrong.

He opened his mouth and then closed it, and for the first time ever, he looked like he was at a loss for words.

Another first for him.

I skated my fingers over him as I glanced down, flushing before bringing my gaze back to him. "You're beautiful, and you're worthy."

He shook his head, jaw tight.

"I don't understand how you can think you're not, and I . . . I don't want you to think that. I don't like it."

Luc sucked in a sharp breath. "God. Evie, you don't . . ." He dropped his head onto my shoulder. His lips kissed my neck. "You don't need to do this."

"I want to." I curled my fingers around his hair as I curled my fingers around *him*.

This wasn't something I'd done often in my life. Once, maybe? I had no idea what I was doing, but based on the catch in Luc's next breath, I figured I was doing something right.

And when his hips jerked, lifting his body and me clear off the bed, I had a feeling he wasn't disappointed at all.

I braced a hand on his chest as he leaned back once more, those glowing eyes flashing over my face and lower, to where my sweater parted and to where my hand moved.

His lips parted as his chest rose and fell rapidly. "Evie." He groaned my name, and something . . . something began to happen.

The pupils turned all white, and thin, faint vessels appeared under his skin, all over his face and throat, and lower even. White light glowed from within him. The air around us became charged. Static crackled around—

Luc reared up, one hand grasping the back of my head, fingers tangled tightly in my hair. He pulled and stretched, and our mouths clashed together. Lips. Teeth. Tongues. Energy crackled, snapping through me. He swelled, and then his entire body seemed to stiffen, every muscle locking up as he panted into our kisses. The air around us seemed electrified, and then I felt the tension slowly ease out of him.

Luc held me tightly but kept a little space between us as he continued to shudder under me, his large, powerful body trembling. When he finally stilled, I pulled back and opened my eyes.

He was staring at me like he'd never seen me before, and that was an odd look for him, because he always looked at me like he knew exactly who I was. There was a softness to his face, and for several moments, we just stared at each other.

"Give me a sec, okay? Don't move."

When I nodded, he lifted me up and over, depositing me on the bed as he rose, disappearing into the bathroom. Using the time somewhat wisely, I fixed my bra as I heard the water turn on.

Luc reappeared. He sat beside me, quiet for a long moment. "You didn't have to do that."

"I know." I glanced at him. "I wanted to."

"I appreciate that. A lot. Like, a lot, a lot." A small grin appeared. "I've never . . ."

My brows lifted. "You never . . . what?"

His gaze met mine. "I've never experienced *that* with someone."

"I thought you said you did things."

"Things, yes. But never that with someone." He lifted a shoulder, completely unashamed to be talking about this. "With myself? Yes. More times than you probably want to know."

A slow grin started to tug at my lips. "Probably."

"But you're the first. I knew it could feel like that, but I . . . I also had no idea." He opened his mouth, closed it, and then appeared to try again. "I didn't hurt you, did I?"

"No." I leaned forward, kissing his cheek. "Why would you think that?"

"I lost a little bit of control there, if you didn't notice. The Source?" He jerked his chin to the lamp. My eyes widened. Holy crap, it was smoking!

I smiled, rather smug that I'd caused him to do that.

He shifted toward me, kissing me back, slowly and languidly. I felt his fingers brush over my stomach. "You know what this means, right?"

"What?" My brows knitted.

"If you get to play, so do I." He guided me onto my back, muscles rolling and flexing along the bare skin of his shoulders and upper arms.

Oh.

Oh my.

Luc kissed me as if he were sipping from my lips, and then his mouth was skating down my throat, around the silver chain as he pulled the obsidian pendant straight. His lips and fingers were everywhere at once, tugging and caressing, licking and nipping.

Every pulse point thrummed as his hands drifted lower, over my navel and then to the band of my sleep shorts.

He paused, gaze lifting to mine. "May I?"

Heart racing, I nodded.

Luc dragged the band down an inch. "Have to hear you say it, Peaches."

"Really?"

One side of his lip kicked up. "Really."

"Yes," I said. "You *may*."

"Then I will." He kissed the skin under my navel, and then he did.

A thrill filled my veins as I lifted my hips, helping him remove the shorts, rocking back as he did so. They landed somewhere on the floor. Even though he still had his jeans on, there was nothing else for him to remove from me.

"I have a very important question," he said, staring down at me, lips parted. "Do you have any idea how much you undo me?"

My chest squeezed and then swelled. "How . . . how do I . . . undo you?"

The tips of his fingers trailed over the crease between my thigh and hip, causing my breath to hitch. "In every single way." The air caught in my throat for a whole different reason now.

He drew his finger down my thigh, and then I watched him lower his head. His hair brushed the skin below my navel. My heart launched itself into my throat. "I . . . I've never done this before," I whispered, my hands opening and closing on the sheets.

His mouth followed his finger. "Neither have I."

"That . . . that doesn't sound right." My entire body jerked as I felt his lips along my skin. "You seem to know what you're doing."

"I really don't." Inching my legs apart, he settled there. "I'm just doing what feels right." His warm breath danced over an extraordinarily sensitive part as he glided a finger up my thigh. "Am I doing it right?"

"I . . . I think so."

"Think so?" His finger came close as he made another pass to where I *throbbed*. "I'm going to have to do better than 'I think so.'"

I was all on board for that.

He chuckled, and I knew immediately he'd picked up on my thoughts. His finger came close again before sliding away. My hips lifted out of instinct, in a silent urging.

"You know what this reminds me of?" he said, lifting his gaze to mine once more.

Breaths coming in short, shallow pants, I shook my head.

"When you were thinking about wanting to climb me like a—"

"Don't," I said.

"Horny—"

"Luc."

"Octopus," he finished.

"I hate you."

"No, you don't." Luc smiled at me then, and it was real and beautiful, softening the hard, striking lines of his face. "You love me."

And then he was sipping from me again, this time from my skin, and every part of me shorted out.

Every part of me shorted out.

His tongue. His teeth. His hands. I was moving with him, twisting and rolling, gasping for air. My pace picked up as my fingers dug into his soft, unruly hair. Tension coiled tight. Everything about me became frantic. My gasps. The way I moved. The sounds that came from me. The way I said his name, over and over, and then it was like when I touched the Source. Electricity rippled over my skin. Light filled me, and Luc was with me through the waves, until my legs were limp and my fingers had slipped from his hair.

Luc eased up, stretching out beside me. He curled an arm around my waist, tugged my boneless body to his chest. The blanket folded over us, and I knew he hadn't touched it.

"You're so lazy," I murmured.

"You're just jealous."

"I am."

Luc was quiet for a moment. "I should've known."

"What?"

He kissed the space below my ear. "I should've known when I saw Diesel."

For a moment I didn't know what he was talking about, but my gaze drifted to the smiling face of the oval-shaped rock.

"I should've known then that you loved me."

35

Luc and I lay in warmth and silence for a little while, his fingers tracing idle shapes along my stomach. A circle around my navel. A triangle above it. A smiley face near my hip while my thoughts flitted from one thing to the next, shying away from things that would shatter the peace that had invaded my soul.

"I just realized I didn't ask you about the Arum," Luc said, his fingers dipping over the curve of my waist. "Did he say or do anything?"

"Nothing really, but . . ." I shifted onto my back, causing the blankets to slip low on my chest, and his fingers found their way to the center of my stomach once more. "Actually, he did speak . . . in my mind."

A frown started to appear on his well-formed mouth. "That's how they communicate while in their true form. What did he say?"

I shuddered at the memory. "He said I wasn't . . . normal. And you know, that isn't the first time. Lore, the other Arum, said the same thing."

His eyes narrowed. "What?"

I realized I hadn't told Luc what Lore had said when he saw me outside the club. "Lore asked me what I was. Like he could sense something . . . off about me. I'd thought it was the Andromeda serum, but now . . ."

"He wouldn't be able to sense the serum." Laziness vanished from his features as he stared down at me. "And you shouldn't have heard him speak."

I digested that. "You know, he sounded like Sarah, and remember when I heard her speak? She said something was done to her, and no one else heard that. Maybe because it was in my head, just like the Arum was. I know it sounds insane, but—"

"It doesn't." He tilted his head down, brushing his lips over my forehead. "I just don't know what it means yet. Everything that I consider is impossible." The muscles along his arm tensed. "Or doesn't make sense."

I watched the shadows flicker across his face. "You don't like not knowing, do you?"

He snorted. "Is it that obvious?"

"Totally."

A brief smile appeared. "I'm not used to not knowing, Peaches. It's not a superpower, you know? How I know things. I can read thoughts, so very little is hidden to me."

Seemed like a superpower to me.

"When I met with Jason and Sylvia, I pried into their thoughts. It wasn't easy," he said after a moment. "Both had shields up. They knew I could read their thoughts, so they were careful."

"What do you mean by *shields*?"

"Many who worked in the Daedalus, especially those who were involved in the development of Origins, learned how to block their thoughts. Mainly by deflection, thinking about random things, but others could make it seem like their heads were just . . . empty. Jason and Sylvia were good at that, but no one is perfect. Not even them. I looked around in their heads, and I didn't find anything that made me think . . ."

Made him think that they were going to turn me into an experiment.

I didn't have to read his mind to know where his thoughts had gone. I rolled onto my side, facing him, and then I snuggled close, forcing his chin up as I tucked my cheek to his chest and wiggled an arm under the blanket, around his waist. He gathered me even closer, tangling his legs with mine.

"Luc?" I whispered after a few moments.

"Peaches?"

"Thank you."

"What are you thanking me for?"

"Being here." I kissed the warm skin of his chest. "Thank you for being here."

The sun had just crested when Luc rose from the bed, stirring me awake. I blinked open sleep-heavy eyes. "You leaving?"

"Grayson needs to see me," he murmured and then kissed the corners of my lips as he slipped over me. "Everything is fine, though. Go back to sleep."

I started to rise, but his hand on my cheek stopped me. "It's early," he said, violet eyes meeting and holding mine. "You need to rest."

It was almost like his words held some kind of compulsion, because I settled back down, and I was asleep before he even left the room. When I opened my eyes again, the room was filled with bright, warm light, and the bed was empty. It took me a couple of moments to remember that Grayson had somehow summoned Luc. Had he knocked on the door and I'd just been so out of it that I hadn't woken up until Luc rose? I doubted Luc had allowed Grayson into the room.

My thoughts drifted over the night before, and I was snagged somewhere between euphoria and grief, feeling whole and yet empty. It was an odd place to be, having the heart-racing joy of realizing what I felt for Luc, admitting that and seeing how it had affected him, and also trying to process the loss of my mother, of life as I knew it.

But I could deal with this. I knew I could, as Evie and as Nadia.

When I rose, my muscles were less cramped and sore, and I figured that had to do with finally getting some rest. Maybe a little too much. It was almost eleven in the morning.

I hurried through getting ready, taking a quick shower and then changing into a pair of jeans and a loose pink-and-white-striped shirt I didn't remember even having in my closet.

Turning toward the door, I took a step and then stumbled as the floor swayed under me and the walls wobbled. The house was moving—no, not the house. It was me.

Air wheezed in and out of me as I doubled over. A powerful surge of dizziness swept over me as I clasped my knees and squeezed my eyes shut.

White light exploded behind my eyes. There was no pain, just *static* until an image of me standing above a body formed. A body of a boy no older than I was. Black ink leaked out of his ears and his nose while I stood there . . . waiting for further instruction.

"Flawless," he said. "I'm so proud of you. That was utterly flawless, Nadia."

I was sucked back as the image faded and the house stopped moving. The churning dizziness dissolved. Slowly, I opened my eyes, and when I didn't feel like I was going to hurl, I straightened.

What the hell was that?

A memory? If so, of what? Because it sure looked like, sounded like I'd . . . I'd killed someone.

Had been rewarded for it.

And had been called *Nadia*.

Wiping my sweaty palms on my hips, I took a step toward the door and then another. I knew that the voice in my head hadn't been Luc's. It had been the one I kept hearing in those brief, random memories, and no one called me *Nadia* except Luc.

I needed to tell him this immediately, because it had to mean something.

Making my way out of the bedroom, I hurried down the hall and was halfway down the stairs when I heard Luc's voice.

"How's Katy?" he was asking.

"Not entirely happy that I'm not with her. She's due any day now, so I need to get home," a deep voice I recognized answered immediately. *Daemon*. "But you knew that when you left your message."

I pressed my lips together. The last time I'd talked to Daemon, he'd said he wasn't leaving his wife again, but here he was.

"I needed your help," came Luc's response. "All of you. I don't ask for that often." There was a pause. "I've never asked, to be honest."

"And that's why we're here," Daemon replied. "Plus, Kat is excited that she's going to get to see you."

"It will be cool to spend some time with her," Luc said. "Can't say the same about you."

Daemon chuckled, apparently unbothered by Luc's statement. "And here I thought you loved hanging out with me."

"I'd rather watch C-SPAN than hang out with you." There was another pause. "Not you, Dawson. I like hanging out with you."

There was a snort, and then another voice intruded, one slightly raspy. "What about me?"

"I can't even look at Olive Garden because of you, and I loved their stuffed mushrooms, so no, I'm not happy to see you," Luc said as I crept down another step.

"I thought you were never going to bring that up again," the raspy voice stated. That voice was vaguely familiar.

"What happened at Olive Garden?" Zoe asked.

"Well . . ." Luc started. "Let's just say that Archer takes things a little too literally. Anyway, what took you all so long to get here?"

"Ran into trouble outside of Texas," answered Daemon. "Saw something pretty messed up, actually."

I reached the opening in the stairwell, quiet as I took in everyone in the room.

Zoe was sitting on the edge of the couch, and Luc was standing before the mounted TV, his arms crossed. Between the way my stomach dipped when I spotted him, and the flutter in my chest, I felt like I had wings.

I looked away from him and then did a double take as my gaze coasted over the two tall, dark-haired guys standing side by side. They had wavy hair and eyes the color of emerald jewels, and their faces could have launched a million fantasies across the world. One of them, the one with shorter hair, was grinning. They had dimples.

Dimples.

Luxen twins. I'd seen both Daemon and Dawson separately, but seeing them now was a bit unnerving. It took me a moment to realize which one was Dawson. He had longer hair, if I remembered correctly.

They weren't alone.

Stretched out on the couch as if he'd always been there was a sandy-haired man who I'd met once before. Archer.

Luc turned to me. Our gazes met. His eyes widened. "Evie—"

Several things happened at once.

One of the twins swore.

"Holy shit!" Archer exclaimed. He sat up, his face draining of all color so fast, I worried he might faint. Could Origins faint? I looked behind me, half expecting Bigfoot to be standing there.

No one was there.

Understanding seeped into Zoe's face, and she paled as she launched to her feet.

"Oh my God." Archer rose, turning to where Luc stood. "Oh my God, *Luc*."

"I heard you the first time, Archer," Luc snapped. "And I would suggest everyone think very wisely before they overreact or say anything. I can explain." There was a pause. "Maybe."

"What's going on?" I asked, starting to get nervous.

Archer's gaze swung back to me. His mouth opened.

"I mean it." The pupils of Luc's eyes turned white.

Archer snapped his mouth shut.

Stepping down from the landing, I stopped because everyone else stopped.

"Daemon . . ." His brother took a step to the side.

Daemon followed his brother's gaze. His head tilted to the side as he eyed me. Veins under his skin turned bright white. "What in the hell, Luc?"

Luc moved as fast as lightning striking. Within a blink of an eye, he was standing between Daemon and me. Tension rippled off Luc, charging the air with static. "Back off, Daemon."

"Back off?" Disbelief thundered through Daemon's voice. "What in the hell is that, Luc?"

"Me?" I squeaked. He was talking about me? "We've met a couple of times. Don't you remember?"

"I remember, but you didn't look like that last time," he said, the white light spreading through his cheeks, down his throat as Zoe moved, darting around the couch and coming close to the stairwell.

"Look like what?" I grasped the back of Luc's shirt, tugging on it. "What do I look like?"

"It's okay," he said, placing one hand on my hip. "And it'll be really okay the moment Daemon backs the hell off."

A whitish glow surrounded Daemon. "What did you do, Luc?" he demanded. "Is *this* how you saved her?"

I sucked in a startled gasp.

"What I'm about to do is going to be something really bad," Luc warned. Crackling white light appeared from Luc's knuckles, spitting into the air. "Let me remind you, Daemon. You may be an alpha, but I'm the omega. Back down, or someone will be very pissed at me, and that someone is named Katy. And I like her. A lot. I don't want to make her cry."

"Are you threatening me?" Daemon sounded incredulous.

Luc seemed to grow in height. The air in the open room became heavy, stifling. A clap of thunder shook the walls, and I jerked back from Luc, eyes widening.

"Daemon," Archer said quietly, his gaze bouncing from Luc to me. "She can't be a threat."

"That's not what it looks like to me," the Luxen growled. "And you want us to bring her back with us? Are you out of your mind, Luc? I'm not bringing that back where Kat and my child—"

Luc shot forward. I shouted, but it was too late. One second Luc was standing in front of me, and the next he was slamming Daemon into the wall with one hand planted in the center of the Luxen's chest. Drywall plumed into the air as Luc rose off the floor, bringing Daemon with him.

Good God . . .

"You, Kat, and your child wouldn't be here if it weren't for me." Tendrils of white light curled into the air, spreading around Luc like the wings of an angel. The walls of the house groaned under the power coalescing in the room. "After all I've done for you and yours, you would refuse me in my time of need?"

Daemon lifted his hands, but they slammed back into the wall. Sheetrock caved in under them. "And you would put my entire world in jeopardy?" he snarled, the tendons of his neck straining as he struggled to lift his head from the wall. "Are you that selfish?"

"You should already know the answer to that," Luc growled. "I am."

"Stop!" I shouted as Archer grabbed Dawson, winging him back from Luc and Daemon. "Luc! Stop!"

"She is not a risk to you or to Kat," Luc said. "She needs your help."

I started toward them, but a gust of wind shoved me back several steps. My mouth dropped open. "Luc!"

"Don't come near us, because if he so much as looks in your direction, that's it," Luc warned, and I barely recognized his voice.

"I don't know what is happening, but you need to chill out," I tried as Daemon fought against Luc's hold. "Please? Both of you. Because I am really starting to freak out."

Static charged the room, making the air heavy. Then the light receded from Daemon's face. "My bad."

Luc stared at him for a moment and then dropped him. The Luxen landed nimbly on his feet. The tense silence stretched out as Luc lowered himself. "That's an awful big oops you almost made right there," Luc said. "Let's make sure you don't make it again."

Daemon's lips twisted in a smirk as he stepped to the side, and once again, I was in the line of his sight for only a brief second. Luc shadowed his movements, blocking him.

The door opened just then, and there was Kent, holding a huge white box. "I have doughnuts . . ." He lowered the box, taking in the scene before him. "Um, what did I miss?"

"Stay right there," Zoe said, and Kent listened.

Daemon took another step back. "I'm not going to do anything, Luc. I'm just really, really curious about her."

Relieved that it no longer looked like Luc was going to kill Daemon, I threw up my hands. "Is someone going to tell me what the hell is going on and why you all are staring at me like that?"

"Your eyes." Luc faced me. "It's your eyes."

"My eyes . . ." I trailed off as understanding blasted through me. I darted over to the rectangular mirror above the mantle and yep, my eyes were black with white pupils. "Oh my God, I don't know why they're doing this." I spun around, and Luc was there. "I got dizzy in the bedroom, and I had a memory. I was coming down here to tell you."

"What did you remember?" he asked, capturing my wrists as I reached for my eyes.

I tried to focus on him, aware of the fact that everyone was listening. "It came out of nowhere, but he called me *Nadia,* Luc. In the memory, he used that name, and it doesn't make sense." I drew in a stuttered breath. "Are my eyes still messed up?"

A muscle flexed along Luc's jaw as he nodded.

"I'm guessing this has happened before," Dawson stated.

"Yes," Zoe answered, staring at me. "Once before."

"I really think you guys should start telling us what the hell happened," Archer said, arms folded across his chest. "All we know is that Foretoken was raided and that you needed our help. That's it."

"It's a long story," Luc replied. "But the gist of it is, something was in the Andromeda serum that was given to Evie when she was sick. I don't know what it is."

"Wait. You don't know what it is?" Daemon blinked once and then twice. "Seriously?"

"Yes."

"For real?" Daemon insisted.

Luc looked over his shoulder. "Yes, Daemon. I don't know what the hell was given to her, because obviously I was lied to."

"Wow." Daemon grinned, and my eyes narrowed. "This is a first."

"Anyway," Archer drew the word out. "She wasn't like this the last time we saw her."

"It was April. This girl at my school. You remember Sarah?" I turned to Dawson, and he nodded. "We think April was like Sarah. Mutated into something we've never seen before. April was killing humans and framing Luxen for it. She nearly killed Heidi, our friend." I looked over at Zoe while Luc moved to stand by my side, his hawklike gaze latched on to Daemon. "Anyway, she had this key fob thing. She pressed it, and it—I don't know—unlocked something that was in the serum. It turned me into this assassin for like two seconds and made my eyes like this, but that's all. I'm still Evie . . . or Nadia . . . or whoever. We don't know what happened."

"A key fob?" Daemon asked.

"Yes," Luc answered. "This girl called it a Cassio Wave. I have the key fob. Was planning to see if Eaton had any insight."

I had no idea who Eaton was; this was the first I was hearing that name.

Archer cursed under his breath as he looked over at the twins.

"What?" Luc gritted out. "I feel like you three know something that may explain Daemon's overreaction."

"It wasn't an overreaction," Daemon said, and Luc's head jerked in his direction. The Luxen held his hands up. "Remember how I said we ran into trouble and that's why we were delayed? We ran into this . . . thing near the border of Louisiana and Mississippi."

Thing? I had a really bad feeling about this.

"It looked human, and it felt human," Dawson said, glancing at me. "We saw it at a rest stop. Archer had to use the restroom."

"Because he has the bladder of a two-year-old," Daemon muttered, and Archer shrugged.

Dawson continued, "Thought it was just a normal human guy, but then he went right at me. Tried to take my head off."

"Never seen anything like it, and you know I've seen a lot of stuff," Archer said, sitting back down in front of Kent. "The guy was like a damn machine. Took all three of us to take him down, and we *barely* took him out."

"Head shot," Dawson said. "It was the only way we could kill him."

"Like a zombie?" Kent quipped from where he stood with his box of doughnuts.

A brief grin appeared on Dawson's face. "Yeah, like a zombie."

"He had eyes like Evie's. Black with white pupils."

"Did he look like an Arum?" I asked. "Like he was made of smoke or anything?"

Dawson's gaze found mine. "He looked like an Arum, but he wasn't one."

I sucked in an unsteady breath as I looked at Luc.

"Well, this just gets more and more interesting." Kent, still standing by the door, opened the box and pulled out a doughnut. "Just so everyone knows, your eyes are really starting to freak me out, Evie Beanie."

"Sorry?" I said. "I honestly have no control over it. I have no idea why they're like this."

Kent bit into the doughnut.

"The last time your eyes turned this way was after April used the sound wave thing," Grayson spoke up, and it was the first time I realized he was even in the house. He was standing in the kitchen, and I had no idea how long he'd been there. "That wasn't the only thing that happened."

I nodded. "Yeah, I also turned into the Terminator."

"Are you the Terminator now?" Kent took another bite of his doughnut.

"I . . . I don't feel any different," I said, turning to Luc as anxiety blossomed. "I mean, I feel normal except for the eyes."

"Is your head hurting?" he asked. "Anything like that?"

I shook my head. "I was just really dizzy, but I feel normal now."

Luc leaned down, brushing his lips over my forehead as his gaze met Grayson's. "I want you out there. Make sure no one is near—"

There was a cracking noise as if a pebble had hit one of the windows, and the half-eaten doughnut slipped from Kent's fingers.

A shiver coursed down my spine as a horrifyingly familiar scene played out before me. Red, bright red sprayed into the air as Kent's entire body jerked backward. The twins and Archer spun around, the latter wiping a hand over his face. Red was there, too, on his cheeks and now on his hand, and Kent's blue hair turned dark, and half his head was gone, completely—

Oh God.

Oh my God . . .

Kent was dead before he hit the floor.

36

I thought I was screaming, but it wasn't me. It was Zoe. She burst past me with blinding speed, reaching Kent's side as Grayson shot out of the kitchen, but it was too late.

"What the hell?" Daemon shouted a second before shifting into his true form. A second later, Dawson joined him. They were twin brilliant lights shaped like humans.

I started toward Kent in a daze, but Luc caught me with an arm around my waist. He lifted me right off my feet and spun around. The room blurred as the entire front window exploded.

Men propelled through, boots first, and they landed with thick rifles aimed. The door flew off its hinges, falling into the wall. The back door followed, slamming against the stove. Men in straight-up tactical gear poured into the house along with the rain, guns drawn.

Not normal guns.

Terror seized my breath as I gripped Luc's arm, recognizing the EMP-modified weapons.

The men quickly spread out, aiming their guns on every living creature in the room. They could easily kill with just one twitch of the trigger. My wild gaze darted around the room as Luc held me close to his chest. Archer had his hands fisted at his sides. The twins were shifting back into their human forms; each of them had a gun leveled on them. Both Zoe and Grayson were rising, fury etched into their features.

All the men, well over a dozen, wore the same kind of ski masks the men who'd entered my home had. They were the same group that had tracked us down to the house in Columbia. They'd found us here.

One of the men spoke. "All we want is the girl."

Luc's breath danced along my cheek. "At the risk of sounding cliché, over my dead body."

"That can easily be arranged."

I tensed.

Luc's chest rumbled against my back as he laughed. "Yeah, that's not going to be easy."

"Well, we can make it easy, or we can make it hard." The man speaking tilted his head to the side. "We prefer the easy way. Give us the girl, or we will start taking each of these people down, one by one."

The air crackled around Daemon.

"And maybe you'll take out a few of us in the process," the man added, voice eerily calm. "But we'll definitely take out a few of you. Willing to risk that?"

I knew Luc's answer to that. Yes, he would risk that.

My heart pounded fast as I stared at the gun pointed at Zoe. She was fast, unbelievably so, but would she be fast enough? Or would she be like Kent? Gone before she even hit the floor? The same for Grayson—even though I was confident he still loathed me, I didn't want to see him die. And what about the others? I didn't know them all that well, but I liked them when they didn't seem afraid of me, and I wanted them to make it home to their families, to their expecting wives.

I shuddered as the back of my throat burned. And Luc? I loved him—I was in love with him, I couldn't deal with him dying.

I couldn't deal with any more people dying because of me.

And some of them or all of them *were* about to die because of me. These weapons would kill them all. A startling realization floated to the surface. There was only one way out of this for me.

"Let us have the girl and all of you will walk out of here," the man said again. "Alive and whole."

Daemon's fingers twitched at his side. "Now I am super curious why you all would want a human girl but would let us live."

I was pretty confident at this point Daemon knew I wasn't an ordinary human, but he was playing dumb.

The man who was speaking didn't take his eyes off of Luc and me. "We have no problems with the Luxen or the Origins."

My breath caught as Zoe's eyes widened.

"Well, obviously you don't work for the government, then," Daemon replied, his tone casual.

Energy ramped up inside of Luc. I could feel it humming through him. His body vibrated with power. He shifted slightly, and I recognized my chance when I had it. He loosened his arm to move me so that I was behind him. I had seconds to make up my mind, but I didn't need them.

I thought of Kent lying on the floor.

I thought of Mom.

I thought of Chas and Clyde and God knows how many others who'd died because of me. And I thought about how Luc had saved my life, probably more times than I ever could realize, and it was now time for me to save his.

I wrenched free, only catching a glimpse of the shock rippling across Luc's face.

"Okay!" I shouted, raising my hands. "You guys have me. I'm right here. You don't need to hurt anyone."

Horror filled Zoe's eyes. "*Evie.*"

"It's okay." I stepped forward, toward the man who'd spoken. "It's going to be okay."

I knew it wouldn't be.

I knew it wouldn't be okay when one of the men gripped my arm and yanked me forward. Things weren't going to be all right as I was propelled forward toward the open door. And I knew there was a good chance they would still try to kill everyone in that room, but I had to do something. I couldn't stand on the sidelines any longer.

My ears buzzed as I put one foot in front of the other. A numbness settled over me as I stepped out on the porch.

Luc didn't say a word, but I could still feel the immense power building behind me, stretching the seams of the house.

Three more men waited there. One stepped forward, taking ahold of my other arm in a tight, biting grip. I wanted to say something snarky as I was dragged off the porch. I wanted to prove that I was brave and I wasn't scared, but I was trembling so badly I couldn't form words.

Rain drenched my hair, tugging the strands free as I walked on weak legs. This was really happening, and I knew what was coming. They weren't taking me outside to have a chat with me. They weren't leading me across the driveway, pushing me through the thick line of trees to take me to a picnic.

"Stop," a man barked.

Soaked and shivering, I obeyed, staring straight ahead. Under the heavy trees, the rain didn't fall as heavily, but the tree trunks blurred in front of me. *I'm going to die.* I couldn't get enough air in. I was going to die before I even got to live my life, before I even knew what my life really was—who I really was.

"On your knees," the man ordered.

My body reacted on instinct, starting to follow the command, but I stopped myself. "No," I whispered.

"What did you say?"

"I'm not going to make this easy for you," I said, my breath catching and releasing. I started to face him, because I'd be damned if I let them shoot me in the back of the head. "I'm—"

Pain burst across my jaw, stunning me. Swaying, I almost went down as I lifted my hand to my throbbing jaw. I tasted blood in my mouth.

A hand slammed into my back, shoving me forward. "Don't let her turn around. She can't see it coming, or it won't work."

Another hand landed on my shoulder, forcing me down on my knees. Eyes wide, I fell forward, my fingers digging into the wet, loose soil. I opened my mouth. Blood dripped out, smacking off my hand.

It was red. Plain, normal blood.

A flare of dull pain lanced across the back of my skull as I saw myself again, standing in a white room, surrounded by men.

Show them before they hurt you, the man's voice whispered in my ear, and they had hurt me, over and over. I had the bruises to prove that, the aches that went beyond bone deep. *Show them what you're capable of. Prove to me you're worth this gift of life. Show them!* the voice screamed in my memories.

It was like a switch being flipped somewhere deep inside my subconscious.

Fear turned to rage, and it was red hot and powerful as it surged through me and then outward, a shock wave that rippled out.

"Shit," someone said. "Put her down. Put her down now—"

I lifted my head to the man who stood in front of me, rifle in hand. I felt the ground under my hands sink and give way. The ground rumbled as I pictured the man before me being swallowed up by earth and rain. I wanted him *gone.*

Rich, dark soil rippled out from my fingertips like a thousand snakes. It reached his booted feet in seconds, forming clumpy, thick vines. He shouted, jerking the barrel of the rifle up as he was yanked backward. The gun fired, shooting into the sky as the ground collapsed underneath him, sucking him up.

And then he was gone.

I rose, whipping around to the masked man behind me. I lifted my hand. "Fly."

A rush of burning wind lifted him up and up, above the trees and higher still, until he was lost in the thick clouds. I lowered my hand. The man followed, slamming into the wet soil with a fleshy *smack*.

I turned toward a man backing up as he lowered his rifle, and I raised my hand.

"No," he said, holding up his hand. "No—"

I curled my fingers into my palm.

His head jerked to the right, and his shoulders caved. His chest crunched, and his legs folded as his arms broke and twisted. He was nothing more than a crumpled mess.

A gun fired, and I whirled. The bullet didn't strike me. Brilliant white light lit up the clearing. A cry of pain split the air. A rush of wind hit the clearing, and the man across from me fell forward, collapsing onto the ground. The gun was still clutched in his hand.

The man's body *smoked,* and that hadn't been me.

My head cocked to the side as I waited.

Another shot rang out, a flash of blue, and the ground trembled. I saw the guns fly upward, ripped out of the men's hands. They disappeared into the trees.

He strode forward as if he hadn't a care in the world. "I am really annoyed that I had to come out here in the rain"—he glanced in my direction, and he had the strangest purple eyes—"*after you.*"

I frowned. "I don't need you."

Movement snagged my attention. I threw my arm out, and the men to my left spun into the air, into the *branches.* They came back down to the earth at the speed of light.

Someone charged the purple-eyed boy, and he tilted his head to the side. "Really?"

The man didn't slow down, and Purple Eyes stepped into the attack, catching him by the throat. There was a sickening *crack* just as another rushed his way.

Laughing, he spun to the left and kicked, sweeping the legs out from underneath the man. Catching him by the front of his shirt, Purple Eyes slammed him into the ground. White light pulsed from his hand.

I stopped, watching Purple Eyes. The man he held to the ground threw his head back, screaming as the glow washed over him. Within seconds, the glen filled with the scent of scorched flesh and earth.

Purple Eyes was strong.

Dangerous.

Powerful.

A threat.

But I was *more*.

I lifted both arms, and the trembling in the ground turned to a roar. All around, the trees thrashed and twisted as a great wind picked up, blowing my hair back. Broken tree limbs rose from the ground. One cut through the clearing, piercing the man closest to me straight in the chest. Another two went down that way, impaled deep into the ground.

Energy charged the air. The smell of burned ozone increased. I rose off the ground, and the trees continued to shake and the ground rolled under me, buckling as lightning struck close—too close.

The trees ripped from the ground, exposing long, gnarled roots. A cloud of rich, wet earth sprayed.

"Holy shit," someone whispered.

I clapped my hands together.

The trees flew across the clearing, and Purple Eyes ducked, hitting the ground as fleshy grunts sounded, followed by shocked screams that ended abruptly. There was a loud crash.

And then silence.

My arms lowered to my sides as I spread my fingers out, bringing myself to the ground.

A twig snapped, and I focused on Purple Eyes. He prowled toward me, and I lifted my hand.

He stopped, eyes widening slightly as his wet hair curled back from his forehead. "Peaches . . ."

I stared at him.

Slowly, he lifted his hands as if in surrender. "Evie, it's okay . . ."

Names.

Names flickered through my thoughts. Nadia. Evie. Peaches. They held meaning, carried weight, but he was *powerful*. He could hurt me, and I could not allow that. Not again. Never again.

"It's me." His voice was gentle. "Evie, it's me."

"You doing some landscaping?" I heard someone ask, and I turned to the sound of the voice.

It was a dark-haired man with emerald-green eyes. Behind him, I saw an identical replica of him, and there were two blondes, and a girl with deep brown skin. There were masked men still alive, survivors, staggering to their feet. They turned, darting off between the trees.

One of the dark-haired men and the tall blonde took off, disappearing after them. The masked men could run, but a . . . Luxen would always, always be faster. They were Luxen. The two who ran after those men. I knew what they were, and they were also threats.

"That wasn't me," the one who'd come to fight beside me said. Purple Eyes. "That was her."

The dark-haired Luxen swore under his breath, and I felt the power rippling inside me again as I moved my head from side to side. A white glow began to form around him, a showcase of his strength.

A challenge.

A threat.

"Daemon," Purple Eyes said. "I'm going to need you to do what I say and *run*."

"What?" the Luxen called Daemon said.

"Now," the other ordered. "Dammit, run, *now*."

Too late.

I lifted my hand and summoned the rage inside me, letting it whip out and find its target.

37

A bolt of inky black tinged in whitish-red light erupted from my palm, striking the one called Daemon in the shoulder. He flew backward. There was a shout of pain as Daemon rolled into the tree, flickering in and out of his true form as I turned my hand palm up, curling my fingers inward. Daemon lifted off the ground, twisting and struggling as I drew him toward me. He wasn't dead. Yet. That would change—

"Stop!" Purple Eyes shouted. "Stop it now, Evie!"

Evie.

Purple Eyes was now standing in front of the Luxen, his wet hair blowing back from his stark face, his shirt tearing around his shoulders.

Everything in me focused on him. I tilted my head to the side as I curled my hand into a fist, picturing his body caving and cracking, giving way to me.

But that didn't happen.

He took a step toward me, lips peeled back in a snarl. "Evie, it's me. Luc. I need you to stop this. Now."

I squeezed my hand tighter.

He made it another step, a hole appearing in his jeans, along his knee. He shuddered as his chin lifted. "It's me. I'm here. Evie, I need you to come back to me."

I didn't understand how he was still standing. I didn't understand why he was here, why his voice was drowning out the other, who demanded that I prove I was the strongest, that I was the best.

The front of his shirt ripped. Pinpricks of reddish-blue blood appeared on his cheeks as his pupils gleamed all white.

Tension poured into my muscles as something or someone began screaming in the back of my head. The shirt tore across his chest as he skidded back a foot. He was caving. I could see it in the way his shoulders bent and in the whites of his eyes and the tautness of his mouth. He was power personified.

But I was virtually a god.

Purple Eyes went down on one knee. "Don't do this," he gasped, head twisting to the side. Muscles along his neck strained. "Don't do this."

I smiled.

He slammed a hand into the ground, barely holding himself up as veins filled with white under his skin. His left hand followed, punching into the loose soil. His back bowed.

"Nadia." His voice cracked.

I jolted, my entire being recoiled. My concentration weakened. The power flickered and retracted in waves.

Nadia.

She was a girl, a sick and helpless girl. Scared and beaten down, and I was . . .

He lifted his head once more, the skin of his cheeks flayed. "It's going to be okay. I promise you."

A tremor coursed through me. I'd heard that before. He'd spoken those words to me before. A promise . . .

I never really left you.

Another shudder made its way through me. He'd made those promises. My eyes found his, and his were a beautiful, stunning amethyst. I couldn't look away from them. My chest rose sharply. Purple eyes. I knew those eyes. Dreamed of them. Missed them. Mourned them. *Trusted* them.

Gasping, I let go of the power, and it coiled tight, deep inside me, snapping throughout the forest. I threw my head back, screaming as fire and darkness erupted inside me. The burning shadow that had tattooed my skin and coated my muscles, that had entwined itself with my bones and was a part of me.

Had always been a part of me.

Trees groaned under the power's weight. The ground moaned as I dropped to my knees and pitched forward, letting my cheek rest on the cool grass.

My head wasn't blank.

My body was once again mine.

I curled inward as a steady stream of thoughts began to trickle in, as consciousness took hold. I was Nadia. I was Evie. I was Peaches. I could feel the cold rain pelting me. It had been Daemon I'd attacked.

Luc I had nearly killed. Luc, who I loved with everything in me.

Oh God.

What was wrong with me?

What was *inside* me?

Hands were suddenly on me, a gentle touch on my shoulder and hip, but I still flinched. I trembled from my head to my toes.

"Evie," the voice whispered. *Luc.* The fingers were at my cheek now, scooping back wet hair. "Evie, open your eyes for me."

I didn't want to. I didn't want to see what I'd done to him.

"Evie, please," he pleaded, and Luc never pleaded.

"I'm sorry," I whispered, squeezing my eyes tightly closed. "I don't know what's wrong with me. I'm sorry."

"It's okay," Luc said, sliding a hand under my cheek, lifting me from the soaked grass and into his arms. "I'm okay. Look. I'm okay."

I shook my head, trying to pull away, to put some distance between us because there was something seriously wrong with me, and I couldn't be trusted.

"There's nothing wrong with you."

A harsh laugh retched from me. "There is something very badly wrong with me."

"Okay." His hands splayed across my cheeks. "There is probably something a little wrong with you."

"A little wrong with me? A little? I tried to kill you! And Daemon!" I shuddered as his lips pressed to my forehead. "I almost did."

"But you didn't. I'm here." Those lips of his glided over my cheek. "I'm here, and so is Daemon. Open your eyes and look."

Taking several deep breaths, I did as he asked. We weren't alone. The Luxen stood several feet away, in his human form. He was alive, but he didn't look exactly thrilled.

"I don't care how he looks," Luc said, guiding my gaze to him. "Look at me. Please."

I looked at him.

Where his skin had started to peel away, there was nothing but faint pink marks along his cheeks. He looked like he had a sunburn, but I could still see him in my mind. Thin strips of flesh giving way, ripping—

"Stop." He cupped my cheeks. "I'm okay. Don't you see? I'm okay, Peaches."

"But I hurt you and Daemon," I whispered, folding my shaking fingers around his wrists. "I was going to kill you both. I stopped, but—"

"You stopped, and that's all that matters."

I wasn't sure if that was true. Stopping wasn't all that mattered. It didn't erase the pain I'd caused them. What if it happened again and I couldn't stop? Then what?

Luc made this sound in the back of his throat as he stared into my eyes. "We will figure this out. I keep saying that, but I promise you, Evie, we will figure this out. Okay? Believe in that. In me."

I wanted to, badly, but this was beyond him—beyond us. My gaze shifted from his to the bodies strewn around us. Nausea twisted up my stomach. I'd done that, and I'd tried to do worse to Luc, who was the most powerful thing on this Earth it seemed, and yet, he had been breaking underneath me.

I didn't understand how it was possible.

"I have really no idea how I did any of that. One of them hit me and knocked me down, and I saw my blood, and it was like a switch being thrown," I told him, sliding my hands down his arms. "I heard his voice in my head, ordering me to prove that I was worth . . . a life. I think . . ."

"What?" His thumbs smoothed over my cheeks, drawing my gaze from the broken bodies.

"I think I've done this before . . . in a white room full of men who had hurt me." I gave another shake of my head. "I don't understand it. I just knew what to do. Picture it and make it happen."

Luc was quiet for a long moment. "These men who you think hurt you . . . do you remember what they did to you?"

I shook my head in his loose grasp.

"Do you know what happened to them?"

I did. "I killed them."

"Good."

My gaze shot to his.

"Are you guys okay over there?" Zoe called out. "Because we're all starting to get really worried."

"You okay?" Luc asked quietly.

I nodded even though I wasn't sure, because I couldn't sit out here in the dwindling rain.

Luc took my hands and rose, helping me up. I let him turn me to where Daemon and Zoe stood.

"I'm sorry," I said to Daemon. "I don't know what came over me. I'm sorry."

His lips were pressed in a thin line as he glanced at Luc and then nodded.

I didn't expect him to accept my apology.

Daemon looked at Luc, and there were a thousand unsaid words in his hard, unforgiving expression.

"I know," Luc said, obviously picking up on Daemon's thoughts. "We'll talk."

Daemon inclined his head. "Yes, we will."

Glancing at Zoe and finding that she was staring at me like she didn't quite know what to say, I bit back a burst of shame and I looked away, my gaze drifting over the bodies, some still—

One of them was still alive, on his side and reaching for his thigh, where I could clearly see a gun still strapped there.

Luc saw it at the same time I did. He shot forward, catching the man's right arm. The crack of bone was like dry twigs snapping. The man's scream of pain was cut off by Luc's hand around his neck.

Lifting the man clear off his feet, Luc held him in the air. The man's face turned ruddy. Spittle flew as he clamored at Luc's grip with his good hand. His feet kicked, but Luc held him there like he was nothing more than a bag of groceries.

"Every part of me wants to drag this out," Luc said, his voice frighteningly calm. "I want you to fear every last second you have left. I want the very last thought you have to be how precious that last breath of air you took was."

Stepping back, I bumped into a broken tree stump. I looked down, a little lost in the burned, ragged edges.

"Stop," Daemon ordered, knocking a tree limb aside as if it were a paper bag as he stalked forward. "Luc, stop."

"Now why would I do that, Daemon?"

"Because it would be wise to keep him alive. They know what she is."

Wetting my lips, I swallowed hard. "Luc, he has a point. He could tell us why they keep coming . . . and maybe what I am."

The man's eyes bulged as Luc increased the pressure on his neck. He wasn't going to stop. I thought about Kent. I wouldn't blame him if he didn't stop. As badly as I wanted to know why they kept coming after me, I could still understand.

I might've held my breath.

With what appeared to be great restraint, Luc took his fingers from the man's throat, dropping him. He hit the rocky soil in a messy heap, dragging in air and sputtering.

Tense silence followed as Zoe crossed the clearing, her eyes full of barely contained wrath. "Are there any more of you out there? Any more teams coming?"

"No." The man coughed. "We . . . we were the only team, but they'll know . . . something is up if we . . . don't radio in by night."

Daemon glanced at Archer, but the Origin was zeroed in on Luc. I knew in that instance that Archer would support Luc if Luc decided to end this man's life right then and there. Part of me thought that Luc might, even though he'd let go of the man. Deadly violence etched into his features, a promise of retribution.

"What is your name?" Luc asked.

Rolling onto his side, the man gagged as he struggled to breathe. "Steve," he rasped. "Steven Chase."

Luc's lips curled. "You're going to talk, Steve, and maybe, just maybe you'll get to breathe a little longer."

I expected the man to put up a fight, because he looked like he was the military sort. In all the movies I'd seen, people who looked like he did required a ton of convincing and torturing before they started spilling secrets.

Not Steven Chase.

He sang like a canary.

"We didn't want any trouble with you guys. We really didn't," he rasped.

"Really?" Derision dripped from Luc's tone as he bent down, grasping the man by the front of his shirt. Dragging him by the shirt, he lifted the man—like he was a kitten—to his feet. "Look around. You got a whole lot of trouble."

"I know." Steven was trembling, his broken arm hanging limply. "But we didn't have a choice. We had a job to do. You all . . . were in the way. We only wanted her. Those were our orders. Take her out, and then we get to go home."

Archer dragged the guy all the way back to the house. Literally. Dragged him by the scruff of his neck. Luc stayed close, but he didn't speak. Not until we reached the house, and Grayson and Dawson returned.

"They were taken care of?" Luc asked, referencing those who had run, and when they nodded, I didn't feel at all bad for those men. He turned to Daemon. "Secure the asshole."

I trudged along, following Zoe, but Luc reached out, catching my arm. "Oh no. Not you. You're staying out here with me for a moment."

Zoe hesitated, and I thought it was for me, but then I realized she was hanging around for *Luc*. She was worried about him.

"It's okay," I said, just wanting to get this over with, figuring I knew why he wanted to talk to me. "He's just going to yell at me—"

"Damn straight," Luc growled.

My eyes narrowed on him. "And I'm not going to kill him."

"You sure?" she asked.

I kind of felt bad for her having to ask that. "Yes." I sighed. "I'm sure."

Ahead of Zoe, Daemon's lips twitched as he glanced back at us. "Come on, Zoe. Help me find something to tie this douchebag up with."

Zoe didn't move for a second, and then she finally turned away, stalking off toward the guys. I watched until the whole group was gone before letting out a ragged, bone-deep sigh. I turned to where Luc stood, vaguely registering the simmering fury etched into his coldly striking face, and I realized just how much he'd been holding back until he made sure I wasn't going to kill anyone.

He drew in a long, slow breath. "I'm going to try to be calm about this, because of what just happened, but I need to get this off my chest, because if I don't, I might actually implode."

I crossed my arms. "I know—"

"You don't know shit," he said, seething as he stepped forward. "I think that is something we have established multiple times over."

I blinked. "Well, that is completely—"

Luc shot forward, moving so fast I didn't have a chance to react. His hands clasped my cheeks, tilting my head back. In a stuttered heartbeat, his mouth was on mine.

The kiss was deep and sudden, beautiful in its rawness, and my body reacted without thought to the almost brutal emotions pouring into the kiss. My hands landed on his chest, and my fingers dug into his shirt. I kissed him back, and it reached deep inside me, burning its way into my soul.

This was far better than being lectured.

By the time we both came up for air, Luc's chest was rising raggedly under my hands. He rested his forehead against mine, and neither of us moved. I didn't even open my eyes. We stood there in silence as the rain started coming down again, a fine sheen that settled on our skin.

"You need to know that I didn't think you were going to be able to do what you did when they took you outside."

"I didn't, either," I admitted.

"And that makes this worse. I didn't know if I would make it to you in time," he said, sending a shiver through me. "I thought that this time, this would be it. No more bargaining or miracles."

Breathing in the scent of rain and woods, I opened my eyes. "It wasn't."

"It could've been." His hands slipped off my cheeks, sliding down to my upper arms. He drew back, and my eyes fluttered open. Raindrops clung to his thick lashes. "Don't you ever do anything like that again. I don't care what you can do."

"I . . . I had to do something. I had—"

"You didn't have to do anything." The hue of his eyes deepened to violet. "I had it handled. That's what I do."

"They killed Kent." My voice cracked. "They were going to kill each one of you because of me. I couldn't just stand there and let that happen."

His jaw hardened. "You will stand there and allow that to happen if that's what it takes for you to survive."

I gaped at him. "Are you serious? You can't be."

"I'm dead serious."

"And you *would've* been dead!" Pulling free, I took a step back, ignoring the fact that I'd almost killed him myself. "Zoe would've been dead. Everyone in that house would've been dead. I don't care how special any of you are. You're not immortal. You're not untouchable, and if something happened to—" I cut myself off, wiping at the mist gathering on my face. "I know what I did was dangerous. I knew that when I made the decision to leave with them, I might die. I didn't make that choice lightly."

His eyes narrowed. "It was a stupid, careless, and reckless choice. I would've handled the situation."

"By jeopardizing everyone's lives in there? Is that how you would've handled it?"

Luc's lips formed a thin, hard line.

"That's how you've handled it before, right? With Paris?"

"Someone's been talking." His shoulders tensed.

I knew it was a harsh thing to bring up, but I had to. "You've done it before. Put others at risk for me. You would've sacrificed everyone in that room, and you can't keep doing that, Luc." Struggling to stay calm, I swept my wet hair back from my face. "That was my choice to make—"

"It was not your choice." Anger filled his voice. "I know I said this to you before, but I feel like I need to repeat myself just so you're clear. I didn't spend half of my godforsaken life trying to keep you alive for you to just throw it all away!"

"I wasn't throwing it away!" I yelled, hands balling. "I was trying to save the lives of people I care about. If you honestly think I would've stood by and allowed more people to die because of me, then you don't know me at all."

38

Everyone in the house studiously averted their gazes the moment I walked through the busted front door. I didn't have it in me to be embarrassed that they clearly had either heard or seen everything.

A quick glimpse around the room revealed several scorched patches on the floor against the walls. There were no bodies. There was nothing left of them.

I didn't even blink an eye.

I headed straight for the man now tied up in a kitchen chair with what looked like bungee cords.

Archer's gaze flickered over my shoulder, and I knew without looking that Luc had joined us. I didn't want to look at him, because I understood why he was mad, but he also had to understand why I'd done what I had.

I kept striding forward, and out of the corner of my eye, I saw that someone had laid a blanket over Kent, covering his upper body. It was Zoe. She was still kneeling by his body, her face stained with fresh tears.

My chest squeezed painfully as I stopped in front of the man. Up close, I saw that he was middle-aged, with fine lines around his eyes and pinched mouth. His dark eyes darted to my face. He looked normal to me, like he'd be married with 2.5 kids. A guy who'd spend Saturday mornings mowing the grass and chatting with his neighbors about mulch and Weed Eaters.

And he'd been sent to either apprehend a teenage girl or kill her, and he'd accepted the job. Didn't quit or anything like that.

Pushing aside the roiling emotions, I exhaled raggedly. "I want to know what I am, and if you even try to lie, I swear to God, I'll break your other arm."

"Dayum," someone murmured behind me.

Steven's gaze darted around the room, and I could feel Luc growing closer. I didn't even want to know how I knew that, but I did. The man's bruised throat worked on a swallow. "My team . . . was hired. I don't know who—"

"You might want to think twice about going down that route." Luc glided up to my side. "You have another 205 bones I can break, and you have a lot of tissues that I can liquify with a touch."

My lip curled with disgust.

Luc grinned. "So you wanna try answering that question again?"

"I'm kind of hoping he doesn't answer." Daemon strode toward the kitchen, shoving a couch cushion out of the way. "I have some pent-up aggression I would love to really work out."

I crossed my arms. "I think you really need to answer the question differently."

Steven's chest rose raggedly. "We don't work for the government. We're a part of the Sons of Liberty."

Daemon sighed. "I don't think you're taking us seriously." He stepped forward, his smile as eerie and cold as Luc's. "I think I need to show you just how serious we are."

"I am being serious!" he insisted, his head swinging around wildly. "They are— We are an organization that was founded—"

"In the original American colonies? Wait." Zoe shoved to her feet, her nose wrinkled. "The Sons of Liberty were a secret society that protected the colonists' rights and were against taxation. You know, the whole 'No taxation without representation'? The Boston Tea Party?"

The room was so silent you could hear a cricket belch.

"God." She wiped at her cheeks with the backs of her hands. "We learned about them in history class. Unlike some people," she said, sending me a pointed look, "I paid attention."

"She's right," Steven said, words spilling out of him in a rush. "The SOL was created to protect the colonists. People think the society was disbanded over the years, but it never was. We were active during the Civil War and during the Luxen invasion. We've always known that the aliens have been here, because we have operatives in every level of the government."

"Oh really?" Daemon replied dryly.

"We have members all over the states, and whenever the SOL is needed, whether it be in times of war or strife, we answer the call." Pride filled Steven's voice and eyes. "We do so without recognition or record, knowing that we could die on any mission and it would be like we never existed."

"Like Batman?" Luc asked.

Daemon snickered.

"You don't believe me? I can prove it. All the members are marked. Pull down the right side of my shirt." Steven nodded at his words. "You'll see it."

Luc did just that. Gripping the collar of the black shirt, he yanked it aside, revealing what appeared to be a tattoo with a snake coiled atop an American flag. It was all one color, shaded in black.

My brows lifted.

"All that proves is you have an ugly-ass tattoo." Luc let go of the shirt, and Steve slumped back into the wooden chair. "This all sounds like a crock of shit, but I've heard stranger things, so I'm listening. Why would the Liberty boys be interested in her?"

Steven worked on another swallow as his gaze flickered between Luc and Daemon. "You think we're enemies. We're not."

"We are," Luc corrected.

"At least we shouldn't be," Steven insisted as frustration rose in his voice. "It's about to happen, and it's going to happen fast if we don't stop it. It'll be over before anyone knew it even began."

Cold air teased the back of my neck. "My mom said something similar." I glanced at Luc. "Right before . . . She was saying something just like that."

"Sylvia Dasher?" Steven said her name with a curl of disdain. "She was a part of it—part of the Poseidon Project."

Dawson groaned as he drifted behind the chair, tipping his head back. "What is it with the Greek names?"

His brother became very still. "What is the Poseidon Project?"

"It was the Daedalus's greatest achievement," Steven explained, his lips thinning in pain. "And it was their most horrific creation."

Stepping back, I rubbed my hands over my hips. "You know about the Daedalus?"

"Of course we do. We monitored them as best we could." His gaze darted from Daemon to Luc. "We don't agree with what they are doing. They're playing God. You all know exactly what they are."

"Are?" Dawson questioned. "The Daedalus is no more."

Steven shook his head, and I remembered they didn't know what we suspected, what we knew. "No, they're still active, very much so. You thought you took them out," he said, fixing his panicked stare on Luc. "But you didn't."

"Obviously," Luc muttered.

"Wait a second." Daemon's hands opened and closed at his sides. "Are you saying that the Daedalus *is* still active?"

"We didn't get a chance to tell you that, because these jackasses interrupted us," Luc said. "Guys, I know you all want to focus on the Daedalus, and I get it, but let's deal with one screwed-up thing at a time. So, a little more detail on the Poseidon Project would be great."

"Wow." Daemon snorted. "That's two things you don't know about?"

Luc looked over at Daemon. "I'm literally in the worst possible mood you could ever imagine right now."

"So? I'm in a bad mood, too. In case you forgot, your girlfriend just tried to kill me after *you* tried to kill me," Daemon pointed out. "And I just learned that the organization responsible for every one of Kat's nightmares is still functioning."

Luc exhaled heavily. "I'm beginning to think I shouldn't have stopped Evie."

"Nice." Daemon rolled his eyes. "That's really helping with my mood."

"Do I look like I care?"

"Guys, really?" I threw my hands up in exasperation, and half the room ducked as if they expected to be tossed into the ceiling. "Can you all not do this right now?"

Neither of them looked like it was something they could control, but they both fell silent.

I focused on Steven. "Tell us what that is."

"The Poseidon Project was their longest program, nothing like what they'd worked on before. Hybrids? Origins?" He shook his head, wincing. "This, if successful, would make every creation that has come before it seem like child's play."

There was no question that Steven knew exactly what the Daedalus had been up to, but he wasn't telling us anything, really.

"I'm getting bored," Luc warned.

"Records indicate they'd been working on the Poseidon Project since the Luxen first arrived—since the Arum first came here. Yes," he said when Dawson let out an expletive. "The project was fraught with so much failure we believed what they were attempting to be impossible—not even a concern. It had to be impossible—the blending of Luxen and Arum DNA."

"What?" Daemon and Grayson thundered at the same time. It was Daemon who continued. "That's impossible. Our DNA is not compatible."

"Isn't it?" Steven challenged. "Would it be impossible inside a human vessel?"

Luc unfolded his arms. "Nothing is impossible."

"They succeeded. We didn't realize until after the war, but they succeeded in ways we never imagined, long before we could've ever guessed. The things they've created—they're unstoppable, wielding both Luxen and Arum abilities, more powerful than their strongest Origin." His gaze flicked to Luc. "They're not vulnerable to obsidian or the weaponized onyx."

That was the stuff that sprayed into the air in an invisible mist. Like the Disabler, it caused the Luxen extreme pain.

"EMP-modified weapons do not harm them," he continued, his chest rising and falling heavily. "Once their mutation is complete, only a shot to the head will put them down, but they are fast—faster than a damn bullet. I've seen it."

"Holy crap," murmured Zoe, her eyes wide. "You said when their mutation is complete? What does their mutation look like?"

"Like a horror show. It's on a cellular level. Their bones break and reform, their blood vessels leak. Fever. Vomiting." He closed his eyes. "Their entire bodies and minds change. They're not like the hybrids. They aren't the same afterward. They are programmed, unstoppable killers."

"Sarah." Zoe turned, thrusting her hand through her hair. "April. Possibly even Coop and . . ."

She didn't need to say it.

Me.

"You've seen the news? About the outbreaks that the media is blaming the Luxen for?" Steven's laugh was dry as old bones. "They weren't sick people. They were humans mutating."

"How?" I whispered, and Zoe whipped back around. "How are people mutating? Why?"

"Some of them were created in the labs. We're pretty confident it took place at the compound in Frederick," he said, referencing Fort Detrick, where my mom worked. "They were like the Origins. They created sleepers and called them Trojans, and just like their namesake, they have infiltrated every level of society. But others are . . . they were normal humans that were mutated."

"How?" Daemon demanded. "How could normal humans mutate?"

"It's a flu," he said, throat working on a swallow. "The Daedalus mutated a strain of a common flu to carry this mutation, and they released it. We don't know when, but that's why some humans are beginning to mutate."

Horror warred with disbelief inside me.

"This is impossible," Zoe murmured.

"It's not," Steve insisted. "Weaponized biological agents aren't anything new, and the Daedalus has had decades to perfect this."

"If what you're saying is true, how come we don't have thousands of these . . . mutated humans running around?" I asked.

"Flu shots. People who got flu shots may still come down with the flu, but it weakens the mutated strain in the virus. They won't mutate," he explained, and it felt like the floor moved under me as I thought about how Mom had even mentioned the importance of flu shots. So much so that I often joked that she must be getting kickbacks from the makers. "Those who didn't get the flu shot, they're either going to die during the mutation, or they'll mutate, and those who got the shot are going to have just about the worst flu in their life."

Silence filled the room, and I thought of Ryan. With the normal flu, people died if they had undiagnosed health conditions like heart problems or autoimmune diseases. People whose bodies probably couldn't withstand the mutation.

"We don't think they've released the virus on a wide scale yet, but there's no way of being sure. At least not yet," Steven continued. "But it's viral. It'll only be a matter of time."

I felt like I needed to sit down.

"No way." Dawson breathed. "This is . . . this is too much to believe."

Archer strode forward, coming to stand on the other side of Luc. "I've never heard or seen anything like this, not once during my entire time at the Daedalus."

"You wouldn't have." Steven twisted his neck from side to side. "It was top secret. From what we could gather, only a very few had clearance to the project or to the key that created the mutation."

"And what was that called?" Daemon asked. "Bullshit 101?"

Fear trickled into Steven's gaze. "It's not bullshit. None of this is. They had three serums. Some of you know them well. LH-11. Prometheus and Andromeda—Andromeda creates the Trojans."

My hands fell to my sides. I tried to speak, but my throat closed off.

"No," Luc said, snapping forward. He gripped the man's shirt, lifting him and the chair off the floor. "You're lying."

"Why would I?" he cried out. "What point would that serve?"

I stared at Luc, wondering why he didn't believe this man and then quickly realizing that he didn't *want* to.

"He doesn't have a reason to lie, Luc." Archer turned to him. "What he is saying sounds unbelievable, but you and I both know the Daedalus was capable of just about anything."

"He's right," Steven gritted out through clenched teeth. "We have been tracking down the Trojans, trying to get to them before they activate and take them out afterward, like we did in Kansas City and Boulder. Something is coming—something big. The ones we haven't been able to capture have all but disappeared. We don't know why, but we know it's not to go live out their days on a farm. Whatever reason they were created for, it's happening now."

It seemed like Daemon was the first to figure it out, because he turned slowly, looking directly at me. "And that's why you're here?"

Luc dropped Steven and the chair landed with a thud. "Don't say it," he ordered, speaking the words so quietly I barely heard him.

Steven ignored him. "She's a Trojan. You saw what she did out there. Have you ever seen anything like that? No, none of you have."

I couldn't speak.

"If you don't believe me, I can prove it," he interrupted, his wide gaze fastening on Daemon. "Try to shoot her."

"What?" I exclaimed.

Archer cocked his head to the side. "I don't think any of us are going to fall for that one."

"You're not listening to me!" Steven shouted. "If you try to shoot her, it won't happen, even if she hasn't been activated. What is inside her will protect her."

"You guys were trying to shoot me in the head outside!" I yelled a sentence I never thought I'd have to.

"From behind," Steven clarified. "If you can't see it coming, you can't stop it."

Breathing heavily, I stared at him. "You can't be telling the truth. I know I did some pretty badass and scary stuff out there, but I can't magically stop bullets."

"I can," Luc said.

I looked over at him, brows raised.

"Do it." Steven's gaze swung around the room. "Do it, and you'll see that I'm not lying."

"No one is shooting Evie," Luc said. "Sorry."

"Well," Daemon said. "If we do it and she stops the bullet, then we know he's telling the truth."

"Did you miss her go all Dark Phoenix out there?" Zoe demanded. "I really don't think we need to risk shooting her to prove what he's saying."

Luc faced Daemon. "We're not shooting Evie."

"I'm just saying we could just maybe aim for her leg or something," Daemon suggested quite helpfully. "That wouldn't kill her if it turns out he's full of crap, and she'll probably kill him."

My mouth dropped open. "There's no reason to shoot me. I'm . . ."

As everyone around me fell into an argument over whether or not it was okay to shoot me, I thought about Mom, and my heart cracked wide open. What little hope I had left that she hadn't been a part of what was done to me was gone. She had to have known—

"You need to take her out," Steven said, breaking the silence. "You need to do it before it's too late."

Luc slowly turned around, facing everyone in the group. "No one is touching her. Does everyone understand that? Because I used up the last of my generosity not killing this man when he pulled a gun outside. That tank is on empty."

No one responded. There were nods, a few long looks exchanged, and then Steven spoke once more.

"There will come a time when you will regret this." Steven lifted his chin. "There will come a time when you will wish you'd put her down, and by then, it will be too late."

That was the same thing Micah had said to us, and when I looked over at Luc, I knew he was thinking the same thing.

Micah had known.

He'd known what I was.

There was no more information Steven could provide, and when I walked out of the house, I wasn't expecting that Steven was going to live much longer.

And he didn't.

I knew he was gone when Grayson carried out Kent, who'd been wrapped in a blanket. Zoe followed the Luxen, and I closed my eyes, seeing Kent's face.

I felt Luc's presence without hearing him. I felt his warmth. "That shouldn't have happened to Kent."

"No, it shouldn't have."

"I know I didn't know him as long as you all did, but I liked him." I opened my eyes, and my lashes were damp. "He was funny, and he was . . ."

"Good. Kent was just all around good," Luc finished for me, and then he took my hand. "Come on."

Luc led me off the porch, toward where Grayson and Zoe had walked. They hadn't gone where the other bodies were laid but behind the cabin, near a stone bench.

We didn't talk about what Steven had told us or confirmed. I don't think any of us were even thinking about it as Zoe lifted her hand and tapped into the Source. Grayson joined her. So did Luc, and by the time there was nothing but ashes left, we were joined by the twins and Archer.

Kent wasn't buried in the mist, and there were no words spoken and no tombstone to mark his grave. Just a patch of scorched earth and heavy, palpable silence.

If Kent were here, there probably wouldn't be silence. He'd crack an inappropriate joke. Probably call me some weird nickname and then have all of us laughing.

All I could tell myself was that he hadn't seen it coming. There'd been no pain. He'd taken a breath . . . and then didn't, and I had to think that was at least some consolation. He didn't hurt, but it wasn't fair and it wasn't right, because, like what Luc said, Kent was *good.*

My tears joined the mist on my cheeks.

I don't know how long we all stood there before Daemon spoke. "We need to leave before more come," he said. "Before it's too late."

39

There wasn't time to shower or change, so we piled into two new vehicles that had been parked in the garage. Both were older models, a nondescript Jeep Cherokee and a four-door Taurus.

Daemon climbed behind the wheel of the sedan, and I got in the back seat with Zoe. Luc was in the passenger seat. Dawson and Grayson joined Archer in the Jeep. It was more than just weird to see Daemon driving. I'd gotten so used to seeing Kent there in a short period of time that it just felt all kinds of wrong.

He should be here.

He shouldn't be dust and ash.

Pulling the blanket I'd swiped from the bedroom around me, I rested my cheek on the cool window. My jeans were cold and stiff in some places, sticking to my skin in others. I was filthy, but I was alive.

I kept replaying everything that Steven had told us. There was a super-scary virus out there that could mutate humans into this *thing* or it could kill them. James had been sneezing the last time we'd seen him. Was he getting sick? Or had he gotten the flu shot?

I didn't doubt what Steven had said. That I was the result of the Poseidon Project, something so incredibly dangerous that a centuries-old secret society had hunted me down. That I was a Trojan, mutated by my mother and hidden in society to eventually be awakened to carry out some nefarious deeds.

Except something had obviously gone wrong with my mutation. I wasn't like April.

But I felt . . . wrong in my skin. Like I didn't know what I would do next, what I was truly capable of, and I couldn't stop thinking about the Trojan Daemon and crew had come across on the way to us. It had tried to kill them.

I had tried to kill them.

Would that happen again? They were taking me to a place where their families lived, to a place where traumatized Luxen and humans had already been through enough, and I . . .

I was capable of anything.

I drew in a rocky breath and slowly let it out.

I was holding it together.

Eleven hours. That was how long this drive would take. Both Daemon and Luc wanted to make the trip with minimal restroom breaks, which translated into one, and I fully understood that. Being seen by anyone was dangerous, especially me since my face had been plastered all over the news.

But I wished we'd saved some of the tranquilizers from the safe house so I could knock myself out.

Minutes ticked into hours, and at some point, Zoe had dozed off beside me while I watched Luc and Daemon, sort of enthralled by their . . . *friendship*? I had no idea how the two of them could go from threatening and slamming each other into walls to chatting and chuckling with each other like nothing had happened.

I still felt like crap for hurting Daemon, but they seemed to have forgotten their skirmish. Or maybe since them threatening each other was something that had happened a lot, it was just an ordinary day for them?

Probably the latter.

Several times, Luc glanced back at me as if he were double-checking that I was, in fact, in the back seat. We hadn't had the chance to really talk after our little showdown outside the cabin.

He looked back at me again now, those amethyst eyes drifting over me. I wished in that moment I could read his thoughts.

"You doing okay back there?" he asked. "Need to stop or anything?"

I shook my head and glanced over at Zoe. "She's out."

"Good. She needs to rest." Luc faced the front. "We're making good time."

I let the blanket fall to my waist. My shirt was dry by now, and my pants were just damp. Keeping my voice low, I asked, "What is this place going to be like?"

"You've been picturing medieval times, haven't you?" Daemon glanced in the rearview mirror.

Pressing my lips together, I nodded. "That or something post-apocalyptic with wild dogs roaming the street and people collecting rain for drinking water."

Luc turned to me, a slow grin tugging at his lips.

"What?" Pretty sure I'd seen those two things in at least a dozen end-of-the-world movies.

"It's not that postapocalyptic," Daemon answered, and I could hear the smile in his voice. "A lot of nature has reclaimed large portions of the city. It's kind of insane how quickly that happened, but we're adapting. Kat and I have been there for almost two years. The same for Dawson and Beth. Archer and my sister have been there longer, helping those left behind."

A huge part of me still couldn't believe that people had just been left behind. I shouldn't be surprised that was the state of humanity, but it was still disturbing.

"And there is still some electricity used in emergencies, like if there is a medical procedure that needs to be done," Daemon explained. "We power them up, using the Source. It's not something we do often. Major outputs of energy can be tracked. So, we've done a lot of scavenging. Batteries are worth their weight in gold. As are camping supplies."

I'd never been camping, so this should be interesting.

"At least it's not summer," Luc commented. "It can get over a hundred degrees and no AC."

My eyes widened. "What's the weather like now?"

Daemon chuckled. "In the seventies during the day, fifties at night. We didn't have as bad a summer as we could've. Part of me wonders if it has to do with the lack of pollution and machines, but we do have ways of keeping the houses somewhat cool. Providing airflow is essential, as is shade. For homes that didn't have porches or trees to block the sun, awnings have been built. Staying on lower levels of homes helps. Basements are few and far between because of the limestone, and the homes that do have basements are used for the elderly or those who are heat sensitive. But when it gets really hot, all you can do is pretend that it isn't that hot."

"What does everyone do in the city?"

"Everyone who can work, works. A lot of people are farming and running cattle ranches who never had any experience with it before. Food is something we don't have to worry as much about as we did in the beginning," he explained. "Life inside the wall isn't very much different from outside of it. There are laws and people to enforce them. Schools run during the days even though there aren't a lot of children. Many didn't survive the first year."

I swallowed hard.

"We have doctors—Luxen and hybrid who came to the city," he continued. "The city is more of a community now. Everyone helps everyone. It's the only way they'll survive."

"How many people are there?"

It was Luc who answered. "In the metro area, before the population, it was over two million. Now it's what, Daemon?"

"A little over twenty thousand, and about five thousand of them are Luxen transplants," he answered.

"Does that mean the rest got out before the cities were walled?"

Neither of them answered for a long moment, and then Daemon spoke. "No one really knows. There was a lot of civil unrest and chaos after the invasion and when the EMP bombs were dropped. Hundreds of thousands had to have died in the weeks and months after, most of it human-on-human violence. Others who had the means and the health got out."

I sat back, twisting the blanket between my fingers. "Why haven't the humans left now? How can you all not be afraid that someone is going to leave and expose you all there?"

"It's a threat they live with daily," Luc said, staring out the windshield. "But many of them simply do not want to be a part of a world that wrote them off."

"I can understand that, but it still has to be a huge risk."

"It is. All exits are heavily monitored, and we don't want to be in the position where we have to stop someone from leaving. So far, it hasn't been an issue." Daemon paused. "We'll just have to cross that bridge if we get to it."

That seemed like a pretty big bridge to cross later.

"But we hope never to get there." Daemon's voice hardened. "We don't plan to stay hiding forever. The city isn't just a sanctuary for those forgotten or hunted. It's also ground zero for the resistance."

Tall oaks and elms gave way to swampy marshes that eventually leveled into long stretches of nothing but prairies. We'd stopped once to use the restroom, and then as night fell, we were on the road again.

Not the highways we'd been traveling.

Daemon took dusty, country roads that bypassed the larger cities near Houston that were still populated, but I knew we were getting close to Zone 3 because we'd stopped seeing any cars out on the road or any sign of life or light in the homes dotting the grasslands, or in the apartments stretching like empty, bare hands into the starry night.

A nervous anxiety filled me as Daemon pulled into an abandoned car wash, followed by the Jeep.

"We walk from here," Zoe said, opening the car door.

I stepped out into the cool night air, making out dust-covered cars in the darkness as I went to the trunk of the car to grab my bag.

Luc joined me, taking the bag before I could drape it over my shoulder. "I got this."

"I can carry it," I told him.

"We have to move fast." He closed the trunk.

"Are we in Houston?" I asked.

"Suburbs." Daemon came around the back as the other three joined us. "Everything here is abandoned. We've got about a mile on foot. You good with that?"

I nodded.

"Then let's go," Archer said from somewhere in the shadows.

Luc took my hand and squeezed. My stomach was churning like a fan set to high as we walked out the back of the car wash and cut through overgrown, empty backyards.

No one spoke as we hurried through the darkness, and I knew that all of them could move a million times faster than I could but were slowing down, exerting far more energy to do so.

I could try to go faster, and considering what I'd done in the woods, I probably could be just as fast as they were, maybe even faster.

But I didn't even know how to tap into whatever was inside me, and if I did, would I turn around and try to kill everyone around me? It seemed like whenever I went badass assassin, I went after anything I perceived as a threat, and since everyone around was either a Luxen or an Origin, I didn't think that was going to end well.

So, I walked as fast as I could, holding Luc's hand with a death grip.

"You're doing perfectly," Luc said as he caught a low-hanging wire, lifting it out of the way.

"Thank you," I whispered.

The mile seemed to stretch for an eternity as we crossed vacant streets and sprawling ranchers, past pools that smelled like moss and knee-high, swaying reeds.

At any given moment, I expected a chupacabra to jump out of nowhere.

Luc chuckled as he looked over his shoulder at me. "Chupacabras aren't real, Peaches."

"I don't know about that."

"Kat would probably agree with you," Daemon said from up ahead. "She's convinced they're real. She says she can hear them howl at night."

"That would probably be a dog," Luc commented.

"Or a coyote," Zoe said. "I definitely think there are coyotes around here."

My eyes widened. "I hope it's a friendly coyote."

Someone chuckled. Maybe Dawson. Then Archer said, "Let's not find out."

Finally, after an eternity, we cleared a heavy thicket, and I saw it in the silvery moonlight.

"Holy crap," I whispered.

A wall of steel stood before us as far as the eye could see. It had to be close to a hundred feet tall, and as we edged around it, staying close to the cropping of heavy trees, I saw no opening.

How in the world did they build this, knowing there were people inside?

"They didn't care." Luc tugged me along.

Up ahead, I saw one of the twins slip into their Luxen form, becoming a brilliant white beacon. "What is he doing?"

"Letting them know we're here," Luc answered.

A heartbeat later, the Luxen slipped back into his human form, and I heard the soft groaning of steel rubbing against itself.

"Daemon?" came a low male voice.

"Here," the Luxen responded, and then we were crossing the dirt trench, heading for an opening I couldn't even see. The twins disappeared into the wall, and then I lost sight of Zoe and Grayson.

My heart launched into my throat as my feet slowed. I really had no idea what awaited me on the other side of the wall. A forgotten city. People who would either welcome us or be wary. Someone in there might know what was going to happen to me.

Could tell me what to expect.

Months earlier, I wouldn't have wanted to know the truth. I would've rather hidden from it. But I wasn't her anymore.

"Evie." Luc's voice was quiet but strong.

Drawing in a deep breath, I nodded. "I'm okay. I'm ready."

And then I stepped forward, hand in hand with Luc, into the unknown.

40

We entered a dark field that had once been a park. There was a swing set in the moonlight, the seats missing from the chains.

I don't know why that was the first thing I noticed, and not the men armed with rifles. They weren't paying much attention to us, and I quickly realized they were guards, obviously protecting the entrance to Zone 3.

We crested the hill, passing the park, and down below I saw rows of homes and a towering, sprawling city, completely dark.

A yellow glow flickered to life several yards ahead, followed by another and then another. Gas lamps casting light along the street. There were people waiting for us.

Daemon disappeared.

That was how fast he moved. He just vanished, and a heartbeat later, I heard a soft, feminine laugh.

"How are you?" I heard Daemon say, and then a plethora of questions came from him. "You feeling okay? No problems, right? You're doing—"

"I'm perfect," came the response. "Especially now. We missed you."

Then Archer was gone. There was a squeak, and I squinted, seeing him lift someone up over his shoulder.

Dawson sighed. "Show-off."

And then he was gone.

There was laughter, male and female, and then a peal of giggles that came from a child, and soft voices, intimate moments of reunions. Zoe slowed down, and I figured, like me, she wanted to give them space. The four of us took our time getting to them, with Grayson hanging way back.

A snapping sound caught my attention. Wind lifted up canopies that were stretched from a house, the fabric rippling.

"Holy alien babies," a female said, and the gas lamp moved closer to her face, revealing a pretty young woman with brown hair and big eyes. "Is that *the* Luc? Has hell officially frozen over? Is there another alien invasion on the horizon?"

"Yeah, it's me." He squeezed my hand and then said to me in a lower voice, "Want to meet Kat?"

I did.

I watched Zoe walk over to where Dawson was standing with another woman. Luc let go of my hand as he moved forward silently, and then he dipped down, hugging someone much shorter than he was, than even I was. He murmured something, and I heard her laugh as he pulled back, straightening.

"Are you sure you aren't having twins?" he asked.

"Good God, don't say that, Luc," Kat replied as I clasped my hands together. "Not exactly prepared for a two-for-one special."

Luc laughed. "I'm sure Daemon is."

"Actually . . ." Daemon trailed off. "The mere idea gives me a series of heart attacks."

"Man up, Daemon; you could be getting ready to have triplets."

"I'm so glad I came to get you," he responded dryly. "So glad."

I cracked a grin as Luc turned to me, and I saw that he was now holding what appeared to be a gas lantern. I inched forward.

"Kat, this is *Evie,*" he said, stressing my name like he always did when it was someone who knew me before.

Now that I was closer to them, I could see how pretty the young woman was . . . and also how pregnant she was. Like she looked as if she were due last week.

Daemon had moved to stand behind his wife, two hands resting on a very heavily swollen stomach.

"Hi." I waved my hand awkwardly, unsure of what to say.

She smiled as she extended a hand, clasping mine warmly. "I'm thrilled to see you. Both of you." She glanced at Luc and then at me. "Daemon said you don't remember . . . meeting me, but I just want to say I'm glad to see you here."

"Thank you. Same. I mean, I don't remember you, but I'm glad to be here," I rambled, sounding like an idiot as I dropped her hand. "I'm just going to stop talking now."

Luc draped his arm over my shoulders as he bent down, whispering in my ear, "You're doing fine."

I wasn't so sure about that.

But Kat was grinning at me—at us—and there was a secret to her grin when she said, "You know, Luc. I always knew it."

"Shush," he murmured, pressing a quick kiss below my ear.

Daemon whispered something to Kat, and her smile faltered as her gaze fixed on me. "I'm so sorry," she said. "To hear about your mother. I know that doesn't change anything or make it better, and I do know. I just want to say I'm sorry."

The next breath I took was shaky. "Thank you. I appreciate it."

Her smile was full of the kind of grief I knew came from first-hand experience.

"Hi!" a bubbly voice broke through, and I turned to my right.

I immediately recognized the stunning black-haired woman standing there beside Archer. "You're Dee," I blurted out.

She blinked. "I am."

"You remember her?" Kat asked.

"No. I don't. I just—I saw her on TV." I turned back to Dee. "I always watched you . . ." I trailed off, wincing.

Archer smiled.

Luc murmured, "Don't worry. That didn't sound creepy at all."

I shot him a dark look I knew he could see.

Zoe laughed.

"So, you've watched me basically talk to a wall?" she asked, smiling.

"If that wall is Senator Freeman, then yes."

Dee laughed as she leaned into Archer, and I couldn't help but notice how both brothers were eyeing Archer like they wanted to punch him into another galaxy.

"Uncle Luc! Uncle Luc!" a child squealed.

Turning toward the sound, I saw a little girl, maybe four or so years old, on Dawson's hip, stretching out waving arms as she wiggled in his grasp. There was a woman standing next to them, her dark hair pulled up in a messy topknot. She had a hand on Dawson's back.

Uncle Luc?

My eyes nearly popped out of my head as Luc walked over to the girl, lifting his hands. The child practically propelled herself out of Dawson's arms into Luc's. She wrapped tiny arms around his neck.

I suddenly remembered what Luc had said when Dawson realized who I was—or who I'd . . . I'd been connected to.

I really don't want to make Bethany a widow and little Ash fatherless.

This was Dawson's wife and child.

Which would mean that since Dawson was a Luxen and Beth was a hybrid, the little girl was an . . . Origin.

The woman was shaking her head in wonder. "She hasn't seen him in years, but she remembers him." She smiled at me, extending a hand. "Sorry. I'm Beth. Dawson's wife."

I shook her hand, wondering if I'd met her before or not. "Nice to meet you."

"How is my favorite Ashley doing?" Luc asked, leaning his head back.

"I'm your only Ashley!" She planted her hands on his chest, pinning him with a rather serious look for such a young child.

He just smiled at her in a way that was a little sad. "You're getting so big, almost as tall as I am."

Her head cocked to the side. "I'm not that big!"

"Uh-huh," he said.

"Nuh-uh!"

My heart . . . well, it did this weird little thing as I watched Luc with this girl. It squeezed and swelled, and while I wasn't even remotely entertaining the idea of babies of any kind, seeing him with her . . .

I sighed.

"That should be illegal, shouldn't it?" Zoe murmured in my ear. "A guy that hot holding a kid."

I nodded in agreement as Luc continued to argue with the child over whether or not she was getting as tall as he was.

Folding my arms over my chest, I looked around, realizing that Grayson had disappeared. "Where's Grayson?" I whispered to Zoe.

She sighed, shoving her hands into the pockets of her jeans. "I think he just needed some time alone."

Kent. Bitter grief rose from what felt like a never-ending well.

I knew whatever I was feeling was nothing compared to what the others were experiencing.

"I want to introduce you to someone very special to me, Ash." Luc turned toward me. "This is—"

"Nadia," the little girl said.

Uh.

"No, this is Evie," Luc gently corrected her.

"No, it's not." The little girl studied me, wrinkling her little nose. "She's Nadia."

Um.

"Okay." The girl's mother swooped in, deftly plucking her child out of Luc's arms. "It is way past your bedtime. I let you stay up to see your daddy, but it's time for you to snuggle in with the bedbugs."

"Bedtimes are stupid," the little girl grumbled as she all but threw herself over Beth's shoulder so that she was facing me. "And I don't want to snuggle with bugs."

I wouldn't want to, either.

Beth turned around. "It was really nice getting to see you guys. I'm sure we'll see you in the morning?"

"Yes." Luc joined me.

Dawson nodded at Luc and then gave me a little half smile. "Take it easy tonight, kids."

"Kids?" Luc snorted.

Beth and Dawson walked off, and little Ash ended up in her dad's arms. She was waving at us, and I waved back.

"Sorry about that," Daemon said. "Ash can be . . . different."

"It's okay, but how did she know? Based on her age, she couldn't have met me before. Right? Did she read my mind or something?" I asked, and then frowned. "Well, that doesn't make sense, because I wasn't thinking about being Nadia or anything like that."

"She can read thoughts," Dee explained. "But Ash is . . . very different. Sometimes creepy, but in an adorable way."

Zoe's brows rose.

"Well, that explains why she loves Uncle Luc," I said.

Luc nudged me with his arm. "Don't be jealous."

"Did you guys run into problems on the way here?" Kat asked, rubbing a hand along her belly.

"Not on the way in, but on the way out, we did." Archer dropped his arm on Dee's shoulders. "We'll talk later. It's getting late."

Luc looked up, beyond the group. His arm tightened around my shoulders. "General Eaton," he announced. "Should I salute you?"

A man drifted into the glow of the lanterns, an older man with white hair buzzed closed to his skull. He was dressed in a white cotton shirt.

"As if you ever saluted anyone in your life." The man was nearly as tall as Luc and Archer, and while he appeared to be in his sixties, he was fit and trim.

Then I remembered Luc saying he planned on seeing if Eaton knew what the Cassio Wave was. This was the man who possibly held all the answers.

"This is Evie—" Luc started.

"No, she's not." The general eyed me over the long, crooked slope of his nose. "I know exactly who she is. Nadia Holliday."

Everything inside me locked up as Zoe exchanged a look with Archer and Dee.

Being called Nadia twice in a span of minutes was weird.

"Well," Luc drawled as he stared down at the general. "Hell of an icebreaker."

The older man smiled tightly. "We'll talk later." He scanned the group. "Glad everyone made it made safely. Archer, I want a debriefing now."

Archer sighed so heavily that Grayson would've been envious. He kissed Dee's cheek before he pulled away. "This shouldn't take long," he told her.

"It won't." Eaton nodded at me before pivoting sharply, stalking down the dark street, back straight as if he were performing for an army we couldn't see.

"See you all later," Archer said, and then he jogged off, easily catching up with the older man.

Kat lifted her brows. "He's been moody lately. Stress."

"I can imagine," I murmured, more than unnerved as I watched the general disappear into the dark.

"Come on, I'm sure you guys are hungry and exhausted," Kat said. "I can show you the house we have ready."

"I'll do it," Dee offered. "Daemon, get back to bed before she gives birth in front of us and traumatizes everyone."

Kat turned to her slowly.

The smile on Dee's face was angelic. "Just looking out for you."

"Uh huh," she murmured.

"Perfect." Daemon started to turn her away. "I want to get Kat in bed."

"No one wants to know that," Dee remarked. "TMI."

"To rest," he stressed, and then he looked at Luc. "Don't forget we need to talk."

"I won't," Luc answered, and a fine shiver curled down my spine. I had a feeling I knew what he wanted to talk about.

We said our goodbyes, and then Dee was leading us down the dark street, lit by the lamp Zoe now carried.

"There are two houses next to ours that are empty and are perfect," Dee was saying. "You'll be able to take a quick shower, but it'll be cold."

I about moaned. "A shower would be amazing, cold or not."

"How do you have the water running?" Zoe asked, keeping step with Dee. "You all didn't have that before."

"We powered up some of the generators in anticipation that you guys would like to freshen up. The drive is ridiculously long," she explained. "And I know that would be the first thing I would want."

"You are magnificent," Zoe told her.

Dee laughed. "I do try."

As we went farther, I could hear the distant hum of low conversation. People were definitely here, hidden in the homes or under the canopies.

"Has anyone else arrived?" I asked, thinking of Heidi and Emery.

"You guys are the first."

"Emery and Heidi probably won't be here for several more days," Luc explained.

I nodded, worrying festering inside me like a wound.

"By the way, Evie has a girl crush on you, Dee," Luc randomly announced.

"Luc!" I gasped as Zoe giggled. I swung at him, but he darted out of the way.

Dee spun around, her long hair spinning around her. "I'll take that as a compliment."

I was going to throat punch Luc. "It is. I mean, I hope it is. It's just that I think you getting on TV and talking with the senator and keeping your calm is really admirable."

"Thank you." She walked to me, threading her arm through mine. "It's not easy. I want to flip a table or find the senator and beat his face in." Her forehead creased. "Which would reinforce all the terrible things he says about us, so unfortunately, I can't do that."

"Too bad," I said, earning a quick grin.

"Taking the smarter road is not fun."

"Do you film here?" I asked.

She shook her head. "We could power up all the necessary equipment, but there's the chance of getting traced back. We leave here to do the interviews."

Zoe stopped suddenly, her gaze tracking over a wooden area. "Are you guys setting me up in the brick house with the white shutters? The one I normally stay in?" she asked, and I was struck again by how little I really knew about Zoe.

"Yep," Dee answered.

"Cool. I'm going to go check out where Grayson went to," she said, appearing beside me. "Unless you want me to hang out for a while?"

"No, I'm good." Slipping free from Dee, I hugged Zoe. "See you in the morning?"

"Sounds like a plan." She turned to where Luc was beside me.

"Go find Grayson," he said softly, taking the lamp from her. "Make sure he's dealing with everything."

"I'll do my best," she said, and then she was gone in a blur.

"You lost someone." Dee brushed her ponytail over her shoulder. "Kent." That one word, just a name, was filled with so much sorrow. "He's not with you."

"Yeah, it was Kent." Luc's hand found mine, and I squeezed his. "There were more."

"I'm sorry," she said, letting out a heavy sigh as she started walking. "It never gets easier. After everything we've all been through, will probably still go through, it never gets easier. I'm really sorry for all your loss. He was . . . he was Kent."

"Thank you," Luc murmured.

Dee led us past the wooden area to a street on our left. "This is where we all live, so we can be all up in one another's business. This house has been made ready."

We followed her up a cracked driveway to a small rancher-style home. She stopped in front of the door, unlocking it, and then she moved in, lighting gas lamps as she went.

"All brick. Keep the extra bedroom doors closed, blinds drawn during the day, and windows open at night, and it stays cool this time of the year." She gestured at the ceiling. "You also get a nice cross-flow that even turns the fans."

The fan was spinning lazily. I looked around, spying several pieces of comfortable furniture and a kitchen.

"I was assuming you two are okay with staying in the same place?" Dee stopped, placing her hands on her hips. "I probably should've checked that first."

Luc looked over at me, the soft light from the lamp casting a glow over his features. He waited to hear what I would say, leaving the decision up to me.

I nodded. "That's fine. I mean, it's okay. Totally."

A smoky little smile played across Luc's lips, and I felt my cheeks flush.

"Good. There are some fresh toiletries in the bathroom. I'll bring over some extra clothes that should fit and some food in a few minutes, okay?" Dee waited at the door.

"That would be perfect," Luc answered.

She nodded and dipped out of the doorway, disappearing into the night.

For several moments, Luc and I stood there, and then he said, "Let's find out where the shower is."

Down the narrow, short hall we went, into a bedroom that smelled like lavender and fresh air. Luc placed my bag on the bed and then walked over to the nightstand. Another gas-powered lamp flared to life. The shower ended up being in a quaint little bathroom behind one of the doors.

Luc placed the lamp he'd carried from outside onto the vanity. The soft glow beat back the shadows. "Why don't you shower first?"

"You sure?"

He nodded, backing up as he looked around. "You're super gross."

I laughed, the sound raspy but there. "Nice."

A grin appeared. "Here're some towels, and there's . . . a robe on the back of the door." Picking up the towel, he placed it on the vanity next to the lamp. "You good?"

"Yeah." I stared down at the towel. It was either pink or off-white. There was some kind of monogram on it.

"You sure?"

I forced a nod as I looked around the bathroom. There were toothbrushes and mouthwash, shampoos and conditioners in the shower. All of this had been placed here by Dee, but people had definitely lived here. "Do you think they made it out?"

"Who?"

"The people who lived here."

"I don't know. Let's just hope that they did."

I decided that was what I would hope, because if they hadn't made it out, and they were no longer here, in their own home, that meant they just didn't make it.

Everything felt heavy, and I . . . I didn't want to think about death anymore.

"I'll be right outside," Luc said, closing the door behind him.

Glancing at the shower, knowing it was going to be ice cold, I didn't give myself time to really think about it. I stripped off my muddy, ruined clothing and then turned the water on. Muttering a curse under my breath, I stepped under the spray.

"Holy shit," I gasped, the air punching out of my legs as the icy spray hit my skin. For a moment, I was shocked into immobility, but I pushed through it. I snatched up a bottle of shampoo and then took the quickest, coldest shower in my life.

I stepped out, shivering as I grabbed the towel and rubbed at my chilled skin. Tiny bumps were all over me, and my hair felt as if it were encased in ice. Freezing, I grabbed the robe and shoved my arms through it, cinching it tightly around my waist. I found a comb and then opened the bathroom door. Luc was walking into the bedroom, carrying a plate of food. My stomach grumbled.

"You look like an ice cube."

"I am." I hopped from one foot to the other. "But I'm just glad to be clean."

"So am I."

"Shut up."

He laughed as he placed the plate on a dresser, along with bottled water. "Dee brought some clothes over along with this. We've got a whole assortment of cheese and veggies."

"Yum."

He walked over to a chair in the corner and picked up some clothing. "There's more bottled water in the kitchen. Not quite sure where they got it, but we're just going to assume it's safe to drink."

I smiled a little at that.

"I'm going to go and freeze to death. You good?"

"Yeah."

Luc hesitated, and then he went into the bathroom, and I focused on eating as many pieces of celery and hunks of cheese as I could without choking. Then I rooted around in my bag, realizing I'd left my sleep shorts at the cabin. Nothing I could do about that now.

But I hadn't forgotten Diesel.

I pulled out the rock and placed him on the nightstand, by the lamp. Then I snatched up one of the bottles of water and guzzled the liquid.

The bathroom door opened no more than five minutes later, and Luc stepped out, wearing a pair of sweats, which hung indecently low on his hips, and nothing else. My gaze got a little hung up on all the hard, damp, bare skin on display.

I really needed to stop staring at him.

"I don't mind," he said.

"Get out of my head." I picked up the plate and walked over to the bed. "You don't even look cold."

"I'm actually freezing, but it was worth it."

I sat on the bed, crossing my ankles. "I guess it's something we'll get used to."

"Imagine so."

I peeked over at him as he lifted his hand to push the wet strands of hair back from his face.

"So . . . when should we see this general?" I asked. "He's the one you think will be able to answer some of our questions, right?"

"Yeah. Tomorrow morning, if you want."

I nodded as I offered Luc a carrot. Curling his fingers around my wrist, he took a bite of the baby carrot and then sat beside me on the bed.

He checked out the plate of veggies and cheese. "You want anything else to eat?"

"No, I'm stuffed. You should eat, though."

"Later." The plate moved off my lap and onto the nightstand, resting next to the gas lamp and Diesel. He tugged on my arm, and I rose onto my knees. An arm curled around my waist, and he pulled me over into his lap. "How are you processing everything?"

"I don't know." I settled against him, a little surprised by the ease of being this close to him. But it just felt right—natural, even. "I'm kind of surprised we made it here. I kept thinking we were going to run into an ambush or something; I keep waiting for something to happen."

"We're safe here." He tucked my wet hair back from my face and then dropped his hand to the space above my knee, where the robe ended.

For now hung unspoken between us.

And there was something else unspoken between us that couldn't stay that way. "Are they safe from *me*?"

"Evie—"

"It's a valid question," I said. "And isn't that what Daemon wants to talk to you about? I know he doesn't want me here, and I don't blame him. He doesn't know what I'm capable of. I don't even know, and neither do you."

"I really don't care what Daemon wants."

"Luc." I sighed.

"That doesn't mean I don't understand his concerns," he added, squeezing my knee. "I do. I also get why you felt like you had to do something to stop everything back at the cabin, even if I didn't agree with it. I do know you, Peaches. I get that you're worried, too. We don't know what's going to happen an hour from now, let alone a day or a week, but what I do know is that we're together. Right?"

"Right."

"Whatever happens, we're going to face it together, and I will not allow you to hurt anyone who doesn't deserve it," he said. "You have to believe in that. I stopped you before. I will stop you again."

But I'd almost killed him when he'd tried to stop me before.

"Trust me," Luc whispered against my forehead. "I need you to trust that I will not let you hurt anyone here."

I closed my eyes, shuddering. I did trust him. Irrevocably. And that meant I was going to have to act on that trust. Taking a deep breath, I nodded. "Okay."

"Okay," he repeated, kissing my cheek.

Several moments passed while I rested in his embrace, the chill on my skin seeping away. "When Kat said something about my mom, it made me think that she'd, you know, been through something like that."

"She has." He lifted his head, and in the flickering lamp, I met his gaze. "Kat lost her mom during the invasion."

"Oh." The heaviness returned, settling in my chest. "That's really sad."

"Yeah, it is."

The weight of his hand on my knee drew my gaze. I placed my hands over it, tracing the bone of one finger to his knuckle. I then looked up, taking in the unfamiliar room. "Everything has changed. I guess it has been a continuous stream of things changing."

"It has been." His thumb moved over my knee. "It's been a lot."

It had been so much that I thought back to the day he'd taken me to Harpers Ferry, and that afternoon felt like a lifetime ago. "What happens next?" I turned to him, finding his gaze in the dim light. "What if we talk to Eaton tomorrow and he has all the answers? He can tell me why this was done and what's going to happen, but then what? We can't . . ."

"We can't what?"

I drew in a shallow breath. "We can't stay here forever, hidden away. That's not the kind of life I want."

"That's not the kind of life I want, either."

"So, what happens next?"

"We dance."

I blinked. "What? Right now?"

"Yes." He lifted me off his lap and onto my feet. He rose, extending his hand.

"But there's no music."

"We'll make our own."

I lifted my brows. "That was . . ."

"Extremely romantic and charming?" he suggested.

"That was pretty cheesy."

"Cheese is awesome, though."

"Yes, it is." I grinned. "But it's also very random."

"Most of the best things are." He wiggled his fingers. "Dance with me, Evie."

Shaking my head, I placed my hand in his, and he tugged me to him. One of his arms circled my waist, and then he lifted me up so that I was standing on his bare feet. My hands landed on his chest. His skin was cool from the shower.

Luc started to sway, and within a few moments, we were dancing even though there was no music. He did all the work as I stared up at him, wondering if there was ever a time that I hadn't been in love with him.

And wasn't that the craziest thing? I was sure I fell in love with him when I was Nadia, and here I was as Evie, and we were in the same place. I loved him.

I reached up, cupping his cheek and drawing his mouth to mine. I kissed him slowly at first, and when his lips parted, I took the kiss deeper. My tongue moved against his, and I loved the way it felt, the way he tasted. The kiss was dizzying in its intensity, and when I pulled back, I felt stripped bare. Would it always be like that?

I had a feeling that it would.

Always.

We'd stopped dancing.

"You asked what we do next?" Luc's lips grazed mine, and my breath caught. "We find the people responsible for this, and then we burn down their entire world. Nothing will stop us."

41

There was a part of me that hadn't expected to fall asleep. Not after everything that had happened or with what awaited us in the morning, and not in such a strange place as someone else's home. I didn't feel like a guest. I felt like a squatter, but the moment my head hit that pillow beside Luc's, I must've passed right out, because when I opened my eyes, there was a sliver of light seeping in under the blinds, traveling across the foot of the bed.

And I was wrapped around Luc like I'd been worried in my sleep that he'd disappear or something. Thin sheets tangled at our hips. One of my legs was somehow tucked in between his. I had an arm tossed over his waist and his was curled around mine, lax and pleasantly heavy. My cheek was resting on his bare chest.

Waking up like this was different. It felt entirely new. Intimate. And I . . . I liked this. A lot.

Closing my eyes, I took a deeper breath. The fresh scent of soap mingled with the lavender that clung even to the sheets. Luc was surprisingly comfortable to lie on. We hadn't gone to bed like this. We'd been together, me on my back and Luc on his side, facing me. Whatever drew us together in our sleep was just as powerful as it was when we were awake. Was it chemistry? All the tiny things that made me who I was and made him who he was were just attracted to each other? Was it the shared past even if I couldn't remember it? Or was it everything that I did remember, everything that came *after*?

Whatever it was, it didn't matter, because I really loved this, and that . . . that felt wrong after losing Kent and Clyde, Chas, and my mother while Emery and Heidi were still out there, slowly making their way here. It felt inappropriate given that we'd taken over the home of someone, possibly even a family that had perished. It made me think it was unfair that I kept getting all these chances when no one else did, and I didn't even know if I deserved them.

If I deserved *this*—waking up in the arms of someone who loved me just as much as I loved him.

I didn't know if I did, because at the end of the day, I didn't know what I was, and neither did Luc. And maybe I didn't and maybe it was unfair, but I sure as hell was going to fight with everything in me to have more mornings like this, to stop losing people I loved, and to have all my friends with me, safe and happy.

When Luc had said we'd find who was responsible for all of this and burn down their entire world, his words had spoken to a part inside me that I hadn't known existed until that moment. I didn't know what it was. Determination. Retribution. Justice. Could be all of them, but what I did know was that I hadn't batted an eyelash when he'd said it. There wasn't a moment of hesitation even though I knew that whatever path we took was going to be a violent one. The Evie who would've pumped the brakes and suggested we call the police had died on the floor along with the only woman I knew as my mother, and the Evie that was birthed in the safe house outside of Atlanta would not stand by and watch anyone else be hurt. Whatever had come alive inside me in the woods sure as hell wasn't going to allow it. I might be dangerous. I just might be a Trojan. But I trusted Luc; I believed that he'd stop me if it came to it. Like he'd already done before.

Because what drew us to each other while we were awake and even in sleep was also powerful enough to blast past whatever resided in me, reaching me.

I opened my eyes and lifted my head. Luc's face was turned toward my side of the bed, his profile visible. I still couldn't get over how he looked in his sleep. His angular features softened in a way they rarely did when he was alert. The otherworldliness was still there, but blurred, and I could almost imagine if we were normal, and this was our bed, and we had days and weeks and months and years of simply living stretched out before us, an infinite time to explore each other and the world, to grow and learn together. Graduate school and figure out what I wanted. Move in together out of want and need instead of necessity. Get married and maybe even start a family in some way, many, many years from now.

But that wasn't us.

Yet.

"Peaches," Luc murmured, startling me. "I wish you'd brought your camera. You would be able to take a picture." His arm around me tightened. "It would last longer."

"Jerk." I smiled. "I didn't mean to wake you."

"It's okay." One sleepy eye opened. "I could never complain about being woken up like this, by you."

A sweet swelling motion filled my chest. "Hearing you say that makes me want to kiss you."

Luc turned his head to me then as his hand on my side slid up my back, tangling in the mess of my hair. "That's an even better way to wake up, so what's stopping you?"

I wiggled up and lowered my head. "I probably have morning breath."

"I probably do, too." His eyes went half-mast. "I don't care."

As I stared down at him, I realized I didn't either. "Did you sleep well?"

"Yeah." His other hand cupped my cheek. "I thought I wouldn't sleep at all, but fell asleep right after you. You're like my perfect dose of melatonin."

I laughed at that, and then I lowered my mouth to his, kissing him. I just meant to give him a quick one, but that wasn't what happened. The moment I started to lift my head, Luc rolled me under him.

"Now, you can give me a better good morning kiss than that," he teased, and this time, I did.

We got a little lost in each other for a while. Kissing. Touching. We knew we had to get up and find the general, but we both seemed to sense that this was . . . it was just as important as all the possible answers in the world were. It wasn't just living in the moment. It was seizing whatever seconds we had because we'd already lost so many, and when he settled over me, the kisses became more urgent, our touches more frenzied as we moved and twisted against each other. Electricity seemed to charge the air as he lifted his head, his chest rising and falling heavily as he stared down at me with pupils a bright, intense white. There was a tension to his mouth that caused my heart to jump all over the place, a question in that odd, beautiful gaze of his, and I knew. I suddenly knew.

This was it.

Him. Me. No clothes. Together. Like, *really* together. It wouldn't be my first time, but it would be his, and this time, in a bed and house that belonged to someone else, it felt so much more right than before.

Luc's eyes flared an intense amethyst. "Evie?"

It was one of those rare moments when I didn't mind that he'd been picking up on my thoughts. "Yes," I whispered. "I mean, if you—"

I never got to finish the question, because Luc kissed me and there was something entirely different about it this time. It was slow and deep, and beautiful, and then it became more. He reached for the shirt I'd donned before going to bed and I shoved at his sweats—

A knock on the front door stilled us. My eyes flew to his as I held on to the band of his bottoms. He had my shirt halfway up my chest.

"It's our imagination," he said, voice rough like sandpaper. "We didn't hear anything."

"I heard nothing." I lifted my head to his, kissing him. His groan rumbled through me. He went for my shirt again, and I yanked on his bottoms as I arched my back. His hands, his gaze was so close—

The knock came again, this time followed by the muffled voice of Kat. "Guys, are you all awake?"

The groan that came out of Luc was nothing like the one from before. He dropped his head to my neck. "We could ignore her."

"We could." I let go of his pants, folding my arms around him.

"She'll go away." His lips coasted over my neck. "Eventually."

I turned my head toward his, seeking his mouth. "She has to."

"Definitely." He kissed me, pressing his body against mine and into the bed.

"Eaton sent me!" Kat's voice rang out, this time closer, as if she was coming around to a different window. "He wants to see you guys and he's super impatient." A pause. "As per usual."

Luc sighed.

A giggle crept up my throat. "I don't think she's going to go away."

"I think you're right. Unfortunately. I've never been more disappointed in my life." Luc lifted his head and then yelled, "Give us twenty minutes."

"I think I'm going to be disappointed," I murmured.

Luc looked down at me, eyebrows raised and his eyes slightly wide. "Peaches. . . ."

The laugh burst out of me before I could stop it, and it felt good to laugh, and it felt even better when he silenced that laugh with another kiss.

Off in the distance, downtown Houston loomed, a graveyard of buildings built of steel and stone. It was the first thing I saw after Luc and I joined Kat, who was waiting for us on the porch. There was something unnerving about seeing a city of that size completely stagnant, and it caused me to remember the faint memories of how quiet things had been after the invasion. I had no idea if those memories were real or something that had been implanted, but the city seemed . . . haunted, a ghost of the past.

"Sorry we kept you waiting." Luc closed the door. "We weren't expecting to be summoned this early."

"Neither were we." Kat rose from the wooden glider she'd been sitting on, one hand on her lower back, the other clutching a floppy, cream-colored hat. While she didn't look remotely comfortable, she looked really cute in the simple pale blue sheath of a dress with long sleeves. "But Eaton was all but banging on our door at the crack of dawn, getting Daemon to go into the Yard."

"The Yard?" I asked, stepping off the porch. I wished I'd grabbed a heavier shirt as it was actually cooler than I thought it would be.

"It's a few blocks over, by the old high school." She slid the hat on, the floppy edges covering most of her face. "It's where . . . well, it doesn't matter. By the way, I don't think Eaton slept at all last night."

It didn't pass me by that Kat had changed the subject instead of telling me what the Yard was being used for. Had Daemon told her about me? It didn't take a leap of logic to assume that he had. It would be the first thing I told Luc. What did she think? Was she worried? Uncomfortable, I dragged my gaze from her to the street across. Homes nearly identical to the one we'd come out of faced me. It was the same both left and right, but there were no signs of life inside, no low voices of hushed conversation. The only sound was the soft snapping of the breeze catching the canopies. It was early, but not *that* early.

"Do people live in these houses?" I asked, thinking the whole place sort of reminded me of the first season of that zombie show.

Luc's hand folded around mine, drawing my gaze. He was watching Kat as she waddled along beside us.

"A lot are at work at the markets or doing what they did before all of this happened," she said, leading us down the street. I realized we were walking toward the way we'd come in. "The kids are in school—not at the old one, but a house that's been set up for the different ages. Others may still be in bed."

I didn't want to think about the fact that one house was large enough for all the kids of school age here.

The streets were clean while most of the yards were taken over by tall, reedy grass, which made sense. I doubted precious fuel needed to be used to keep the grass at a certain height. There were only a few cars parked in the driveways. Maybe five. All were at least a decade or so old, and I realized that was because they would've been made pre-electric ignition. As we continued on, the distinctive feel of being . . . watched crept over me, and every dark window we passed, the sensation grew.

"Is Eaton in the same place? The blue house near the park?"

Kat nodded.

"Why don't you go head back and rest," Luc offered, stopping. "I know the way."

"It's not bad for me to walk. I think I'm supposed to be doing it, actually, but I am so freaking tired." She laughed, patting her belly. "Who knew cooking up a baby could be so exhausting."

I smiled at that. "You're due any day now, right?"

"I think I'm actually a day or so overdue," she said, worry tightening her voice. "But that's normal. Or people keep telling me it is. It's just . . ."

"You're going to be okay. Both of you are going to be just fine," Luc assured her, and I wondered if he was picking up on her thoughts or not.

"I know." When she lifted her chin, I could see the smile on her face. It was faint and weary. "I know," she repeated. "I'm going to head back. Come find me when you guys are done. We have a lot of catching up to do."

"We will."

I was quiet as I watched Kat make her way back the way we came. "If they have to induce labor or . . . do something like a cesarean, do they have the stuff they'd need for that? Or doctors who can do that here?"

Luc was quiet for a long moment. "There are a few doctors, and I think one or two surgeons. There's medical supplies, things left behind and stuff others have scavenged." He tilted his head to the sky. "She's a hybrid and she has Daemon—she has her family. None of them will let anything happen."

His words were meant to cause relief, but I still worried for the girl I didn't know. Special alien abilities or not, women have died giving birth since the beginning of time, even when they had access to every life-saving measure.

"She'll be okay." His voice was softer.

I nodded, and then we started walking again, crossing the street. Out of the corner of my eye, I saw someone by one of the front porches of a small home, and when I looked over, he moved under the canopy, seeming to disappear into the shadows. I thought about how Kat hadn't wanted to tell me what was going on with whatever the Yard was, and I had a sinking suspicion that not everyone was at work or in school. They were in their homes or hidden, because—

"It is because of us."

I shot him a look.

"I know what you're thinking—and no, not because I'm reading your mind." He squeezed my hand. "Well, I kind of did, but just a little."

"Really," I replied dryly.

"It was an accidental mind reading."

"Uh huh." A small dog trotted out from one of the narrow streets, tail wagging as it continued across. "People are hiding because of us."

"Because they don't know us," he explained.

"I can understand that." And I did. "She doesn't trust me, does she? That's why she didn't tell me what the Yard is used for and changed the subject."

"It's not personal."

"How is that not personal?"

"In the same way you wouldn't trust anyone showing up here, in a place that is one of the few last safe spaces for everyone, and especially when that person was believed to have died," he said, being all logical. "They've all been through a lot. Trust is not given and it's rarely earned when you're asking for it from people who've been betrayed over and over."

I fell quiet, because Luc had a point. Not that I hadn't thought of that originally. I couldn't blame any of them for being wary around me when I was also wary of myself, but it was still hard knowing you weren't trusted . . . and knowing there was a damn good reason for it.

About two blocks down a narrower street, I saw the park up ahead. The breeze was swaying the seat-less swings and toying with the weeds that were as tall as the still merry-go-round. The blue house sat between what appeared to have once been a corner market and a home that was identical in shape but painted a red that had faded.

Luc led me along the cracked cement of the walkway and onto wooden steps that groaned under our weight. He knocked on the door, and it wasn't more than a few seconds later that it opened.

"I figured you two would be here first thing in the morning." General Eaton stepped aside, revealing a small room that smelled of must and was lit by a gas lamp in the corner. "Didn't think I'd have to send someone to retrieve you."

Luc simply grinned. "It was a long trip here."

The general huffed in response.

"You've been good?" Luc asked, letting go of my hand and letting me step in first. He closed the door behind me.

"Been better and been worse." He turned, walking back to a leather couch that had a tear down the back. He picked up a bottle of amber-colored liquid. "I'd offer you something to drink, but all I have right now is warm beer and you two are still underage."

Luc snorted. "Really? We're still following laws around here?"

"If we don't, we lose civilization." He sat. "And we can't have that."

"No, we can't," Luc murmured while I tried to figure out if the general normally drank beer this early in the morning.

Scanning the room, I saw piles of books and rolled maps stacked against the wall. It was like he'd pillaged a library or a bookstore, which was totally possible. This home didn't resemble the one we were staying in, where it still had the remnants of the previous owner's personality. This house, at least this room, was gutted and stark, looking every bit the way a home would appear after an apocalypse.

"I know why you both wanted to talk to me. Especially you." That was said to me. Leather creaked under his slim frame as he leaned back against the cushion. "You want to ask about what you are."

I nodded, liking that he cut to the point.

Luc sat on several reinforced crates. "Something I got to address. She was around after the invasion, but you never met her when she was Nadia."

"You're right. I never officially met her, but I did meet the real Evie Dasher," he replied.

That I wasn't expecting.

Luc straightened. Apparently he hadn't expected it either. "When did that happen?"

"When she was a young girl, a few years before her death." He took a sip of his beer. "The resemblance between you is uncanny."

"I . . . I wasn't sure how much I looked like her. I saw pictures of her, but. . . ."

"You could've passed as cousins. Maybe even sisters. The resemblance was pure luck," he said.

"Really?" I asked.

He nodded. "You were a part of the Poseidon Project, the blending of human DNA with that of a Luxen and an Arum. You were a sleeper—a Trojan, living like a human until you would be activated. Just like what is happening all across the United States as we speak. They can't be detected, not by RAC drones or any developed technology."

"Well, you definitely do know what she is." Luc rested his arms on his bent knees. "What is the purpose of the Poseidon Project?"

"Not world domination," Eaton answered, taking another drink. "But domination of the universe."

"Really?" Luc's tone was as dry as the desert. "Did we slip and fall into an Avengers movie?"

"When has it ever been anything else for the Daedalus? When have they ever had a different purpose?" the general responded, and I crossed my arms. "They want to be grand puppeteers, pulling the strings of everyone, from world leaders to city council officials, and whatever exists out there, in the vastness that is the universe. In their minds, they're striving to create a better world. They're not the villains. At least they don't think so. They believe they're the heroes of the story. That has always been the Daedalus, and you know that, Luc, better than most."

"How is that possible?" I asked, remembering what April had told me. "How do they not know what they're doing is wrong?"

"Throughout history, a lot of very smart people have convinced themselves that what they believe in, what their ideologies are, is better for the general masses. This has happened a thousand times over. This is nothing new."

"How exactly do they plan to make the world a better place by forcing Luxen to mutate and turning ordinary humans into Luxen-Arum hybrids?" I asked, thinking that was a damn valid question.

So I had no idea why he laughed.

"Because at the end of the day, those who control the Daedalus and who run our government, and the world, are the one percent of the one percenters. That is also nothing new. Everything that ever happens in this world happens to the benefit of them, billionaires and CEOs, old money and new, and they're in the pockets of all the politicians since the beginning of time."

Luc pressed his lips together and nodded. "Thanks for the sucky but accurate history of U.S. Civics not taught in schools, but that really doesn't answer our questions."

"But it does. These powerful men, their families, and their companies have never had their rigid control of the world questioned. They may be flesh-and-blood humans, but to the everyday, average person, they were gods. Nothing could challenge their power. Not until the Luxen first arrived. Everything changed then." Eaton lowered the bottle to his leg. "Suddenly there were these beings that could look human, could adapt rapidly, more advanced in nearly every way than a human, and were walking weapons. It takes no leap of logic to think that if the Luxen went unchecked, they'd eventually take over. Hell, things could possibly be better if that happened. Maybe the human race itself just doesn't know better."

"Possibly." Luc paused. "Except for the murderous invading Luxen."

"Yeah, except for them." Eaton smirked, and I blinked. "These people founded Daedalus, placed it within the Department of Defense with the function of assimilating Luxen, but also to study them. You know the history of the Daedalus, so I won't bore you with that." His finger tapped on the bottle. "You just need to remember that they wanted to be able to create something better and stronger than the Luxen, something that could be controlled. They started with hybrids and made their way to Origins, but they didn't stop there. They wanted to create something that could be programmed genetically, and as you know, Origins still had too much sense of . . . self for that to work."

Luc inclined his head. "That we do."

"Nancy just couldn't let the Origin Project go. It was her pet," he said, and Luc's jaw immediately hardened.

I didn't know who Nancy was and I made a mental note to ask about that later.

"Meanwhile others within the Daedalus were developing the Poseidon Project, messing around with the hive mentality the Luxen and Arum both have," Eaton went on. "Their first success was in the nineties. That's how far back this goes. It was a lot of trial and error, just like it was with the hybrids and Origins, but they had enough success to know that through the Trojans, they could gain real control. They just needed the right scenario for it all to come together."

Luc seemed to figure it out before me. "The invasion?"

He nodded. "The Daedalus knew it was coming, had intercepted the communication between the Luxen here and those who hadn't arrived yet. Plus, they worked with enough Arums to know that the Luxen, just like humans, were not all peaceful."

"They knew it was coming. Why?" I breathed, horrified and sickened. "Why would they do that? So many people died."

"And the herd was thinned out. Population is a real problem. Well, it *was*." He sipped from his beer. "But it also served another purpose. The invasion created fear and then hostility."

I thought about what Dee had said on TV, and then April. "And that's why they continue to frame the Luxen for things they're actually carrying out?"

He nodded once more.

"Because humans can't go toe to toe with the Luxen." Luc leaned back, thrusting a hand through his hair. "Luxens are outnumbered, but there's more than enough on this planet to seize sizable control, maybe even complete control. Damn." He shook his head. "They truly want to eradicate the Luxen, and they're doing it by turning humans completely against them."

"Not just the Luxen at this point. They want the hybrids and most of the Origins gone," Eaton added. "They're using fear and ignorance, which are the greatest and most powerful weapons of mass destruction ever created."

Feeling a little dizzy, I turned halfway around as I tucked my hair back from my face. "This is what Mom meant, isn't it? When she said that they let this happen but it got out of hand. She was talking about the invasion?"

"I imagine so," he answered. "If they're successful in eradicating the Luxen and the rest, then there's nothing to stop the Trojans from taking power."

"And what happens then?" I faced him.

"I imagine it will be pitched as a utopia. In reality, it will be something quite like a dystopia, but much worse."

"But you aren't hiding here with no purpose," Luc reminded him. "This isn't the only Zone brimming with Luxen ready to storm the gates. The Yard isn't being used for play fighting. You guys are training and preparing."

The Yard.

That was what the Yard was being used for.

"How much longer do you really think we're safe here? It's only a matter of time before we're found out."

"Then we fight," Luc said, and I found myself nodding. "Isn't that what most of us were bred for?"

Eaton's faded blue eyes tracked over me. "I want to know what you know about your abilities—when they started. Everything."

So we told him everything we knew about what was done to me, leaving nothing out. When I finished, I was exhausted even though Luc and I had shared the task.

"You're different than the rest. I imagine it has to do with you being given different serums beforehand. The hive mentality programmed into Trojans hasn't fully taken hold," he said. "But you said when you attacked the men that came for you, these Liberty men, you weren't yourself?"

"No, it was like . . . I was there but I was viewing things differently, like it was a task for me that needed to be carried out. That's the best way I can explain it." I started to pace in the cramped space between the stacks of books. "And I don't know why it happened. It was like a switch being thrown."

"Is it possible there was another sound wave weapon nearby that was used?" Luc asked. "The Cassio Wave?"

"I don't think so. As I said, it most likely was the multiple serums. You're a fluke in a way. Those serums you confiscated from the girl's house? Would've been interested to have seen them."

"Yeah, they're gone," Luc said.

Eaton was quiet for a moment and then he looked to where I stood. "The Daedalus really would love to get their hands on you. You're not like the others, and they'd want to take you apart, bit by bit, to figure out exactly why."

Well, that statement sure didn't leave me feeling warm and fuzzy.

"You're going to need to get your abilities under control," he said, still looking at me, and then, after a pause, "If you can."

If I can?

Wow, that was motivational.

"She can," Luc insisted. "I'll help her."

General Eaton took a swig from his bottle. "Of course you will."

Luc frowned. "What is that supposed to mean?"

"You two are a disaster in the making, how can't you see that?" Eaton looked down at the bottle he held while Luc and I exchanged a long look. Then Eaton laughed. "Well, one of you would see the truth if you'd stop letting yourself be distracted by emotion and the past."

Well, that could honestly be either of us.

"I think it's time for you to put down the drink," Luc suggested.

Eaton lifted his gaze to Luc. "Do you think that this wasn't planned from the beginning? You're smarter than that, Luc. You know how the Daedalus operates. They know how you operate."

Luc clamped his mouth shut.

"What is he talking about?" I demanded.

Eaton didn't take his gaze off of Luc. "You two were made for each other."

A fine shiver skated over my skin as I turned back to Luc, recalling that he'd said the same thing to me. *We were made for one another.*

"You think it wasn't designed from the moment you left the Daedalus, Luc? That they didn't know that eventually you would find someone out there that you'd do anything for? You know how they manipulated the Luxen that were close to humans. Look at Daemon and Dawson. The Daedalus damn near engineered their relationships in hopes that they'd mutate a human."

My brows flew up. "Engineered their relationships?"

"A Daedalus operative was connected to both Bethany and Kat," Luc explained. "He didn't put them with Dawson or Daemon, but he was able to report on them and help . . . aid things along, whether it be the final step of the mutation or turning them over."

"God," I whispered.

"And you think the same wasn't done to you?" Eaton challenged, and Luc's head whipped toward him. "Did it ever occur to you that they knew about *her* the minute she ran away from her house and into your waiting arms? That they weren't tracking both of you, keeping tabs on you? They just got lucky when she got sick."

Luc's jaw clenched as he stared at the general, and I felt like I needed to sit down.

"Her cancer was their perfect opportunity. They knew you were trying to get the serums to give to her. LH-11. Prometheus. Each one not healing her, but prepping her for the final serum. Andromeda. They just had to wait until you were desperate enough to take that risk and take her to the Daedalus."

Luc's features turned stark, and I had to speak up in his defense. "He didn't take me to the Daedalus. He took me—"

"To Sylvia Dasher? Child, I know you believed that woman to be your mother, and maybe in some small way, she was, but she was very much a part of the Daedalus up until the moment she decided she couldn't do what was required from her," he said, and if I thought my heart had broken back when Steven had begun to talk, I'd been wrong. It was breaking now. "Those things you said you were able to do? The fighting. The shooting. What you did to those men outside of Atlanta? You were trained by the Daedalus, handed over by Sylvia, and then your memories were wiped."

I did sit down then, in a worn, squeaky computer chair.

"What do you mean her memories were wiped then, after the training?" Luc demanded. "The serum—"

"Caused a fever, but never took her memories. Sylvia lied to you. She gave you the serum and then you were mutated. Once Sylvia knew you were going to survive the mutation, she handed you over to the Daedalus. You would've known exactly who you were until you completed training. Then the Cassio Wave was used to fry your short- and long-term memory bank," he said, and I knew in that moment if Mom . . . if that woman hadn't died, Luc would've hunted her down.

And killed her.

I knew it, because it was in the way he turned and stared at me, in the horror creeping into his features as he realized I'd been Nadia when I woke up from the serum and I'd been Nadia when I'd . . . I'd been trained.

Luc paled, and even though I couldn't read his mind, I knew that while I couldn't remember what it was like to be trained within the Daedalus, *he* did.

"For whatever reason, Sylvia had a change of heart. It was the one thing the Daedalus hadn't planned for." Eaton looked between Luc and I. "Love." He laughed then, shaking his head. "They hadn't anticipated Sylvia caring for you as a mother would for their child. She may have had a change of heart and tried to get you out, but make no mistake, she knew what was in those serums. She created the Andromeda Serum herself. Worked on the early trials, chronicled all their failures and their successes. The Andromeda Serum wouldn't have existed if it wasn't for her."

I pressed my hand to the center of my chest, over my heart. I couldn't speak.

"You weren't their first success, far from it." He was back to staring at the bottle. "But you were different. Not just your mutation, but because of him." He nodded in Luc's direction without looking up. When he spoke again, his voice was tired—tired and bitter. "You had to know, Luc, that they would find some way to reel you back in."

"They'll never reel me back in," Luc said, his tone as cold as the Arctic. "That I can promise."

General Eaton looked up then. "You so sure about that?" His gaze flicked to me. "You didn't recognize him out in those woods, right?"

"No," I whispered. "I saw him as . . ."

"You saw him as a threat and a challenge and you needed to dominate. One of the three things you were coded to do." The corners of his lips turned down. "You were coded to answer to one person only, and that isn't that boy sitting here."

"What the hell does that mean?" Luc demanded.

I had a better question. "Are you saying that what happened in the woods could happen again, and I won't remember him? *Again?* He won't be able to reach me?"

Sadness crept into the general's rheumy eyes. "You were coded to answer only to one person—"

"Stop saying that I was coded!" I shot to my feet, chest rising and falling. "I'm not a damn computer! I'm a person—"

"No, you're the Burning Shadow and he's the Darkest Star, and together, you will bring about the brightest night."

I jerked back.

"What?" Luc said.

Eaton chuckled hoarsely. "Code words. That's what he used to call both of you."

"Darkest Star? Burning Shadow? That sounds like a load of crap," snarled Luc.

"No. It's not." I shook my head. "Micah . . . he called you the Darkest Star. I didn't think it was a name, but . . ." I drew in a shallow breath. "Who in the hell is *he*? And how do you know all of this?"

"I know all of this, because I tried to shut down the Poseidon Project when I became aware of it. I failed." His knuckles were bleached white from how tightly he was gripping the bottle. "I underestimated him. Won't do that again."

"Who?" Luc rose and stepped toward the man, and I thought that he might strangle him if he didn't answer. "Who is she supposedly coded to? Who is behind this? Tell me so I know who I need to kill."

"You already did," Eaton replied. "At least, you thought you did. That's what you were led to believe."

A shiver exploded along the nape of my neck and powered down my spine. "No. No way."

"Dasher," Eaton said, his arm cocking back with a speed that betrayed his age. The bottle flung across the room, shattering upon impact with the wall. "Jason Dasher."